HEALING FAITH

JENNYFER BROWNE

VOLUME ONE OF THE **IN YOUR WORLD** *SERIES*

Cover Design by JBR Designs

ISBN 978-0-9894966-05

CHAPTER 1

The bus rumbled along the highway, the mottled landscape a ghostly blur under the late night moonlight. I wasn't concerned with what was outside as we traveled, but what I had left behind. So many memories and so much pain that if I dared to sleep; it would only bring on the nightmares that would surely leave me panicking and then dumped off on the highway in the middle of nowhere.

I shifted in my seat and tried to get more comfortable, the bruises on my hips feeling a little tender from sitting for so long. But I was used to the pain Sean caused. There wasn't a day that I didn't feel some kind of discomfort. I frowned at the notebook in my hand and leafed through it once more, the proof of the pain there in black and white. I rubbed at my chest to quell the unease I felt at running away and studied the journal again, needing the proof to secure my decision to flee in the first place. Pages upon pages of entries about my relationship with my boyfriend sat in my lap.

Sean Miller was in every entry of my journal.

The good was few and far between.

The bad made me more resolute.

I hid the bruises on my arm from Dad today. Even if it were warm out, Dad wouldn't question the sweatshirt. It was what I always wore to cover them.

Sean was late picking me up for the party. I guess it was okay we didn't go. My leg still hurt from where he kicked it.

Sean brought flowers today. He was really sorry.

My finger is healing crooked. I don't think anyone noticed how swollen it was.

First time in the face. Dad believed the softball excuse.

His touch repulses me. I will never like it.

I should have never said no. I should have just let him do it. It's not worth it anymore.

The black and blue faded, but what I had written over the last year and a half reminded me again and again why I was on a bus fleeing my home in California and traveling across country. My only option it seemed was to run.

Get away. Save myself.

The anger in Sean's black eyes had told me that this would be the last time I ran from him if he ever found me.

I rubbed at the bruise on my hip again and looked outside at the darkness in the window, seeing more than my reflection staring back at me. I could still see him in my mind. I could still feel his hands on me, grabbing and trying to convince me that I should just let him do it. I had let him wait long enough, he kept saying. His friends sat there laughing, urging him on. I should have let him. Instead I had kicked him and ran, hoping maybe this time I could find the nerve to tell my father. Every time I tried to confess to my father though, he was always in a rush. An important city council meeting, or public speech engagement was always more important.

No, my father was too absorbed in his political career to notice his family.

It was his way of dealing with the death of his wife and the reminder of her, which were my sister, Stacy and I. Many times I think if we had died in the car accident with her, he would have been able to manage his grief better. Instead we were a reminder of his pain and he chose to ignore it. Ignore us. Stacy intentionally applied to schools across country to get away and make a clean break. I was left to finish school and pretend that our home life was picture perfect, despite the tragedy.

When Sean and I started dating, my father couldn't have been happier. Sean was the perfect boyfriend, the son of my father's best friend and therefore a good match for me. I would be taken care of, and my father could look forward to furthering his career without the baggage of his family. The trouble was, with Sean, my father turned a blind eye and because of that, I found myself trapped in a relationship.

I moved to the last page of the journal, to the list my sister suggested I write while waiting for the bus. It was a short list of things I wanted that I couldn't have if I stayed.

Safety. Purpose. Love. Family.

I had none of that while I stayed.

Sean never made me feel safe, more like guessing which version of Jekyll and Hyde he would be when I saw him. Purpose? My hopes and dreams were quashed when Sean refused to let me go to San Francisco to study cooking. And I had no idea about love. While my parents put on a public front of dedicated love, the heated arguments at night that kept us up and huddled in our beds provided proof that love had long since vanished between my mother and father.

My sister's words from my frantic call the night before played in my head again.

"Kate, you won't ever get anywhere if you stay there. You can come here, but you need to decide what it is you really want to do with yourself. Come to Illinois. We'll figure it out once you're away from him."

Escape was my only option for a chance at happiness. Perhaps what was ahead of me would be my salvation. I needed something to hope for. Somehow, on the three-day bus ride to Illinois, I would figure out how to make a life away from what I knew. I had nothing to lose. I closed my eyes to that hope and forced my mind to think of those things, rather than what I had left behind.

The bus jostled me awake roughly, the stench of burning oil filling the cabin at an alarming rate. I bolted from my seat, grabbing my backpack when I heard the driver hollering for us to get off the bus. We tumbled out in a panic, unsure whether or not it would explode at any moment. I squinted into the bright sun and moved far from the smoking mass until I could breathe a little easier. Looking around, we were surrounded by nothing but corn.

Miles and miles of corn.

I had no idea where we were, the bus route taking us in and out of just about every state between California and Illinois. All I could tell was that it was in the middle of nowhere. I looked around for any sign of civilization but found none. The corn rustled and hissed in the breeze, and I felt at any moment some crazed killer would come barreling out of the tall stalks with intent to kill us all. I rubbed at my burning eyes, trying to pull myself together from the paranoid and stressed out person that I had become.

The bus driver talked into his cell phone and was waving his arms around for several minutes before he finally turned to us, the heat of the early afternoon already turning his face a glistening pink.

"All right, folks! Another bus is on its way from Ottumwa. It'll be here in a few hours. There's a little town about a mile or so back. If you all want, we can make our way back there and the bus line will pay for lunch!" he announced.

I huffed and pulled my backpack a little higher onto my shoulder. A mile wasn't much, but it was ninety plus degrees and the afternoon sun was blazing down on us with no shade in sight. We set out, and less than five minutes in I was helping the old lady beside me with her bag so she could walk a little easier. It took us about an hour to walk, and by the time we arrived, we were all hot and thirsty.

The town we had converged upon wasn't much; it had one main street with only half a dozen storefronts and the one diner beside a deserted gas station. The diner was overwhelmed with us, being able to only handle about half of the bus occupants. I stood outside with the other travelers, watching as a few cars passed by, the drivers waving to anyone that they passed. But it was the horse and buggies that travelled down the main street that confused me. Sleek black buggies, with strong looking horses would stop at the general store across from me, a man in a light colored shirt and straw brim hat entering the store before coming back out, hands laden with seed or something in large bags. The riders looked like Amish people. But I was pretty sure we were in Iowa. There weren't any Amish people in Iowa, right?

Who knew?

Iowa was full of corn and I was more than ready to get on the road again. The town was quaint like some of the coastal towns north of where I lived, but without the rocky beaches and towering redwoods. The blistering sun beat down on me, making my skin pink almost instantly. I had been used to the fog and coastal temperatures. This place was nothing like my past. While it might have been refreshing to stay someplace such as this town for my new start, I had to continue on my way. I needed to get as many miles away from Sean as I could.

7

Impatient standing around to wait for a seat in the diner, I followed a couple of my bus mates across the street to the small general store and bought a bottle of water and some interesting looking corn cakes. I settled into one of the rocking chairs on the front porch with a good view of the street out of town. I figured if I could see the bus first, I could get a better seat.

Texting my sister about the delay, I shook my head at the lack of bars on my phone and wondered if she'd even get the text. This little town was as far removed from modern conveniences as I had ever seen. Tucked away in the quiet and far from the hectic day-to-day dealings of politics and industry. It was quaint.

I chewed on the corn cake thoughtfully, enjoying the sweetness of it on my empty stomach. I was starving, having not eaten since my first bus transfer in Sacramento and the cakes were delicious. I was working on my second one when another horse and buggy pulled up, this one with a back end full of fruits and vegetables.

I watched as the man got out of the buggy, his striking red hair shining under his straw hat. His beard was fairly long, but his face looked quite young. He was maybe in his late thirties or early forties. He looked a little like a young Santa Claus, especially with his kind blue eyes as he regarded me when he passed.

"Pleasant day to you," he said, his deep voice friendly and warm, with a slight accent that made his words almost melodic.

"Hi," I murmured, not sure how to address this odd stranger.

The Amish looking man nodded, making his way back into the store and leaving me to my corn cake. He passed by me twice more, his arms laden with baskets of food. On the last pass, he paused, his smile breaking out across his face again while he regarded me.

"Are you enjoying your cakes?" he asked.

I looked down to find only a few crumbs left trailing down my shirt and blushed.

"They were good, yes," I replied, embarrassed by him taking notice of me.

His eyes brightened and he chuckled.

"I will make sure my wife learns of your enjoyment. She made them. Pleasant day to you, child," he said as he tipped his straw hat and walked back into the store.

I couldn't remember the last time a total stranger spoke with me, let alone in such a friendly and open manner. It made me feel welcome, even though I knew I would never see the man again. I glanced down the road once more, hopeful to see the bus and be on my way. It had been almost two hours and the bus driver had said it wouldn't be long. Looking down the long expanse of roadway, the road appeared deserted. I stood and stretched, ready to step inside where it was cooler when I caught a reflection in the corner of my eye. A car was coming down the road, shimmering in the heat mirage.

A sleek and brilliant red Mustang, marred only by the dust from travelling.

And as it neared, maybe a quarter mile from the city limits, I heard it: the unmistakable muffler that made me tense in fear. Sean was here, the nightmare coming to life as the car rumbled towards the far end of town. Panic coursed through my body while I searched around for somewhere to hide. Sean would surely get out and look around to ask about me only to find out I was here and stranded.

How had Sean found me? All the way to Iowa from California? After all the bus transfers? Had my dad traced my bankcard? I hadn't used it since Sacramento, pulling out as much cash as I thought I might need. But with Sean's father a deputy sheriff, it wouldn't have been difficult to have him trace my money trail.

My heart hammered as I searched in vain again for somewhere to hide. Inside the store left me trapped with people who had seen me. The diner was across the street. I felt my body shaking, the panic verging on a full-blown attack. Just as the car moved close enough that I could confirm it was definitely his, I hid in the only safe place where no one would look.

I hid in the back of the buggy.

I peeked through the small window as I watched him step out of his car and look around, a cold feeling of dread passing over me. Sean looked like he had been driving non-stop; his usual meticulously spiked black hair messy and windblown. His tight t-shirt was wrinkled along the back, and sweaty from the heat, probably from sitting in his car all those hours. Every muscle on his imposing body seemed tense as he stood there, surveying the town and the people standing outside the diner.

He looked around briefly, my body tensing as his dark eyes traveled over the buggy I hid in before they scanned past me towards the diner again. He hitched up his jeans on his hips and slowly made his way towards the diner, his normally pouty lips set in a thin, tight line. Sean's swagger told me he was determined in his mission. He was going to find me, and I would be his, with no one to protect me or stop him from doing whatever he wanted on the return trip.

There were a lot of ditches and lonely roads between here and McKinleyville, California.

I trembled in the corner behind the burlap sacks in the buggy, sure that at any moment, the bus driver would nod and point over my way, and Sean, who always seemed to know where I was like a blood hound in the hunt would find me.

I wasn't prepared for the owner of the buggy to come back so soon.

"Thank you, Eli! Pleasant day to you! I will be sure to tell Fannie that you need more of her cakes!"

The buggy rocked slightly as the man climbed up onto his bench seat in front. I heard him make a noise, and the buggy jolted into motion. I bit my palm to keep from crying out; I had no way to escape now, not without raising suspicion and being caught. My heart rose in my throat when the buggy stopped abruptly.

"Hey man. I'm looking for this girl. Have you seen her?"

The sound of Sean's voice made shiver in fear. It was purposeful, direct and commanding. He had never had much in the way of manners when it came to addressing his elders, and I could tell his irritation at having to ask around for me only made him more direct. I slunk further into the darkness amongst the bags and boxes, praying that I couldn't be seen. It was stifling in the back where I hid; the sweat dripping down my skin as I silently wished the buggy to continue its trek. But the Amish man had seen me and spoken to me. He was sure to tell Sean he had seen me. I clenched my eyes shut and waited for the end.

"Did you check the diner, son?"

"Yeah I was heading there. Thanks," Sean muttered and turned away from the man.

"Pleasant day to you," the man called out and once more we were moving.

I tried to hold in my tears, but the stagnant heat and the overwhelming need to escape made it difficult to breathe. I couldn't hide my yelp when I heard my phone chirp loudly in my pocket. I watched in horror as the Amish man's head whirled around, his mouth opening up in an exclamation until he saw my fear. His face immediately became more guarded and I could feel the buggy slowing down once more. Sean would see and would wonder why.

"Please," I pleaded in a strained whisper. "He'll kill me if he finds me. Please, help me."

"How did you come to be in my buggy, child?" the man asked his voice more authoritative than it had been when he had spoken to me before.

"Please. Please, I just need to get away from him. He'll kill me," I pleaded again.

He pursed his lips and turned to look back out towards the expansive road ahead, licking his bare lips above the gleaming beard. His glance drifted from me to what I assumed was Sean behind us, his eyes thoughtful before he redirected them back to the road where he urged his horses along at a brisk pace.

"It is not our place to intervene in Englisher troubles, child. But if he is determined to hurt you in some way, I cannot let that be. You have asked for sanctuary. I will offer it to you, for that is our way. I am Jonah Berger, child. And you are?" he asked, his tone suddenly very formal.

"K-Kate. Katherine Hill, sir."

"Welcome to West Grove, Katherine Hill."

CHAPTER 2

I struggled with the hooks on the dress, frustrated at there being no zippers or buttons. This would have been so much easier with my t-shirt and shorts, but I had been told as long as I stayed in their community I had to wear their clothes. A dress whose skirt was much too long for me, and a shift underneath made me sweat just trying to put them on in the heat of the house. I wished regretfully for the fog and chill of home.

I grimaced at that thought, shaking my head in disbelief that I had actually had the ridiculous idea of to wanting to go back.

The hooks finally done, I looked around for a mirror. There was none to be found in the room I had changed in and had to wonder if this family didn't believe in them. They seemed a quiet and guarded group of people. And stuck in the pioneer days, judging by the bonnet I had to wear and the lack of electricity. I knew virtually nothing about the Amish, but I had an idea I was going to learn firsthand by hiding with them. Smoothing my hair into a bun at the base of my neck like I had seen with some of the other women on the road back, I turned to tuck my old belongings into my backpack.

I looked at my phone one more time, the message that had given up my hiding place still there on the screen. My sister's warning about Sean:

He's coming. He knows. I'm sorry. Run.

Feeling the sense of panic run through me at her warning, I shut off the phone in a rush and shoved it in my bag. Sean was out there somewhere, and until I knew how he had found me, I wouldn't give him any way of finding out I was here now. I straightened my dress one last time and made my way down stairs, the well-worn stair treads creaking as I went.

Turning the corner and still fiddling with my head covering, I didn't notice the tall figure in front of me until my face met with his solid, heated chest. I stumbled back, nearly falling until strong hands reached out to right me. I steadied myself before looking up to apologize to the man I had run into. My words died in my mouth when I found myself gazing into the dazzling green depth of his eyes.

"I'm so sorry," I stammered, feeling the heat rising in my cheeks as those eyes continued to look through me.

I was incapable of moving, he had rendered me immobile in hands that held me as if I would break if he squeezed too hard. He continued to stare intensely at me, his eyebrows knitting together as he seemed to come to his own senses and shake his head slowly. He let me go, his strong hands slipping away cautiously until he knew I was able to stand on my own.

"No, I must apologize. I did not see you there. Did I hurt you? I… I do not know you," he said, his voice soft and cautious with a similar cadence as Jonah's.

I shook my head and tried to smile up at him. It was hard to concentrate while I took in the man before me. He was tall, so much so that I had to crane my neck slightly to look up at him. His short, mussed hair was streaked golden as if he spent most of his days in the sun. Judging by the soft wrinkles around his eyes and sun kissed cheeks, I assumed that he must. I watched as he licked at his full, dry lips, swallowing hard enough that I could hear it over the rushing in my ears.

"Uh, I'm Kate. I'm… visiting." I extended my hand out to him in greeting.

He paused; eyeing my outstretched hand like it was diseased before looking back up to offer me a timid smile. His face softened as he regarded me and the suspicion that had been in his eyes before was replaced with a friendlier crinkle around them.

"Welcome, Kate. I am Nathan. Are you staying with Elder Jonah and his family?" he asked, never taking my hand. Instead he moved his hands to grip the suspenders over his chest, as if fighting some temptation to touch me.

I blushed and put my hand down, assuming I must have violated some strict Amish custom in my handshake. I took a step back hesitantly, to put more space between us. I was already warm in all the layers of clothes I had to wear and his nearness didn't seem to help the heat. I still felt the ghost warmth of his solid chest against my face, a tingling sort of feeling everywhere I had made contact with him.

He was broad across the shoulders like I would expect a farmer to be, but his height made him look a little lanky, as if he had grown too fast and his trim body was still catching up. He couldn't have been too much older than me, perhaps twenty. The sun had aged him like the surfers and sailors at home so it was difficult to guess. He had a roughness about him that told me he worked a hard life, but that was where the roughness stopped. His eyes held a kindness I wasn't used to in a man. He was not as imposing in stature as Sean, but still he was a man and I knew well enough what men could do. Even with this man's gentle smile and the way he had held me, he was a stranger to me.

"Katherine!"

The forceful voice startled me, and I jumped again, this time forward towards Nathan, who awkwardly grasped me by the waist to steady me again. I was sure I had stepped on him, because he lurched away abruptly, his hands pressing me against the wall before retreating a step. He shook his head as if to clear it, darting his glance down the hallway towards the voice before he turned and rushed out of the back door without another word.

I watched his strong back as he left in the waning light, his cream shirt stained with sweat and his neck long and almost elegant under the black hat he pulled down over his hair. He glanced back once, a troubled frown on his face before he turned around again and quickened his pace up the hill and through the field away from the house to disappear behind the hill.

"Katherine, are you dressed? It is supper. Come! The family is waiting," the voice said again from down the hall.

I turned from the strange man and made my way down the hall, into a lantern lit dining room. At the head of the table sat Jonah, watching me with a kind smile as he waved me in. Around the table sat a few other people I had not yet met. To one side of me sat a small, frail looking girl with dark wispy hair peeking out of her head cover. She was possibly my age, maybe a little older, but she was shorter than even me, stunted somehow. Her large dark brown eyes took me in openly, and her smile was very welcoming.

In stark contrast to her was the tall red-haired girl across from her, who barely glanced my way before looking back towards the window and the darkening sky beyond. Next to her sat another girl, a child with pale blonde hair that was bound in braids that wrapped around her little head. She looked up at me with the brightest blue eyes I had ever seen with open curiosity as I slowly moved to sit beside the dark-haired girl.

"Family, please welcome to our home Katherine Hill. She is visiting us from the outside. Please assist her in blending in to our ways while she is here," he said warmly, glancing to his right and his left at his daughters.

The dark haired girl beside me turned and smiled warmly as I sat beside her.

"I am Emma. I am happy to have you as a sister while you are here, Katherine," she whispered, beaming.

"Oh, you can call me Kate," I corrected, only to close my mouth when Jonah cleared his throat.

It was not aggressive or accusatory like my father would do, merely commanding in an intense sort of way. It still frightened me a bit, unsure of this man's temperament.

"We shall abide by your God-given name as your parents thus named you. We will go by Katherine, even if it be an English name," he explained.

I nodded and laid my fidgeting hands in my lap, suddenly nervous that anything I did now would be construed as "outsider" or English as I had learned they called people like me. Jonah had filled me in a little of his community on the buggy ride in from town. I was an outsider, and would raise suspicion if I acted as such. I would pose as someone from another community visiting their home.

It was just for a couple of days, but I wanted to pay my way to this family, however I could. A few days dressed up like a pioneer wouldn't be so bad if it kept me hidden long enough for Sean to give up and go home. I needed all the help I could in order to blend in and live by their rules judging by the man, Nathan's, reaction to me.

I let my gaze wander as I felt the sisters regard me, until finally Fannie, Jonah's wife portioned out our supper. Fannie was pretty, in a plain sort of way, tall with long dark hair that plaited and wrapped neatly beneath her hair covering, and large warm eyes that seemed to observe every detail. She was very welcoming with her warm smile and soft voice. I knew immediately that she was a kind and gentle person. I

17

couldn't explain the sense of security I felt every time she looked towards me.

She was what I remembered my mother was like when I was a child, before politics got in the way of the family. Before the alcohol that slowly consumed my mother and left her a shell. Before everything that distanced our parents from one another and their daughters. Fannie and Jonah Berger were nothing like my parents. They seemed interested in their daughters' lives based on Jonah's conversation.

"Is Mark coming for supper tonight, Hannah? The wedding is a couple of weeks away. There is much to plan still," he asked, a blush blossoming across the tall girl's cheeks.

"No, Father. With the sick mares, he has to work later than he wished to get the field cleared," she replied, her voice somewhat aloof as she spoke to her father, glancing at me briefly before returning her eyes out towards the window once more.

"Abigail, do not stare so," Fannie admonished quietly when the youngest of the daughters continued to watch me. She blushed and looked down at her lap as her father recited meal prayers, and I found myself copying her movements, only raising my eyes when he had finished.

We were quiet as we ate, Fannie smiling at me and offering more food than I could possibly indulge in, and Emma and Abigail hid their smiles every time I glanced their way. Jonah remained silent for most of the meal, breaking the silence only when he complimented his wife on a good supper. I felt terribly out of place and awkward as I ate, unsure of where to put my hands, whether to eat the leg of chicken I had on my plate with a fork or with my hand, whether to butter my bread with my own knife or use a communal knife that seemed to have disappeared from the butter dish.

When the meal was done, the girls stood to clear away the table, and out of fear I moved to do the same. Fannie stopped me with a smile and a light touch on my shoulder.

"It is your first night with us, Katherine. You can help with the drying of the dishes so you can find your way around the kitchen. Do you like to cook?" she asked as she moved me towards the deep wash sink.

"I do, actually. I don't know if anything I cook will be acceptable though," I murmured nervously. My father had never been very complimentary on my dishes.

She hugged me around the shoulders and handed me a dishtowel.

"Well then, tomorrow you can spend the day with me and I will show you the ways we cook. We will be busy in the next few days, and your able hands will be most welcome. We have a Frolic to prepare for!" she said happily and turned to the dishes, washing and handing them to me as she finished.

"What's a Frolic?" I asked, feeling dumber by the moment.

Emma moved in close and took the dishes from my hand to put them away.

"A Frolic is a social gathering in our community. The men help with a task while we arrange the food. The community comes together for each other when one needs many hands," she explained.

I nodded, thinking carefully of all the Amish references I knew, which sadly were only from movies and television. I remembered one movie my mom had watched when I was young, with a number of men building a barn.

"So like a barn raising?" I suggested, smiling when Emma's eyes lit up.

"Yes! Precisely! Day after next we go to help Elder Wittmer clear his field and mend his fences. The rains and heavy snow last winter caused much damage to his land," she explained.

"And maybe someone will get to speak with young John Wittmer," Hannah teased as she wiped away the remains of supper from the table.

Emma frowned and looked away bashfully at mention of this John Wittmer. Abigail giggled beside Emma and looked up at me with a wide smile on her face as she relayed the story.

"John likes Emma but Emma will not talk with him," Abigail stated in a shrill voice until she noticed her mother's pursed lips and shake of her head.

"We do not discuss such things," Fannie stated and handed me another plate, the matter closed.

Talking about boys was obviously not something they did, and I was sure there was some strict code to dating. I doubted Amish teenagers made out in their buggies. Staying here, trying to blend in was going to be a lot harder than I ever thought. I somehow knew I would offend or embarrass the Bergers or myself every time I opened my mouth. I wasn't used to their pure ways.

My world was much different than theirs.

We finished with the dishes, and by the time we had wiped down the table and counters, I could feel my eyelids drooping. I doubted it was even past nine in the evening. Jonah came in through the back door and clapped his hands together, startling me back to wakefulness.

"Another beautiful day by God's graces. Let us turn in and get some rest. Early day tomorrow!" Jonah said brightly and ushered us up the stairs.

Emma and Abigail pulled me into the room I was to share with them and began to undress for the night. Abigail was in her small bed before I had even removed one hook to my dress, her eyes already closed. I stalled my hands on my head cover as Emma slipped her own off, revealing her hair to me. Thin and almost black in the dim lighting, her hair was terribly short, with the back much shorter than the sides, as if it didn't grow at the same rate or had been shaved at some point. I realized I was staring when she turned, dragging her hands up to her head self-consciously. I turned away, feeling awkward at her embarrassment.

"I'm sorry, I didn't mean to stare," I stammered.

I felt her hand on my shoulder, turning me softly so that I could look into her penetrating gaze.

"You have no need to be upset, Katherine. I feel so close to you already, I forget you would not know. Come; let us ready for bed and I will answer your questions. It is a bit of a melancholy story to sleep to, but it must be told so you know me," she whispered and turned away to slowly remove the layers of clothing she wore until she was down to her thin cotton shift.

I followed her routine, hanging my clothes on the hook on the wall beside hers. I was learning that observation was my ally in learning to blend in with the Amish. Dressed down to our shifts, we slid into the small bed beside Abigail's, the weight of us making it creak in defiance. I settled on my side, Emma turned towards me with her hands under her head as if in silent prayer. She closed her eyes, as if collecting her thoughts before she spoke, her voice whisper-soft.

"I was very sick, you see."

Her eyes opened up but seemed to peer off away from me, unfocused as if to remember her memory better.

"I was always a bit dreamy, often finding myself in trouble with the schoolmistress for not paying attention. But school bored me. I hardly ever paid attention, but still did well. I did not talk much, but when I did it was often rushed and difficult to understand. My thoughts worked faster than my mouth I suppose. Some said I had demons, but it was not witchcraft," she said, her eyes focusing on me pointedly for a moment until I nodded and she continued.

"It was not until the pain and the vision problems that my family understood that there was something truly affecting me. The doctors in our district tried home remedies, but my vision grew cloudier, the dreams more vivid until I thought they had truly happened, and the pain in my head grew worse. It was then that we finally sought an English doctor," she said softly, her eyes closing.

"You guys don't go to our doctors regularly?" I asked, clasping my hand over my mouth at how rude that had sounded from my lips. "I'm sorry."

Emma's smile seemed to brighten the dim room as she giggled beside me. Abigail mumbled in her bed and we were quiet for a moment before she settled into a steady breath once more fast asleep. Emma let out a soft breath and looked back towards me.

"We do see your doctors. Do not be embarrassed. We keep much of ourselves private. You will see. It is better to handle our issues within the community, but sometimes, like with me, we need Englisher aid," she explained and continued her tale.

"The doctors listened to my ailments and offered a grim prognosis. I had a brain tumor. They used their machines and found it, a slow growing tumor in the top portion of my head. It had spread towards the front over time, which explained the vision loss and dreams."

"I'm so sorry, Emma," I whispered.

I didn't know why I felt some kinship with this girl, but her family had taken me in, she was telling me a private part of her life. I knew that was special. As reserved as these people were, they had shown me more of themselves than even my neighbors whom I had known all my life. Emma had known me for a couple of hours and already I felt a keen friendship forming. She pushed back the hair that had tumbled across my cheek and smiled.

"I am well now. I had the surgery, and they removed the tumor. You can feel the scar here," she said and lifted her fingers to a small lump I could make out on the top of her head above her ear.

"Does it hurt?" I asked, touching it tenderly with my own fingertip.

"No, not anymore. But that was the easy part. The medicine was the worst of it," she said and grimaced.

"You had chemo?"

It was so strange to think of the Amish undergoing chemotherapy. But here was Emma, with her thin black hair that was obviously just growing back from her recovery. I was discovering that she was not so different from any of my friends back home.

"How long ago was this?" I asked.

"I took the last of the medicine four months ago. My hair just started growing back about a month and a half ago," she murmured and smoothed down her hair self-consciously.

"That must be a relief, though. To have it growing back?" I asked.

She frowned and ran her fingers through her hair repeatedly; in what I was discovering was her nervous tic.

"I only wish it would grow a little faster. I do not look like a woman. I will not gain favorable attention like this," she mumbled, her eyes regretful.

I reached up slowly and touched her hair along the side of her head, feeling how soft it was. I wondered if her words were true. Did the men here look on women with judgment of their beauty and nothing else? I had hoped that was untrue, just something that Sean had always said to berate me when I didn't look good enough for him. I looked at Emma again, finding she really was pretty, even with the short hair that was perhaps not the Amish style. She looked like she belonged in a trendy club in a busy city.

"I think it's beautiful. And it will grow back," I said, smiling into her timid eyes. "Think of how much cooler it is in this heat right now."

A small grin crept across Emma's face.

"I knew we were meant to be great friends. You see the benefits in what God gives us. Thank you for helping me to see that," she replied and leaned in to offer me a hug.

"Thank you for taking me in. I only hope I don't embarrass you all," I replied, remembering the strange look the man, Nathan, had given me.

"We have a few days to help you with that. And our community is very welcoming. I think you will find you will have many friends here by the end of our Frolic," Emma quipped.

I raised my eyebrow at her and shook my head.

"We'll see," I replied, skeptical. I had never made many friends ever.

"Come, we need to sleep. Father will have us up for the cows in no time," she murmured and yawned as if to illustrate the point. Her yawn was contagious, reminding me of how long it had been since I had had a good night's sleep.

It had only been two days on the road. But it felt like forever ago I had enjoyed a dreamless night. I shivered at the idea of what my dreams would bring, and how Sean might never leave me alone, awake or asleep.

I watched as she blew out the candle on the nightstand, throwing us into the darkest night I had ever known. It took several minutes until my eyes could adjust to the dim light, my mind playing tricks by imposing images in the dark. Not the same images that had haunted me for the last few days, these were startling in a different way.

Deep green eyes and a strong back as it walked away from me took me into my dreams.

Why did my mind linger on the stranger?

I had obviously offended him.

Not that it mattered; I would be gone in a few days.

But his manner had me perplexed; his shy smile had made me a little uneasy. My mind lingered on his face, his brief, timid smile as he spoke to me those few moments and the sea green eyes that drew me into his world. Everything else that had happened to me over the course of the day drifted into oblivion.

But the Amish man, Nathan, haunted my dreams.

CHAPTER 3

Katherine.

My name sounded strange coming from his lips. Sean never called me by my formal name. Was he trying to trick me? Lure me back?

Katherine.

I struggled against his iron grip, turning before he could push me to the ground again. I felt him nudge me and I whimpered, knowing that he was seconds from ripping at my clothes. I had to get away. I looked around for anything to fight with, freezing in fear when I saw a silhouette of a man behind Sean coming towards us. The wide brimmed hat looked eerily familiar. The light from the hallway caught a flash of green, and I was trapped in the stranger's stare. Warm and crinkling eyes offering me a way from the biting grip on my body.

Help me.

"Katherine."

My eyes flew open and I sat up quickly, nearly toppling out of the tiny bed that wasn't my own. I wasn't home, and it wasn't Sean's voice that woke me. Looking around in the murky darkness, I found Emma, fully dressed and pouring steaming water into a basin on her vanity. I pulled my hand through my hair, feeling disoriented and unsettled as I tried to get accustomed to my surroundings. The culmination of the last few days swirled and coalesced into muddled memories in my head in the form of my nightmare. I could still feel Sean's hands gripping my hips, holding me still. I could still see green eyes staring down at me.

Emma whispered my name again, shaking me out of the dream still playing in my head.

"We have to get ready for the day, Katherine. There's fresh water here for cleaning, and I have set out a new shift for you to wear today. Do not dally. Father will have us looking after the pigs if we are late."

I nodded and moved to get up, my body stiff from the soft bed. I felt dirty, disheveled and road weary sitting there in Emma's crisp and clean bed linens.

I was desperate for a shower.

"You were whimpering in your sleep," she said in the darkness as I pulled the dress I had worn the day prior from the hook.

I didn't turn to look at her; I could tell from her voice that she was concerned.

"Just a dream," I murmured and held the dress to me tightly as if to hide how raw and exposed I still felt from the dream, let alone her questions. Emma must have understood because she turned silently and left me to get ready, the door closing quietly in the darkness. I looked towards the little girl Abigail's bed to find it empty and neatly made.

I made the bed I had slept in with lightning speed and then stumbled through a fast cleaning routine, the sponge bath cold merely for the briskness of the predawn air. Once again I struggled with the layers of clothes required of me, tripping several times on the hem of my skirt that was just a few inches too long. When I made it downstairs, Jonah gave me a cursory nod before looking off to Emma and Abigail who waited by the door with large silver jugs.

"The cows are needy. Show Katherine how we appease them," he said softly before taking another smaller bucket off the back porch and making his way into the darkness.

Abigail looked up at me and smiled as she handed me her silver jug.

"Have you ever milked a cow, Katherine?" she asked, giggling when I shook my head. She took my hand and dragged me out into the predawn towards the large barn, Emma already a few steps ahead of us.

I had a feeling this was going to be a long day.

"My good wife, these cakes are heavenly this morning," Jonah beamed from the end of the table during breakfast.

Fannie smiled and nodded towards me.

"Dear husband, our newest daughter did make them this morning. She is proving to be quite helpful in the kitchen," she commented, pursing her lips when Hannah let out an exaggerated breath.

Emma leaned in close and whispered, "Hannah is not gifted in matters of the kitchen."

Abigail laughed into her juice while Hannah merely sat up straighter, feigning indifference.

"My quilts are well sought after. God graced me with a steady hand for stitching. I am content with that."

"Quilts do not feed the family," Fannie said, winking at me as I looked from person to person in this odd interchange. I continued to be surprised by just how personable this family could be, and yet still so foreign to me in so many ways.

Hannah's cool glare bore into me, her smile tight and never reaching her eyes.

"Well, I suppose if Katherine were to remain here among us, she will have no trouble finding a husband. Her cooking renown will precede her, no doubt. Too bad she will only be here for a few days."

I blushed and looked away at her remark. I had no intention of staying. I was an outsider after all. This was not my world. She was right.

I'd be gone in a few days, even if my dreams had centered around one particular Amish man.

We finished up breakfast and I was clearing away the last of the dishes when I overheard Jonah and Fannie talking near the doorway.

"Nathan works too hard to go without eating. I cannot understand why he would not come for supper. That is most unusual for him," Jonah was saying as he picked up his hat and made his way towards the door.

"I will take Abigail and Katherine with me to bring him some breakfast. I will speak with him about supper tonight. He cannot say no to me," Fannie suggested as she straightened her husband's shirt.

"This is why I love you, Fannie. You see the need in those around you, and you tend to it without worry. Nathan would do well if he found someone such as you," he murmured and leaned in to tuck a stray hair that had worked free of Fannie's bun.

I watched their interchange in fascination. Jonah smiled down at her, his eyes bright while his wife doted on him. She eyed him playfully and grinned up at him when he pulled her a little closer in a loose embrace. I lingered by the stove, feeling as if I were intruding on the simple way Fannie took care of Jonah.

I had no reference to a normal married couple. My mother had been aloof and reticent to any affection my father had given her, which was just as well. He had never made much effort to do much for us, his work with the city taking precedence. They had fought constantly, and too many times I remember my mother drinking herself to oblivion and disappearing for days. My parents were the quintessential dysfunctional couple.

Now I was in Amish country, with a married couple that loved one another so simply and yet so completely. You could tell in the soft smile that graced Jonah's face that he loved his wife. In public, he was stoic and straightforward, even a little forbidding. But with his family, he was gentle. He treated her like a partner rather than a possession. I was learning that love was more than physical, was more than simply having it to use. It was about sharing, and taking care of one another.

In the twenty-four hours I had been with this family, I had not once heard Jonah belittle his wife like my dad had done all those years. If anything Jonah Berger worshipped his wife, and she him. It was completely foreign to me, for I had never seen my family act as the Bergers did. Maybe it was the Amish way.

I was discovering that Englishers such as myself had little understanding of how the Amish truly lived.

We seemed to judge the Amish unfairly, simply because of their strict beliefs. They were perhaps strange in that we didn't understand them. I was finding out that their beliefs weren't much different from our own. We just clouded our beliefs with prejudice. I felt suddenly ashamed at how I had thought of them just the night before, making fun of the obvious choices they made at keeping their life uncomplicated.

The Amish kept it simple. There was no need for television or cars that took you away from your home. They had everything they needed. Simple was fine for them. They had a purpose in their lives. If given the opportunity, I wondered if I would prefer the simple life to all that my world had to offer. As I thought of a life here, those haunting eyes of the Amish man entered my mind once more.

I pulled myself out of my thoughts when I heard Fannie clear her throat and look at me curiously. I must have zoned out on the two of them, because I was still staring at her when my eyes focused on her bemused smile. Jonah was nowhere to be seen.

"And what has you so transfixed, Katherine?" she asked, her eyes full of mischief.

Mischief.

These people were so confounding.

I cleared my throat and wiped down the tabletop absently.

"I'm sorry. I admire your sense of family I guess. Your love for Jonah is rather beautiful," I whispered, feeling my face burn with embarrassment.

She patted my hand and her smile grew.

"You do not have love in your world?" she asked while she pulled out a large basket from a nearby cupboard.

I shook my head and laughed.

"We have love; it's maybe just a lot more complicated. Here, it seems so pure. We seem to muddy it up and taint it somehow," I replied and avoided her eyes.

Fannie was quiet beside me for a moment before she turned and busied herself spooning some of the egg casserole she had made into a deep bowl and covering it with a linen cloth. Her silence made me assume that perhaps I had overstepped in my observations, and rather than apologize and embarrass myself further, I set to helping her. I wrapped some of the corn cakes into another cloth and laid them carefully into the basket. I was proud of my corn cakes, Fannie having shown me how to make them before I had fully woken up. The cakes had turned out so well that Jonah had mistaken them for Fannie's.

It seemed my cooking was not so lackluster as my father and Sean made me believe.

We packed everything up into the basket and set out for the Fisher farm, Abigail skipping ahead of us up the hill. She'd find a flower in the grass and pull it out to make a small bouquet in her hands before rushing off again, laughing in the breeze. I was less enthusiastic about this errand.

I was extremely nervous about seeing Nathan again.

Nathan Fisher.

Even his name left a strange feeling in my stomach.

A tense knotting that was not quite painful, but left me finding it hard to breathe.

Or it could have been the hill we climbed.

Forget what people say about Iowa being flat. They had hills. They were just long sloping hills that caught up with you. But it was beautiful, and the quiet in the air was rejuvenating. I remembered the day before and how the corn had sounded in the breeze. It had scared me then with its angry brushing of drying stalks. But it seemed different here somehow. Melodic as they rustled in the soft breeze, and the occasional birdsong offered one a chance to reflect. Perhaps it was because this corn was still green, at its peak. It had the feeling of life and hope as it swayed, whereas the corn yesterday was screaming its last death cry.

The quiet here was peaceful and calming.

We were nearing the top of the hill when Fannie finally spoke.

"This is my favorite time of year, when the harvest is nearing, but the freshness of spring is not quite forgotten. To see the occasional sweet pea flowering amongst the corn. Smelling the earth after the rain. You can feel God's hand at this moment, I believe," she said, letting her eyes close for a moment at the top of the hill to take it all in.

"Does Jonah tend to the fields as well? He told me he was the healer. How do you tend the fields if he is healing?" I asked, pinching my lips together on instinct that I had overstepped once more.

She opened her eyes and laughed at my expression, hugging me close to her as she started down the slope.

"You look abashed when you ask your questions, Katherine! We are not a secret society. Please ask your questions. We are happy to tell those that are curious of our way of life. Knowledge is power, and only by educating can there be tolerance and understanding," she said.

I hugged the milk pitcher to me a little tighter and let out a breath.

"I just don't want to offend, or break any rules. You've all been so kind to take me in. Thank you for that," I said and smiled when she leaned in to offer me another hug.

"It is our way. Please, ask your questions. If it is something we cannot speak of, I will tell you. And maybe, when you are ready, you might offer insight into your world and your life," she replied and we continued on our path towards the house at the bottom of the hill. Abigail had made it to the porch steps, fidgeting as she sat to wait for us.

I was quiet for a moment as I reflected on her comment, wondering what I would be able to tell them of my life. It seemed so sordid compared to how they lived. I was surprised they had not questioned me already regarding the flight from my world. They were a very patient people.

Simple, patient, and loving.

The amorous display between Fannie and Jonah played in my head once more.

"How long have you and Jonah been married?" I asked, wanting to understand how their love seemed so fresh and genuine whereas my parents had been at one another's throats since I was in grade school.

"We were wed the autumn of my eighteenth year. Jonah courted me for six months before that. I was the reason he became a healer," she said with a blissful look in her eye.

"Why is that?"

"He resurrected me, just as Lazarus. I fell into a ravine near Bloomfield, slipping on the edge. He slid in after me and carried me to safety. He did not even know me. My family was from the neighboring community. When he could not find my breath, he breathed his own into me. I awoke shortly after with a broken arm he had splinted and cuts that he had bandaged. But his breath flowed in me and I knew then that he was to be my husband," she said, smiling into the sun as if recalling the memory.

"That's beautiful," I murmured, taken by the love she held for Jonah just in her tone as she recited their story. I let my thoughts wander at the idea of ever finding that sort of love.

It seemed too good to be true.

No one fell in love at first sight.

We were nearing the side of the house, a two-story white structure that stood sharply against the blue sky. It was large, like something a family of ten could live in comfortably. But the yard and garden surrounding it looked untended, the vegetables falling off the vines to rot on the ground, the green leaves wilting from lack of water. I heard Fannie sigh in dismay as she climbed the steps to the porch.

"Nathan needs to ask for help. He cannot tend his home alone. He is so proud, it will be his ruin," she murmured, low enough I assumed she had not wanted me to hear.

"Where is his family?" I asked, looking around and noticing the neglect around the home a little more. The porch had a worn path of dirt leading to the door, the windows glazed with a thin film of grime. There was a deep sense of abandonment surrounding the home. It was far too quiet for a large family the house suggested to living there.

"He is alone, Katherine," Abigail said, her tone much more somber than I had heard from her since meeting her.

Fannie sighed again and stroked her daughter's cheek distractedly.

"His mother and father died last winter, as well as his brother and sisters. The flu took them this past winter," she replied and turned to knock on his door.

"The flu?"

She nodded and knocked again, a faraway look in her eyes.

"It was a hard winter. One of the most brutal winter storms I can remember. It was days before we could get help. God works in his own ways, but it still does not make our loss less painful."

"Nathan never smiles now," Abigail whispered.

I stood there absorbing what they had said.

Nathan was alone.

His family had been taken from him less than a year ago.

The tension in my stomach pulled, and I frowned at the strange overwhelming need to do something for Nathan. I had no idea what; I didn't know him. After last night I was sure he wanted nothing to do with me. The pinching of his brow when he looked back at me as he left made that clear.

Fannie turned away from the door and nodded towards the barn.

"He must have begun his day. Come let us check the field. Perhaps he is there," Fannie said and stepped off the porch towards the sprawling barn to the side of the house. There was enough room in the barn for an entire herd, but again there was only the quiet. The Fisher farm seemed utterly desolate the more I observed it.

As we turned the corner of the barn, I caught sight of him in the field, behind a piece of machinery that dug into the earth as it was pulled by a large black horse. I blinked several times at the sight before me. Nathan worked behind the till, his arms tensed and straining as he gripped the handles to hold the blade in the earth as it cut through. His forearms were well defined, and shining with sweat already in the early morning. His shirt clung to him as he walked; open around his neck to reveal a light smattering of chest hair. He wore his hat back on his head a bit, and his hair looked damp as it plastered to the side of his brow that was tightly knit in concentration until he caught sight of us by the side of the barn.

He pulled his horse up short when he saw us. Wiping his mouth across the back of his arm, he moved to unhitch the horse, his face unreadable as he glanced our way again. I watched him as he worked, his nimble fingers tugged at the leather straps around the harness with practiced ease. He made quick work of the harness, drawing the great monstrous horse with him as he made his way towards us.

The horse shook his head and snorted, clearly upset at having his job stalled. I kept still behind Fannie, timid of both beast and owner as they came to a halt in front of us. Nathan took off his hat and clutched it to his chest, glancing at me briefly before looking down at the ground by my feet.

"Fannie, Abigail. A good morning to you," he murmured, his eyes flickering towards me again. "A good morning to you, Kate."

I could feel the blush rising on my cheeks at the sound of his voice saying my name. It was soft spoken, trembling in his chest. He wasn't loud or brash like Sean. Instead his voice seemed to vibrate through me, the flutter in my stomach growing because of it. I tried to open my mouth to speak, but found my nerves had closed it up. Abigail saved me from my awkward silence.

"You know Katherine?" she asked, looking from him to me curiously. Fannie tilted her head to glance at me askance, a slight smirk on her lips when she noticed my blush darkening.

"Yes, yesterday before supper," he replied, still avoiding my eyes. "I nearly knocked her down her as she came down your stairs. I am afraid I may have startled her."

Fannie was quiet as she glanced between the two of us before nodding and letting out a soft laugh.

"That should not have deterred you from staying for supper last night, Nathan. You are family. Your company was well missed last night," she replied and he dipped his head down again at her words, his ears turning bright red.

"I was just from the field. I would have made poor company. I had supper here. Thank you for thinking of me," he replied and looked up finally into her eyes.

Fannie tutted and motioned to the house.

"Will you not sit with us a moment? We brought you food to break the fast. You must be hungry? Come, put the horse to pasture and rinse the field off. Break fast with us," she said, not offering him a chance to refuse before she was turning and walking back to the house.

He let out a small noise that sounded suspiciously like an exasperated sigh before he frowned and put his hat back on, fidgeting with the horse's bridle before he turned to the beast and mumbled a quiet command, letting him go. The horse snuffed against his chest, glancing at me for a second before flicking his head and turning towards the meager grass growing near the shady side of the barn.

Nathan hesitated in following Fannie and Abigail, gesturing with his long arm towards the house, wanting me to lead. I blinked out of my trance and willed my legs to move, mindful of the man beside me. His soft voice filled the air once more.

"I must apologize once more for yesterday, Kate. I did not mean to frighten you," he said, my name sending another tug into my gut.

"No, I'm sorry. I wasn't looking where I was going. I should have been paying attention," I started to explain, only to have my feet tangle in my long skirt yet again.

I let out an exclamation; words I was sure the Amish didn't use and braced myself for a frontal impact into the dirt, seemingly in slow motion as I extended my arm holding the pitcher of milk to keep it from spilling. I clenched my eyes tight, but the ground never came. Instead, a different hardness caught me.

I felt hands around me once more, and the hot sturdy frame of the man beside me as he pulled me up and into him, jogging me a little hard. My body recoiled on instinct, so that the contents of the pitcher splashed up and drenched Nathan across the chest when I made to push away.

"I'm so sorry!" I wailed, mortified beyond measure that I had stumbled, and then worse, spilled the milk all over him when I reacted.

His eyes pulled together, lips pursed as he pulled away from me carefully. He flapped his shirt a bit to separate the wet fabric from his skin while I stood there clutching the near empty pitcher thoroughly embarrassed. He let out a soft breath of exasperation and shook his head, avoiding my eyes.

"It was not your fault, Kate. I should have assisted you across the wheel ruts. Just as well, this shirt needed laundering. I just have not had a moment to do so," he muttered and stepped away towards the water pump to rinse off, effectively leaving me to stand dumbly in the middle of his yard.

My humiliation only continued when I felt Fannie pulling me up the steps, a low chuckle escaping her lips. She had seen. She would know how out of sorts I was around her nephew.

"God did not grant you grace, Katherine. Busy yourself with Nathan's food and set it up on the table while I go fetch him another shirt.

Abigail has gone to fetch a plate and glass for Nathan. It will be all right, child," she soothed, guiding me to the small table on the porch. I nodded and watched as she disappeared inside the house in search of clean clothes.

I had managed to ruin my second interaction with Nathan.

Why did he unnerve me so?

As if to answer, I looked off towards the water pump, only to feel my breath stutter once again. Standing there, hat tossed on the ground and his shirt open nearly to his navel, stood Nathan, glistening wet in the sunlight. He leaned over and worked the pump forcefully until the water sprang forth into the basin before him.

When it was nearly full, he stood taller and glanced around. I turned my head quickly, busying myself by pulling out the cakes I had made to keep my eyes distracted. But my periphery vision was excellent and soon my eyes were turning to watch him again.

He turned from me a bit, so that I could only see his profile. He slipped his suspenders from his shoulders and shrugged his shirt off, hanging it on the handle of the pump while he bent over to splash water over his face. The water bounced against him, soaking his hair around his temple until fat droplets fell back into the water basin. He splashed across his chest, slipping his hands up and under his arms to rinse off. His body shimmered in the bright sunlight, water pooling off of him as he splashed and scrubbed, the mud and dirt that had caked on him slipping away from his body to leave him much cleaner than I had yet seen him. His chest was pale, seeing little of the sun he worked in, but his arms and neck were tanned from his time in the field.

He dipped his head into the water, drawing it up in an arch of water that splayed out in a rainbow before him as he raised his head upwards and shook out the excess. Toned back muscles rippled as he tugged his fingers through his hair and across his face. Reaching for his soiled shirt he found the small remaining dry spot on it and rubbed his face dry, moving down to soak up the escaping water rivulets across his broad chest and down to his abdomen where a soft trail of dark hair disappeared into his unbelted trousers.

I heard footsteps behind me just as Nathan's head lifted and his eyes captured mine. I was frozen at being caught ogling the beautiful Amish man by my host, and by the man himself. I could see the turbulent green of his eyes from across the yard, could see the uncertainty flicker across them before those delicate brows pulled together and he turned away from me, his lips a thin tight line.

I looked away just as the door opened and Fannie walked past me down the stairs towards Nathan. I kept my eyes averted as she offered him a clean shirt, his soft thank you carrying in the air. My throat was dry and burned as I worked to control the uncontrollable fluttering in my middle. My face felt hot and my heart wouldn't stop its thunderous beating, even while I distracted myself by setting the table full of food. I held my breath when I heard his boots climb the steps, followed by Fannie.

Abigail came out of the house seconds later, and seemed to remain oblivious to the tension between Nathan and I as she set his dishes down on the table, smiling up at him in the hopes to make him do the same.

He was quiet as he settled into his chair, Fannie and Abigail sitting down beside him. I was forced to sit across from him, where he steadfastly refused to look. His lips were still set in a thin line, opening long enough to take a bite before closing once more to chew silently. I sat ramrod straight before him, trying hard not to watch him eat, looking at anything but his face.

My eyes wandered to his long fingers as they carefully tore apart my corn cakes.

His shoulders as he hunched over his plate.

His sharp, angular jaw as he chewed, just starting to show signs of whiskers this early in the morning as if he hadn't shaved yet.

His hair had begun to dry; haphazard now in how it sat against his head. My eyes traveled back up to his red lips as he took a drink of the last of the milk, leaving a white line across his lips until he brought his hand to them.

In no time at all, he was standing quickly, turning to Fannie.

"Thank you for this delicious meal. It is more than you should have to do, and I am grateful. I need to return to my work before the sun is much higher. I would like to be off of the field before mid-day," he murmured softly and moved to leave.

"Let us stay and tend to your house, Nathan. You should not have to tend to both," Fannie started, only to have Nathan shake his head and lift his hand abruptly.

I flinched on instinct at the movement.

My reaction didn't go unnoticed by either, but they said nothing.

Nathan continued.

"I could not impose on Elder Jonah. You have your home. Thank you again for the meal. Pleasant day, Fannie. Abigail," he said, pausing before he glanced at me with tight eyes.

"Katherine."

My name sounded wrong when he said it. His eyes took me in for just a moment, hesitating before he stepped off the porch and disappeared behind the barn. I didn't follow his progress around the barn because Abigail was watching me with those bright blue eyes that seemed to see everything. She glanced back at Nathan before dashing off towards the failing garden beside the house, the strange farewell quickly forgotten to her.

I busied myself with helping Fannie clean up until we were ready to depart. I turned to leave, anxious to get far away from Nathan Fisher, but Fannie stalled me with her hand at the top of the stairs. She glanced in the field, searching for signs of him before turning to me with determined eyes.

"He may not want to impose, but he is my sister's son and therefore my own son as she is gone. Come, we must to tend to his house while he is in the field," she whispered.

"But... but he said no," I stammered, uncomfortable with standing outside his house let alone stepping inside.

"Katherine," Fannie replied, her eyes holding mine hard. "He cannot have the experience to know what he needs. He has not yet taken his Rumspringa. As much as he believes himself to be a man, he is just a boy. He will have his house tended to," she said and pulled me towards the door.

I glanced back towards the field, Nathan still unseen as we entered the house. I looked around nervously, so much closer to a private side of this Amish man than I had ever thought possible. I was immediately taken in by the simplicity of Nathan's home.

Rooms sat quiet and still, with white cloth sheets over most of the furniture save a chair here, a small table there. It looked like our lake house when I was young, sheets covering furniture to repel the dust while it sat vacant. But this house was occupied, if by only one soul. My heart stuttered at the loneliness the house seemed to exude. Fannie stood silently for a moment, not in sad reflection as I did, but in thought about where to start first. I was still taking in the lonely chair and desk in the sitting room when she started to give her orders.

"Clothes, linens, anything that looks like it needs tending to that we can carry home, gather up and bring here," she said.

I gaped at her in surprise.

"Linens? I can't go into his bedroom! I don't even know which one!" I replied frightened, my stomach flailing at the thought of pulling sheets that his bare chest had laid upon.

Fannie nodded, pushing his dishes into my hands and pointed towards the kitchen.

"To the kitchen then. He has neglected that for far too long I am sure. And when you are done there, a rag to wipe up the dust in the sitting room. Go! We do not have the luxury of time!" she ordered and turned and swiftly disappeared up the stairs.

I all but flew at her command towards the back of the house, finding the kitchen easily. Nathan's home and the Berger's had a similar lay out, so I felt more comfortable than I thought I would have given that I was invading a stranger's home, even if just to clean it.

It was still a stranger's home.

A stranger who made my heart hammer as he washed in front of a water pump.

I shook my head and concentrated on the kitchen before me.

By my father's standards, it was spic and span. In my world or theirs it always seemed that a man could put up with disarray. But by my standards and apparently Fannie's, it was a mess. Breakfast or dinner plates were on the table, a used cast iron skillet left on the stove. Remnants of a loaf of bread had already attracted the ants, and they were devouring the bit of jam dropped on the edge of the table.

I rushed about, setting a pot to boil, as Fannie did when she needed hot water for washing the dishes, and wiped down anything I could as I waited for the water to heat up. By the time the water was steaming, I had swept the kitchen and main entryway, wiped down the table in the kitchen, and had made a small pile of dishtowels for the laundry.

I was amazed at how much information about their way of life I had retained in just an hour in Fannie's kitchen this morning, but soon I had the kitchen clean and I was making my way through the rest of the ground floor with a broom and a wet rag. When I made it to the sitting room I had every intention of keeping to the task and not letting curiosity win over.

That was my intention until my eyes flashed on a bit of paper lying on his small writing table. There was a pile of papers and journals lying on the table, strewn across it haphazardly. My fingers moved to straighten the pile up, in an effort to dust, until words leapt out from the top paper.

I forgot to breathe as I read the words on the page, written in neat script.

The colour of fresh turned earth
Gold spun wheat at harvest in the gentle breeze
The pureness of fresh drawn milk
The gentle bend of the elm tree
The melody of breaking day
The tranquility of a cloudless night
The moon as it dances across the starlit sky
The sun's kiss on the horizon at dusk
The depth of the universe.
These are but trials to what I see
In her perfection
The Lord must surely have dreamt as I didst
A haunting image in slumber of beauty beyond all nature
Kate.

I touched the note softly with my fingertips, reading the words once more to be sure I had read them properly. Nathan Fisher, the strange and beautiful Amish man to whom I had just met, had composed a poem.

About me.

Apparently I was not the only one haunted by dreams of a stranger.

CHAPTER 4

We made our way back to the Berger house before midday, a large bundle of clothing held between us as we walked. To have Nathan Fisher's clothes in my hands should have been exciting, if I didn't also know that these were the clothes he had sweat in, been spilled on, had slept in. And thoughts of plunging his soiled shirt into the water and scrubbing what remained of Nathan in his clothes made my face rage as my thoughts drifted to images of him bare-chested in front of the water pump trying to get clean.

"Are you all right, Katherine?" Fannie asked as we neared the house. "You are quite flushed."

I swallowed to wet my dry mouth and tried to smile.

"Just hot. I'm not used to wearing so many clothes," I said, only to feel my blush deepen.

It sounded like I walked around naked in my world.

"That is why I do not wear shoes!" Abigail exclaimed. "The earth is cool on my feet."

I laughed and looked down at my sneakers. They hadn't given me shoes to wear under the dress.

"I don't think I could handle the rocks and dirt," I confessed.

Fannie laughed and guided me towards the back porch of the house, resting the mound of Nathan's clothes on the floor before turning to me.

"Our worlds are quite different I am sure. I forget you have modern conveniences to help you along. Although I might enjoy the air conditioning you have. That is something I wish sometimes," she said, her smile growing when she saw my own blossom.

"I do miss cool air," I replied and followed her into the house, which was much cooler than outside. I let out a relieved breath at the temperature difference.

"We will make midday meal before we tend to Nathan's clothes. He does not have much; it should be quick. I do not know what the boy has been doing for himself all this time. The shirt surely never gets fully clean if he is doing it," she replied and pulled out meats and cheese from a hidden cabinet near the back of the kitchen that I soon realized was a refrigerator.

"It is powered by propane," she explained when she noticed my confused look. "We Amish have made some improvements to some of your devices, if only to make things easier."

"Why not just use electricity?" I asked, truly curious. It seemed like cheating.

She smiled and nodded as if reading my mind.

"Electricity ties us to the world beyond," she explained. "It shows a certain dependence on the outside world. But with propane, we are self-sufficient. It is strange I know. One day we might even think of solar power. But it is important not to tempt us with too many conveniences. You will never see a true Amish person with any of the diversions in your world that would only make our life more complicated. We have enough to do to keep us busy."

I nodded as if I understood what she was saying. It still seemed like cheating to me if they had refrigerators and mixers that were simply adapted to do the work. What I really wished they had was good running hot water and a shower. I felt sweaty and dirty from my morning trek and it seemed like forever ago I had stood in a hot shower to scrub away the dirt.

We worked quietly for a while before I heard footsteps coming down the hall. Half expecting Nathan to burst in to yell at us for cleaning his house, I was relieved to see Emma and Hannah as they stepped in with a basket of vegetables from the garden. Emma offered me a bright smile and began to set the table.

Bread sliced and vegetables cut, Fannie and I plated up sandwiches for everyone. I watched as she took two she had made and wrapped it carefully in a cloth. She smiled at my observation and nodded towards the window. I glanced out and watched as Jonah passed by the window in a large farm contraption behind his horse. Behind him walked a large man in a light blue shirt and straw hat. His dark curly hair peeked out from his hat.

Fannie excused herself to bring the food to the men outside, leaving me with the three sisters. I was comfortable with Emma, and even Abigail. But Hannah watched me as I ate, her eyes calculating and unreadable. Emma on the other hand was full of energy and talked animatedly through lunch.

"The sow finally gave birth. I always love seeing the little piglets before they grow up and become surly. One suckled my finger this morning thinking I was its mother," she said brightly.

"Could be the disgusting color you are wearing today," Hannah muttered around her sandwich.

Emma tutted and smoothed out her dress, admiring the soft muted pink. It wasn't so much pink as it was almost peach colored. And it brought out the color in her pale cheeks. I liked it, although I would never wear it. I preferred the darker dress I had on, an almost forest green in color. It reminded me of home, of the redwoods in California. You wouldn't find trees like that in Iowa. Plenty of sun in Iowa; the shade seemed hard to come by. And although I was from California, where I grew up had fewer sunny days than one might expect. It remained cool for most of the year and sunny only in the mid summer when the fog didn't obscure it.

But the trees were something to behold.

And the ocean.

And the cool breeze.

I missed home.

I frowned into my sandwich at the revelation.

I missed it to some degree.

I wondered if my father was worried.

Did he have people searching for me, or was he glad to be rid of me? He had trouble coming to terms with being a father too. He ignored me half the time and yelled at me for not doing something other times. It may have even taken him a few days to realize I was gone.

I had left a note. Perhaps he had bloodhounds out on the search. Which reminded me of Sean again.

How had he known where to find me?

Only my dad would have been able to track my bankcard, which was why I had refused to use it after buying the bus ticket to Illinois.

So if my dad had traced my card, he would have been the one to tell Sean.

He had sent my nightmare to me, to come and fetch me.

"You are frowning, Katherine," Abigail said, pulling me out of my thoughts. "Do you not feel well?"

I put my sandwich down, nodding and trying to look unaffected.

"I'm fine. Just the heat I think. I'm all right," I said softly, watching as the sisters eyed me carefully for a moment before there was a booming voice in the hall.

I jumped in surprise.

"It is no trouble, Fannie! I will look at your machine and get it running in no time!"

In through the hall came the giant man from outside, his face clean-shaven and a wide smile on it as he approached our table.

"Ladies," he said, grinning at Hannah for a moment longer the rest of us before his attention zeroed in on me.

There was a playful mirth in the big man's eyes, the blue of them brilliant next to his bronzed skin. He was young I knew, older than I was but it was hard to tell with the men in this community. The sun and work seemed to make them more mature than any of the college guys Sean hung around with. He was certainly friendlier than most of the Amish I had met so far.

He removed his hat and offered me a merry smile.

"You must be Katherine. Jonah has mentioned you much this morning. Welcome," he said and extended his hand out towards me.

I hesitated in taking it, sure that it was not Amish custom to shake hands based on my previous night's attempt with Nathan. But apparently this man didn't abide by the usual stoic rules, judging by his broad grin and twinkling eyes. I took his hand tentatively, feeling the strength and roughness of his hand as it all but swallowed mine up.

"Yes, I am Katherine. It's nice to meet you," I said, leaving my sentence lingering since I really didn't know whom this hulk of a man was who was grinning down at me. I suddenly hoped Jonah had not just betrothed me to this man. Surely that was not how they worked.

"This is Mark," Hannah explained, watching me like a lioness watches her pride.

I slipped my hand from his and looked away from his amused gaze.

"Yes I am. Mark Bowman. And soon to be happily wed to my dearest Hannah," he said, smiling adoringly at Hannah.

I didn't know how to act. In many ways Hannah and Mark did not fit the image I had constructed of a good Amish couple. If anything they reminded me of the popular kids back at home. But Mark's smile changed the instant he heard heavy footsteps coming down the hall and he straightened his stance before us. Like a sudden transformation, his manner was more polite as Jonah and Fannie walked back in.

Fannie took in the scene and raised her eyebrow at Hannah, who feigned indifference, but I was sure my uncomfortable smile gave them away. Jonah clapped Mark on the back briskly and brushed past him to step out on the back kitchen porch.

"Mark, son! Come help me with this machine. Show me how to keep this contraption working!" he called as he walked out.

Mark offered us a glimmer of his mischievous grin before he followed Jonah out, the sound of metal and grunting soon following. I glanced back at the noise in confusion until Fannie explained.

"It is our clothes washer. It stopped working a week ago. Mark seems to have a gift for anything mechanical. Let us hope he can fix it fast or we will be elbow deep in Nathan's underclothes!" she said and turned to wash the remaining dishes.

She didn't see the color drain from my face at the mention of my elbows in Nathan's anything, but Emma and Hannah did. Emma's eyes grew wide for a moment before her smile overtook her, but Hannah simply raised her eyebrow and slipped out of the room silently. I watched her leave with a feeling of trepidation in my bones.

I had no feelings for Nathan Fisher, regardless of how my stomach knotted at the mere thought of him. Regardless of the fluttering I felt over the poem I had found, or the mortification I felt at upsetting him, I'd be gone in a few days, searching for a place to live without the threat of Sean overshadowing me.

I didn't belong here.

"Come girls!" Fannie admonished. "Until they have that machine fixed, I am afraid it is the old fashioned way!"

I cleaned the meal away quickly, Emma grabbing a pail of something that looked like powdered laundry soap as we made our way out to the porch where Nathan's clothes lay. Fannie had her hair pulled up tight under her head covering, her hand on her hip as she surveyed the workload.

"Emma, fetch the wash tub from the barn and bring it here. Katherine and I will start hauling water. Abigail, you can sort the laundry," she said, and we split up on a mission.

The heat of the day was at its worst, so Fannie found the only shady spot near the clothesline to wash. Several trips with buckets of water from a water pump and finally the large tub was filled. Fannie brought over the first bundle of clothes, what looked like a nicer pair of trousers and a light blue short-sleeved shirt. Under that were the undergarments. She passed the bundle to me and laughed when I looked at her, horrified.

"Please tell me you have hand washed clothes in your world?" she asked, hands on her hips once more.

"Yes, I have but," I stammered hopelessly.

Plunging and scrubbing; I remembered that in some movie. Simple.

"But?" she asked, that eyebrow rising once more.

I had not really intended on getting that close and personal to Nathan's underclothes. I swallowed and shook my head.

"Nothing, Fannie. I'm happy to do it," I said and moved towards the basin as she talked me through how to properly wash their linens.

"Take out his undershirt there, yes. It is thin, to help breathe on hot days and wick the moisture away. But it is delicate, so do not scrub too hard on the washboard. Otherwise we will be adding mending to our chores and we have far too much to do today as it is," she said and watched as I drew Nathan's lightweight undershirt out from the pile.

I knelt by the washbasin, handling the material delicately with my fingers. Already fine wear marks were evident where Nathan must have scrubbed too hard to clean. The sleeveless shirt was paper thin, light as a feather in my hands, and soft. I realized, as I looked it over that he had not been wearing one in the morning. Nor had Fannie brought him one to change into. I glanced at the mound of clothes and realized that we must have taken all of his clothes with us to wash.

How long did he go until he had to wash his own clothes, living alone and fending for himself? I shook my head and I plunged the garment into the water, taking the soap that Fannie offered me. I was bound and determined to get Nathan's clothes clean for him. I had made him uncomfortable; I had spilled on him, making his life more difficult than it already was. If there was something I could do to help out, I would. He only had himself to depend on and that was not enough.

I scrubbed and rinsed out the soap, wringing it carefully to get most of the water out before Fannie swapped with me and gave me the next garment, what looked like linen shorts. I blinked for a moment before understanding settled in and quickly pushed the underpants into the water in a rush.

I may have scrubbed a little longer, terrified to bring the pants up to the surface and have to look at them once more. But Fannie was pushing me along, and I knew there were many more in the pile. My random thoughts had to wonder if Nathan had not been wearing an undershirt, had he run out of underpants as well?

"Katherine, I admire your enthusiasm, but you will wear yourself out with your scrubbing! You're flushed from working so diligently!" Fannie said, smiling behind her hand when my blush grew.

I handed her the next garment in a rush, deciding that silence was a better friend to me than having to explain my embarrassment. It was silly really. I never got embarrassed over my father's boxers, so why was I so unnerved by some random stranger's undergarments?

We worked like that for some time, Emma taking over when I was huffing over the basin and ended up nearly as wet as some of the clothes. Fannie had a large wicker basket that she had been laying the freshly washed clothes into; she handed me clothespins and set me on my way with Abigail to the clothesline, working together to hang the wet garments. This I knew, since our dryer at home was constantly on the fritz and no matter how many times Sean had come to fix it, it never seemed to work.

I shuddered at the thought of Sean again and pinned Nathan's trousers with a little more zeal. I was here because of Sean, hiding like an outlaw, instead of comfortable at home. I thought again about whether I had made the right choice, how long I would stay, why I was even here when I could have simply asked Jonah to drop me off down the road so that I could hitchhike to the next big town and continue on my way to Illinois. I grew more frustrated with each article of clothing, with each new thought that made me question the very reason for hiding in this small Amish community.

I was working on the last pair of trousers in the basket when Mark stepped off the porch to speak with Fannie. He glanced my way, at the vehement way I pinned and let out a soft cough. It was a laugh, but he was good at disguising it.

"You seem to be quite focused on making sure the clothes stay on the line, Katherine," he said with a hint of mirth in his voice.

I shook my head and remained silent. I continued with securing the clothes, putting the last of the undershirts on the line before turning to see Fannie smiling behind me. I wondered if she could possibly know why I was so flustered.

"Come, Katherine. Mark has fixed our machine. Help Emma and Abigail to empty the water and I will show you how our machine works. We can do much more now and prepare supper while it washes the clothes," she said and made her way up to the porch with my empty basket.

I walked over to the sisters, who were drawing buckets into the washtub and emptying out in the nearby row of bushes. I joined them and soon we had a fire brigade going that made us laugh at seeing who could be fastest. With the bin emptied, I helped Emma return it to the barn. Stepping in to the barn my eyes widened at the size of it.

From the outside it was big of course, but on the inside, it seemed monstrous. The hayloft above seemed a good place to hide and read, with bright sun filtering through the beam and the window above it. There were enough stalls for the Berger's four horses and the dozen cows we had milked earlier. I hadn't noticed how big it was at five in the morning in the predawn light.

Awake, it seemed like a cavern.

And the men of this village had erected it by hand. It was simply amazing.

"Come, Katherine! The day is wasting!" Emma said excitedly.

For all their simplicity, I had to wonder why they didn't stop and enjoy what was around them. Maybe it was because they had so much to do. I stepped back out into the heat and followed Emma a little more slowly up the porch, stopping when I looked at the contraption Mark and Jonah had been working on. It was an old style washer, like what my grandmother had owned when I was little. I looked at Fannie questioningly.

"It is also gas powered. We do have some conveniences," she explained with a smile. "Perhaps one day soon, Jonah will repair the water heater and main water line so that we can have hot water in the house again. There are just too many things to do."

I smiled and shook my head.

"I won't complain over this convenience," I replied, earning a smile from Fannie. My fingers were already pruned up from all the washing so I was grateful for this added bit of technology to their simple ways.

"Every little bit is a blessing," she said simply.

I helped Fannie put a load of bed sheets in the washtub, carrying yet more water from the water pump to the machine before she added soap and started the machine. It wasn't a complicated process, but it cleaned three times as many clothes as we had done in half the time. I was happy about that. The less I had to handle Nathan's underpants the better.

We let the machine run and retreated back into the house to prepare supper. Since four thirty this morning, we had been busy. I was beginning to understand why they went to bed so early. I was exhausted, the last few days and the new lifestyle taking its toll on me. Fannie seemed to take pity and let me simply peel potatoes while she made the bread and Emma peeled away the beans. When we heard the washer finish on the porch, we left our food and worked as a team to get the laundry on the line and the second load in the wash. Between the clothes and the linens, Nathan only had a few loads. Fannie looked over the clothes as we hung them to dry, frowning at some of the holes and bad patches that covered some of his rougher clothes. It looked like we'd be mending his clothes as well as washing. I hoped they had a gas-powered sewing machine as well; my hand sewing would take days otherwise.

Back in the kitchen, mountains of potatoes were peeled, as well as carrots and rutabaga. It seemed like more than what the family would eat, until Fannie reminded me of the Frolic coming up in the next few days. We would prepare most of the feast's dishes the day before so that the Frolic day would be easier. I sighed in relief when the last potato was peeled and I could retreat back to the clothesline. It was nearing sunset once more, and I thought about all I had seen in the last twenty-four hours. I smiled to myself as I folded the clothes, feeling a sense of utter accomplishment at all I had done in that time, even if I was dead on my feet.

I had successfully milked a cow; made the fancy corn cakes I liked so much, cleaned a man's house, and had been elbow deep in his underwear. I laughed softly at the thought of how embarrassed I had been over it when I heard someone come out of the back door.

"Fannie, do you want me to separate the clothes that need mending or should I bring it all in and we can look after supper?" I called out. When she didn't answer, I pushed the sheet aside to reveal familiar green eyes staring at me.

Nathan surprised me with his closeness, so much so that I lurched back in fear, toppling backwards with a loud exclamation that should have sent Nathan running. Instead he reached out to my hand that I had thrown out to try to balance and pulled me back, propelling me again against him. I impacted with a hard thud, grasping onto him to steady

57

myself. Every time I was around him I seemed to find myself buried in his chest.

It wasn't a bad thing.

"Kate."

My whispered name was on his lips was like a quiet request. It made me shiver against him. His hands moved to pull me away and right me once more, but only after lingering for just a little longer than was necessary along my hips. He provided a solid foundation as I stood there swaying from the headiness of having him near. Judging by his thundering heartbeat against my hand as I steadied myself against his chest, he had to have felt something.

How and why I didn't understand. I was not his kind, and my mind made sure to remind me that I would be gone in a few days. This was only temporary.

"Kate?" he asked softly, his voice melting my name. Meeting his eyes, I could see the uncertainty in them as he stood there before me.

I smiled up at him and slowly pulled away, just far enough that I could see his face better. He licked at his lips and continued to stare down at me, frowning. But this time it didn't appear out of agitation, but concern. And still his hands cradled me by the elbows as if to protect me from falling once more. Hands that didn't grip me hard, but with a care as if he were afraid he'd break me. He was nothing like I expected.

He was a puzzle that needed figuring out.

"I'm okay. Good evening, Nathan," I said trying to wipe the worry from his face. He pulled away a bit more and his face softened.

"Pleasant evening, Kate. I am sorry I startled you," he murmured, still holding me. "Again."

I noticed the slight flicker of amusement playing in his tremulous smile.

"You didn't startle me," I replied, swallowing hard when his smile widened at my words.

It was like a million suns had exploded in my stomach. He was beautiful when he smiled.

"So you make it a habit of falling around me then?" he asked, his eyes sparkling with mischief.

I laughed quietly and shrugged.

"I'm not used to the skirt. It's too long," I replied and tugged up at the long material, revealing my tennis shoes underneath.

"I see," he murmured and pulled away from me, glancing towards the porch before returning his gaze back to me, bashful. His hands, now free of me, moved to his suspenders as if determined not to touch me again. Instantly I saw the change in him.

Guarded. Distancing.

What had I done?

He looked at the pile of clothes in the basket and then at the remaining linens on the line and shook his head, that brow puckering again in agitation. The smile that had lit up his face was gone faster than it had appeared. He finally let out a breath and looked back at me in resignation.

"I did not wish Fannie to tend to me. Nor you, Kate. I am sorry if she involved you. I can take care of myself," he said softly, his eyes now downturned as if embarrassed.

I stepped a little closer to him.

"I didn't mind. I learned a lot today and it was really no trouble, Nathan. We all need help. You shouldn't have to do it alone."

His frown grew and he took a measured step away, his hands gripping the leather of his suspenders tight.

"I am not yours to tend to, Kate. I do fine on my own. Fannie worries, but she has her own house to worry over. I thank you for your attention, but I wish you had not," he said and bent over to retrieve the basket.

"Nathan," I started, but his eyes stopped me. They held more than embarrassment, they seemed almost angry.

"Pleasant evening, Katherine. You have no need to be burdened by me. Good night," he said and strode away towards his house, the heavy basket in his arms forcing him to struggle up the hill.

I stood there and watched his broad back once more as it retreated from me, so similar to the night before. I didn't know what I had done to upset him, but once again I had turned him away. He disappeared over the hill and I felt the sadness at his leaving. I didn't know what it was, but whenever he was near, I felt the pull of something comforting. Safe even, despite his acrid tone to me a moment ago.

I shook my head and forcefully pulled down the sheets that remained, folding them quickly before striding back into the house and wanting to forget all about Nathan Fisher. He was nothing to me. I needed to forget the Amish man.

Regardless of his poem.

Regardless of the way he stared at me.

I would still leave.

It was better this way.

CHAPTER 5

"Nathan was here and he left?" Fannie asked, surprise in her face.

I simply nodded.

"What did he say? This is the second night that he has not come for supper! I do not understand what is amiss with that boy!" she exclaimed and turned towards the kitchen porch as if to leave.

"Fannie, my lovely wife, he is his own man. If he wishes to starve that is his own right. I am sure he is upset that you took him in order. Give him a day or two to bury his pride. He will return," Jonah said softly from the head of the table.

She paused in the doorway, looking out towards Nathan's farm before turning back in resignation. Maybe it was the lighting in the room, but her eyes looked glassier than usual. I didn't have the courage to tell them that I was the reason he didn't want to stay for supper. Perhaps it was selfish of me to want to hide the fact that he was troubled to be around me.

We sat and ate a quiet meal, Fannie watching Jonah as if to have a silent conversation across the table. Even Abigail was quiet, glancing at me occasionally before returning to her meal. I was hungry, my body wanted sustenance, but I picked at my meal, eating little while my stomach churned. When the meal was finished, we cleared away the dishes and made quick work of putting the food away for the next day. I fought my yawns behind my hand until Jonah finally announced the end of the day, just as he had the day before.

"A good day by God's graces! Let us to bed, tomorrow will be a busy day!" he said, following us up the stairs.

Emma closed the door quietly and turned to smile at me.

"You have had a busy day, Katherine. If I did not know better, I would say you are taking to our Way better than most. You may even find yourself happy here," she said and winked at me before she started her ritual of disrobing.

Down to my shift, I climbed into bed gratefully and yawned once more. Abigail was already asleep in her bed, drifting off immediately just as she had the night before. Emma slipped in quickly and set the candle into a small lantern holder, smiling as she settled in next to me. I waited quietly for her to extinguish the candle so that we could fall asleep. Instead, she continued to watch me, fingering the casing of her pillow as I shifted under her scrutiny.

"Nathan is an interesting boy," she started. Already I could feel my stomach knot just at his name.

"I guess," I whispered, trying to sound disinterested. Even I could hear the lame attempt.

She shifted in the bed, her eyes thoughtful.

"My mother told you about what happened to his family?"

I nodded.

"Nathan feels guilty over it."

I frowned at her statement and propped my head up on my elbow to regard her better in the dim light.

"Why does he feel guilty, he didn't give them the flu, did he?" I asked.

She shook her head and sighed, a sad faraway look on her face.

"No, he did not. But he was away when they became ill. He was in Missouri with the Bishop on a missionary trip for our community.

Nathan was always concerned with others. It was said that he could easily be voted in as a minister, if not chosen by God to become Bishop, he was that driven to do God's work. When he received word of his family's health, he rushed back, only to return to his mother's deathbed. The rest of the family had died the day before. He was left to take over the farm, despite my father's assurance that our family would take care of it for him while he found himself during his Rumspringa," she explained, her voice a low whisper, as if Nathan's story was the most private secret of the community.

"What is Rumspringa?"

"The Rumspringa is a time when our youth is allowed to explore themselves, to see if the way of the Amish is the right path," she explained. "We come of age at sixteen, and from then, we are to make our way in the world, see for ourselves what is right for our destiny. Some go out into your world, to see how the English live, and some stay here to openly court the one they wish to make a life with. Ultimately most return and are reborn into our faith."

"So you get to choose this life?" I asked, only to put my hand over my mouth again at how insensitive that truly sounded. Emma only smiled and nodded.

"Yes, Katherine. Do not be embarrassed. I can understand from an outsider's point of view how it can be surprising that more do not remain in your world, with all its diversions and temptations. You have only seen the small part of our lives. But we are all joined with a purpose, to live life fully and enjoy the benefits of what God has given us. Rumspringa allows us to see not only your life, but what we have to offer, and to respect our lifestyle that much more," she replied.

I thought about it for a moment and could see their logic. I supposed college was our equivalent to their Rumspringa. We left home to find ourselves. To experiment with that which was unknown but tantalizing to try. Some found their way, some did not. But ultimately, we found our place in the world. Not that I had.

Yet.

Maybe this experience of running away and coming to live with the Amish was my Rumspringa in a sense, my place to figure out who I was. It was a way to find what I needed. Peculiar that I had found them by chance, and discovered more about their simple life and how it drew me in. I was learning more about myself every moment I spent with the Amish.

What an alarming revelation that I found myself here.

Emma might be right, in that I could possibly find happiness in this lifestyle.

But I had only been here a day. Nathan had been Amish his whole life.

"And Nathan hasn't done this Rumspringa yet?" I asked, thinking again about how much Nathan had on his shoulders, and how he had lost his chance at finding who he was. He felt some sense of responsibility that I doubted many men his age even had a clue about.

Emma shook her head and sighed again.

"He had decided long ago that he would forgo searching the outside when he chose to follow God's Word. He would have taken the baptismal classes this last spring. Everything changed when his family died. He turned his back on everything. The church, his chance to explore the world, everything. My father and mother worry for him in that he is a proud person, even if we do not accept pride in our hearts. He is determined to succeed. He would rather starve than admit he is in need. I am sure he is hungry tonight. Your meal this morning is the only meal he has eaten in a couple days, I am sure," she said softly, her dark eyes penetrating mine.

If I didn't feel guilty before, I certainly did after her observation. I had made Nathan uncomfortable, I knew. So uncomfortable that he would willingly starve than sit near me at a meal. I couldn't sleep peacefully while he sat in that large house, alone with a solitary table and chair and a bed, and nothing else. Not while he was hungry and I was full.

His suffering only made me feel worse.

"Did you know that you can follow the moon to his house? I did so many times at night to play with his sister when our parents slept. It is not difficult to find."

I looked warily into Emma's eyes, her thoughts unreadable as she waited for me to respond. I blinked at the thought that played in my head.

She wasn't suggesting I go there, was she?

"Mother and Father sleep soundly, but the back porch squeaks."

I opened my mouth to ask her if she meant what I thought she was saying when she smiled and yawned widely.

"Goodnight, Katherine. I will leave the lantern in case you feel the need to get a drink of water from the kitchen," she said and closed her eyes, a sly smile on her face.

I sat there in the semi dark for several minutes, trying to make up my mind as to whether I should do as she suggested. I waited until her breath slowed before slipping out of bed quietly. I scrambled to get my clothes back on, leaving my shoes off as I snuck downstairs into the kitchen; the only light that of the little candle lantern of Emma's. I put my shoes on in silence, tiptoeing towards the refrigerator. On a shelf, right in front, sat a large, cloth-covered plate with a meal large enough for a growing young man. I glanced towards the staircase, half suspecting Fannie to appear behind me, fully clothed and preparing to do the same thing I was about to do.

No one materialized out of the dark, and as I quietly made my way out through the front door, and down the porch steps, still no one came after me. With the lantern in one hand, and the moon as my guide I made my way towards the field I had watched Nathan disappear into twice now. I had no frame of reference in the dark, and that scared me.

The idea that I could be walking in the wrong direction, a plate of food that coyotes would fight for, only to get hopelessly lost made me question the sanity of my actions. The fact that Nathan had gone without food pushed me forward. He might be a stranger to me, but he suffered because of me. Perhaps I had a little too much pride as well. I wouldn't let him suffer on my account. It was in my nature to make sure I took care of those that needed it.

The breeze fluttered through the corn, the sheaths making an eerie rasping sound as I passed. I could make out the lay of the land as I crested the low rising hill, and I breathed a little easier when I saw the large white house at the bottom, its white siding seeming to glow in the near full moon. The entire hillside was bathed in its cool blue brilliance, painting an almost alien landscape.

I made my way down the hill, fully intending to simply leave the plate by the doorstep, to knock and run for my life. But as I neared the house, I noticed a warm glow coming from the front room, the same room that held Nathan's solitary table and chair. My heart sped up at the thought of him writing another poem. Although I had no idea what it might be about, given the course of events during the day, I hoped that perhaps it might be about me.

Curiosity is a wicked thing.

Perhaps the Amish would be able to recite a passage regarding one's downfall from curiosity. I could barely remember my purpose for coming as I slipped in silence onto his porch and to the nearby window. I felt like a peeping Tom, but the desire to see Nathan, at his desk and writing beat down any moral conflict I had over spying into his private life. I closed my eyes in preparation and let out a calming breath.

I didn't realize the window was open. My eyes opened to Nathan at his table, pen poised over the paper, looking towards the window I hid behind. Dark, lonely eyes locked on mine for a second before I stumbled aside and pressed myself against the sidewall, my heart racing at being caught.

I wanted to flee.

Run. Run away. Again. But my feet were rooted to the floor of Nathan's porch.

Even when the door opened and Nathan stood there, silhouetted in the soft candlelight from his house, I could not run. He was clothed in one of the sleeveless undershirts I had washed for him and soft grey trousers, the suspenders dangling at his hips. His strong shoulders were framed in the doorway, a long graceful arm holding the battered screen door open. The candlelight seemed to set his face in fiery relief, his stubble glowing along his strong jaw. He let out a soft breath, just a whisper.

"Kate."

The energy in the air changed dramatically, from a soft breeze to a crackle of electricity that seemed to exist only between Nathan and I. I swallowed as I watched him take a step towards me, his hands moving to his mouth, rubbing the rough golden stubble around his lips. Still my feet would not move. A dangerous warming filled my gut, expanding through my body as he took another tentative step towards me.

I knew I should run.

He was a stranger.

I was alone.

Another step and the charge heightened so that the hairs at the base of my scalp now tingled.

He could overpower me so easily.

No one knew I was here, except Emma who was surely asleep by now.

"What are you doing here, Kate? It is late," he asked, his voice barely audible over the rushing blood in my ears.

Run. Flee. Another step.

Those troubled, dark eyes watching me warily, the fear I felt inside mirrored in the insecurity I could see in his. What was he afraid of?

"You must be hungry," I whispered, the only words I could think of. It was the reason I was there.

Nathan licked at his lips, sucking the bottom lip into his mouth for a moment as his eyes wandered down to the covered plate in my trembling hand. He swallowed hard and cast his eyes back up to mine, more guarded as he watched me shift on my feet before him.

"It is not wise to be out this late, Kate. Does Elder Jonah know you are here?" he asked, and I could see the renewed turmoil in his eyes.

I swallowed and shook my head slowly, pushing myself back against the side of the porch as he took another tentative step towards me in the dark. I could feel my heart racing, and my breath struggled under his gaze.

"You could get lost in the dark, Kate. How did you find your way?" he whispered, taking another slow step so that he was a mere foot or so from me. His eyes continued to hold me there, unable to move, or to think. I tried to calm my breaths, to will myself to be brave.

He paused before me, his eyes holding me in place with the raging uncertainty swirling in them. He really was afraid.

Of me?

Or himself.

Run.

"The moon," I stammered, feeling the heat of him with another slow step.

So close.

His breath tickled my forehead and blew at the stray hairs that had come loose from under my head covering. I continued to hold his stare until he leaned in, his eyes closing as his head dipped slightly. My eyes fluttered closed at the intense heat I felt against my temple when he sighed out softly, stirring the air around me. I let my breath out slowly, only to inhale once more to the scent of fresh soap and the scent of him. The soap I recognized as what I had scrubbed his shirt with, but his scent was new. Clean, and yet a hint of musk of a man that worked hard. Less intense from every other time he had come close, but definitely familiar.

Nathan.

My eyes opened to the soft pull of the plate from my hands, finding Nathan's eyes downcast as he regarded the meal before him. He licked his lips again in anticipation, swallowing as if he were salivating. He had to be starved. The amount of work he did in the day could not be maintained by breakfast alone. And as he stood there, in only his undershirt and loose trousers, I could see the effects of his struggling lifestyle.

His cheeks were a little thinner than they should have been, tightly hewn muscles along his shoulders and arms, not a measure of fat on him to speak of. He was trim and solid, all his energy going towards the muscles necessary to work on his farm, but not an ounce more. He could have been broader by the look of his wide shoulders, but his modest living had forbid him that luxury. He could easily waste away in the matter of weeks, if left to continue to struggle on his own.

He took a step back, fingering the cloth that covered his meal hesitantly; as if afraid to take the offering I gave him. The indecisiveness appeared once more on his face, his mind clearly battling on what to do. Would he deny it simply because I had brought it to him?

"I should get back," I whispered, stepping to the side to edge my way past him. My courage was failing and I wanted to be gone from the strange pull he had on me.

I felt the heat of his hand wrap around my wrist gently, so light it seemed to be just a brush of his fingers. But the warmth flooded through me and I was lost in his deep eyes once more as he drew close once more. His hand on me should have scared me, but the gentle manner to which he held me put me at ease. Again I felt an odd sense of being safe near him.

"Thank you, Kate. Your kindness towards me is too much. I do nothing but offend, and yet you return with such charity and selflessness. I only wish I could return it," he murmured, looking away towards the darkness.

I turned towards him and touched his arm tentatively, feeling his skin quiver under my fingertips and hearing his breath intake with a stutter. When his eyes drew up to mine, there was something there, something I could not quite discern. It was something akin to longing.

"I'm happy to do it, Nathan. It is something I can do, and not feel like an outsider in your world," I said.

He stepped away again, his hand falling away from me. He let out another soft breath before looking off towards the Berger house, nodding as if to himself. He was resigned again.

"You should go. You are an outsider, and it is not a wise choice to sneak away, in your world or mine," he said and took another determined step back towards his door.

I blinked at his words, feeling a deeper meaning to them, even if he did not mean it as such. In that moment I was sure he understood all too well. I would not be there for him because I didn't belong, and that no matter what we might feel, it was something that could not be. Perhaps he understood more than I did.

No matter the beauty of his poetry.

He understood and had better scruples than I to keep a distance.

No matter what his eyes were saying as I watched him take another step away.

"Good night, Nathan," I said and made to leave.

"A pleasant sleep, Kate," he replied in a whisper.

I made my way back up the hill, glancing back every few moments to see him still in the doorway, watching me as I retreated. The plate of food in his hand was untouched even as I lost sight of him when I descended the hill towards the Berger house. I ran the rest of the way, a little frightened on my own in the dark. Somehow I had felt safe as Nathan watched me climb the hill. I let out a soft sigh of relief when I closed the door quietly behind me, pulling my shoes off to sneak back up the stairs.

I expected Jonah or Fannie to intercept me before I reached the bedroom, but there was no one to greet me after my excursion. I quietly closed the door to the bedroom and stripped once more. But as I slid into bed and made to blow out the candle, Emma's voice made me pause.

"Safe journey?" she whispered.

I smiled at her closed eyes.

"I have no idea what you're talking about," I replied softly.

She smiled but kept her eyes closed.

"Sunrise will arrive sooner than you wish it. You will want to be rested for your second day. Perhaps we might have a guest at breakfast tomorrow," she said, her grin widening when she opened her eyes to regard my blush.

"Good night then, Emma. I'll never fall asleep with you talking," I teased.

I blew out the candle and settled in, still too confused to sleep.

I could still feel his hand on my arm, and the scent I now associated with Nathan still lingered in the air around me. I wondered if he was in his bed, with the freshly laundered sheets I had cleaned for him, and if maybe he was thinking of me. Or would he be up all night writing? Would I find a new poem in his home the next time I cleaned? I was already thinking about next time. Would I stay a little longer, just to see if he felt anything?

Would it matter? He seemed to know whatever attraction there was simply couldn't be.

But what if?

I let out a soft sigh when Emma interrupted my thoughts in the darkness.

"Of course, we must explain how Nathan's plate disappeared from the refrigerator."

"Will Fannie be upset?"

She was quiet a moment before responding.

"She will see God at work, not to worry. Pleasant dreams, Katherine."

"Pleasant dreams, Emma. And thank you."

I listened to her breathing slow, taking in the summer quiet as I slowly drifted into slumber, with his soft voice ringing in my head.

Nathan Fisher definitely had a hold on me.

I drifted off to the warm feeling of his touch on my arm and the look of longing on his face as he watched me go. There had to be something there.

I just had no idea if it was worth the leap to stay a while longer.

CHAPTER 6

I knew it was early.

It felt like I had just fallen asleep. I'd slept poorly, the anticipation of seeing Nathan playing idly in my head. The more I thought of him, the more nervous I became to see him at breakfast. It would be the first time I would be able to interact with him with others present. How would he act towards me?

Aloof? Distant once more?

I knew there was something there. The poem had said it clearly. His soft touch confirmed he was just as drawn to me as I was to him. Even when he retreated from me, I could see the want in his face. It was something different than I had seen in Sean's face. It seemed a lonely and conflicted desire to not be alone anymore. Not the lustful air Sean gave off.

The night had been spent wondering what it would be like to stay and discover that gentler side I had seen in his eyes, the same as Jonah towards Fannie. But I was learning that just being attracted to someone did not permit you to pursue that person in this community. And I was not just anyone.

I was an outsider. An English.

It would be wrong for me to pursue him, I knew. But Emma pushed me to bring him his meal. Fannie smiled at the way I blushed around him. Perhaps it was not so taboo to be interested in the beautiful Amish man. As the precious few hours slipped away from me, I thought about him more and what could happen.

What was I doing?

I would be gone in a day or two. They wouldn't let me stay.

This was nonsense.

But his touch, and his eyes on me confused me.

Round and round my mind whirled around deep green, until my head ached and my eyes crossed and a small hand jostled me lightly. My heavy eyelids slowly opened to the dim smiling face of my sleeping partner. I knew I had to get up and start the day; milk cows, feed pigs or whatever else they had planned for me. But the bed was warm and I had just fallen asleep.

"I've drawn you a bath, Katherine. Come, before Father sends us on some chore. You want to be fresh for today, and the bath will wake you," she whispered, jostling me once more.

I fumbled getting out of bed, my legs asleep and sore from all the walking the day before. Emma led me into the adjacent room, a small bathroom with a claw foot tub and small commode. I stripped and climbed into the tub, the water still warm. Instantly I felt the aches and pains wash away, and I hummed in appreciation over the healing water that smelled like delicate flowers. I allowed myself only a short soak, not wanting to appear too indulgent. I scrubbed my skin until it was pink, and dug into my bag to find my favorite shampoo.

Clean and dried off, I slipped back into my room to find a fresh dress lying on the bed. I got into it quickly, beginning to finally understand the hooks before I pulled my hair into a soft braid that I then wrapped around to hide it under the cover. I hoped I had cleaned up well; it was difficult to know without a mirror. Taking a deep breath, I quietly made my way down the stairs and towards the kitchen.

We repeated the same chores as we had the morning before, and I found I was gaining some expertise in milking the cows. At least I sprayed the milk less out of the jug and more in the jug, and Abigail lectured me less in how to do it, much to my enjoyment. She was very friendly and always smiling, but her skills far surpassed mine and I had to wonder when she had first started milking cows.

I looked towards the hill that hid Nathan's house and tried not to be disappointed when I didn't see him there. He didn't come for breakfast, much to Fannie's dismay, and perhaps my own. Hannah seemed to watch me over her glass and every time I glanced her way, she would smirk and look away. I had to wonder if she had seen me walk to Nathan's the night before or if she suspected something. Emma remained quiet about the missing plate, and Fannie didn't bring it up. Instead she instructed us on preparing foods for the Frolic.

"We need to make some bread and desserts Katherine, would you like to help me in the kitchen this morning?" Fannie asked as I helped to clean up.

"I wouldn't know what to make. I like to make pie, but I don't know what you might like."

"I love pie! Oh will you, Katherine?" Abigail asked loudly.

I looked from her to Fannie, pointedly ignoring Hannah and her dramatic sigh by the sink.

"What kind of pies do you like?" I asked, wondering if maybe I could make my Gran's apple pie.

Did they even have everything I needed?

Suddenly I was nervous to do what I loved best.

"The blackberry vines are bursting," Fannie said as she pulled out ingredients from her cupboard.

"And we just picked some of the first apples from our tree. Can you make apple pie? I will cut them for you!" Emma asked, her eyes begging.

I laughed, the fears I had felt from earlier beginning to fade in my memory at Emma and Abigail's excitement. Of course, Hannah knew how to break the camaraderie with a loud groan and throaty laugh.

"Apple would be perfect. Very symbolic, Katherine. Of course we can always go with cherry," she mused, closing her mouth when she noticed Fannie's warning glare.

"That will be quite enough, Hannah! You can gather the blackberries. Fill the bucket please," Fannie ordered and all but shoved Hannah out of the kitchen.

I stood there, uncomfortable with the conversation made over pie. I just wanted to help. There was no symbolism in pie.

Emma pulled me out of my dark thoughts.

"Do not worry over Hannah. She is nervous about starting her own life away from home. It is no secret she is not one made for the kitchen," Emma said soothingly, and pulled me over towards the sink.

"I just don't want to cause trouble," I mumbled and swallowed hard at the thought of finding my own way back in my world.

At least here, Hannah would have the support of her family.

I couldn't depend on my family save perhaps my sister, who must be worried about me. I hadn't been able to contact her since she had sent me that warning text. My father would no doubt be upset I had not surfaced.

And then there was Sean.

Was he still around, or had he left? Was it safe for me to leave yet?

Why did the idea of leaving make me unbearably melancholy?

"So Katherine?" Fannie exclaimed with a bright smile as she walked back inside. "I will make the bread pudding and milk pie if you will help me make the fruit pies."

I nodded and remained quiet as I took in the ingredients Fannie had pulled out. Lard, flour, salt, sugar, spices and as I took it all in Fannie pulled out bowls and a rolling pin. She smiled a little wider when she took in my soft smile.

"I take it you know how to make a proper crust?" she asked.

"You could say I'm an expert at making pie. It's something I love to do," I said proudly and took the tools from her as well as the apron she handed me.

She watched me with an appraising eye for a moment, checking on my measurements before moving away to start her bread pudding. I was fast learning that the Amish loved bread. And anything that could be reused found its way into a new meal. The bread pudding took the mornings bread and made a raisin and cinnamon baked dessert.

We worked quietly, laughing now and again when Abigail would steal an apple that Emma cut. Hannah came in shortly after with a large pail full of ripe blackberries and handed them to me before stalking off, volunteering to gather up chairs and blankets for the day. I felt a moment's frustration at her attitude, but washed it away just as I washed the berries, preparing them for the first round of pies to be baked.

Fannie watched me a little more closely as I rolled out three crusts for the blackberry pies, nodding when I added the right amount of sugar and lemon juice. I was a little nervous, I'll admit. My mother had never watched me when I baked. But Fannie truly seemed interested in how I managed around the kitchen. And I would admit, I showed off a little when I added the top crust with little overlaid crust leaves on top, sealing it with a light egg wash. Even Emma was impressed.

"You make it look so pretty. I will not want to eat it," she giggled and helped me place it into the heated oven.

Turning back to the table, I pulled out the next batch of dough balls for the apple pies and set to rolling them out. Fannie took that time to settle in beside me and roll out her crust for her pie as well. She was quiet as we labored, the kitchen already starting to grow warm with the morning sunlight and the heated oven. When she finally spoke, we were just starting to form the crust into the next line of pie plates.

"You seem to enjoy baking, Katherine. It is not a common practice for girls your age in your world, yes?" she asked softly.

I shrugged and worked a little harder at the mixing up the apples into the sugar and cinnamon.

"No, I just found I loved to bake. I wanted to go to school for baking, but Sean," I started, only to close my mouth tight and frown into the apple-laden bowl. I could feel my heart thumping hard just at mention of his name.

"Your Sean did not approve of you learning to bake?"

I shook my head and let out a low laugh.

"No, he just didn't want me to do it for other people," I replied, spooning the apples into my crusts to distract myself from the fear I could feel welling up inside.

"Is Sean your betrothed?" she asked softly.

I shook my head again vehemently.

"He was my boyfriend. Not really my betrothed as you think of it, but he was rather possessive of me," I said, glancing at her cautiously.

Would she understand what I meant without having to tell my story?

She simply nodded as she continued with her custard pie. She did not ask and I felt relieved to not answer. They'd want to know eventually, but for now they were being patient. They respected my silence.

But they would ask, I knew.

I made the same fancy embellishment on the top of my apple pies and set them into the oven over the blackberry pies, which were nearly done. Glancing out the window it looked to be still early in the morning, perhaps a couple of hours after dawn. At home I would be just getting up, starting my day. Here, I had already eaten and made half a dozen pies.

I thought again of my sister and I wondered if my cell phone had service this far out. I needed to call her. I excused myself for a moment, sneaking back upstairs to my backpack. Digging around, I found my phone buried deep in the bottom. Turning it on, I sighed in frustration at the lack of service and shut it back down. I'd have to go into town to make my call to let her know I was all right and somehow figure out my next move.

Surely Sean would be gone. It had been three days. I made the decision then that I would leave tomorrow. I closed up my bag and shoved it back under the bed before turning to find Emma in the doorway, her large eyes sad.

"You cannot leave yet."

I blinked at her words.

Had I spoken my thoughts out loud?

"What do you mean?" I asked cautiously.

She came into the room a little further, her arms folded tightly across her chest.

"You are thinking of leaving us. You cannot leave yet. Please," she whispered. Her plea was so genuine; all I could do was nod. She grasped my hand and pulled me back downstairs, her voice a whisper as she led me back into the kitchen.

"You have much to experience still, Katherine. And you have a reason for being here, I am sure of it," she said with a smile. Again my thoughts leapt to the Amish man, and then to his discomfort around me.

"I'm hiding like a coward, Emma. There is nothing special about that," I replied as we came back into the kitchen. Fannie caught the tail end of our conversation and frowned.

"There is hiding and there is fleeing, Katherine. I have a suspicion it is more the latter in your case," she said and started removing the blackberry pies from the oven to make room for her bread pudding and custard pies. When she turned back to me, I saw the question in her eyes.

"So Katherine, which is it? Are you hiding to avoid your duties to your life, or are you fleeing for your safety?" she asked directly.

I felt the table against my back as I leaned against it, suddenly very weary. I looked away from Fannie's worried gaze and let out a long breath, preparing to detail my life and why I was running away. Somehow I knew they would see me for a coward and admonish me for not staying strong in my relationship with Sean. I should have toughed it out. When I looked up into her eyes again, they had softened.

"Is he bad for you?" she asked.

I swallowed the lump in my throat and shook my head.

"He wasn't always like he is now. He used to be sweet and loving. But things changed after we started dating and after he graduated from high school. He changed," I began, not sure how much I really wanted to tell them. They remained silent while I gathered up the courage to talk about Sean Miller.

"I've known Sean since I was little. He's my father's best friend's son, so we spent a lot of time together. It was simply the next step when we started to date. He and I had a lot in common. His mother had left them shortly before my own mother died in a traffic accident. It wasn't until later that Sean became abusive," I said, letting my eyes drop to my fidgeting fingers before me.

"I am sorry for the loss of your mother. That must be difficult for you, to be without her. To have someone to go to when you found he was hurtful," Fannie replied softly.

I figured the story of my mother could wait. It was difficult enough to discuss Sean and his ways. The fact that my mother was distant and the opposite of what Fannie was as a mother was a discussion for another time.

"I was never really close to my mother. My sister and I took care of each other. When she left for school, I had to stand on my own."

"You have a sister?" Emma asked. I nodded.

"Where is she?" Fannie asked me and sat down beside me at the table.

"She's in Illinois. That's where I was going when the bus broke down," I explained. "And then I saw Sean in town, and got a message from Stacy that he knew where I was."

It was quiet for a moment as they thought on what I had said.

"Why would your father approve of someone who hurt you?" Emma asked softly.

"My dad liked Sean as the son he never had. He was captain of the football team and had a future ahead of him in college football. But then he blew out his knee the summer after he graduated and that was the end of his career. He lost his scholarship. That had been his way of getting out of town. Even when the community rallied and got him a scholarship to the local university, he resented it. He was stuck there. He hated that, and it changed him. I was just an easy place to project his anger," I said, shaking my head at memories of trying to explain the bruises away at first to hide the shame, then trying to tell my father the broken arm wasn't a bike accident.

Of course he believed Sean. I had made such a good show of it being accidents. How could I say it was Sean?

"Katherine, no," Emma said, her voice breathy as she stepped up to me. "No man should raise a hand to a woman. It is forbidden in His eyes."

"Do you not have laws? Could you not go to your lawmen and seek help?" Fannie asked, aghast.

I laughed bitterly and shook my head at their innocence.

"Sean's dad is the law. He's a deputy sheriff and my dad is well placed on the city council. Sean was the golden child to the community. It would only make them look bad, or it would make me look like a liar. I tried to tell my dad once, he didn't understand. It was easier to ignore it instead," I explained and turned to clean up our table, hoping to end the conversation.

Instead, I felt Fannie's arms around me, followed by Emma's as they held me close.

Their emotion took me by surprise, after so long admitting that the life I led was how it would be, I fell into a world so foreign and yet completely as life should be. It was difficult not to let out the tears I had refused to shed over Sean and my misunderstood circumstances. Instead I let them hold me until I softly cleared my throat.

"We'll burn the pies," I mumbled and slid from their grasp to check on the apple pies.

They seemed to sense my need to drop the subject and helped pull out the pies, leaving them to cool on racks on the table. I watched the sun brighten the window, turn to midday, and still no appearance of the man over the hill. We worked in the garden in the early afternoon, the heat bearing down on us as we pulled weeds from the flourishing tomatoes and green beans. By the time supper was being set on the table, I had decidedly resigned that Nathan wouldn't be showing up again.

"He was here earlier," Jonah replied when Fannie said something about his absence.

"Why did he not come to supper then? I do not understand his behavior of late," she said, clearly frustrated at her nephew.

"It has only been the last few days," Hannah mumbled and glanced at me.

Fannie heard the comment and shook her head.

"He would not choose to miss meals simply because we have a guest," she said.

Abigail, who had been silent most of dinner piped up.

"It is not Katherine," she said and smiled at me. "He could not stop watching you when he came to speak with Poppa. Poppa had to repeat himself twice for Nathan to understand him."

I glanced over at Jonah and noticed he had slowed his chewing to regard me. He swallowed and looked back down at his plate, an amused smile on his lips.

"We will see him tomorrow at the Frolic, and I will not allow him to be rude to our guest," Fannie said, offering me an apologetic smile.

I didn't know what to say to everything that had transpired at dinner. I was still surprised to hear that he had watched me while I had worked. Once upstairs in our room, Abigail pulled me with her towards the small bed and made me sit beside her while she watched me with her innocent eyes.

"Do not be upset with Nathan," she said simply.

"I'm not upset with him," I said hesitantly.

I was to some degree. He confused me, and he had no business doing so.

"He is just lonely and looking for a friend. Maybe you can be his friend," she said and pouted when Emma snorted from her bed.

"I don't think he wants to be my friend, Abigail," I explained gently. "I'm an outsider."

"But I am your friend," she said, confused. "He should not think of you so."

Emma stood, chuckling at her little sister as she tucked her into bed.

"I am sure Nathan thinks Katherine is nice, Abigail. But he is conflicted," she explained.

Abigail slid into her bed, a frown on her usually merry face.

"He should be nice to Katherine," she muttered. "Talk to him tomorrow, Katherine. He will see what we see."

I hung up my dress and slid into bed with Emma.

"And what do you see?" I asked.

Abigail closed her eyes and snuggled deeper into her blanket.

"You are our new sister. He should be nice to family."

I remained quiet and closed my eyes at her words.

It was nice to hear that she thought of me as family, but it just made it more difficult to explain that I would be leaving, in part because I didn't want to leave now.

I fell asleep to the same conflicting thoughts I seemed to have every night since arriving to this place. The peace and simplicity was soothing, but the haunting specter of the man on the other side of the hill perplexed and frustrated me.

Perhaps Abigail was right, the next day would offer some answers.

Perhaps he just needed a friend.

CHAPTER 7

The routine of waking up early was getting easier.

Up in the darkness, clothed and to the cows for their milking, and I was learning a little more every day. Both Abigail and Emma showed me how to gather eggs from the chickens and laughed when I yelped at the persistent pecking.

The sun was just starting to break its way over the horizon when we reached the kitchen door, and stopped at the conversation in the other room.

"She does not understand our laws, Mother. She will shame us."

I swallowed hard at Hannah's words.

"She is our guest. It is up to us to show her our way. She has honorable intentions."

Fannie's words made me blush. She had so much faith in me, a stranger. But Hannah's logic made me want to get in touch with my own sister that much more. I needed to get back on track. Hannah had only clarified how much I didn't belong here. She seemed to be the only one who saw me for who I really was, an Englisher simply pretending so she could hide.

"She dotes on Nathan. Surely you see the scandal that would bring, and just before my wedding, Mother."

"Nathan needs something to pull him out of his sadness. Perhaps a friend can do that. I think Nathan knows the law well enough to keep a proper distance, Hannah. Perhaps that is why he keeps his distance now.

And if it were to become something deeper, you should be glad for him, and for her. Perhaps that is why God brought her to us. She needs something as well, or she would have remained in her world. We are here to provide whatever she needs to find her way."

"Just do not ask me to include her in my wedding."

It was quiet for a moment in the kitchen.

"Your wedding is of course your own. I am sad you would not welcome your sister into your celebration."

"She is not my sister."

The voices in the kitchen grew too low for me to hear, but I had heard enough. Emma and Abigail whispered out my name as I walked away down the hall. I was intent on going upstairs to find my things and leave. Regardless of the friendships I had made with this family, it was bound to end sometime. At least Hannah had in her head that I would not remain here, and I respected her for her standoffish behavior towards me. She had been honest. The part of their lives that they had allowed me to experience was well and good for learning about them. It didn't mean I would make a life here. I was moving towards the front door to avoid them when I heard footsteps ahead of me at the door.

"Pleasant morning, Katherine," came the booming voice as the door opened towards me. Mark stood there, Jonah in his shadow. I shuffled to a stop from my retreat, plastering a stilted smile on my face at the men before me.

"Pleasant morning, Mark. Jonah," I replied, nodding to both of them and turned reluctantly to make my way back towards the kitchen.

I entered the kitchen to four sets of eyes watching me. Emma tried to smile apologetically as Fannie moved towards me and hugged me quickly before moving to set the table. Hannah simply turned back around to finish cooking the eggs in the large skillet. It was obvious that

Emma had said something about us overhearing the conversation. The tension was overbearing as I stood there, watching Jonah and Mark take in the scene. It took Jonah's bright voice to break the awkward silence.

"I am famished! Hannah, whatever you are cooking smells delicious! I am sure Mark is excited to break fast with you every morning if he has to look forward to this every day!" he exclaimed and rested his hand lightly on my shoulder as if in support for a moment before moving to his seat.

Mark moved past me and settled in next to Jonah, speaking softly about the day's events. I helped Emma with bringing out the meal, avoiding Hannah's cold stare every time I passed. It was only once I was seated beside Emma that Hannah spoke up.

"I wonder if Nathan will join us this morning," she said lightly, sitting comfortably beside Mark. Her eyes flicked over to me for a moment, a knowing smirk on her lips at my blush.

Jonah shook his head and reached for the biscuits.

"I spoke with him at dawn. He sends his regrets at not breaking fast. He wanted to be on his way to Elder Wittmer's," Jonah said pointedly and passed the biscuits around. I remained quiet, focused on the eggs on my plate.

Did the Amish gossip as much as we did in our world? Or was I simply that obvious about my conflicted feelings? I had a feeling the day at the Frolic was going to be nothing short of humiliating, with either him making a show of ignoring me, or of providing gossip for this community and me stammering like an idiot. And for that, I was determined not to embarrass Nathan or myself at the Frolic.

I would behave myself and remain distant, regardless of what Emma or Abigail thought.

The Amish man didn't need any more drama in his life, certainly not from me.

Emma watched me carefully as we cleaned and packed up everything to prepare to leave. I tried to offer her a smile, to let her know I was fine with what I had been through, but her eyes seemed to penetrate through me, as if she could see all my sins.

Fannie ushered us out with our food, patting me gently on the shoulder as we made our way outside to the waiting wagon. We placed the food in boxes in the back of an open wagon, where half a dozen chairs and piled quilts lay. Jonah finished pulling the harness on his two large horses and turned to us, a bright smile on his face.

"Shall we? The men are sure to be hungry when we get there!" he said and climbed up into the bench seat in front.

Fannie followed, settling in beside him, pulling a dark cover over her head. Hannah was already seated in the back of the wagon, nestled between the chairs. Emma and Abigail scrambled up and sat with their backs to the bench, smiling towards me expectantly. I let out a sigh and climbed in.

Climbed in might be an understatement.

It was more like clawed and scrambled and stomach rolled once I had a leg up gracelessly to hitch myself into the bed of the wagon. By the time I had slid up and crawled over to sit beside Emma, all eyes were on me. I shook my head and hunkered down holding onto the box that held the pies as we started off. I could only imagine having to get back down again.

I sat quietly as we rode, the sound of the horses and the loud rolling of the wagon the only thing I could hear in the bright day. The sun was already beating down fiercely, and it was not even noon yet. It was bound to be a scorching day. I squinted against the harsh glare of the sun to take in the landscape as it passed by.

Iowa was the corn capital, and at a glance, it seemed that the Amish did indeed grow plenty of corn. But as my eyes adjusted to the glare of near midday, I noticed other fields, brighter here, duller there as we travelled down the dusty road. It seemed they also grew plenty of wheat and small pockets of leafy vine plants: grapes and berries and tomatoes. And with every house we passed, few and far between, there was a large garden beside the house bursting with life.

There was a fair share of newly turned fields as well. It was mid summer, I could only assume that crops had been harvested already and the soil preparing for something new. I didn't know anything about farming, but it seemed reasonable. I had to wonder how the Amish survived on just their crops and quilts. Did they trade with us Outsiders?

Surely they did, and then purchased what they could not grow or make. There was so much to them that I did not understand. How could something so simple be so mysterious and complicated?

I let my thoughts drift as the sun beat down on us. We made our way towards Elder Wittmer's farm in silence. Emma was strangely quiet beside me, and Hannah merely ignored the two of us. It wasn't far, but with some of the blankets and food, it was easier to ride than walk I supposed. It was fairly obvious when we neared the Wittmer farm. The buggies on the side of the road and the milling people around a field by the house gave it away.

That and Emma's sudden fidgeting.

I glanced her way, trying to offer her some encouragement, but the look in her eyes gave me pause.

She liked the son, John, didn't she?

Why did she look suddenly ill?

"Are you all right?" I whispered near her ear, watching as she swallowed and tugged her bonnet over her hair nervously.

"Emma is nervous to see her John," Hannah teased.

Emma swallowed again and grew paler at Hannah's words. I had had enough of Hannah and her teasing. But I remained quiet, not wanting to cause any more problems. Instead I took Emma's trembling hand and squeezed it encouragingly. I was going to help her, whatever it took. The wagon slowed to a stop, drifting backwards for a moment on the slight hill until we turned into the hill and stopped with a jolt. A few of the men in the field started to make their way towards us, their straw hats bobbing as they walked. I glanced towards them, hoping for a sight of the black hat, but there was none that I could see. I helped Emma with the box of pies, slipping out of the wagon with a little more grace than I had getting in. As the men joined Jonah, we followed Fannie towards the house, where tables had been set up in the shade for the bountiful spread of food for everyone.

As we approached, the women around the tables turned and regarded us quietly. I felt every eye turn to me when they noticed me just behind Fannie. One woman, who seemed to be the one giving the orders turned and nodded towards Fannie as we drew near. She was an older woman, stocky and grey haired; she stepped forward with a brisk smile.

"Welcome, Fannie! We are happy to see you and your kin today," she said, her voice gravelly with age. She looked my way, waiting for my introduction. I couldn't help withdrawing just a bit into myself at her perusal.

"Sarah, this is Katherine," Fannie said simply, motioning towards me. "She is visiting and welcome in our family."

Sarah moved closer, several of the older women falling in line behind her as if in solemn judgment. I turned my eyes down, not sure if I should look her in the eye or simply be the obedient outsider. Which may be why I was surprised when strong arms wrapped around me. Sarah held me briefly before pulling away to smile down at me.

"Welcome, Katherine. We are happy to have you with us today. Please, come. We will get you settled with a duty for the day," she said and just like that, I was making my way down the long table with Emma to set out the pies before being shuttled off to gather water for the men in the field.

Emma came with me, still pale as she looked around timidly. I noticed that no one spoke with her and she seemed more withdrawn as we walked amongst the women. The younger women, those that were about our age, stared at us as we passed, some frowning before turning away. I waited until we were at the water pump to ask Emma.

"Why are the other girls like that? Why do you look so upset, Emma?" I asked softly, pushing on the pump to get it started. The water gushed out, filling our bucket quickly.

Emma glanced back towards the house and shook her head, grimacing.

"It is nothing. We should go. It is hot and the men will want a drink," she replied and struggled to pull the heavy bucket out of the basin.

The bucket's handle was shaped so that two people could carry it, as if it were made especially for two women to haul. I put my hand on my hip and refused to lean over to pick it up until she answered me. She looked at me pitifully, her eyes pleading for me to drop it. When I didn't she finally let out a long breath and looked at me hard.

"I said no to John Wittmer."

I blinked at the hard edge to her voice, and to the words she had said.

"I don't understand. No to what?" I asked, stepping a little closer to her. She huffed and dragged the water bucket out of the basin, splashing it over the edge roughly. I jumped forward and helped her before she spilled it all over herself. For someone so small, she had a lot of force when she used it. I followed along beside her for a moment, walking towards the field where the men worked on the fences. She finally let out a breath and slowed down.

"I am sorry. I do not mean to be rude. It is something that I will regret it for the rest of my life, I know."

"Emma," I said, slowing her down to a stop to look at her. "Can you please speak without all the drama? What did you say no to him about? And why do the other girls look at you like that?"

We both glanced back to where the women busied themselves with laying out food for the mid day meal, catching quite a few of the younger women looking after us. When Emma turned back at me, she shrugged and let out a pained laugh.

"They do not like me because I broke John's heart. I told him I did not wish to be his wife," she said and pulled us along again.

"Wait," I said and pulled her to a stop again, sloshing water over the side again.

"Katherine, we have work to do."

"Tell me why."

Her exasperated look turned suddenly to shame and she looked away towards the men.

"I did not want to leave him a widow. He said he would love no other."

I walked beside her when she pulled us along, realizing what she had done. Emma had thought she was going to die, and chose to deny her love, John. And to see her, who always seemed so excited about everything, now so at odds with being near him once more, it made my heart hurt.

"But you're better now. He can ask again, can't he, or is that forbidden?" I asked, speaking a little quieter as we drew near to the first group of men.

The men paused in their work, leaning in to take the cups we had and dipping them into the cool water to take a drink. The men did not introduce themselves; they merely drank their fill and passed the cup around, ignoring us. When they were done, one of them nodded and we moved along towards the next group of men.

As soon as we were out of earshot, Emma answered me.

"Of course he can, Katherine. But I broke his heart. I shamed him by denying him."

"How do you know that? If he will love no other, then he still loves you," I whispered, afraid that the men near us could hear our conversation. She didn't answer me until we were on our way once more to the next group.

"You do not understand, Katherine. He is a faithful man. But his father is most pious. He did not approve of me breaking his son's heart. I denied his family. I am not the wife John needs," she said and pulled me along roughly only to come to a stumbling halt before the next group of men, all young and beardless.

Her breath caught as the first came towards us, a good-looking man with wavy blond hair and deep brown eyes. He seemed a little older than the rest, perhaps a year or two older than Nathan. His smile was quick, like a radiant blast of sunshine before he restored himself to a more stoic demeanor. He tipped his straw hat back a bit as he walked towards us, his long gait bringing him to us quickly. The other men followed him a little more slowly. I recognized Mark among the young men of this group.

But their leader was looking intently at Emma.

And again, the briefest smile on his face.

"Pleasant day, Emma," he said softly, tipping his head towards her, his eyes never leaving hers.

Even I could see the adoration in them.

This was John Wittmer.

And there was no way that he did not absolutely love the girl beside me.

He looked on her for longer than any of the other men, his eyes never leaving her even as the cup was passed around. Emma kept her eyes downturned, avoiding his gaze until the men turned to leave. When they were far enough away, she glanced towards me and nodded.

"John, this is Katherine. She is visiting our family. Katherine, this is John Wittmer," she mumbled.

John's adoring gaze drew away slowly so that he could finally look my way, his smile suddenly polite as he nodded to me.

"Welcome, Katherine. I have heard much about you. I am most happy to see you have made friends with my Emma," he said quietly, his voice resonating in the hot air.

"She is a wonderful friend. I am grateful to meet you," I replied, feeling my own heart flutter at how he seemed to watch her.

His smile widened for a moment before he looked off past my shoulder, a flash of amusement passing across his face before the more polite look slipped back into position.

"I am keeping you from your duties, I must apologize. Emma, may I sit with your family at mid day meal?" he asked, his focus back on Emma.

She nodded and blushed, staying silent as he nodded and turned back to the work on the long wood fence. I glanced at Emma as she let out a soft breath and shook her head slowly, trying to pull herself together. I put my hand on her shoulder gently and urged her on, quiet as we walked to the next group of men.

We emptied the bucket, heading back twice more for water before we made it to the last group of men at the top of the far field, mending the fence beside what looked like a large cow pasture. It was the last group of men that made me stumble like Emma had when she had seen John.

Before me with a large sledgehammer in his hand was Nathan Fisher.

I heard Emma let out a soft giggle and tugged me back into motion. My eyes couldn't look away from him, drawn, as they seemed to be from my first glance at him. His arms moved, the sledgehammer rising in the air in a perfect arch to land squarely on the fence post, driving it into the ground. The man across from him copied his movement, but somehow, it was not nearly as mesmerizing.

Nathan swung again, his body moving with a graceful rhythm accompanied by a low grunt as the iron met wood. Again the man copied him, then again Nathan swung.

Swing. Thump.

Every movement was crystal clear in my head as I watched in awe. A flash of moisture escaped, flying from his head as he swung and the noise of the hammer connecting in the background to the noise that escaped Nathan's lungs on impact made me flush. The damp shirt clinging to his back that moved when his back moved, bunching up and pulling out around the suspenders was a sight I would remember long after the sun went down. The way his bottom lip slipped into his mouth when he noticed I was standing there, watching him work, only made me much more aware of his pull on me.

I looked away hurriedly and kept my eyes turned towards Emma as the men slowly moved to take a drink, Nathan lingering in the back of the line until everyone had had their fill. I watched as his scuffed boots stepped up beside me as he took his turn to drink down the cool water. I chanced a glance up towards him, hoping to give away nothing of the draw I felt, but the steady blush on my face was a dead give away to my conflicted feelings.

And his sweet, bashful smile only made me blush more.

"Pleasant day, Emma. Kath...Kate," he said softly around his cup, the first part of my name barely audible before he was swallowing down a long drink of water.

"We have missed you, Nathan," Emma said sweetly. "Will you eat with us today? I know Fannie is hoping to see you."

Nathan glanced at me for a moment, as if to read my thoughts on the matter of him eating with us. I looked down at my feet, fighting to keep myself calm and neutral, but I could feel my cheeks burning as he watched me. Nathan returned the cup to the water bucket and took a step back to return to the task.

"Please tell Fannie I would be grateful to sit with you. Until mid day," he said and turned to return to his work, his back yet again the image burned into my mind as he picked up the hammer once more.

I felt Emma tug me along, realizing after a moment that I was still staring. We hurried back to the water pump, filling it up and carrying it back towards the gathering of women, who were busy making final preparations for the meal. Fannie saw us and motioned us toward her.

"Excellent, Emma. Would you two help Sarah with setting up the food tables?" she asked and turned back to the task of cutting up the chicken in front of her.

We made several trips in and out of the house heavily burdened with casseroles and bowls of food. My arms had begun to feel numb by the time Sarah finally dismissed us and sent us out to find a place to settle in to eat. It seemed Fannie had made a comfortable spot by an old oak, providing room and much needed shade in the worst heat of the day. She waved us over, looking off towards the field when an old fashioned bell rang out.

I followed her eyes and watched as the men turned as one and made their way towards us, separating to find their families. Jonah walked towards us with John and Mark in tow. Fannie turned to us and handed us small hand towels. I looked down at them, confused.

"The men will need to clean up," Fannie explained, pointing to our bucket that was sitting by the tree, full of water. I looked down at the towel again and blinked at the idea that I would get to see Nathan washing up again.

Hannah stood by Mark, who grinned down at her own smiling face. I watched as Emma took a deep breath and moved towards John, who was watching her intently. He took the towel with a soft thank you and hidden smile, causing Emma to appear even more bashful. I smiled at the thought that he did really care about her. It was simply a matter of time before he asked her again.

I looked around our little gathering for the familiar black hat, seeing nothing but straw as I craned my neck to find Nathan. He was nowhere to be seen. I felt a bit left out, standing there alone as the other couples tended to one another before settling into places on the quilts Hannah had laid out. I moved towards the bucket, the vantage a bit higher so that I could see well. But still there was no sign of Nathan.

The men reclined on the quilts while Fannie and her daughters made their way towards the tables of food, where plates were being filled and passed out. I looked a final time towards the gathering of men as they mingled and found their places before I sighed and tucked the towel into my waist and started towards the food line where Fannie and her daughters waited.

I stood quietly behind them, listening to the conversations as they flitted past.

New babies.

The Schmidts had to put their bull down.

It would be a tough winter again.

A simple life.

Not if the Giant's had scored.

Or the new movie that had become a blockbuster.

Nor the newest trend in fashion.

I glanced around again, catching a few eyes looking my way, but for the most part I seemed to be ignored. I found that odd. Perhaps it was because I was with the Bergers. I watched as people passed Fannie and smiled and wished her well, looking back towards our camp out to see Jonah speaking with several men before they ventured on their way. I was learning that they held a respected position in the community.

Abigail pulled me along, laughing quietly as she watched me take in the surroundings. All work had stopped, families sitting close together but the entire community within hearing distance so that the Bishop, a tall man that Emma pointed out could speak as we made plates of food.

I was making my way back to the Bergers when I noticed Nathan.

He was standing off by himself, behind the tree where the men had cleaned up. His eyes were tracking me, and the knowledge that he had been watching me made my skin tingle. Emma looked his way and let out a frustrated sigh.

"He is nervous, Katherine. I would say he is worried about sitting too close to you, or maybe too far," she whispered, grinning when I grunted and shrugged.

"I don't care where he sits," I muttered, although to be honest I was hoping he would sit near me. Then perhaps I could speak with him.

Figure him out.

He continued to watch me, his eyes flickering briefly towards the plates before he would look away, sucking on his bottom lip as if trying to make a choice in something. We arrived to our blankets, the men sitting up and smiling in anticipation as Fannie and her daughters handed the men their food. I was left standing with two plates, glancing towards Nathan as he slowly made his way towards us.

I pretended to ignore his approach, placing his plate near the edge of the blanket, as if bribing a wild animal closer. I sat down carefully, tucking my legs under me and sitting straight with my back to Nathan's plate, wondering if he would finally sit down and eat with the family. Jonah's booming voice gave him no alternative.

"Nathan! Please come sit with us! Katherine has brought you a plate. Come sit with us, do not linger there!"

I felt him draw near, hearing his voice soft as he thanked Jonah and sat down near me. I continued to sit facing away from him, waiting patiently for prayers to be said. The Bishop stood and raised his arms to call for silence. He was a tall man, with a strong presence. He looked around as the community quieted down, his voice carrying in the quiet afternoon air. His voice was deep and carried across the yard, so that it was easy to hear his words.

"Brothers and Sisters. This is a blessed day. Once more our community comes together to help one in need. I am thrilled to see the commitment of so many young sons and daughters help out one of our

Elders. As you know, Elder Wittmer was in need of our assistance, after a hard winter, one that so many of us felt deeply," he said, his booming voice carrying through the trees.

At mention of the winter, I heard a soft sigh leave Nathan from behind me. I knew the Bishop's words had made him remember his loss.

Without looking behind me, I leaned back, letting my hands rest behind me on the blanket. I could sense Nathan behind me, could feel his foot touching my extended hand as I sat stock still, willing some energy his way. I felt his fingertips brush against mine; one finger curling with my pinky finger for only a second and then it was gone. Just that brief touch filled me with the fluttering feeling I always felt when I thought of him.

The Bishop's prayer complete, everyone turned to the food, the buzz of conversation building once more. I chanced a glance towards Nathan behind me, swallowing when I noticed he was watching me. He offered me a tremulous smile before turning his attention to John and striking up conversation. It was difficult for me to concentrate through the meal with his voice so close behind me. I sat there listening, forgetting to put the fork in my mouth many times. His voice was melodic as he spoke of typical mundane things.

Abigail leaned in close to me and looked over my picked meal.

"Do you not like your food, Katherine? You have eaten very little."

I shook my head.

"Oh no, it's all very good. I just can't eat this much in one sitting. I'm full and we haven't even gotten to the pie yet," I said.

"Did you make pie, Katherine?" Mark asked, grinning like a hungry Yogi Bear.

I blushed and nodded, ignoring Hannah's glare.

"Well, I am looking forward to it," Emma said happily. "Apple is my favorite!"

"It would be," Hannah muttered under her breath, noticing Emma tense.

"Hannah," Jonah warned quietly from far end of the quilts.

"I just mean to say that it did not do Adam well, the apple," she said and glanced at Nathan with a knowing look.

I heard a breath behind me, as if Nathan made to interject, but I beat him to it. This was something I knew.

"The forbidden fruit is never truly referred to as an apple, Hannah. Artists depicting Adam and Eve used the apple because of its appearance. Scarlet, round and full of juice and heavenly goodness that can only be sinful if stolen from the tree. Some scholars have argued that it might be the pomegranate, or dates or even figs. But the Forbidden Fruit is knowledge itself, is it not? The more you know, the more you are bound to the Earth and the sins of man. The apple, however is discussed in the Bible in more than one occasion as a positive entity," I said, watching as Hannah's eyes narrowed at my knowledgeable explanation.

Just because I was an Englisher, did not mean I didn't know anything. True, I knew little about God and the Bible. I didn't go to church. But what little I did know would be my talisman. I was suddenly thankful for that Religious Studies class I had taken my only semester in community college.

Nathan's soft voice startled me.

"Keep me as the apple of your eye; hide me in the shadow of your wings."

I turned to look at him, his eyes contemplative as I nodded.

"Psalm 17:8," he whispered, his eyes focusing away from me as if embarrassed to have spoken.

"That's right," I replied. "The Bible refers to the apple of one's eye as the pupil of one's eye, or the center. It is a reference to Israel, and the center of God's love."

Nathan cleared his throat and looked up towards Emma, smiling.

"So by loving apple pie, Emma, it seems that you are one with God's love," he explained.

I grinned at the clever interpretation Nathan had come up with, watching as Hannah scowled in the corner near Mark while Emma and I rose with Fannie to take the empty plates away. Emma pulled me close as we walked, glancing back towards Nathan before she laughed softly.

"How did you know that, Katherine? You surprise at every turn! I think you impressed Nathan with your knowledge," she exclaimed softly.

I shrugged and glanced back to find Nathan still watching me. When our eyes met, his lip would twitch upward and he would look away hurriedly. His glances did not go unnoticed. The Bishop, standing by a tree near the food tables, cast a long contemplative look towards Nathan, and then to me. His face was unreadable as he turned and walked away, sitting with the elders.

As we neared the table where the desserts were laid out, we were joined by some of the girls that had watched Emma and I earlier. Their leader, a tall redhead, offered a simpering smile to Fannie as they passed. They lingered behind us as Emma and I cut up slices of apple and blackberry pie to take back. Fannie and Abigail loaded up with plates and made their way back. As soon as Fannie was out of hearing range, the redhead spoke up.

"Katherine, is it? You do not act like one of us, with your laughter and willful arguments with your family. Are you from a neighboring community that has looser laws?" she asked, her voice high and nasally.

"She is visiting, Joanna. She is a guest," Emma replied coldly.

103

Joanna ignored Emma and continued on.

"Surely you do not plan on remaining here? Or are you looking for a husband?" she asked and glanced back at Nathan with a smirk when she caught him watching me.

I straightened and gathered up the plates in my hand, turning to the redhead with determined eyes. After Hannah, I was finding my courage.

"I'll stay for as long as the Bergers allow me. I am happy to help them with whatever they wish of me. They have made me feel welcome," I replied, trying to sound calm. Joanna glanced back towards the Bergers and laughed, her laughter sharp like glass breaking.

"Yes, the Bergers are most charitable. I am sure they are not the only ones that have made you feel welcome," she said and turned on her heel and disappeared into the crowd.

I let out a breath and shook my head at Emma as she huffed beside me on our way back.

"I thought you were all friendly and welcoming. Who knew you had catty bitches just like in my world," I muttered, squinting hard at the words that had flown out.

They felt dirty somehow in the presence of Emma. But Emma let out a chuckle and looked back towards where the girls had gone.

"Our worlds are not so different, Katherine. Evil can be found anywhere," she replied and moved a little faster towards her family.

Emma handed John a slice of pie, his grin widening over her choice of apple. I had come with three plates in my hand. Not sure what Nathan would have wanted, I brought him a choice. I stood beside him, my back towards the family and smiled down at him nervously.

He sat up at my approach and fought to hide the eagerness on his face.

"Would you like apple or blackberry?" I asked softly, struggling to hide my smile when I watched him lick his lips as he eyed the plates in anticipation.

"You made these?" he whispered and looked up at me with those penetrating eyes, glimmering with excitement.

I nodded and felt a surge of pride wash over me when his smile brightened.

"Must I choose?" he asked, a hint of mischief in his expression, the same amusement he had shown me when I had tripped on his laundry.

I glanced back towards the family, their chatter distracting them from our quiet conversation. I looked back down at Nathan, his eyes still on me. I tipped the slice of blackberry onto one of the apple plates and settled in beside him, offering him the double slice. He took it from my hands eagerly, his fingers brushing over mine as the plate slipped from my hand to his.

His soft blush and downturned eyes made my skin burn more than the touch had. He was so much different than the men I had known. Shy, hesitant. Never overbearing.

"Thank you, Kate," he murmured and cut off a sizable piece of the apple, slipping it into his mouth.

I watched as his eyes closed, his jaw moving slowly as he chewed. He hummed softly, the deep tenor of it rumbling through his chest. But his lips had me mesmerized as he chewed. They moved with his jaw, turning up slightly in contentment as he took another bite, this time from the blackberry.

Again a soft hum and smile, his eyes opening lazily to look down at me, in a slight daze. A silent conversation seemed to move between us, and more than anything I wanted to touch him, to feel that connection. I knew it wasn't allowed, so instead I tried to eat. His voice startled me.

"You make pie like my mother did."

I blinked and stared at him, unsure of what to say. He looked back down at his plate and cut another piece.

"She loved to bake. She made the same leaves on her crusts. Did your mother teach you?"

Green eyes searched me out when I didn't answer right away, so deep and expressive with the sadness that swirled in them. I shook my head slowly, afraid to say anything that would make him think about his mother any more. It was clear he missed his family.

"However you learned, you can tell it is what you must enjoy doing. Baking that is," he continued, a smile playing on his lips as he looked down and took another bite. "Your talent will be well known before the day is out."

"Hannah says it's my bargaining chip for finding a husband," I blurted out, cringing when he stopped mid-chew with widened eyes. He recovered quickly, the playful smirk returning once more.

"An honest man would look for more than the ability to make a good pie," he replied. "He would spend his energy to find what she enjoys in life so that he could please her."

His eyes continued to hold onto mine, the world falling away from us as I read every emotion roil through him. Fear, hope, caution, and concern. Was he asking me what I enjoyed? Did he want to know me?

"Are you enjoying your time here, Kate?"

I blinked and concentrated on the pie on my plate.

"I am. It's different than my old life, that's for sure."

"Do you miss it?" he asked, his voice a little closer. When I glanced up, I noticed he had slid a little closer, his knee brushing my own as he settled in beside me.

"Miss it?"

He nodded and took another bite from his blackberry pie. I could tell he was trying hard not to devour it like Mark across the blanket. And he was still trying to figure me out as he watched from the corner of his eye.

I shifted beside him, so that my shoulder sat close to his, our faces a little closer for quiet conversation. No one bothered us, although I could see Emma and Abigail glancing time and again towards us.

"I don't really miss it, no," I finally answered. "There wasn't much to miss really."

He frowned and fingered the chip in the plate he was holding.

"Surely there are people to miss. It must be hard to be away from family? Your loved ones?"

"My family's nothing like what you have here," I replied, feeling a sudden sense of longing for what Jonah and Fannie offered as parents to their daughters. I would never have that, not unless I worked at it.

"But your mother? She must miss you?" he asked, his eyes capturing mine in an inquisitive gaze.

I cleared my throat and looked down at my plate, shaking my head.

"My mother died seven years ago," I whispered.

"I am sorry," he replied quietly and I felt a warmth work through me when his hand brushed over my own on my lap. It was tentative, hovering before he squeezed it with a gentle pressure. I was transfixed on his hand over mine, so much bigger than my own, and tanned from days spent out in the field.

And warmer than I would have thought.

Comforting.

Safe.

Mark's booming voice broke the spell, Nathan's hand jerked away quickly as if startled from a dream.

"Katherine, that was delicious! Do you think there is any more left? Nathan, come let's get another piece of Katherine's pie before it is gone!" he exclaimed, jumping up and nearly dragging a flustered Nathan along with him.

I tried my best to pretend to ignore Nathan as he walked away, but his back was so familiar to me now, and his brightening smile cast in profile as Mark seemed to tease him made it nearly impossible to ignore. It was nice to see Nathan opening up, and a little more relaxed.

Fannie's voice finally broke me from my thoughts.

"Katherine, come. We must help with washing."

I followed Fannie dutifully back to the tables, where food was being separated and brought into the house for storing; cups and dishes were being moved to the wash basins laid out near the porch. Fannie grabbed a stack of dishes, nodding for me to take one as well and followed her to the washbasins. We stood there and worked as a team to clean many stacks, washing and rinsing and passing along to Emma and Abigail to dry and stack. It took most of the women a considerable part of the afternoon to return the Wittmer yard to its original state, with men gathering up the long benches and an army of girls taking the silverware and plates to a large wagon where it all seemed to get packed up with expert efficiency.

With chores completed, I joined Fannie and some of the women on the porch to sort through clothes that needed mending. I was reminded of Nathan's clothes that we had never mended. Needle and thread in hand, I set to the arduous task of sewing hooks back onto vests and trousers, graduating up to patches in children's clothes as the older women watched me work. A few of the women chuckled at my work and remarked at it teasingly.

They were in agreement that I was by far a better pie maker than seamstress.

The afternoon passed quickly, the fence and house repairs completed before the sun had dipped down too far. I was tired from the heat and the work, my eyes drooping as I rested against the porch railing. Fannie's soft hand on my shoulder had my eyes slamming open, blinking away the sleep. She smiled and put her needle and thread back into her sewing basket.

"Come Katherine. We should gather our things and make our way home. Would you collect our plates from Sarah? Jonah appears to want to depart soon," she said and stepped towards our wagon.

Emma, Abigail and I picked up our dishes from Sarah in the kitchen and said our goodbyes. The wagon was already hooked to the horses and the blankets already packed for our departure. John and Mark stood by the horses, nodding to us as we passed. I made a better attempt at climbing into the back of the wagon, settling in next to Emma once more.

Looking around, I didn't see Nathan.

It was on the second scan of the buggies that I noticed the familiar black hat down the line of tethered horses. Nathan was frowning and nodding at the Bishop as the man spoke to him, the elder's hand moving in succinct movements that told me that he was being lectured sternly about something. Nathan glanced our way and looked away quickly, his frown deepening at the words of the Bishop. Our wagon began to move, away from the two men. As I continued to watch, Nathan glanced our way once more, his eyes meeting mine, the emotions running through those dark eyes left me feeling gutted.

He looked regretful.

The Bishop followed his gaze, and I frowned when his glare reached me.

It was obvious now what the Bishop had been telling Nathan.

He most certainly did not approve of me.

Nathan did not come to supper again that night, Fannie tutting and shaking her head as she looked out the window repeatedly for some sign of him. She finally turned away when it was clear he would not be joining us. We cleaned in quiet, tired from the long day. Even Jonah's bright announcement to the end of the day was a little worn.

"A blessed day, our fatigue reminds us of the hard work we accomplished. Let us retire and enjoy an easier day tomorrow," he said and ushered us up the stairs.

As I was following Emma into our room, I felt Fannie's hand on my shoulder, turning me toward her. Her face seemed troubled, looking off worriedly towards her bedroom before pulling me in for a tight embrace. She let me go; I could tell she wanted to say something, but her resolve had failed. I offered her a weak smile, which put her at ease as she left me for her own room. I entered my bedroom, stripping off my clothes quickly and sliding into bed beside a yawning Emma. She opened her eyes and let out a long sigh, reaching for my hand to hold it tight.

"Nathan will be all right. He is probably already asleep. You saw how hard he worked today. Do not worry about the Bishop. He has always had his eye on Nathan. He still wants Nathan to be a part of the community. He is impatient to see Nathan join the Way. You will see, tomorrow Nathan will be himself again," she murmured and closed her eyes.

I heard Abigail shuffling around in her bed and then her small voice cut through the dark.

"He likes you, sister. Nathan smiled today."

"You will see, Katherine," Emma murmured. "I have said you are here for a purpose. You will see."

"I guess," I whispered, not sure as I thought on the look he gave me as we left.

I lay there fighting sleep, struggling to figure out once again what I was doing.

The regret in his eyes then, as well as him not coming for supper once more had me questioning his motives. The Bishop seemed to know where to steer Nathan's feelings.

I closed my eyes and thought on what Emma had said.

Would he be himself tomorrow?

Was I really here for a purpose? Was this where I should be?

Was Nathan the reason for me to stay?

I made a resolution there in the dark that I would find out.

I had no claim, but I wanted to know what he thought of me.

Tomorrow I would find out.

CHAPTER 8

I was up before the dawn.

Up before the sisters, amazingly.

I was up so early I surprised Jonah in the hall as I stepped out of the bedroom. I cringed at his startled exclamation and put my own hand over my mouth to keep from crying out anything inappropriate. He motioned me ahead of him down the stairs and followed me into the kitchen where Fannie was already brewing coffee. She turned and her eyes widened when she saw me.

"Katherine, you are up early! Could you not sleep?" she asked, touching her husband gently along the cheek as she passed him.

I felt that maybe I was intruding on their quiet time until Jonah sat in his seat and motioned for me to sit by him. Fannie brought over three cups of steaming coffee and sat beside me, her hand lingering along my neck where my hair was bound up. They were both quiet for a long moment, glancing at one another over my head until Jonah finally let out a heavy sigh.

"You have been a most welcome addition to our family these last few days, Katherine."

Glancing at Fannie I could see there was something left unsaid in Jonah's words. She smiled and nodded.

"But you have many worries," she said softly.

I nodded.

"I feel like I might be making things more difficult here by staying," I said and watched as Fannie frowned.

"You are no trouble, Katherine," Fannie started, closing her mouth when Jonah cleared his throat.

"I think perhaps it is a good time to talk about what you ran from and what you wish to gain by remaining here with us," he said softly, his eyes finally capturing mine in a fatherly gaze.

I swallowed against the sudden dryness in my throat and nodded. I owed them an explanation. Especially if they found me gone later today. Or worse, here to stay past my welcome.

"You met Sean, that day you discovered me in your buggy," I started, trying to figure out how to best describe the events of my life so that they would understand and maybe not judge me too harshly.

"Yes," Jonah replied. "He seemed to be worried about you. But there was something in his eyes I could see. Something dangerous perhaps."

I nodded and clenched my jaw at the thought of having to flee like a scared lamb from the big bad wolf.

"He has hurt you," Jonah stated, looking at his wife with a guarded expression.

Fannie already knew some of my story; I relayed briefly some of my history to Jonah, watching as Fannie shook her head sadly. I couldn't look them in the eye as I described the fear I felt the night that made me decide to run. I had tried not to think much about it, the memory of his hands on me lingering deep in my thoughts only in the dark of night. My fingers twined together as I whispered the events that forced me to run. Images that continued to haunt my dreams were still crystal clear in my head.

Sean, a little drunk as we sat around at his friend's house.

Sean pulling me in for a possessive kiss and me trying to pull away because the taste of the cheap beer made me retch.

Sean's friends laughing when they noticed me struggling in his grasp. His dark eyes that flared with anger at being embarrassed in front of them. His whispered threat that he was done waiting. The pawing of big hands, followed by the cheers by his friends. Shadows closing in, hands everywhere. Struggling to break free when I heard the fabric ripping at my shoulder.

Screaming.

Breaking free when I kicked and connected with soft tissue.

Running out of the house, blind into the dark night.

Running. Fleeing. Hiding.

"Katherine."

My head jerked up to the sound of Jonah's voice. He whispered quietly, the calm in his voice helping me to focus in the present.

Safe.

"Katherine," Fannie started, her hand covering mine as they fidgeted on the tabletop.

"I couldn't stay there anymore," I whispered, ashamed at what I had revealed finally.

"And no one of your world could help you?" Jonah asked, his voice low.

I looked up and saw the pain in his eyes.

Or disappointment.

I shook my head.

"I tried with my father," I replied and shrugged. "But Sean always had an excuse, or he found a way to distract my dad. Honestly there were days I thought my dad was happier having Sean around than me."

"I do not believe that," Fannie replied gently. "He must love you. You are his child."

"Maybe it wasn't that way, but it felt like it most days, especially after my mother died," I amended. "Sean was everything my dad wanted in a son. But something changed in Sean after the injury. He was meaner. He didn't like that he had to depend on people."

"And he took that aggression out on you," Jonah said, straightening up in his chair.

I hesitated before nodding.

With Sean there was always more.

He always wanted more out of our relationship, even when we were younger and just friends, he had always wanted more. I had never really felt that draw to him, had thought that it would happen eventually. But I also had learned from my parents' mistakes that I wouldn't just let him decide when we would make the relationship more. My parents had started too young, had been too reckless, and the result was a loveless marriage, two daughters and my mother's regrets that eventually made her drink too much, ultimately ending in the car accident that killed her.

My dignity was nothing to Sean, who was more like my father than I cared to think about. Brash and demanding, thinking only of himself and not what might happen should I give in to him. He wanted more and he knew I would break down eventually. It became a game to him. He had tried so many times, but had never truly been forceful, until that night. And saying no to Sean that last time was the final straw.

"I cannot believe your father would not wish to help you find peace," Fannie said quietly, pulling me out of my thoughts once more. I looked up to find Jonah and Fannie sharing a solemn and silent conversation between the two of them.

I knew it was only a matter of time that they would want me gone.

I was everything they were not.

"It's okay," I murmured, looking down at my folded hands. "I'll understand if you want me to leave."

"Why would we ask you to leave?" Jonah asked, surprised. I looked up into his compassionate eyes and shook my head.

"I don't fit in your world. I'm not good. I'm," I stammered, closing my mouth when Jonah shook his head and placed his hand over his wife's that rested over my own.

"We do not judge, Katherine. There is nothing but love and acceptance in our home. What happened was not your doing, nor your fault. Whatever happened in your past is behind you. It is your choice where you wish to go next. Until then, you are welcome in our home as our daughter," he said, looking deep into my eyes.

Fannie held me close, nodding in agreement with her husband.

"You should contact your sister. She must be worried," Fannie said.

I nodded and thought on that.

"I don't want him to have a way to trace me back to here," I started, thinking about my phone and again how Sean had found me so easily. "I should probably go into town and call her to let her know I am alright. I just don't know if he is still there."

"It has been a week, with God's grace he has left," Jonah said and scratched at his beard in thought. "We must go to town tomorrow. We can take you then."

"Thank you," I murmured. "I don't know how to repay you for everything you've done. I've felt more at home and at peace here than my own home."

Fannie's smile widened and she glanced at Jonah.

"We live by kindness and peace, Katherine. That is what we know. We do not start our life until we have chosen the path. You came here because you needed a path to find. Perhaps it is God's way of telling you that you have found yours," she said and turned to busy herself in the kitchen. Jonah watched me thoughtfully for a moment, as if contemplating something serious.

"You have had much to process these last few days. You have enjoyed it here?" he asked over his coffee.

I smiled as I thought about all I had done. And whom I had met.

"I have enjoyed it here. I feel like I am accomplishing something when I'm here," I replied.

"Then we shall enjoy having you here with us a while longer," Jonah replied with a smile and rose to walk out the back door, heading for the barn. I helped with breakfast, my heart a little lighter in the knowledge I had a place to be for the time being.

Nathan didn't come to visit for breakfast, much to Fannie's frustration. Jonah remained quiet, but I sensed his worry as well. I caught him watching me with that thoughtful air over his coffee before he let out a sigh and stood to start his work.

I had helped Fannie with clearing the dishes and setting them back in the cupboard when we heard voices and hard footfalls in the hall before turning to see Mark and Jonah returning to the kitchen. Mark's face was flushed, as if he had come from running.

Jonah grabbed a bag by the door and turned to Fannie.

"The Bishop's daughter has gone into labor, and it appears to be breech. I will need your help Fannie. We must leave this moment," he said hurriedly.

I watched as Fannie leapt in to action, tugging her apron off in an instant. She gathered up a basket and turned to us.

"I am sorry, you will need to finish up here, girls. The garden needs tending, as well as the chickens. We may be delayed. You must take care of things while we are gone," she said and followed after her husband.

Mark touched Hannah's cheek lightly before following after, leaving us in the quiet of their departure. We heard the buggy pull away just as Hannah turned to look at us, scowling.

"I am not doing all the chores today. Mind the animals while Abigail and I see to the garden," she snapped and left through the back door, leaving Emma and I alone in the kitchen.

Emma sighed and shook her head sadly.

"I wanted to show you around today. I suppose it will have to wait. I will tend to the stalls. Mother made Nathan a plate that you can take to him. I am sure he is hungry," she said, grinning when she took in my awkward frown.

"I don't think he'd like me just showing up," I started.

Emma groaned and moved to the refrigerator, grabbing the plate and shoving it into my hands. She raised her eyebrow at me when I made to push it back towards her.

"Mother would have taken you there anyway this morning, the way she was acting at the table," she explained. "Besides, you have matters to discuss with Nathan."

My mouth dropped open and my eyes widened at her words. She laughed and pushed me towards the door.

"Emma, how do you figure?" I asked, doubting how I could ever hide anything from this family.

She laughed again and squeezed me tight as we walked out together.

"Katherine, I can read people. When they make a decision, their body language changes," she explained. Then she giggled and blushed.

"You also talk in your sleep," she quipped and skipped off the kitchen porch on her way to the barn, leaving me on the steps, gaping at her mischief.

I shook my head in wonder at her outgoing nature and started up the hill towards Nathan's house following the well-worn path between the houses. I had to wonder if Nathan shared all his meals with the Bergers.

At least before me.

I sighed at the silly notion that Emma and little Abigail had put into my head about Nathan. If he liked me, then why didn't he come to meals?

I crested the hill and immediately caught sight of Nathan, the black hat a striking beacon as I watched him pulling bundles of hay off of a wagon and toss it near the entrance to his barn. He held strange metal hooks in his hands that grabbed at the tight bundles, allowing him to grip them easier before hauling them off the wagon and through the air. He seemed to toss them effortlessly, his arms never seeming to tire, even with the weight of the bundles and the heat of the morning, already causing the sweat to stain his clean shirt along his back. As always, I noticed just how elegantly he moved as he twisted and tossed, his lean form reminding me of how hard he worked, all alone here on his farm.

He noticed me as I neared, tossing one last bundle of hay and wiping at his forehead before tossing the hooks up into the wagon. He didn't pause in his work to greet me; he jumped up into the back to drag the deeper bales closer to the edge where he could toss them off unceremoniously. I stopped just out of throwing distance and waited quietly as I watched him work. He was silent as he labored, his eyebrows tight, glancing over only once before frowning and returning to the task.

That quick frown was enough to make me question why I had come. His silence seemed to confirm what I had thought the day before. The

Bishop did not approve, and had told Nathan just that. Of course Nathan had listened. Gone was the soft smile and tentative glances from the Frolic. Now there were tight lips and a furrowed brow. Today there was a stiff back and a determination to ignore me.

I contemplated turning and dropping the plate onto his porch, so that I could run away once more. But I was tired of running. I glanced at the porch, wondering if he would follow when I heard him clear his throat near me. I turned to find him standing in front of me, looking down with a glare that seemed to be fighting a maelstrom of emotions, all dark.

"Pleasant morning, Katherine," he said low.

Katherine.

Just in a name I seemed to have my answer in how he felt towards me.

"Good morning, Nathan," I said, my voice much stronger than I felt. I was trembling on the inside.

"Did Fannie send you? I have already broken fast. She need not dote on me," he said. His voice was gravelly as he spoke, as if he were fighting to keep his voice measured.

"She was called away. But she wanted to bring this for you," I replied, deciding that the partial truth was probably best.

He didn't seem interested in the plate in my hands, and certainly didn't seem excited to see me with it. He looked away towards the way I had come and nodded, his lips pursed tightly.

"I appreciate your selfless spirit to look after me, Katherine. Please thank Fannie when you see her next. Would you leave the plate in the kitchen? You undoubtedly know where to find it, yes?" he asked, pointedly staring down at his gloved hands.

I blinked at the harshness of his words, so unlike the day before.

"Of course," I murmured and turned to head back to his house, my breath hard to find as I made my way up the steps to his house.

I went directly to the kitchen and set the plate into his refrigerator, not wanting it to spoil. Looking around as I made my way back out, I noticed not much had changed since I had last been inside. There were no dishes mislaid, not even a crumb on the table. I wondered if he had been truthful in that he had eaten.

As I walked past the small table in the sitting room, my heart sank at the sight of the bare tabletop.

Not a note out of place, or a paper resting there. Had he thrown out the poem?

I didn't linger to find out.

He was still where I had left him when I walked back out, his eyes on me as he watched me walk back towards him. When I drew close, his cold gaze faltered and once again he looked down towards his hands. We were quiet for a moment, an awkward silence that seemed to stretch on forever before he finally straightened and stepped back away from me.

"I have much to do today. A pleasant day to you, Katherine. Please offer my thanks to Fannie," he announced and turned back to the stack of hay, grabbing the farthest one and strode in the barn with it, not waiting for me to respond.

I stood there dumbly until he came out and took the second bale inside, never looking my way as he moved. He had effectively dismissed me and I was standing there like an idiot waiting for more humiliation.

I turned from him and strode in the opposite direction, back to the Bergers. With the hope of being able to stay with them, I had set myself up thinking there was truly something there between Nathan and myself. Only there was not. The Bishop, someone he probably looked up to, had reminded him of our differences. I was a stranger, and he would of course see the error of his ways when someone opened his eyes.

It still destroyed me.

I should have known better.

I was halfway up the hill when I heard a loud rustling behind me. Not used to the sounds of the farm I hurried my pace, afraid of something coming at me in the stalks of corn. I trudged through the uncut wild grass, hoping to shorten the distance between the Bergers and me. I heard a muffled exclamation and whirled around just as Nathan burst through the corn to my left, his face red and his body winded from the pursuit.

"Please, Kate. Wait," he panted.

I turned away from him and started back up the hill, struggling with the skirt and the tall grass that wrapped around my feet as I tried to speed up.

"You made yourself clear, Nathan," I said as I struggled to stay ahead of him as I fled.

"Kate, please just a moment to explain," he begged and reached out for me.

The feeling of radiating heat from his hands as they wrapped around my waist and pulled me back to him made me falter. I felt him against me, a burning solid mass against my back as he held me gently. His breath blew across my neck, the scent of hay and soap causing my nose to burn slightly as I inhaled deeply. He breathed in as well, a soft sigh sounding against my ear before he pulled away slightly, turning me around to face him. One hand ghosting along my hip, the other cradling my shoulder, he seemed to understand I needed tenderness instead of force. His fingers held me so loosely, as if he were afraid to grasp too hard.

If he only knew how his light touch affected me.

So unlike Sean's forceful grip, Nathan's was like a caress.

And his eyes held so much emotion as he looked down at me, asking me.

Asking me for what?

"Kate, forgive me," he whispered and let his eyes close as he took another deep breath.

Perhaps it was the plea in his voice, the question in his eyes before they slid shut. Or maybe it was the alluring way he held me close that made me react.

I don't know. I only know that I was a magnet to him, from the first moment I had stumbled into his life. And every touch from him seemed to set off my senses to wanting to be closer to him. I felt myself leaning in a dreamlike haziness. He stood there, the heat of him radiating into me as my head strained up towards his. My hands moved up and touched his cheeks reverently just as my lips reached his, partially open as they breathed in the air around us.

The instant my lips touched his, a tingling flush rushed through my body. He gasped and trembled between my hands, as if to pull away, but his hands gripped me a little harder. His eyes shot open, looking down at me in surprise when I pulled away slightly. He darted a glance from my eyes to my lips, turmoil raging in the darkness of them. I could feel the heaviness of his breath as it washed over my cheeks. He seemed undecided as to what to do.

Push me away or continue what we had been doing?

Daring to take the chance, I pulled myself up on tiptoe once more, my lips connecting to his quivering ones with a little more pressure. Nathan shook against me, this time a soft moan escaping his lips as they tentatively moved with mine, mimicking as I tasted him carefully. My fingertips traced along his jaw, at the smoothness there of an early morning shave until I traced up to thread into his hair along the nape of his neck. His bottom lip found its way between my teeth, and I sucked him in gently before releasing his lip slowly.

He tasted like apples.

Forbidden fruit?

Perhaps in this instance.

He moaned again and staggered a step towards me, his hands gripping me a little more possessively, clinging to me as if he might fall. His lips, so soft and full as they captured mine, seemed to learn quickly, and sucked in my bottom lip as I had done to him a second before. When he released it, he sighed and moved to reclaim my mouth eagerly as his breathing became more ragged through his flared nose.

Another moan as I touched my tongue hesitantly to his lips, feeling another tremor work through him and his mouth opened willingly. He mirrored me again, the tip of his tongue grazing against mine as if to take in the taste of me before his arms wrapped around me and held me tighter to him, his mouth enveloping mine in a passionate kiss that rushed through me and made my knees collapse underneath me. He held me up against his rigid body, a tinkling of fear playing in my head under the rush at being held so tightly. I could feel him shaking against me, or perhaps it was both of us, as our bodies were forced so close.

And then a tattered whimper and he was tearing himself away, shoving me away as if I had burned him. He stumbled back, hands going to his mouth and his eyes clenched shut as he struggled to catch his breath. I balanced myself, hands on my knees to keep from falling, my breath ragged in the air. When I straightened, his eyes opened wide and he took a step back, shaking his head emphatically.

"This is not," he stammered. "We cannot... you must leave. Kate. I cannot."

I took a step towards him, to apologize for what I had just done; sure I had just sullied any hope for getting to know him with my brazen attitude. He staggered back another step and put his hand up to stop me from coming closer.

"Please, Kate," he rasped. "You must go. I cannot."

He turned and fled down the hill towards his home, tripping on the steps of the porch before retreating into the house and shutting the door hard, leaving me without a doubt that I was absolutely the worst thing for him. So much so he had told me to leave.

I turned and ran.

Ran away.

It was what I was good at.

CHAPTER 9

No one was in the Berger house when I burst in, to which I was thankful. I couldn't bear to see Emma's face when she heard I was leaving. She would convince me to stay, and I would be forced to see Nathan again. And see the pain in his face as he looked on me shamefully.

Why had I kissed him?

Why did he turn from me all the time?

Why did I go and shame him?

I was such an idiot.

I dug into my bag and pulled out my old clothes, flinging the dress off hurriedly. The tears refused to come, which made me more frustrated as I struggled with the buttons to my shorts, finding them difficult after a few days of hooks and eyes. I threw on a tank top and ripped off the cover on my head, completing the transformation back into the old me in a matter of minutes. Folding the dress neatly and laying it on the bed, I took one last look at the room I had felt more at home in than any other and turned from it, closing the door and not looking back.

I snuck down the stairs quietly, afraid at every turn to discover one of the sisters there to stop me. But the house was quiet. Slipping out of the front door, I skirted along the edge of the house away from the barn, finding myself at the edge of the garden. I was half way to the road when I noticed someone watching me from the row of vines towering in the sunlight. Hannah's red hair had worked loose and framed her face as her eyes tracked me.

It was her expression that alarmed me more than anything. I had assumed Hannah would rejoice on the day I left her family. Instead, her eyes seemed worried, her mouth set not in a frown of disapproval but of concern. I shook my head and turned from her, not wanting to see any more regret on my behalf.

I chose my life.

It should not affect anyone else in how I chose to screw it up.

Shouldering my backpack a little higher on my shoulder, I set off quickly down the road; back towards the town I had first met Jonah a week ago. It felt like months, but in a good way. The more I thought about the last few days, the more upset I became at my brazen attempt to force a response from Nathan. The response had been forced out of him, to be sure. I didn't like being treated like that with Sean.

What had I expected?

A happily ever after?

Did I think I would fit in with them?

I laughed out loud at the notion of spending my life there, milking cows, with several children running around and the Amish man smiling at me as Jonah did to Fannie. But my laugh choked and I swallowed against a dry throat when I realized that that life was not nearly so bad as what I was walking towards. In fact, the idea of seeing Nathan smiling down at me every day seemed worth all the pre dawn chores and life without television or the Internet.

And that one forbidden kiss had been the best kiss I had ever experienced.

I kicked at the gravel that piled up on the side of the road and walked a little faster, amazed that no cars or buggies passed on my trek. I walked under the blaring sun for what seemed like hours, until it beat down on me from directly overhead. I was beginning to think I had taken a wrong turn when I noticed an intersection in the distance, and beyond that, buildings shimmering like a mirage in the heat. With the end in sight, I quickened my pace.

Within minutes, I was stepping into the general store, where everything had changed for me. It seemed a lifetime ago. I dug into my bag and pulled out the last of my cash for a tall bottle of water, ignoring the little corn cakes that had gotten me into trouble in the first place. The man behind the counter eyed me suspiciously as I asked for a restroom, eventually pointing towards the back of the store. I disappeared into the restroom, the incessant flicker of the fluorescent lights irritating as I rinsed the dirt of the road off of me.

The water was cool and it helped against the burn that was starting along my shoulders and cheeks from the late summer sun. I looked in the mirror, the first time in days and grimaced at the image before me. A girl, flushed and gritty, with her hair still tied up in a simple bun stared back at me. I looked so plain as I traced my hairline, my cheek. I knew I was plain.

Dull blonde hair, overlarge dark eyes and tender pink skin from the sun. I was nothing spectacular. But now, having lived the plain life, I felt even less so. It was then that I felt the prickling of the tears. I didn't belong in my life; I certainly didn't belong in his. I had nothing to show for my life, or where I might go.

Shutting off the water forcefully I dug around in my backpack looking for my hairbrush until my fingers wrapped around my phone. I pulled it out, hesitating before I opened it to retrieve the number. It was only a matter of time before Sean might find me again.

I dialed Stacy's number and she answered on the first ring.

"I've been so worried!" she said in a breathless voice. "Are you all right?"

"Yeah, I didn't have cell service and was afraid Sean was tracking me with my phone," I replied, relieved to hear a familiar voice.

"I'm sorry, Katie. Dad called and threatened to cut off paying my tuition if I didn't tell him where you were. And then Sean called me," she said and I could hear the fear in her voice.

I closed my eyes at the pain I had caused her.

Sean would never stop.

"I shouldn't have gotten you into this mess," I whispered and leaned against the sink, exhausted.

"Just tell me where you are and I'll get you here," she started.

"No," I said and shook my head vehemently. "Then Sean will just come there."

"Then we'll get a restraining order, Katie. Where else do you have to go?"

"I shouldn't have left," I whispered. "I should have just dealt with it. Given him what he wanted."

"You know that would have ended with you in the hospital or worse," she argued. "Come here, maybe Dad will be happy to have you out of sights. And the police will take care of Sean."

"The police will only help if he actually does something, Stacy," I shot back. "And I don't want to think about what he has planned for me. You didn't see him the other night."

She was quiet for a moment, thinking things over.

"What are you going to do?"

I sighed and closed my eyes.

"Katie, let me talk to Dad. I'll get him to wire some money and then we'll get you set up here. You can start over again."

I knew as soon as she told our father where I was, Sean wouldn't be far away. Chances are he was having my phone traced as I spoke to her.

"I'll call you as soon as I know where to wire some money. Just don't talk to Dad yet. I need to figure things out," I replied.

I hung up before she could answer.

I needed to figure out what to do next.

I contemplated hiding in the bathroom all day, but I was sure the man behind the counter was already counting the minutes I was in here. I splashed water on my face again and paced the room, weighing my options.

I really didn't have many options left. I took a measured breath and stepped out of the restroom, trying to decide where to run next. I'd get to Stacy's, and figure it out then. For now, I needed to get out of this town, away from the last week and more importantly, away from the threat of Sean.

I pulled out my phone and dialed up Stacy once more. It was ringing as I stepped out onto the porch of the store.

One ring.

Looking down the street I caught a glimpse of one of the many buggies I had seen in the last few days coming towards us from the community.

Two rings.

I glanced off towards the diner and noticed an old couple entering the diner, walking past a dusty car that was parked in the alley next to the restaurant.

Three rings.

My heart stopped at the recognition of the car, red under all the dirt.

Four rings.

"Kate."

"Katie?"

I startled at the meaty hand that grabbed my phone, as I looked up at black eyes in wide-eyed terror.

"Do you have any idea how worried I have been, Kate?"

Large arms wrapped around me, arms that suffocated and gripped me too tight as the heat of Sean's body overwhelmed me in the hot summer sun. I stood there frozen in fear as he held me against him, his nose burying deep into my neck to lay a kiss at the base of my neck.

Run.

He let out a relieved sigh and kissed me again, the steamy wet heat of his breath uncomfortable in the heat of the day.

"I was so worried, Kate. But I found you. Everything is okay now. Shhhh, it's all right. Don't be afraid. I found you," he whispered along my neck, making me tremble. I felt trapped, swallowed up from his massive frame tightly wound around me.

"I missed you," he said and pulled away enough to look down at me, his smile too wide as he took me in.

"Sean," I croaked, trying to carefully extricate myself from him.

His smile widened further at my attempts to escape and his hands wrapped around my wrists hard, a flash in his eyes told me he knew I was trying to flee.

"Uh-uh-ah," he tutted. "I won't let you go this time."

"Please, Sean," I pleaded, feeling his hands tighten on my wrists enough to make them burn. "Please just let me go. I promise, I won't run. Please. You're hurting me."

He shook his head and narrowed his eyes, as he looked me up and down.

"You hurt me, Kate. By leaving. I'm not letting you out of my sight anymore. I'm taking you home. I won't have you rushing off again.

You're mine," he explained in a voice that was too calm, tugging me to his side as he stepped off the steps towards his car.

I slowed my steps, until he was practically dragging me across the street. I looked around, trying to get someone's attention. I thought to I cry out and get someone to help me, but there was no one. The old couple was safely inside the diner. The buggy I had seen way down the road was still too far away to call out to.

I was alone, and quickly approaching the car that would deliver me back to my cage.

"Please, Sean. I don't want to go," I whispered, struggling in his grasp.

I felt him tighten his hold on me, whimpering at the ache in my wrists from the compression. I stumbled and tried to pull away, only to have him grip me around the waist and shove me roughly towards the car. I had just a split second to veer away and make a run for it. I turned and bolted, but hands moved in and grabbed my arm roughly and spun me hard into the side of the car, Sean's imposing body sandwiching me until I could not move.

I shuddered as he moved against me and grabbed at my chin to bring his lips to mine in a forceful kiss. A kiss that only lasted a second before he pulled away and shoved me harder against the side of the car, his eyes raging.

"Have you been kissing someone else? You reek of a man, Kate! Have you been whoring? To get across country? You won't let me, but you'll let some stranger do you?" he grated and held my jaw firmly in his hands until the pain made my eyes tear up.

"Have you? Answer ME!" he yelled.

"No. Please Sean, you're hurting me!" I whimpered, sagging against the hot metal of his car.

"Get in the car, Kate! I wasted so much time on you, only to find you screwing around in some nothing town. I should just let you stay here, let the guys you hooked up with have their way and throw you out like the trash you are. But I couldn't do that to your dad," he ground out, his face an inch from my own.

"I didn't, Sean. Believe me," I whispered, trembling in his grip.

"You're a whore, Kate. Telling me you were saving yourself, but I bet you were screwing around before we even started dating, weren't you?" he spat and forced himself against me harder. I could feel he was aroused; clearly excited by scaring me.

I felt sick to my stomach.

This was not the Sean I had fallen for. This was the beast, the terrifying dark side of him. His Jekyll and Hyde.

"Get in the car. I'll pretend you are the pure little thing you profess. For your dad's sake, but you will always be my little whore. Maybe now that you give yourself so easily, you'll finally let me have it," he said and grabbed my face for another violent kiss.

It was cut short by the voice behind us. A voice I knew, and thought I wouldn't hear ever again.

"Let her be."

CHAPTER 10

The voice startled me.

It startled Sean more.

He lurched away from my face, his eyes blazing at the intrusion. He looked at the man at the opening of the alley, his dark hat obscuring his face into shadow as the sun hid behind the building. But I didn't need to see him to know who he was. I knew because his profile haunted my every thought. And his voice was like a beacon of hope.

Nathan took a step towards us, his hands bunched into tight fists beside him as he moved closer. I saw the glimmer in his eyes as they flickered my way for an instant before settling back on Sean. Taking in how Sean pulled me possessively against him. Taking in the hand around my upper arm that was squeezing it until it burned with pain. Taking in the way Sean regarded him.

Sizing one another up.

"Get in the car, Kate."

Sean's voice was low, almost a growl as he opened the door and tried to shove me inside. I fought him, angling myself against the side of the car to avoid being pushed inside.

"I said let her be," Nathan said again, taking another step towards us.

"Mind your own business, farm boy," Sean growled and grabbed a hold of me and pushed me towards the door, my head not dipping fast enough before it met with the top of the car hard.

I cried out, everything a blur as I struggled to pull away from Sean once more. I felt his hands shove me roughly towards the car before I was suddenly free and slipping to the ground as my knees gave way under me, crashing to the asphalt beneath me. Gripping the doorframe I pulled myself up and swayed slightly at the dizziness, but the scene before me cleared my head immediately.

Sean circled around Nathan, who stood as still as a statue in the middle of the alley. Sean leered at me for a moment before returning his gaze back to Nathan, looking him up and down and laughing.

"Seriously, Kate? You'd do the little country boy here and not me? Does he screw you like he screws his sheep? Do you get on all fours for him?" he said, watching as Nathan's hands closed and opened slowly. Nathan's eyes held mine, calm under the tightness of his body.

"Stop it, Sean," I whispered.

I could tell Sean was trying to get a reaction from Nathan. And as he circled, he moved closer and closer.

"Stop it? Why do you always say that, Kate? Do you tell him that? When he kisses you? Do you tell him to stop? Is that why you reek of him? Did he have a little roll in the hay with you?" Sean taunted.

"Stop it, Sean! Please! It's not like that!" I cried out, struggling to stand, only to cringe back against the car when Sean rushed over to me, his face an inch from my own.

"It's not?" he hissed, forcing me to flinch away from him. His hand moved lightning quick and caught my wrists in his large hand, squeezing hard until I bowed over in pain.

"Let her alone. She has done nothing wrong."

I was aware of Nathan beside us, and of Sean's body tensing at his closeness.

Nathan's fingers slipped over my forearm like cool water, wrapping around Sean's fingers with determination. I felt Sean's fingers tighten on me as Nathan's pried at them. All the while Nathan seemed eerily calm, staring intently at the man who held me captive.

"This is not how Kate should be treated, you are hurting her," Nathan said, his voice low. Sean's eyes widened at the statement.

"How would you know about Kate? She's mine. I'll do what I want. Stay out of it!" he growled.

Nathan's hands never left me, even as Sean moved to block him. I felt one vice give way, followed by a shove from Sean as he continued to berate me. Nathan stood his ground, never pushing back. He continued to work at releasing me from Sean's strong grip.

"She's a lousy lay, you know that? Cold and limp. Of course I guess that's better than the farm animals you're used to. She's not even worth it. At least you can get something out of livestock," Sean prodded.

Nathan remained where he was standing and looked down at me, his face a mask of calm. But his eyes burned as he looked at me. Anger and determination made that calm exterior fierce. Something I had never seen in him before.

"Kate, you do not need to hear this. Wait for me by my buggy. I will take you somewhere safe," Nathan was saying.

"You won't take her anywhere! She's going with me!" Sean hissed and tried to grab me just as Nathan's fingers had pried the last finger away.

I watched in horror as Sean pushed Nathan, Nathan holding his own, as he stood there, solid against Sean's shove. It frustrated Sean, his nostrils widening as he puffed out his chest and moved towards Nathan once more. Sean was almost as tall as Nathan, but he was definitely wider, having trained for so long with football.

"She's coming home with me. Go back to your farm," he said and shoved Nathan a little harder.

Again, Nathan did not budge from his spot beside me.

"Kate, please. You do not need to stay with him. Go, it will be all right," Nathan said to me, taking his hand and moving it carefully towards my shoulder.

"Don't touch her!" Sean yelled and pushed Nathan with an explosive force that sent both of them past me. I heard the impact of the two of them as they careened towards the dumpsters of the diner, Sean gripping Nathan by the collar and shoved him against the dumpster hard before stepping away, laughing.

"You won't even fight. You see that, Kate? He doesn't care. He just used you for a good screw. Get in the car, we're done here," he said and turned to push me back towards the car.

"Leave her be. She does not wish to go with you."

I knew by the flash in his eyes that Sean had had enough.

Nathan stepped in to intervene between us, to block Sean from grabbing at me once more, but Sean was intent to get to me. I felt Sean's grip on my arm tugging me away from Nathan. I wasn't prepared to see Sean's arm as it swung around to an unsuspecting Nathan. Nathan stumbled back a step, surprise on his face as Sean stepped towards him again, in an effort to frighten him off. But Nathan stood there, hands clenched at his side.

I cried out when Sean moved closer, arm raised. My cry distracted Nathan, his eyes flashing towards me for a second too long when Sean's fist hit him across the jaw, forcing Nathan to retreat back another step. Sean took advantage of his distraction to push him again, knocking Nathan back and stumbling towards the wall of the alley. I knew if Sean cornered him there, Nathan would become a punching bag, no matter how fast he dodged.

I acted on instinct.

An instinct I never thought I would have. Perhaps it was because I hated the idea of someone like Nathan coming under attack from someone like Sean, because of me.

I leapt for Sean's back, tugging and scratching at bare skin as best I could to distract him from pummeling Nathan. Sean faltered, stumbling back towards the car long enough to provide Nathan a chance to get way from the wall. I clung to Sean as he grabbed at me, finally wrenching me free and tossing me off of him like a rag. I landed hard against the door and fell to the ground, the wind knocked out of me. I lay there for a moment, stunned, feeling like a limp ragdoll.

"Kate!" I heard Nathan cry out.

I crouched on the ground, heaving to try to get the air back in my lungs, the ground spinning before me. Noises reached my ears, garbled as I struggled to breathe. There was a loud crash and then silence. As the quiet rang in my ears, my lungs suddenly exploded, the air rushing back in.

With the first breath I was calling out.

"Nathan!"

I felt the door push past me, and hands pulling me upright to sit. I flinched at the suddenness of it all, until I felt the gentle pressure of Nathan's fingertips along my jaw, his eyes coming into focus as my vision cleared.

"Kate? Are you all right?" he was asking.

His hands searched my face, tracing along my temple and down my cheeks, his eyes taking in where his fingers searched. I nodded dumbly, trying my best to speak, to ask him if he was all right. He had an angry cut along his cheek, extending up towards his ear, and his bottom lip was split and bleeding. I reached up and took his hands in mine, hearing his relieved breath.

"Where's Sean?" I whispered, suddenly terrified of what must have happened.

Nathan's eyes seemed more pained at my question and he shook his head.

"We should leave, Kate," Nathan whispered.

I looked around us, not seeing Sean at first. When I finally found him, I gasped and struggled to stand. Nathan helped me to my feet and pulled me in the direction of the alley entrance. I slowed and shook my head.

"We should leave, Kate," he repeated, the fear in his voice apparent this time.

"I have to see," I whispered, pulling away from Nathan to make my way towards the unmoving form in the half darkness.

Nathan released me; my feet slow to move as I took in the image before me.

Sean's body lay crumpled amongst the trash of the diner; his arm limp over his face. I took a tentative step closer, afraid of getting too close and having him spring to life and tear me apart.

Afraid of getting too close and finding him dead.

"Is he?" Nathan stammered several feet behind me.

I knelt down and carefully moved Sean's arm away from his face. Sean let out a soft noise but didn't stir, though his chest rose and fell. The bleeding gash across his forehead from where it seemed he had hit it along the dumpster was already starting to slow. It looked worse than it was; he'd have a bad headache when he woke up.

But he was breathing, and that was enough for me.

"He's alive," I whispered, scrambling to my feet and rushing back to Nathan, who let out a relieved breath and held me close.

"I am sorry, Kate. He pushed me; I just wanted to get past him to get to you. He pushed. I had to...he fell," Nathan stammered, pausing when Sean moved slightly.

"We need to leave," I said in a rush and grabbed my bag and Nathan's hat off the ground.

Nathan watched as I gathered our things, apprehension clear as he glanced at Sean repeatedly. He stood there frozen until I reached for his hand and held it carefully as I could in my own. My touch seemed to jog him back to reality and he turned, grasping my hand. We walked swiftly out of the alley and towards his buggy that stood across from the diner. His hand never left mine until he helped me up into his buggy, climbing in quickly to sit beside me.

A flick of the reins and we were off at a fast pace, the town fast disappearing behind us. I looked back several times, sure that we would see the red car following at any moment. It was only when I felt the heat of Nathan's hand over mine on the seat did I turn finally to find him watching me.

His cut had stopped bleeding; leaving a darkening red line across his cheek, and his lip was caked in dried blood, the plump part of his lip growing plumper by the minute. The hand that covered mine squeezed gently, just a ghost of pressure. I picked his hand up and held it up to my lips briefly. I felt him tense slightly when I lowered it to rest on my lap, onto bare legs.

He cleared his throat when he pulled his hand gently from my lap, turning to concentrate on the road ahead. I knew I was grossly underdressed for his sensibilities. I shifted in my seat, trying to shrink as far into the corner and hide as much of me as I could from Nathan's uncomfortable gaze. He glanced at me several times, his eyes darting back to the road when they ventured anywhere partly exposed. I suddenly felt more like the whore Sean had labeled me while I sat awkwardly half-dressed next to Nathan. I had never felt so exposed when I had worn my own clothes, but I was in a different world. And I was going back to it, with the Amish man that had told me to leave, and yet had come to my rescue.

Why had he come to find me?

Why was he taking me back?

"I thought I had killed him."

His pained voice pulled me from my thoughts.

"But you didn't, Nathan. It wasn't your fault."

He shook his head and frowned hard.

"But I thought I had. You do not understand, Kate. We do not fight. It is our law. But he hurt you, and then he pushed. I only pushed him so that I could get to you; to be sure you were not injured. I was sure I had gone too far," he said, his breath coming a little harder as he gripped the reins hard.

"It's all right, Nathan. You didn't do anything wrong," I said softly, watching as his frown deepened while he seemed to contemplate what had happened.

"Who was he? Does he have a claim on you?" he whispered, his eyebrows buried together at the idea.

"No one has a claim on me," I said a little too forcefully.

I would never be anyone's possession again.

"I did not mean to presume. It is not my place," he stammered, looking away hurriedly.

"No, Nathan. I didn't mean to be rude. He is just," I said and trailed off, leaning into the side of the buggy and curling into myself, embarrassed to talk about this with him.

He'd think me cheap. Or worse, dirty. Certainly not pure and innocent, something he deserved.

"I am sorry," he whispered after a long silence.

"I should be saying sorry," I replied. "I dragged you into something you don't need to trouble yourself over. It's not your problem."

"I was worried for you."

I looked over to find him watching me again, his eyes regarding me with such intensity.

"I don't know why," I murmured and looked away.

"You have something about you, Kate. Something that pulls me," he started, only to stop and look back out towards the road.

"I'm an outsider, Nathan. English. I'll only shame you," I whispered and retreated further into my corner of the buggy.

I felt his gaze on me again, but I refused to look into those deep eyes and see the truth of my words in them. His quiet exhale made me finally turn to face those sad green depths, losing myself in them as he continued to watch me intently.

"I shame myself, Kate. You help me to see there is a light in the world by your kindness, and I push you away," he replied softly, looking away from me finally and off into the fields of corn.

"Why did you come after me? You told me to leave," I asked softly, afraid to hear his admittance.

He shook his head, a rueful smile playing at his lips.

"I did not mean for you to leave forever, Kate. I meant for just that moment. I was afraid. You kissed me and I felt an overwhelming urge. I was tempted. I was afraid I would shame you if you remained in that moment," he said, his ears turning bright pink.

"Shame me?" I asked, confused by how he could possibly shame me, the dirty Englisher.

His blush grew, and he frowned, his eyebrows drawing up tight on his forehead.

"Kate, you have an indescribable hold on me, since the first moment I met you. You are like nothing I have ever known. I have tried to deny it, to say it is merely temptation wanting to lead me astray, but it is more than that. Perhaps you are here for a reason that only God knows. But it is only a matter of time before you realize that you miss your home and leave us," he said and looked towards me, his eyes drawing me in to their tormented depths once more.

I slid a little closer to him, his eyes widening for a moment and his mouth opening in protest before my finger tip touched his battered lips gently.

"I have no interest in going back there, Nathan. I can't go back to that. I don't know where I belong. But here? It's daunting I admit it. I know I will mess up. I don't understand most of what you do here. I know there are rules but I don't know them. I'll break them, I am sure. But I'd like to find my way here if I can. If it's even possible," I whispered softly.

"Anything is possible," he said. A hint of a smile cracked at his lip, causing it to bleed again. I traced the wound, wiping away the blood before it could run. He seemed to sense my distress over his injuries and pulled my hand back into his own for a moment before returning it to my lap. His fingertips lingered against the flesh along the top of my thigh as he held me.

His touch was feather light as it moved with a tentative curiosity along my arm and up, brushing lightly across the welt I could feel pounding along my hairline from where I had struck the door. I winced at the slight pressure, knowing the bruise would hurt more tomorrow.

"I thought he had struck you dead," he whispered, his breath coming a little harder when he turned away to concentrate on the road ahead, his hands returning to the reins in a white-knuckled grip.

"I was scared he'd hurt you. He's strong," I said, watching his jaw clench.

"I am not afraid of him," he murmured. His hand flexed slightly, as if to temper his anger.

I was quiet while we traveled, wondering if he truly was unafraid of Sean.

"I am sorry you had to hear what he said," I whispered after a while, terrified that perhaps Nathan believed the things Sean had said.

"He had no right to behave as he did. What he said, what he did to you? That is not allowed in my world. You deserve better than what he has done. That would not happen here. I would not," he started before shaking his head, sliding away from me as another buggy approached.

I slipped back over to my side, unsure how it would appear with Nathan to be riding with someone like me. The buggy passed, the occupant waving to Nathan who returned it and continued on. I was contemplating how things had changed when I felt his hand brush across mine and take it lightly into his once more. Looking over, I caught the brief smile flicker across his lips and he let his eyes close for a moment, his thumb lightly stroking across my knuckles.

He had come after me, had stood up to Sean, and his gentle smile as he grazed my hand sent shivers through my body at the thought that I had made him happy. He was truly interested in me. I just had no idea how to continue by their standards. What I had experienced so far suggested I was well out of my league in matters of dating. I had a feeling everything I had learned from Sean would be taboo in Nathan's world. Just the kiss had sent him running. Would he ignore me when others were around?

"I don't know how to act around you," I murmured.

He opened his eyes and his smile fought the tightness of the cut. But his eyes danced as he took me in.

"I do not know as well. Our ways are much different I know. You are correct; there are rules and it will take time to learn them. I would like to show you our ways, if that is what you would like. I would like to know more of your world, so that I may understand you. But we must abide by the law," he whispered, his eyes thoughtful as he watched my reaction.

He was saying he wanted something. Wanted me.

"So what next?" I asked, feeling the blush creep along my neck as his thumb returned to brushing across my knuckles. Just his touch was certainly taboo, right? It felt entirely too good to be right.

"I shall take you home," he said, his eyes sparkling at the mention of home.

"And then?" I asked, my smile breaking out across my face.

"And then I would request Elder Jonah to allow me to see you again."

His thumb skirted across my hand a little faster, excited.

"And then?"

He brought my hand up to his lips, kissing my knuckles lightly before smiling down into my eyes.

"And then perhaps I would like to steal a kiss under the moonlight, Kate. If you would allow me," he said and offered me a smile that made my insides melt.

I squeezed his hand in mine, eager to find out more about this man.

We travelled back in silence, my hand in his, each of us deep in thought of what was to come. And for the first time in a long time, I felt truly safe. Whatever laws we had to abide by, I was excited to learn.

I'd learn his ways.

I'd learn and find my place in his world.

CHAPTER 11

Nathan held my hand all the way back to the Bergers. When we turned onto the long drive to the house, he squeezed it as if in promise of returning to it when he could before his hand slipped from my grasp. It was sunset when we finally came to a stop, in front of my new home. He carefully helped me down from the buggy and released me quickly into the arms of Fannie and Jonah, back from their duties and worried for their newest charge. Our bruises alarmed them, but Nathan promised to relay the story before supper, insisting that I needed a few moments.

By a few moments, I was sure he meant to get some clothes on. He refused to look my way as I stood there, half clothed by his standards. I was ushered into the house by Fannie and Emma, Jonah staying with Nathan outside. Leaving me to change in the bedroom I looked out the window and down to find Jonah patting Nathan's shoulder softly, nodding as if in serious conversation. Nathan was shaking his head, taking the familiar black hat off to scrub at his hair roughly. He hung his head for a moment, Jonah taking Nathan by the shoulder towards the house, his head turned in to speak softly.

A knock on the door drew me from the window. Opening the door, I was startled to see Hannah there in the doorway, a new dress in her hands. She offered it to me, her gaze taking in the cut along my hairline before she shook her head and looked me in the eye, the same look I had seen in the garden. Her voice was unnaturally soft when she spoke.

"I took in the length of the dress for you. I can show you how to do this if you like, Katherine."

"I would like that, Hannah. Thank you," I murmured, unsure how to respond to her.

"I would of course help you make another pie for tomorrow night, if you would allow me," she suggested. I laughed nervously, drawing her eyes up to me in confusion. My emotions were a little raw.

"I would like that very much. Maybe we can make dinner together tomorrow?" I asked, watching as she looked at me cautiously for a moment before nodding, her face still troubled. She lingered at the door a moment before her hand came up to touch my bruises along my arm gently. I couldn't help the flinch.

"No one should be allowed to do this. Too many fall victim, I am sorry you are hurt," she said, her voice strangely distant.

Before I could respond, she excused herself and left me there alone. I stood in the doorway for a long moment, contemplating what had just happened with Hannah's sudden warming. I was left feeling more confused than ever.

Jonah ushered me into the front room of the house when I had changed, Fannie lighting several lamps near a chair that sat near the front window. Jonah motioned for me to sit, turning to his bag that sat on the table nearby. I sat hesitantly with my hands folded in my lap and watched as he turned and paused beside me, pursing his lips towards the dark corner of the room. I followed his gaze and noticed Nathan standing in the shadow, his body hunched slightly as he watched me. His arms were folded up around himself, one hand rubbing at the side of his head worriedly.

"Nathan," Jonah sighed. "Just a few minutes alone if you would."

Nathan's eyes darted to mine, unreadable in the half-light, but I could tell by his tight lips that he was worried. He nodded, scrubbing at his neck before slipping through the door, watching me until the door closed him off to me. I swallowed at the sudden separation, not realizing just how much Nathan's presence comforted me after my altercation with Sean.

I could feel it significantly as Fannie and Jonah regarded me carefully.

Was I in trouble?

For running away? For putting Nathan in harm's way?

Was Nathan in trouble for hurting Sean?

I waited while Jonah circled me slowly, taking in my appearance and sighing softly.

"Katherine," he said softly.

Finding the courage to look up, I was caught off guard by the amount of concern etched on his face, but also the fact that he refused to look me in the eye.

"Katherine, I need to ask you questions. Questions we do not typically ask. I have spoken with Nathan, he has told me of your English boyfriend and the violence he inflicted upon you," he said quietly, standing very still before me.

I concentrated my focus on my hands, at the bruises that were darkening along my wrists. I took a startled breath when he squatted down before me, his hands gently hovering over mine.

"May I look to your injuries, Katherine?" he whispered quietly.

I swallowed and extended my arms out to him slowly, struggling at slow measured breaths as his hands ghosted over my wrists. Jonah's fingers were cool and gentle as they traced and pressed at the bones. I winced slightly at the tenderness, but remained quiet as he frowned and moved on towards the bruises up my arms. Fannie stood beside me with her hand beside my head, tucking back the stray hairs from my bun as if to distract both of us from his exploration. It was when Jonah moved up to my face that his eyes finally caught mine fully. The kind face was back in place, but examining me saddened his normally vibrant eyes.

He waited until I could nod to let him continue and then traced his fingertips over the tender spot on my forehead, where I had hit the car door.

"This will need cleaning, but I do not think stitches are needed. It is not as deep as Nathan feared. Does it hurt?" he asked.

"No more than I am used to," I whispered, my voice trembling slightly.

I heard Fannie's harsh exhale.

"Do you hurt elsewhere, Katherine? Anywhere that I cannot see in the moment?" Jonah asked, the meaning coming through strongly.

They thought the worst. I shook my head, embarrassed at his words. How was it that a stranger such as Jonah worried about my health, but my father could not see?

"He did not touch you, Katherine?" Fannie whispered.

"Only to get me in the car. Nathan was there before anything could happen," I said, looking up into her eyes and pausing at her tortured gaze.

"So only bumps and bruises, then? I will want to watch you this evening, with the bump on your head," Jonah stated and stood to go to his bag again.

He handed Fannie a cloth and a bottle of something that smelled like rubbing alcohol. She took it and he stepped out of the room, letting Fannie take care of my cuts in private. She was quiet while she worked, her hand light as she wiped away the dirt and blood I had not known was caked on my forehead. No doubt I looked much worse than I actually was.

For once I was glad for no mirrors in the house. I didn't need to be reminded of the damage Sean could produce, and judging by the soiled rag, I was a mess. Nathan must have been worried. He had seemed so brave in the buggy.

"Is Nathan all right?" I asked my voice a little loud in the quiet room.

Fannie smiled as she worked.

"He is well. Jonah saw to his wounds while we discussed what happened. He was more worried about you than himself. He wanted Jonah to look to you first, but it was best that you changed," she said as she worked.

"It wasn't his fault," I said hurriedly, trying to explain Nathan's actions. "Sean's all right. Nathan was just trying to get to me."

Fannie smiled down at me and pressed her palm against my cheek in comfort.

"I know, Katherine. Do not worry. Nathan is not in any trouble. It is done and past us now," she whispered.

She was quiet for a moment, changing to a balm that she swiped across my forehead before returning to clean my jaw.

"Would you like to tell me why you left, Katherine?" she asked quietly.

I frowned and shrugged, embarrassed to tell her how I had tempted Nathan, and scared him into fleeing from me.

"I thought maybe it was best if I left," I replied quietly.

"Even after our talk this morning?" she asked and I could hear the hurt in her voice.

"I wasn't sure if I had made the right choice to stay."

"And did you get in contact with your sister?"

I nodded and looked down at my hands.

"And what does she say? Or your father? He must know where you are, if the boy knows."

I remained quiet as she pushed my hair back and cleaned up around my neck. What would I say? Even they thought perhaps that my father was the reason why Sean could find me.

"I have never understood how a parent can turn their heart from their own flesh and blood," she whispered and placed her hand against my chin, tilting it up so that she could look down into my eyes.

Fannie looked at me much as a doting mother would and I had to wonder why she and Jonah didn't have more children running around, as was the Amish way. She seemed suited for having enough love for an entire town. She smiled and cleared her throat, nodding as if having made a private decision. She moved away and closed up her husband's bag. When she turned around once more, she was all determination.

"Let us go and see what the girls have prepared for supper, my daughter. I am sure it will be something to remember," she said and held me around the shoulder as we walked down the hallway.

We stepped into the kitchen, all eyes turning towards us when we entered. I caught sight of Nathan immediately, his hair a damp mess as if he had just cleaned up and tried to comb it with his fingers. He smiled in relief before glancing away to listen to Mark who was speaking softly to him from the table. Mark looked my way for a moment, pausing in his conversation, before turning back to Nathan, nudging Nathan slightly to draw his attention from me. Jonah nodded and offered his wife a knowing look before settling into his seat at the head of the table to watch his daughters busy themselves in the kitchen.

I lingered in the doorway for only a second, weighing my next move. Did I sit, or did I help out with serving the meal? Feeling more comfortable with Emma and Fannie, I busied myself with pulling out the plates for the table. I could feel Nathan's eyes on me as I moved around the table, until finally Mark spoke up in his loud booming voice.

"Have you heard nothing I have said, Nathan!" he exclaimed, causing me to jump and Nathan's head to jerk back towards Mark, his face bright red.

Mark let out a chortling sort of laughter and shook his head. Jonah cleared his throat and looked at the boys as if to admonish them.

"That will be enough of that, Mark. These two have been through enough today. We do not need to make them feel more uncomfortable," Jonah said, fighting a smile as I set his plate with shaking hands.

I glanced at Nathan on my way back to the safety of the kitchen, and caught his soft smile as he regarded me. Not a look of fear. Not a feeling of the need to flee. Perhaps this would be easier than I thought. Judging by the way little Abigail hugged me and continued to smile at Nathan, I thought that maybe we would have some support in the family.

Dinner was a quiet affair, even with Mark seated across from me. I was a little intimidated by Mark, if I was being honest. He watched me throughout supper, his playful eyes staring right through me. And as if I was not nervous enough by his attention, Nathan sat across from me as well and tried his best not to look up at me. Every time he did, his mouth would turn up slightly and he would quickly look away again.

Hannah was the most talkative one of the bunch, which was most peculiar. She and Fannie spoke of the upcoming wedding. At mention of the wedding, Mark would shift in his seat and smile endearingly towards his future wife, who would pretend to scowl and ignore him. Emma was the only one who did not speak at all throughout the meal. I looked over at her a few times, but couldn't read her mood as she picked at her meal and kept her eyes on her plate.

Maybe I had been knocked on the head a little harder than I thought. Everyone seemed a little off. Even Jonah seemed to smile more when he would catch Nathan looking my way.

I must have suffered a concussion.

The men ventured out to the porch while we cleaned up. I was setting the last plate into the cabinet when Fannie and Hannah, who had been chattering on about menus for the wedding reception grew quiet. I looked around to see why it was silent when I caught sight of Nathan from the doorway. He cleared his throat and held his hat a little tighter to his chest.

"I wanted to wish you a pleasant night," he said to no one in particular, his eyes focused on the table rather than any of us.

I glanced around the room, at Fannie smiling behind her hand as she held Abigail who was grinning and swaying, Hannah with her arched eyebrow, and Emma with her pout as she stared at Nathan.

"Pleasant evening, Nathan," I said quietly, sounding more like a question than a statement.

He lingered at the door a moment more, shifting his weight between his feet as if contemplating a hasty exit. I wasn't sure what else to say. I wanted to thank him for saving me, but I wanted to do that in private. Really I wanted to hug him and kiss him. But I didn't think that would was allowed.

"Katherine, perhaps you could walk Nathan to the door," Fannie suggested, motioning to the back door that Nathan glanced at repeatedly.

It was then that I realized what he was about. He was trying to get me to walk him out.

"Okay," I murmured and walked stiffly towards the back door, feeling all eyes on us as he followed along behind me at a respectable pace.

As soon as the door closed behind us, I felt him move in closer, the heat of his body radiating against me without touching me. I heard him swallow, his head so close to mine behind me. I made to turn around just as his hand tentatively brushed against mine, taking it gently into his own. I glanced back towards the door, the light from the kitchen bleeding through the door onto the dark porch as we stood there. Everyone seemed to understand our desire for privacy as they continued with the work inside, albeit with wide smiles on their faces.

Nathan's gentle squeeze of my hand brought me back to look up at him. He was smiling timidly down at me; the corners of his eyes crinkling up a bit.

"I would like to call on you tomorrow, if that is all right?" he asked quietly, his lips trembling slightly as he watched me.

"I'd like that. But you're coming for breakfast, right?" I asked, wondering if his hunger strike was finally over.

He laughed quietly and nodded.

"Yes, I will come for breakfast, Kate. And after my chores, I would like to sit with you," he replied, his smile widening slightly.

"Okay, is that how we start?" I asked, utterly clueless.

He squeezed my hand again and laughed a little louder, glancing back towards the door for a moment before returning that intense gaze to me.

"This is how we start, yes. So tomorrow, Kate. Finish your chores quickly, so that we might sit and talk for a while."

I nodded and watched as he slowly pulled away, indecision playing in his eyes for a split second before he leaned in and kissed me quickly, his lips searching mine for only an instant before drawing away. That brief touch was enough to make me breathless. He stepped away, his hands moving to his hair before he settled the hat on his head once more. He licked at his lips and nodded in thought, his smile turning tender as he regarded me from the first step down.

"I am happy you are safe, Kate. I cannot think about what would have happened," he whispered, his eyes closing for a moment as if in pain.

"You are the reason I'm safe, Nathan. Thank you for coming to find me," I replied, taking a step towards him.

I wanted just one more touch. I reached out, placing my hand against the side of his cheek and smiled at the rough stubble there under my thumb. He closed his eyes at my touch and leaned in to my hand.

"How did you know to find me?" I asked, suddenly curious about his timely rescue.

He opened his eyes and sighed, taking another step back, off the porch and into the night.

"I would have never thought that Hannah would admit it, but she was concerned for you. She came to me, demanding to know what I had done to upset you," he replied, shaking his head in wonder.

"Hannah?"

Inconceivable. Why was she concerned about me?

"Hannah cares more than you know. She is," he started, only to press his lips together and take another step back.

"She is what?" I pressed, confused by her strange change in feelings.

He shook his head and looked down at the dirt.

"She is a loyal and fierce sister. And I have no place speaking of her without her knowing," he murmured and shuffled at the base of the stairs.

He glanced towards the door and let out a soft breath. Reaching for my hand once more, he held it gently in his own and pulled me closer, nearly toppling me off the top stair. But his free hand steadied me as his lips brushed across my cheek for an instant before settling me back onto the top step, away from him.

"I must leave. I do not want to. Promise me you will still be here tomorrow? So that we may talk?" he asked. His eyes held mine, a tender vulnerability that struck me hard.

"Of course I will. I'm not leaving, Nathan," I whispered.

His grin lit up his face and he released my hand, stepping backwards into the night.

"That makes me happy, Kate. Until tomorrow then. Pleasant dreams," he said and walked backwards into the dark, his eyes vibrant in the glow of the light behind me.

"Pleasant dreams, Nathan," I said softly after him, watching him as he offered me one last flashing smile before turning towards his hill. The moonlight made his shirt shine in the closing night, and as always, I was sad to see his back walk away from me.

It was a small consolation that he walked a little lighter.

It was still away from me.

I didn't notice the smiles as I walked back inside; I was in my own little world. I could still feel Nathan's lips against my cheek, the stubble around his lips scratching my skin like electricity. And his hand's warmth still radiated in my own. Seeing him leave made me miss him more, and made me question just how plausible this relationship could be. I barely registered Jonah's call for bed, or the gentle touch on my shoulder from Hannah and Fannie as I made my way up stairs.

It wasn't until I was slipping into the bed with Emma that I was pulled out of my Nathan induced trance and into the conflicted eyes of my friend.

"I am so upset with you!" she whispered harshly.

My eyes widened and I opened my mouth to ask her for what, but she beat me to it as her thoughts tumbled out of her head.

"You left! Not a word! You simply left! I came back to find the house empty, Hannah gone, your dress neatly folded here. Not a note to explain! Not a goodbye! You left us!" she whimpered, her voice cracking at the last and I could see the tears reflected in her eyes.

I pulled her close, holding her as she fought to pull away until she relinquished and hugged me tight.

"I'm sorry, Emma! Truly I am. I didn't mean to hurt you. I ran. I didn't think. I just felt like I wasn't wanted. I was afraid," I whispered into her ear, every excuse sounding lamer as I uttered them.

How was it I could hurt so many nice people?

She pulled away and looked me sternly in the eye.

"You cannot do that again! I told you, you have something to do here. You are my friend. You are my sister. Do not leave us like that again, Katherine. I was so upset," she said, shaking her head.

"I promise I won't leave like that again. I'm sorry, Emma. It was just a lot to take in today," I mumbled and settled back into the bed, my head beginning to hurt.

"We forgive very easily, Katherine. I am still a little upset, but more for what has happened and could have been avoided had you simply stayed here. You scared us. You terrified Nathan," she replied, lying down next to me, her head close to mine.

"I'm sure I did," I mumbled.

"He was beside himself when he came to see that you had truly left. I have only seen him that upset once before, Katherine. It is not something I wish to see again."

"I'm sorry, Emma," I replied. "I don't want to hurt him like that, believe me."

"So then why did you run away?" she asked and then lowered her voice and glancing back at Abigail who was sound asleep before she continued. "Did he kiss you?"

I fidgeted with the sheet that covered us. It was embarrassing to have to explain.

"Um, no," I whispered, pausing before I confessed to Emma. "I kissed him."

Her eyes widened as if in shock, before she burst into laughter. Laughter that was loud enough to cause her to cover her mouth with her pillow when we heard the bed creak in the next room. I glanced at the door; sure that Jonah would come banging to tell us to settle down. The bed creaked again and then fell silent, Emma's laughter muffled in the pillow. I waited awkwardly until she pulled herself together and let out a few calming breaths.

I had no idea my kissing Nathan would be so hilarious.

"I am sorry," Emma wheezed, fanning her face until she could speak. "It is just, I am sure you are his first. He must have been alarmed when you kissed him!"

"You kissed Nathan?" Abigail squealed from her bed.

"Shhh!" Emma hissed, throwing her pillow at Abigail who simply caught it and threw it back, sticking out her tongue at us for not being included in the gossip. Emma sighed and motioned Abigail to join us, which she did so with a flourish by leaping into our bed and snuggling in between us, all smiles.

"Did he not like it? He must have. He could not stop staring at you tonight," Abigail whispered, her innocent smile widening when she noticed me squirm uncomfortably.

"I just surprised him, that's all," I admitted, trying to keep the conversation clean for her sake. But I frowned at the memory of him fleeing towards his house. It was an extreme reaction to a first kiss.

When he had kissed me tonight it was much better, even if just a peck on the lips. Such a simple thing, maybe I had been too brazen. I was sure the Amish didn't believe in having the girl make the advances.

"I think maybe I was too forward with him," I muttered and ground my head into the pillow, hoping to alleviate the pain that was starting to throb there.

Emma chuckled softly and shook her head at me.

"I am sure anything you did to Nathan would have been too much for him, Katherine. He is not used to girls. He never spent his free time searching out a girl. His sister and I used to make fun of him for being so shy," she said and then hummed sadly as she thought of Nathan's dead sister.

"You were close to his sister?" I asked softly.

She nodded and let out a soft breath.

"Rachel was my best friend. She and I did everything together. And she and Nathan were very close. Nathan is like a big brother to me in many ways," she whispered.

"Aren't you mad that I kissed him, then?" I asked, perplexed.

She giggled and shook her head.

"No, of course not, Katherine! I want him to be happy. And you make him so. It has been a long time," she said, her voice growing soft, as she seemed to reflect on the evening.

"He smiles now when you are near," Abigail murmured, sighing as her eyes grew heavy.

"He most certainly does," Emma said and leaned in to kiss her little sister on the top of her head.

We were quiet for a moment to let Abigail fall asleep before Emma spoke again, her voice a whisper.

"It must have been a relief to see him when you did in town?"

"I was afraid he'd get hurt. Sean doesn't take competition well," I replied, remembering how he had threatened the boys at home just for talking to me.

"Were you afraid when you saw Sean?"

"Yes," I whispered and closed my eyes.

"Is this how he hurt you before?" she asked and touched my head tentatively.

I shook my head and touched the lump there. This was mild.

"It is not over, you understand," she said, forcing my eyes to open in a panic. She shook her head and offered me a gentle smile.

"I heard Father speaking with Nathan and Mark about it before you came down. Nathan fears he will search you out. Mark agrees. Jonah intends to speak with the Elders about it in the morning. Your English may try to bring the law here. They will want to know you are not being held against your will, Katherine," she explained.

"Of course I'm not!" I rebuffed, shaking my head at how much of an idiot I was.

I should have suspected this. Now I was endangering the Bergers, and maybe the entire community. How would I ever be allowed to fit in if I caused trouble? When would I be able to stop hiding?

"Do not worry, Katherine," she murmured. "Father may be old-fashioned in his ways. But we will protect you. Nathan will protect you. I know it."

"I don't want any of you to get hurt," I argued, but Emma's soft laughter stopped me short.

"We do not fight, Katherine. But we take care of those we care about. We will find a way," she replied and settled in to the bed a little deeper.

I slid down under the blanket, hugging Abigail close to me after Emma blew out the candle, the moonlight the only light in the room. I could see the shine of Emma's eyes as she regarded me.

"If you want this to be your home, Katherine, if you want a life with Nathan, we will help you. I will help you with our ways. It will not be easy. There are many who would deny you. But you have a good heart and Nathan cares for you. We will help you if that is what you want," she said in the darkness.

"I want to try," I whispered and felt her hand squeeze mine under the cover.

"Then it is settled. I will help you with Nathan. And you will be my sister," she sighed and closed her eyes contentedly.

I smiled at how simply she had forgiven me. She was truly a good friend.

"And I will help you with John," I whispered back, grinning when I saw her eyes fly open in surprise.

I closed my eyes, smiling at the fact that perhaps I had something to offer this family for once. I'd see my friend back with her true love. And I'd make Nathan smile again tomorrow.

Because his smile meant a good deal more to me now.

CHAPTER 12

My head hurt when I woke up before the dawn. It throbbed like I had cracked it wide open. My body felt like a train had struck it. My wrists hurt when I moved them. But I sucked it up and got out of bed.

I was not going to let Sean win. I wanted to show everyone I was strong, even if my dreams had made me whimper in the night. Dreams of Sean chasing after me, and tossing Nathan into the dumpster so that it was Nathan on the alley ground and not Sean. If Emma or Abigail had heard, they remained quiet about it when I awoke. Emma and I started our chores with little encouragement from Jonah.

I was getting into the routine. I was learning. I even milked half dozen cows as opposed to leaving Emma to pick up the slack. Abigail met us outside the barn just as the sun was cracking over the horizon, her basket full of eggs from the hen house. She smiled at me and motioned towards the hill.

Nathan's hill.

And there as the first rays of sunlight licked at the hillside, I watched as Nathan made his way towards us, his signature black hat tipped back on his head and a smile on his face. He walked a little more slowly, and as he drew closer I noticed the cut along his cheek had purpled over night. But his eyes shone in the early morning light as he took one of the milk pails from my hand and followed us into the kitchen silently.

We made quick work of breakfast, Fannie having prepared the ham and corn cakes while Emma and I had been in the barn. We settled into our usual seats, Nathan sitting across from me. Morning prayers said, I tried my best to avoid his eyes while we ate, but it seemed every time I looked his way, he was looking my way at the same moment.

We had to be incredibly obvious to everyone else.

As if to confirm my suspicion, Jonah cleared his throat and stood from the table to address the family.

"Today is a day of reflection. We have chores to do so that we may relax this afternoon and thank God for what we have. Nathan? I believe we have a meeting of the Elders before midday? Let us go while Fannie and the girls take care of things here. My wife," he said, smiling at his wife briefly before glancing around the table. His gaze lingered on me for a moment, a thoughtful purse to his lips before he stepped outside to wait for Nathan. Nathan excused himself hurriedly, offering me a timid smile before grabbing his hat and following Jonah outside, leaving me to glance around the table at the women.

"It is all right, Katherine," Fannie said. "They will speak with the Elders and we will have resolution on how best to keep you safe."

I remained quiet throughout our clean up routine. I had a feeling Nathan and Jonah were walking into a heated discussion over me. I could still be asked to leave, and then any feelings I had for Nathan would be pointless. Fannie seemed unfazed by the men going to speak to the Elders, but Hannah watched me curiously as we worked. I felt an instant of fear when she asked me to join her in the sewing room.

Emma raised her eyebrow but dutifully followed Fannie out to the garden to gather vegetables for the afternoon meal while I made my way behind Hannah to the front room of the house. Hannah opened the windows to let in a breeze and settled in on the bench seat by the window, motioning me to share it with her as she pulled out one of the dresses I had first worn. She was quiet as she sorted through her needles and spools of thread, finding finally the same color as the dress and turning to smile carefully. Regardless of Hannah's sudden warming to me, seeing her smile still frightened me. She was like a tiger ready to pounce as she sat there, poised perfectly with her hand working the thread through the fabric neatly.

"I found great joy making these dresses when I came of age," she said after several moments of silence. "It is good that they can be used. Emma will never grow into them and Abigail has years to go yet."

I watched her as she worked, unsure of what to say. Another few minutes of silence and then she spoke again.

"Of course I had high hopes that I would pass these to my sisters. I suppose the sickness is what made Emma so small. She was frail for so long. And a bit dramatic if I must admit. She has a good loving man in John Wittmer. I can only hope she has not passed it by," she murmured as she handed me the needle and thread and the half hemmed skirt.

"I don't know what to do," I stammered, feeling odd with the dress in my hands.

"Follow my stitching there. I have pinned it for you. Just follow the line. You will get better with practice. It is how we all learn, by doing. Abigail is already quite good at needlework and she is only ten," she replied and pulled out another dress from the pile beside her.

We sat in uncomfortable silence as I stitched, following her straight line with one of my own that wavered slightly. My wrists began to ache as I worked, my stitching slower until I finally had to stop and rotate my hands to relieve the ache. She paused in her sewing to glance down at the purpled skin around my wrists.

"Are you in pain?" she whispered, her face unreadable.

I shook my head dismissively.

"Not really, I'm just not used to this. You are much better at this than me," I replied, trying to offer a compliment in her awkward company.

She nodded as if to agree and went back to sewing, glancing at my hands when they resumed the stitching.

"The bruises will fade. Father says you were not broken. That is good. Broken bones and scars remind you of the nightmare," she murmured.

I touched my forehead gently.

"I don't think this will scar. Do you think it will scar?" I asked nervously.

I had scars from Sean. No one had seen them, but Hannah was right. They made me remember. She eyed my forehead thoughtfully and shook her head.

"No, Mother was sure to use the same balm she used on me. You will not scar."

She went back to her stitching.

I paused my stitching to watch her as her words sunk in.

The same balm she used on me.

I watched as Hannah's stitches wavered, as she pulled them out purposefully and re-stitched.

A slightly crooked line.

A breath.

Pulling the threads out.

The silence became rather loud in the still room.

Another breath.

She tried again.

"It was not Mark's fault, you understand," she said suddenly, her voice strangely distant.

I remained still beside her as she worked, afraid to break her from this uncomfortable discussion. Afraid she would harden and be unwilling to let me in once more. She let out another breath and straightened a bit, shaking her head as she pulled out the threads once more on her dress.

"There are many things that happen during Rumspringa. We do not discuss it for we are wiped clear of those sins when we accept our place here. I was stupid to step away from Mark that night. I am so very blessed that he found me. Regardless of what he thinks, I do not blame him for it," she continued.

I swallowed and remained frozen beside her, praying now that she would simply return to her stitching and leave her story untold. Why was she telling me? I didn't want to know. I didn't want to learn of her scars.

"The English boy was a friend of Mark's. They worked at the mill together. I knew him; he had always been nice to me. I did not think anything of it when he told me Mark had a surprise there for me. It was my birthday after all, and Mark was always offering me little gifts as tokens of his love for me. I thought maybe he had finished the rocker he had promised me as a betrothal gift. But it was not. He was not there as his friend had said," she whispered.

I felt my heart hammering in my chest as I watched her. Hannah was as stoic and reserved as I imagined all the strong Amish women were. But I could see her trembling hands as she stitched and spoke. She struggled like anyone would. She struggled like I had so many times when I had tried to hide my injuries. Had tried to be strong. Hannah was still a woman who hurt.

She took a long measured breath and clasped her hands together to still them, looking down at the un-hemmed dress.

"Mark found me, that is what matters. If he had not, I would not be able to show you how to stitch, and I would not have met you. I was forgiven of my past the day I took my baptism. Bruises heal. Scars leave memories. I am sad for my scars. My husband will have to remember every time, every time," she stammered.

"Hannah," I whispered, feeling helpless to offer any comfort.

"I will be a good wife, regardless," she whispered and straightened and looked up at me, her eyes determined.

I could only nod, fighting back the tears in my eyes. She would be upset if I cried for her. I didn't know Hannah well, but I knew she didn't want pity. I knew I would not in her place. It seemed Hannah and I had much more in common that I would have ever realized. She was determined, just as I hoped to be. I hoped I could be a little like her, with her strength of will.

Her faith.

Her faith had healed her suffering.

She nodded and turned back to her stitching, much straighter the fourth time around.

I returned to my own stitching, unsure of what to say to Hannah, fearful that I would mess up the strange truce we had. Instead, she spoke again after I had completed my attempt at hemming my dress. She looked it over, laughter escaping her throat as she picked at my loose threads.

"It is a good thing you are good in the kitchen, Katherine! With time you might be able to stitch something that will hold for a season. Let us hope I can learn to bake easier than you can sew! Otherwise Mark will starve!" she said brightly and rose to stretch.

Just like that.

Hannah was strong again, feisty and sure of herself. Hannah did not bring up her story again, and I did not ask. And she did not ask me about my bruises again. They did not discuss these things.

That was the Amish way.

I followed behind her as we made our way into the kitchen, back into the routine of preparing the midday and late meals for the day. I stood a little taller, shoved the pain of my injuries further back into my head while I worked.

Because Hannah was the strongest woman I knew. I had so much to learn from these people if I expected to remain, if they'd let me. I glanced at the door, wondering what Nathan would say to the Elders on my behalf. And what he would tell me when he returned midday. I might not have a choice in staying.

So I hid my pain and took a page out of Hannah's book.

I'd hide my scars.

I'd be strong.

I'd have faith.

I'd learn.

CHAPTER 13

"Katherine, come away from the door! They will be home soon. Do not worry," Fannie chided, causing me to blush and pull away from the door once more.

"I was just checking to see if it was shady out by the garden yet," I replied lamely.

"It is midday, Katherine," Hannah sighed, exasperated. "There is no shade."

Emma chuckled by the table, glancing my way as Hannah burst into laughter.

I sighed and busied myself with stirring the potato salad we had made earlier. It didn't really need stirring, but I needed a distraction. Jonah and Nathan had been gone for a few hours now.

And my morning chores were done, as Nathan had asked.

A thrill went through me at the idea of being able to sit and talk with him, finally.

The decision of the Elders weighed on my mind, but the idea of him sitting next to me for the afternoon made everything pale in comparison.

"They will be thirsty when they arrive, Katherine. Come help me finish the tea," Fannie said, taking pity on the over-stirred potatoes.

Chores done, potato salad stirred, tea made and soon we were all growing antsy for them to return. Abigail came charging through the door when they finally crested the hill. Hannah let out another exaggerated sigh and rolled her eyes. I was finding her irritation endearing somehow now. I stepped into the flurry of activity to get the midday meal out and ready.

I heard their footsteps and the murmurings of Jonah's voice before the door opened and he stepped in, followed by Nathan. Jonah smiled comfortably towards his wife, glancing my way before turning towards the sink to wash up. Nathan stepped in quietly, his eyes turned down towards his hat in his hands before he glanced up, the green of his eyes shining through his lashes. I held my breath, worried that his hesitation was confirmation that this could be my last meal here.

And then he offered me that soft smile, creeping up from one side that made his eyes crinkle a bit. I let out my breath and smiled back, causing him to blush and fight the wider smile that tugged at his lips. Jonah's bright voice brought us out of our little moment.

"Katherine, my newest daughter! The Elders have agreed to provide you refuge with us!" he exclaimed and moved towards me to hold me between his hands.

He smiled softly and leaned in, kissing me softly on the forehead.

"Welcome to our home, Katherine. You have nothing to fear here," he whispered and squeezed me gently between the shoulders.

I didn't have much time to offer my thanks. Emma, as well as Abigail and Hannah, came running in to hug me. Following soon after Fannie hugged me tightly and refused to let me go. From the corner of my eye, Nathan was still smiling.

Our meal was the most pleasant of any of our meals so far. I felt a lightness that I had not felt before, and as I looked on my newly adoptive family, I discovered how much I had missed in life with my estranged family. Hannah engaged Emma in lighter conversation and Jonah left his stoic nature at the door. The only quiet one at the table was Nathan, but it didn't mean he was unhappy. He smiled and laughed quietly at Abigail's excitement at having another sister to have around, and glanced my way often, his eyes betraying the fact that he was happy to be sitting across the table from me.

Nathan excused himself immediately after lunch, promising to return shortly. I watched as he left and felt the distance when he disappeared behind his hill. When we had finished cleaning up from the meal, Jonah and Fannie stepped out to the front of the house, his hand moving in discreetly to hold hers as they stepped outside. Emma dragged Abigail upstairs with a quick grin, knowing that somehow the youngest sister would want to eavesdrop. Hannah lingered in the kitchen with me, pretending to clean the table with a wet rag.

"You should have something for him to drink when he returns," she said with a smirk on her face.

I nodded and paced the side of the room.

Why was I so nervous?

I liked him, and he liked me. It was simple really.

Except there were all these rules I didn't know.

"What if I do something wrong?"

She let out a noise that sounded like a snort and shook her head.

"Katherine, I do not think you can do wrong with Nathan. He just went to stand up to the Elders for you. I think he is intent on making you his wife," she said and watched as my eyes widened at her words.

His *wife*.

I hadn't really thought much past simply having tea with him on the porch.

And maybe kissing him.

I had definitely thought of kissing him.

But his wife?

Why did that scare me? Surely I knew that was inevitable, right?

I had never been excited about marriage before. Sean talking about it had made me sick to my stomach because it was a sentence with him, but the idea of Nathan talking about it with me left a different feeling in my stomach.

"Katherine, you do not need to worry yourself. He is as nervous as you are. He does not know much about courting a girl. Just enjoy simple conversation," she chuckled and stepped up to me, halting my pacing.

"Simple conversation, right," I said, nodding.

Simple conversation about life. Farming, gardening, having babies.

I flushed at the thought of babies with Nathan.

If the first kiss disturbed him, I doubted he had given much thought to the mechanics of having children.

I, on the other hand had thought a bit about that. Every time he looked at me through his thick lashes, every time he blushed and looked away. Every touch that sent a flush through me. He made me feel very different from how Sean had when he touched me.

But then again, Sean's touch wasn't gentle or kind.

Sean's touch was demanding. Forceful. Painful.

"Katherine," Hannah said, breaking me from my intense thoughts.

"What do I talk about?" I asked.

She laughed and stepped away to pour tea into two glasses.

"What do you talk about in your world?" she asked.

Sports, movies, where to go to eat. Unimportant things here.

I was going to have a harder time than I thought.

She turned and handed me the glasses of tea.

"You will do fine. Tell him of yourself and he will do the same. That is what is expected. Now go, he comes. The swing is quiet on the porch. No one will hear you speak from there," she said and ventured upstairs, the smirk never leaving her face.

I looked outside the back door and there, coming down the hill was Nathan. He looked flushed and I realized he must have run both ways, he had not been gone that long. Taking a big breath to calm my nerves, I pushed my way carefully out the back door and sat down in the swing, nervously watching him as he walked across the yard towards me.

He slowed his gait when he saw me on the swing and looked around to see if anyone else was around. My heart sped up when I noticed his smile brighten as he stepped up onto the porch. Nathan took off his hat and ran his hand through his hair tentatively before stopping just in front of me. He looked down towards the floor and cleared his throat.

He looked so nervous.

"Um, do you want to sit?" I asked, my own nerves showing through my higher pitched voice.

Nathan offered me that quivering lopsided smile I was learning was my favorite and sat carefully beside me, off to the side and leaving a rather large space between us.

Placing his hat on his lap he sat there awkwardly for a moment, looking off towards the garden in front of us. His skin was still flushed from the heat of his walk, his forehead damp and marked red from the inside of his hat. And his hand tormented his hair as he repeatedly pushed it back off his temple.

I couldn't tell which one of us was more nervous.

It was kind of nice. I felt like we were on the same level somehow, both of us testing the water with no pressure to dominate the other.

I liked that especially.

He shifted in his seat and turned towards me slightly and cleared his throat again, watching him as he licked his lips and swallowed hard. It was then that I remembered I held two glasses of tea.

He had me a little distracted.

"I'm sorry, I have tea. You must be thirsty," I rushed out, offering him one of the glasses, which he took gratefully.

"Thank you, Kate," he murmured and drank down most of the tea before taking a breath. I watched in rapt fascination as he swallowed.

I couldn't imagine why something as simple as eating and drinking intrigued me, but it did with Nathan. And my attention to him seemed to make him more flustered.

I liked how his ears would turn red before his cheeks.

I dragged my eyes from his long throat and took my turn looking out at the garden, watching as the house started to cast shadows in the afternoon light. We were quiet as we sat there, I sipping my tea and Nathan lightly tapping his hat on his lap. The silence seemed to only add to our nerves as the minutes dragged on.

One of us had to make the leap.

"It is hot today," he offered and then let out a soft grunt and shook his head as if embarrassed. I laughed softly and tilted my head to watch the blush extend down his neck.

"Yes, it's been hot since I've been here. I like it though. It's a nice change," I replied and realized just a week ago I had been lamenting on how I missed the fog.

Now, not so much.

"What is it like where you are from?" he asked, turning towards me a little more and laying his arm carefully over the back of the swing. His fingers were inches from my shoulder.

"Um, it's cooler, and the sun isn't so bright, which is weird I guess since it's California," I stammered, my nerves making me blather on. "But when the sun does come out it's nice. It's never too hot."

"I did not know you were from California. I thought girls from there were always tan. You have more color since you have come to us," he murmured and hid his nervousness by finishing off his tea.

"Do you want more? I can go get more," I asked and slid over to take his glass, our knees just touching. He straightened a bit and his eyes widened when my hand came in contact with his over the glass. He looked down at my hand over his and shook his head.

"No, I am fine, thank you."

I set our glasses on the table before us and was settling back into the swing when he surprised me with capturing my hand in his. He glanced briefly behind us, as if he were afraid to be caught touching me before he smiled and resumed his timid exploration of my hand in his. His touch was so light, his fingertips just touching the inside of my palm to coax my hand towards him. He studied my hand carefully, grazing over the pads of my fingers and then down to my palm to trace the lines there before turning it over to stroke the tops of my knuckles. His fingers were rough from work, but I didn't mind.

It added to the beauty that was the man beside me.

Hardworking, honest in his life.

I could feel my heart thrumming against his index finger when he found my pulse at my wrist.

"Does it rain here?" I whispered, trying to distract myself from wanting to vault across the swing and kiss him.

Talking of the weather seemed to be our starting point in conversation.

He shook his head and didn't look up from my hand in his.

"Not as often as we need. This summer particularly has been dry. We need the rain for the crops. Do you like the rain?" he asked and finally looked up at me with questioning eyes.

177

"I do," I said and held myself very still while his fingertips traced back over my palm before holding it finally in his lap.

"What of your family? The day at the Frolic, you seemed hesitant to speak of your mother. And Jonah told me that your father has not helped you," he said, his brow puckering at that.

"My dad is a councilman and busy with work," I replied. "My mom died in a car accident."

"I am sorry," he whispered and I could tell by his voice that he was thinking of the tragedy of his own family. We were quiet for a bit, both of us unsure how to continue.

"I have a sister that lives in Illinois," I said, hoping to drag us both out of the awkward silence that had enveloped us.

"Is that where you were going when you came here?"

I nodded.

"You must miss your sister."

I nodded again and looked away out into the field.

"She and I are a lot like Emma and Hannah. But she has always been protective of me. She was really all I had after our mother died. My father dealt with his loss by jumping into politics," I replied and felt a moment's sadness over not being able to call Stacy after Nathan rescued me.

She'd be worried again.

He was quiet for a time, and I felt hesitant to bring up his family, knowing how much pain he had at their loss.

"Do you live in a large city?" he finally asked, perhaps trying to move us away from lost families.

"No, it's not a big as San Francisco, but it's a college town, so there was always something to do there," I replied and continued to watch as his face reacted to my questions.

"We must bore you with our simple ways," he whispered and pulled away a bit, his look a little forlorn.

I laughed, bringing his head back to me in surprise.

"There is so much to do! I can't see anyone getting bored too easily here!"

That timid smile fluttered on his full lips.

"I just mean you must miss the conveniences of your world. Your music, and television. And electricity? You must long for those things?" he asked and shuffled a little closer to me so that he could hold my hand closer to his chest.

The beating of his heart against the back of my hand momentarily distracted me before I could answer.

"I don't really miss any of that. Music perhaps. Music was how I escaped from things," I murmured. "And reading. I miss reading."

"My mother had a collection of books, I can show you one day if you would like," he offered.

"I'd like that," I murmured and returned his soft smile with my own.

We sat for a long while, talking over things I liked to do, and the general questions every boy asks a girl. He had many questions about my life before, his face a little sad when I spoke of my friends, how few I had. How I kept to myself mostly. We never spoke of Sean, and barely touched on my relationship with my family again. He smiled when I spoke about my love of baking.

And then he finally asked about religion. I fidgeted beside him and looked down into my lap where my free hand lay.

"We don't really go to church much. It was never really important to my mom or dad, except at Christmas and Easter. I don't know much really," I confessed.

He nodded, as if contemplating something.

179

"You believe in God, though?" he finally asked.

Knowing how important religion was to the Amish, I knew this would be one answer that might determine whether I would be accepted in this community or not, based on my beliefs.

"I believe in God. I just don't know what to think after that. I've never really read the Bible or anything," I replied.

He pulled to let go of my hand and leaned away from me. I thought perhaps I had offended him until I noticed he was pulling out a small black book from his pocket and sucking on his lips in the nervous way he did. He held the book gently, and I could tell it was very old and well used, but taken care of through the years. It seemed very precious by how he regarded it.

"This was my mother's. It was her Bible that she carried with her always. I would like you to have it," he whispered and placed it in my hand.

I hesitated in taking it, the immensity of him offering it to me a little overwhelming.

"I can't take this, Nathan. This was your mother's."

He shook his head and pushed it back into my hands, covering them with his own.

"I want you to have it. She does not need it anymore. I think she would have wanted you to have it, Kate. And it is something to read, at the very least."

I held it tenderly, tracing the worn leather of the cover with my fingers. It was indeed old, and soft to the touch. His offering of this to me was more than any bundle of flowers or chocolates a boy could give. This was something of his heart and soul. This was his way of life he had handed to me.

"Thank you," I whispered and leaned in to offer him a small peck on the cheek. He blushed and pulled away before I could kiss him.

Rules. Right.

"Sorry," I mumbled and pulled away embarrassed.

"Would you like to take a walk? We can talk and stretch our legs around the yard," he suggested.

Smiling, I nodded and took his hand briefly to stand. He released me almost as soon as I was standing, motioning for me to precede him down the stairs. He fell in step beside me when we reached the grass, walking beside me at a respectable distance.

We made small talk once more. This time I asked about him. I learned the names of his horses: Magnus, the great black he used in the field and Molly and Strider, his wagon horses. I learned about his enjoyment in writing, of which I already knew, but I smiled and nodded as he spoke about prose and how he would read some of his mother's books on poetry when he was younger.

It was poetry that made him want to become a faith leader.

"Do you write a lot?" I asked, hoping that perhaps there were more sheets of poetry in his house.

"Lately, yes," he whispered and his smile seemed to blossom. "I am inspired when I read or when I see beauty around me."

He tugged at his suspenders at his words, clearly feeling a little vulnerable at his admission, while my heart skipped a beat at the thought that I had inspired him that first night. He moved closer to reach for my hand. I looked around before taking his hand, the barn blocking our view of the house.

"We have a few minutes to ourselves if anyone were to be watching," he murmured and stepped a little closer to me, walking beside me so that our arms touched. His hand trembled slightly in his loose grip until I held it a little tighter, offering him some encouragement at his gesture.

The barn offered a little shade on our side, and it was much cooler as Nathan slowed his pace until we stopped near the door of the barn at the deepest part of its shadow. He turned and touched my other hand gently, silently requesting it. I slipped my fingers through his, the warmth rushing through my body when his long fingers wrapped around mine.

"May I kiss you, Kate? Like yesterday?" he asked softly. I felt his hands pull me towards him with a gentle urging. I swallowed and looked up into his dark eyes. His breath was heavier and I could see his heart hammering in his chest where his shirt lay open.

"I would really like to kiss you," he murmured and leaned in just a bit, keeping enough distance to wait until I agreed.

I could only nod.

His eyes conveyed the need he had; I could feel it myself through this energy we shared whenever we touched. I could see it in the soft pout to his lips as he dipped his head down and soft breath of my name, and then I was closing my eyes to feel him against my lips.

A gentle brushing, to reintroduce us to one another, and the burgeoning heat that built within me grew. He let out a soft hum and moved his lips against mine with a little more purpose, having learned from yesterday that taking my bottom lip into his mouth would cause a trembling in my body. I stretched on my toes, our joined hands pulled to our sides as I craned my neck to offer him my mouth willingly.

He moaned when he felt my tongue brush against his lips, allowing me in with his noise. It was just an explorative entry, to introduce him to more than just lips. The tip of his tongue met with mine, curled slightly as if in hesitation. Another soft noise from him, a moan in my mouth and then I felt his hand slip up to touch my cheek, feather light fingertips brushing along my jaw until they stretched to apply gentle pressure along my neck.

Drawing me closer.

Gently. Asking. Not taking.

It was my turn to moan. He paused in his exploration; cautious of my sound, but I drew him against me with my hands, sliding up his back until they found a place along his shoulders. I pressed myself to him, so that the heat and drumming of his heart soon pounded through me. His body tensed against mine for an instant at the contact, before melting and seeming to enfold around me in a welcome embrace.

One hand along my neck, the other wrapped loosely across my back, he deepened the kiss and I shivered at the sound of his groan as he gave in and kissed me with much more enthusiasm. His breath was labored and his hand along my back flexed between my shoulder blades, holding me to him. It wasn't until I pressed my body fully against him that he gasped and pulled away hurriedly, his face flushed and his eyes clenched shut.

"I am sorry," he gasped, bending over slightly with his hands on his thighs, propping his body up from falling over.

"No, I'm sorry, Nathan. I shouldn't have been so forward. I didn't mean," I stammered, watching as he struggled to stand up straight. It was obvious that he was struggling to calm his body.

He shook his head and tried to smile, but through his breaths it looked a little pained.

"Please do not apologize, Kate. I should not have asked. I just wanted to kiss you. It is difficult to stop with just a kiss," he said and chuckled awkwardly at his words.

I smiled down at him and touched him gently on the cheek, drawing his face up to mine.

"If it matters at all, Nathan, I enjoyed it. Is that wrong?" I asked and pulled him back to stand.

He shifted before me, his hands immediately tugging at his suspenders. He was blushing as he regarded me with a shy smile.

"I would do it again if you would let me," he whispered, looking at me through his eyelashes.

My heart skipped a beat at his words.

"I would like that, Nathan."

His smile widened and he leaned forward, allowing only his lips to touch me, soft and lingering for a moment before pulling away and letting out a sigh, his eyes closed.

"*Thy lips, drop as the honeycomb: honey and milk are under thy tongue,*" he whispered and let his eyes flutter open. I was completely taken with this man. His mouth, both in how it moved and what he said to me had me enthralled.

"You are my sustenance, Kate. You feed me with your kindness and your beauty. I have been blessed with your coming here," he murmured and stepped close to take my hand in his again. He leaned in once more, his lips scorching against my forehead as he pressed them softly there, before letting out a soft sigh.

"We will be missed. We must come from behind this barn unaffected," he sighed and held me for a moment more.

"I don't think that's possible," I murmured. Nathan drew away slowly, the color in his face brighter, and his smile appling up his cheeks a bit. I was sure I suffered the same effects. There was no way we would be able to re-emerge as we did before we kissed.

He held my hand quietly as we walked around the barn, squeezing it lightly before releasing it as the house came into view. I felt the separation as we walked slowly back up to the porch, sitting together once more on the swing.

A little closer than before, but still apart.

Those were the rules after all.

But I had a feeling our walks would come often.

We sat for some time into the late afternoon, talking softly. Nathan read from his mother's Bible. Scriptures of respect and love. Something of the kindness to strangers and good will. To be honest I heard very little of what he was saying. I was entranced by the soft timbre of his voice. Deep and clear, but it washed over me like a melody of a song. I found that missing my music was less important to me now.

Hearing his voice as he spoke his words were enough. Perhaps that was his talent; he could sway an entire congregation. Because what he spoke of came from his heart, not just his lips. Regardless of whether I heard all the words, I felt the meaning.

He was happy to have me here. And he would see that I remained happy.

In his world.

As he left that night, I could feel the happiness run through me when he smiled more brightly. He wished me a good night as he always did. But in the cover of the darkness of the porch when I walked him out, his kiss was more tender and sure, if only too brief. I watched his back as it disappeared in the dim moonlight.

I couldn't wait until morning when I would see him return.

CHAPTER 14

I wasn't even half way undressed before Emma and Abigail were chattering at me, asking me the questions I knew would come.

"What did you talk about?" Emma started and then the floodgates opened up before I could get a word in.

"Did he ask to see you again?"

"Is he going to keep coming back?"

"What did you do while you walked?"

"Did he kiss you this time? Tell me he was respectful or I will have to have words with him!"

"He smiled all throughout supper! That is good!"

I was about to admonish them for all the questions when the bedroom door cracked open and Hannah snuck in, lantern in hand and in only her shift, her hair braided down her back. I let out a sigh and hung up my dress.

It seemed it was girls' night tonight.

I had no idea what that meant, in my world or theirs.

I settled into the corner of my bed and slid out the Bible Nathan had given me. It was such a meaningful gift; I was hesitant to show it at first. But Emma's wide eyes and Hannah's smirk made me think they understood.

"He gave you Aunt Elisabeth's Bible?" Emma breathed.

I nodded and opened it carefully, smiling at the thought that just a few hours ago, Nathan had held this in his hands, reading it to me. As I thumbed through the pages, a small piece of paper fell out.

I wasn't fast enough to grab it; it was in Hannah's hands before I could even make a noise. I recognized the paper for the same that Nathan had written on before, for my poem. Hannah opened the tidy folded piece of paper carefully and her eyes widened at the lettering on the page.

"What does it say?" Abigail asked excitedly, covering her mouth at the loudness of her voice.

Hannah held it for only a moment, a blush rising across her cheeks before she grinned and passed it over to me finally.

"I am sorry," she whispered. "I could not resist. But it is for your eyes only unless you choose to share."

I took the paper from her hands slowly, my heart hammering at the idea that she had read his poem he had written me the other night. I knew she didn't mean to be rude, but I had wanted to keep that part of him secret.

"It's all right, Hannah," I murmured and then my smile faltered when I read the first lines.

> *So much beauty in your being,*
> *Surely you are an angel sent down to me.*

I blinked and let out a gasp at the words.

"It's another poem," I breathed.

"Another?" they asked in unison, excitement clear in their voices. I blushed and dragged my eyes away from the poem I desperately wanted to read now.

"He wrote something a few days ago. I saw it on his desk when I cleaned the other day," I explained nervously. I was not sure what they would say about my snooping around his personal things.

"Katherine! Do not leave us in suspense! Read what he wrote!" Emma whispered urgently.

"Emma, this is private," Hannah admonished.

"You read it," Abigail whined.

"All right!" I said to end the arguing. "I'll read it out loud just so I can read it too!"

Abigail bounced a little on the bed and clasped her hands together in glee. Hannah merely let out an exaggerated sigh and lay down on her side at the foot of the bed, Emma joining her with bright eyes. I swallowed and cleared my throat, knowing my voice would do nothing for his beautiful words.

> *"So much beauty in your being,*
> *Surely you are an angel sent down to me.*
> *Such warm eyes as you regard me,*
> *Surely to draw me into your pure heart.*
> *Such sweetness in your voice,*
> *Surely must be Heaven made.*
> *Such a tender embrace,*
> *Surely to offer me His strength in your arms.*
> *Such soft lips,*
> *Surely offering God's love.*
> *Such kindness,*
> *Surely to remind me be true.*
> *Such luck I have at Heaven sitting beside me,*
> *Surely to assure me of my Earthly duties as a man.*
> *Such amazing beauty,*
> *I see in you.*
> *Kate."*

I read it again silently, a great smile tugging on my lips as I read his words.

He had written me another poem.

He had grinned at me knowingly that afternoon when I asked how much he had written, knowing he had slipped this into his mother's Bible.

I sighed and looked up from the paper, into Emma's dreamy stare. She hummed and closed her eyes and nodded.

"He is writing again," she whispered happily and flopped back against the headboard.

I looked at her askance.

"Nathan wrote the most beautiful words for Sermons before," Hannah explained. Her sad smile told me when he had stopped writing.

His family's death had changed so much about him.

It made my heart soar that I could bring him a little happiness back.

"Katherine," Hannah whispered, pulling me out of my pleasant daze. I looked up into her contemplative eyes.

"He has written you prose. He has given you his mother's Bible. You must understand this is serious," she whispered, Emma and Abigail nodding beside her.

I swallowed and looked down at the paper once more, at Nathan's clean script and meaningful words. I knew it was serious. I could feel it in my bones. The conversation with Hannah flitted through my head again.

He is intent on making you his wife.

Very serious.

Is that what I wanted?

I had only known him a few days, how would I know that?

But this was a different world. Perhaps they did it this way. I had no idea. The idea of trying to impress him, or the Elders made my stomach clench. I had no idea what I was doing. The panic on my face must have alarmed Hannah and Emma because they both moved close to me and extended their hands to hold onto me, comforting.

"How do I make this all work?" I asked, clueless.

My words must have surprised them, for Hannah pulled away with wide eyes and Emma let out a happy laugh.

"I knew you liked him as much as he did you!" she said merrily.

"But what do I do?" I repeated, exasperated and collapsed back onto my back in the bed, covering my face.

If this were my world, we'd go out again, move on to touching and feeling, and probably be called boyfriend and girlfriend. Did they say that here?

"We will help you, Katherine. It will be all right," Abigail whispered hugged me across the waist.

"So then what do I do now?" I asked, growing more nervous as I thought of how to impress Nathan and not cause any trouble.

Hannah leaned back into the bed and thought seriously for a moment.

"I must ask you, Katherine," she said and held my hand to focus all my attention on her. "Do you truly wish to be one of us? Would you give up everything, to live this life?"

"I would," I whispered, knowing in my heart that it was true. I hadn't felt more at home anywhere than I had since coming to West Grove.

Emma reached over and held my hand over Hannah's. Abigail mimicked her sisters.

"Tomorrow, Katherine," Emma whispered, "When we do our chores, we will talk about what you must learn then. It will be much, but we pledge to help you. And we will help you with Nathan, for he is hopeless when it comes to courting."

I laughed quietly with my new sisters; sure that poor Nathan would be traumatized if he knew what they thought of him. Hannah wished us goodnight and Emma and Abigail tucked under their covers while I opened up my new book to the very beginning. I knew that their world revolved around this book.

I needed to get familiar with it.

So that I could get familiar with Nathan's life.

I opened up to the first page, the words coming to me easily. Maybe some of the most famous words to this book:

In the beginning, God created the Heavens and the Earth.

I might know some, but I knew I had so much more to learn.

Tomorrow.

CHAPTER 15

"So there are public gatherings just for the purpose of courting?" I asked, digging out the carrots from the ground as I spoke.

"Yes, we will go to one after the next Sermon. Hannah and Mark will be married in a couple of days, it is expected that everyone will be here to celebrate that, but it is also a chance for couples to mingle and speak together," Emma explained and wiped the dirt from her fingers.

She had three times as many carrots pulled as I did. I was still learning.

"So you don't go out on dates then, by yourselves?" I asked and stood to stretch. I was covered in dirt where my knees had been shuffling around.

"That is not allowed, Katherine. Except during Rumspringa. But that is not talked about," she whispered loudly, as if it were a secret that couples could sneak away during their coming out.

This had been our thing for the last several days. One of the sisters would be with me while we did our chores and they would expound on the ways of the Amish.

First it was the basics.

Abigail recited the Amish week for me over and over.

The days of the week all had assigned duties to be completed.

Monday, laundry.

Tuesday, baking for selling at the local market.

Wednesday, a deep clean of the house on top of our daily cleaning chores.

Thursday was a day of reflection, and many times celebration. Like weddings and Frolics.

Friday was gardening day to harvest and replant anything not done daily.

Saturday was canning and preparation for Sunday meals.

Sunday was a day of rest. Every other week, the families met for Sermons together at the house of a member of the community.

Duties were more or less assigned to each family member, to even the load. I was starting to understand why the Amish had so many children; except Fannie and Jonah. They had to be struggling with only daughters. Jonah managed his crops with help from Mark and occasionally a man I did not know. But like Nathan, it was difficult. How much of the Amish life was always a struggle to make ends meet?

I had learned so much in only a couple of weeks, but knew I was terribly behind on how they really lived. And loved.

Courtship was secret. The couple didn't announce themselves until the man had the Bishop come and ask the girl her thoughts on their union. That little bit of information made me sick to my stomach.

The Bishop asked the girl if she wanted to marry the boy?

And the Bishop asked her father for approval?

Well, that would go over well.

I had no intention of having my father agree to anything in my life. He had done such a great job already. Emma must have seen my reaction when she told me. She leaned in and offered me an encouraging hug.

"It will be all right, Katherine. Father will be sure to say yes. I have no doubt," she said and walked off towards the kitchen, allowing me a moment to let my emotions get the better of me, for just a moment.

Jonah would say yes. How welcoming this family had been to me, that they made me a part of their family, without question. So much kindness, it was amazing the amount of love this community had. And the assumption that Nathan would want to marry me, would go through with having the Bishop ask me was a giant leap. Jonah would answer for me, instead of my father. They had taken me as their own with no worries that I wouldn't be accepted into the community.

Would the Bishop let me marry one of his own? Would he allow an Outsider to be a part of the community? Would he allow me to be a part of Nathan's life? Did he have a choice? Surely love was more important than duty.

Was it love? I had no idea. I knew I had an undeniable draw to Nathan.

And Nathan's affections seemed clear.

Yes, Jonah would say yes. He seemed intent on making sure his family was happy. It was a remarkable feeling, having so many care when really it was not their duty.

I wiped my wet face with dirty hands, not caring if I smeared the dirt under my eyes. I didn't want them to see I had been crying. I wanted to prove to them that I was strong. All the information crammed into my head would be used well.

How strange it felt, having a sudden determination to make this work. To make the firm choice that this was what I wanted. I wanted a life here, in this simple world. I wanted a life with Nathan, a man I barely knew, but felt something so strong, it was meant to be. These people had strong convictions. I would too.

I walked back to the house, head held high, determined to learn it all. I was determined to get through my Book, so that I understood everything about it. It was an integral part of their lives. It was an important part of Nathan's life. I would learn it all.

We had worked hard all week in preparation for Hannah and Mark's wedding. Our chores had more meaning, knowing that we were preparing for a special event. We had to prepare our home for the neighbors and guests that would be filling it the coming Thursday. The days had seemed to fly by, and I was happy to finally be able to feel the rhythm that was daily life here take a hold of me. The women showed me how to live the Amish Way, and I was learning that baking was most definitely my strength. My pies sold well at the local Amish market as well as the General store.

I was learning to make a life here.

I was pulling out the last of my boysenberry pies from the oven when Nathan came in with Jonah from outside. Every time he walked in the door it was like a rush through my body. The soft smile and dip of his head as he tried to hide it would always make me smile in return. You would think after being with the Bergers for almost two weeks, with him here for meals and evening sittings, I would be used to his timid glances and smiles.

Even when he appeared sweaty and dirty from the field, I found myself staying close to him regardless. There was something about a man who worked hard for a living that was just incredibly attractive. He smelled like the earth and an honest man. Not disgusting in any way, I assumed those nights when he came in cleaner from the field, he must have washed up, worried that he would turn me off from a particularly grueling day. Nathan wanted to please me as much as I wanted to please him. So when he would walk in, covertly smiling towards me while I helped Fannie bring in the meal, I would do what I could to make sure he was happy. Seeing him smile was more important to me than making a good pie, truly. I wanted to please him as well.

My sisters would giggle and make fun of me in the evenings after he had left. It was strange to have family that knew about our interest in one another, all the while respecting our privacy when we went for our walks. We were supposed to be secret after all. We would talk mostly while we walked together in the evenings, learning of one another's world and each other. But the energy would always intensify when the barn came into view, when we would disappear from prying eyes behind it.

Nathan seemed to be able to time exactly how long our walk should take and how long that meant that we could spend kissing. He always seemed to pull away just as I felt sure I would collapse from the intensity of it. Always the same, just as he would feel me pull against him and open up to him, hoping for more than his hands cupping my head, or cradling my back. Every time, he would pull back and let out a long breath, putting me back at arm's length.

It wasn't like I didn't know he liked it. But instead of trying to cop a feel or move to the next level like Sean always did, Nathan would pull away and take my hand to resume our walk, ending up back in the swing seat, talking quietly. It was a little flustering, until I remembered we had only known one another for few weeks. Less really, given Nathan's avoidance those first few days. With that in my head, I would take a deep breath and enjoy his hand in mine whenever I could, and smile at the intensity of our feelings.

I enjoyed this slow progression. It was a nice change from the pressure I had always felt with Sean. Nathan was gentle and tentative, respectful. Even if our bodies craved more, I liked the fact that I felt safe with Nathan. This was how a relationship worked. Evenings sitting and talking, a stolen kiss, and the tender heat of his hand in mine. It was a natural progression. Eventually, something more would happen when the time was right for both of us.

For now, I enjoyed the simple with Nathan. Nights relaxing after a long day were better when I was with him. If the light of the early evening allowed, he would read to me passages from the Bible. I was delighted to hear him read, especially when he touched on passages I had read earlier in the day. Any time I could spend quietly, I was reading from his mother's book. I found the stories fascinating. And integrating them into their lives, I felt I understood the Amish lifestyle more.

The Amish lived their lives based on the words in the book in my hands, quite literally. As I read something that struck me as familiar, I would find an example of it in the daily life of the people around me. Living the simple life, not drawing attention to oneself, not being vain. Respecting ones Elders, treating strangers with kindness.

So many things that they lived by.

The Amish were an honest God-loving community.

Listening to Nathan every night as he recited words of wisdom, I heard more than his gentle voice, I heard the meaning of what he said. I was starting to see that he had a purpose to his passages. It seemed to offer him some solace as well, reading to me, allowing me to learn from him. Perhaps it was a way of healing his broken faith.

But on some nights, he seemed more reflective than others. Like this night.

We had taken our walk, our brief time behind the barn a little shorter as he settled us back into the swing, his brow slightly furrowed as he cleared his throat and fiddled with his mother's Book in his hands. He

197

read tentatively, as if he was troubled by what he read. I touched him gently on the arm, drawing his attention to me before he started.

"Are you all right? You seem nervous tonight," I said, watching his lip disappear into his mouth.

He brushed his hair behind his ear and sighed.

"My thoughts weigh on me tonight," he said quietly and tried to smile.

"Did I say something wrong to offend you?" I asked, worried that perhaps I had done something wrong.

He shook his head and let out a nervous laugh, fidgeting beside me as we listened to Mark and Hannah laughing inside. It was the night before their wedding, and the excitement seemed to spread throughout the house, except on the porch where we sat.

"Tomorrow your sister will marry," he said after they quieted down inside.

I nodded, confused at his reaction when he glanced at me from the corner of his eye and let out a heavy breath. He cleared his throat again and traced the edge of the Bible as a distraction.

"She is very happy to be wed," he said.

Again I nodded.

It was all she had talked about when we weren't trying to teach me about the Way.

"Weddings are important in our community, as much so as the baptism of new members."

I straightened up a little with that.

"I was going to ask you about the baptisms," I said, watching as he let out a relieved breath and turned to listen to my questions.

"You get baptized when you're older," I started.

"Yes, it is our belief that you choose your way," he said.

"And you do this after your Rumspringa?"

He frowned slightly and nodded.

"Not everyone takes their Rumspringa. Some know before that. And some," he said and his voice trailed off.

"You haven't been baptized," I pressed gently.

"No, I still must take the classes and choose my path."

"You need to take classes?" I asked, curious.

"Yes, and then once you have completed them you can choose. It is assumed that once you start taking the classes, you have already chosen. But some still choose to leave," he said and shifted in his seat.

"So I will have to take the classes too," I said, thinking out loud.

I still had much to learn.

He was quiet as I sat there thinking about everything I needed to accomplish.

"You would choose this life?" he said finally, looking at me with those deep eyes.

I looked at him, a little perplexed.

"Of course."

"And you would be happy?" he asked and slid a little closer to me, his eyes inquisitive.

"Are you sure you're all right?" I asked, his questions making me nervous.

He nodded and laughed softly.

"It is just that tomorrow will be your first Sermon," he said and swallowed, glancing at me. "And your first wedding."

I narrowed my eyes at him.

"Is that what you're nervous about? The wedding?" I asked, laughing when I saw his ears brighten.

"My sisters were always so unbearable when it came to weddings. Emma as well," he said and watched me warily.

"Ah, well," I said, not sure how to put him at ease. "I'm not your average Amish girl."

"No, you are not," he said and he was grinning.

"I'll try not to moon over you tomorrow, if that makes you feel better," I teased.

"People will know regardless," he said, clearing his throat.

"I thought this was all supposed to be secret," I said, feeling his nerves now.

He grinned again and made to stand up.

"It may be secret, but I cannot hide my feelings for you," he replied and leaned in to kiss me quickly. "I am happy to know that you want this life. I am sure there will be questions of your choices tomorrow when the community sees you."

I swallowed at that thought.

"Be at peace, Kate," he said soothingly. "They will see you for the angel that you are. Pleasant dreams, Kate."

I watched him as he walked to his house, a new feeling of nervousness welling up inside of me.

Tomorrow, people would figure out I wished to stay.

Tomorrow they would see me with Nathan.

I had a feeling tomorrow would be a judgment day for me.

CHAPTER 16

It was difficult to sleep that night, the morning coming too quickly. I thought I had just fallen asleep when Emma was pulling me up to bathe and get dressed. And all the while my brain strained to remain calm over what today would bring. Breakfast was a haze, the only welcome part to it was the green eyes that smiled and watched me as I picked at my food. I was sad to see him disappear after breakfast, Jonah and Nathan heading to his home to finish the chores that must be done every day, even on wedding days.

I didn't have time to miss him; Abigail and Emma were rushing around to prepare for the ceremonies. I still had the fear of judgment in my head as I helped Hannah into her newly made dress. Her wedding dress was simple, dark blue to bring out her eyes against her red hair. Her dress would become her church dress after her wedding, the dress of a wife.

With Hannah dressed, Emma and I disappeared downstairs to greet people as they filed into the house, every room filled with chairs and extending out into the yard. I caught sight of Nathan helping some of the older women into the front room. He glanced my way and smiled as he spoke softly with one old woman, her face turning up to smile at his charm. He sat her carefully near an open window, turning to help another older woman to her seat. Each time he turned towards me, his eyes would brighten and he would smile.

It helped calm my nerves.

Emma pulled me towards the front of the room, sitting close to the older women that Nathan had assisted. She pulled out a book from under the bench, thicker than the Bible I had been reading from. She opened it up, leaning in to whisper into my ear.

"This is the Ausbund. It is our hymnbook for Sermons. We sing only in reverence to God. I did not wish to alarm you, what with everything that has happened," she said, her eyes showing her concern.

She handed me the hymnbook, opening it up to one particular page. It was in German. I paged through the book, looking at each page, finding it all in German. With having taken German in high school for a couple of years, I could make out maybe half the words.

"You can whisper along, Katherine. No one expects you to know this," she whispered and patted me gently on the arm.

I didn't have time to ask why the songbook was in German, opening my mouth only to shut it again just as the Bishop entered the room. I looked around to find Fannie and Hannah towards the front of the room. Nathan stood by the door leading to the other room adjacent, also full of people.

I had no idea there would be so many people here.

The Bishop raised his hands, the congregation falling silent. He looked around the room and nodded in approval.

"Today is a special day in God's eyes. Today we welcome young Hannah Berger and Mark Bowman into the bonds marriage. Today is a blessed day," he said loudly, his voice carrying through the house.

We listened as he spoke, talking of commitment and honor, of God's blessing on the couple that would be joined today. I listened and took it all in. Marriage was sacred, a commitment as important as their baptism into the Way. The joining of two people meant the continuation of their way of life. And we were witness to the union.

The Bishop pulled out his hymnbook and called out a page. I held the book for Emma, finding the page quickly. There was a shuffling of paper, and then the most beautiful voice I had heard began to sing the first line.

Standing between the doors, stood Nathan, singing to lead us in our hymn. I watched as the congregation sang to the rhythm that Nathan timed out in his hand. Hands moved in time, cutting through the air in time to Nathan's song, singing in perfect melody to his lead. There was no harmony, no accompaniment of musical instruments, only voices as they rose up and sang.

They sang in German, and I could only catch snippets of it, but I understood the jist of it; to love and respect your mate. That life had meaning, and that in choosing the right path, you found enlightenment. If you asked me what it meant to understand God before I had come to this way of life I would not have been able to tell you. Seeing the dedication this community had for their ways made me see it anew. They lived to serve their God. And they followed their ways happily. I was amazed at how much I could feel God in the moment as everyone sung. The melody of their voices united was uplifting. Spiritual.

I could only sit and watch in fascination, unable to follow along fast enough with the difficult words in the book. I felt a moment's apprehension when I noticed the Bishop's eyes on me. He watched me during the last verse, my face feeling hot as I looked away and tried to follow along in the book.

With the end of the song, the Bishop called Hannah and Mark. They stood and faced the congregation, and at once I could see that Hannah, usually so cool and stoic, was smiling. The Bishop walked out with them, to hear their vows in private as we continued with the Sermon.

One of the ministers took up the Sermon, letting Nathan lead in song as we waited for the couple to re-emerge with the Bishop.

After what felt like forever, a mumbling could be heard behind us. Emma and I turned with the rest of the congregation to watch as Mark and Hannah followed the Bishop in. Mark was grinning happily, Hannah blushing as she held his hand tightly. She glanced towards us as they stepped to the front of the room, her smile growing as we smiled back.

"Let us look on these two now, and know that they have bound themselves to each other. What they vow will keep the Way pure, and we shall hope for the line to continue with them. Let us be joyful on this blessed day! Please welcome Hannah and Mark, man and wife!" the Bishop exclaimed.

The rest of the sermon flitted past in a blur, most of it lost on me when the Bishop spoke in broken bits of German and English. We sang one last song, my eyes catching Nathan's as he sang to lead us, his eyes brilliant as he shared a moment with me from across the room. I knew I should turn away, but the bright green of his eyes and the distinctly pleasant aura around us made me feel comforted.

As the sermon ended, Hannah and Mark made their way outside so that they could receive the congratulations from those attending. Emma guided me into the kitchen, where Fannie was already pulling out the roasts from the oven. She still looked teary eyed when she looked up to see us pulling together the food for the lunch. She motioned us to her, hugging us tight for a moment before taking a deep breath and wiping her eyes.

"I am sorry," she said. "I have waited for this day for so long, and now that it is here, I am not prepared."

We hugged her once more before we moved back into the routine of serving for the guests. We followed Fannie out with bowls of food, setting them up at a shaded table where I recognized a few of the women helping there. They were the same women who had been at the Wittmers. Sarah turned and helped Jonah with the roast; glancing our way and giving instructions to set the food down and bring out more. Emma and I worked quickly, bringing out the pies, the breads and vegetables in record time.

I was turning to go back into the house when I saw an older man struggling to get up the stairs. I rushed to his side just as he looked about to collapse.

"Here, let me help you," I said softly, his eyes lighting up at my gentle touch at his elbow. I felt his bony hand reach for my shoulder, my arm moved around his waist to help him up the last step and guide him to the swing I knew well. Helping him to sit, he watched me as I stood before him.

"Would you like me to make you a plate? A glass of lemonade?" I asked, smiling down at him.

"That would be nice, child," he replied, his voice crackling with age. "My family is sitting in the sun and I prefer the shade."

I looked back at the food table, Fannie laughing and seemingly more relaxed with everything from the sight of it. It seemed I could spare the extra time for the old man who reminded me of my grandfather I had met only a few times before he had died.

"I will make you a nice plate of food and be right back," I replied and turned to make my way to the serving table.

I had just finished setting a plate for the old man when I caught sight of Nathan, off near the side of the house, speaking with the Bishop and another older man. Nathan looked frustrated, shaking his head and looking around as if to locate someone. I was sure it was for me.

I grabbed the closest glass of lemonade and hurried back towards the old man. Stepping onto the porch he waved me over with a smile. I placed the plate in his hands and set the lemonade by him on the table, smiling when he hummed at the taste of the potato salad. I stood there for a moment, unsure if he would be fine on his own, until he finally spoke.

"You are most kind, dear girl. Thank you for helping me. You can go find your friends, dear. I am sure Fannie must need you."

"You're very welcome. I'm happy to help, sir," I said softly and turned to leave.

"You may call me Ezekiel, Katherine," he said, his words making me pause and turn back around to look at him.

He knew my name?

Perhaps more people than I realized knew who I was.

That was a little disconcerting.

He did not look up from his meal, cutting apart the meat and putting it in his mouth in quiet bliss. I stepped off the porch and walked back towards the food area, catching sight of Emma and John at a nearby table. I waved to them and picked up a plate to prepare something for myself. I felt someone's hand on my shoulder, causing me to jump in surprise. I turned to find Hannah and Mark standing beside me.

"I am sorry, Katherine! I did not mean to startle you!" Hannah said hurriedly and pulled me into a tight embrace.

"It's all right, Hannah," I breathed, returning her embrace. "Congratulations. You looked so beautiful."

She pulled away, grinning at me.

"I can not believe how I feel right at this moment, Katherine. It is an amazing feeling," she replied happily when Mark pulled her close, shaking hands with guests as they wished them well.

I watched after them for a few moments, at the happiness they shared. I smiled inwardly and finished preparing my plate, excited about sitting with my new family. But when I turned to come away from the table, I stopped short when I noticed Nathan had arrived at Emma's table, sitting next to her and watching me worriedly. His eyes were wide and he was glancing back towards the porch behind me. I looked back and saw the Bishop standing beside the old man, Ezekiel, speaking softly. Walking towards me was the other man whom Nathan had been speaking with. I swallowed and turned to face him. The older man's lips were drawn in a thin line, a stark contrast to the dark beard and dark eyes as they stared me down.

"Katherine, Elder Ezekiel would like to speak with you more. You may leave your plate here," the man said, towering over me.

Looking back towards Ezekiel, I noticed the Bishop seemed smug as I nodded and put my plate down. I followed along behind the man, my nerves working through me when I saw the Bishop helping Ezekiel to his feet. The old man smiled at me and patted me on the cheek, waving me inside.

"Come inside where it is cool, Katherine. We have things to discuss, child," he said, and entered the house with the Bishop.

I turned one last time before entering the house, the place I had called home for the last couple of weeks, and looked towards Nathan. He was standing and his eyes were glued to mine. Gone was the beautiful smile on his face from earlier in the day, replaced with a look of uncertainty.

I stepped into the house with a feeling of trepidation. I just knew I was going to say something wrong.

I was walking towards an end.

CHAPTER 17

I walked into the house with an intense feeling of dread. I was going to screw up. Nothing in my life was easy.

Why should I be given this wonderful bit of life now?

I followed along behind the Bishop, wondering how they felt so at ease in the Berger home that they could just walk in and sit someplace to speak. Their comfort was the last thing I should be worrying over. If anything, their ease in the Berger home and my confusion was simply a reminder that I was the stranger here and they were the ones that would decide whether I remained.

I was heading to an Inquisition. I could just feel it.

We sat in the front room, the Bishop setting chairs up for the three of them to sit.

I wasn't sure whether I should sit or not, so I remained standing before one of the front benches from the wedding. Old Ezekiel was situated in the center, the Bishop taking one chair, the man who had approached me sitting in the remaining seat. Ezekiel smiled at me and motioned for me to sit, his smile offering me some hope this wouldn't be a firing squad.

"Please, Katherine. Sit. No need to stand and be fearful. We wish only to know you, child," he said sweetly.

I sat carefully, hands my lap, trying for my best posture and innocent look. I glanced at the Bishop and felt my stomach turn from his countenance. He made me incredibly nervous. He seemed to have perfected the same look my father had when he chose to remark on my failings. I could tell the Bishop was cut from the same mocking cloth. His dark brooding eyes never left me, and seemed to shoot his accusing glare straight through me.

I took a careful breath and focused my attention on Ezekiel, the only friendly face in the room.

"Katherine, do you know who we are?" the third man said.

I looked over at him and cleared my throat. I was parched suddenly.

"You are the Elders, sir."

He offered me a curt nod, never smiling.

"That is right, girl. You have met Elder Ezekiel Schroeder. I am Eli Jennson, and this is our Bishop, Samuel Yoder," he replied, offering what seemed to be the official introductions.

I nodded to each of them and tried to smile.

"I am pleased to meet you. I'm grateful for your kindness in letting me stay with the Bergers."

The Bishop let out a noise, something like a snort and smirked.

Had I said something wrong? Had they already made their decision about me?

"Katherine, we do not want you to think that this is an inquest in any way," the Bishop said smoothly. "We just need to know your intentions."

Intentions. And that smirk again.

"Yes, sir," I replied quietly, trying to hide the nerves.

"So," Eli started. "Where is your family from, Katherine? Jonah had very little information about you when we agreed to shelter you."

"I'm from California. A town north of San Francisco," I answered.

"California," the Bishop interjected. "That would explain your worldly behavior."

I shook my head hesitantly, confused by his statement.

"You have seen more than our youth. California is full of deception and no sense of self. There are too many opinions and not enough faith," he continued, interrupting any chance I had at a rebuttal.

I swallowed and looked down.

"I came from a small town, Bishop Yoder. Much like the town near here. I don't think of myself as very worldly," I murmured.

In truth, I felt more sheltered than the Berger sisters these days. They knew more about life than I did.

"Jonah mentioned that you wish to remain here. Is that true, Katherine?" Eli asked, moving the discussion along.

I looked up at him and nodded. He was younger than Ezekiel and his eyes were more cautious as he regarded me, one hand scratching at his dark beard.

"If you will have me. Yes, sir," I replied.

"And why is that?" the Bishop asked, an edge to his voice.

"I feel comfort here. I feel like I was meant for this life," I replied quietly, watching as the Bishop's eyes narrowed in irritation.

The tension was thick as I struggled to remain perfectly still on the bench. Three pairs of eyes bore down on me. Even Ezekiel seemed to be watching me closely. I waited in the silence for them to continue. The silence seemed to go on forever.

I was going to crack.

I could feel it, with my dry throat and airless lungs.

"What do you think it is to be Amish, Katherine?" the Bishop asked, his lips fighting that smirk.

"To do God's work. To live an honest life. To live, to love as He would want us. To live simply, and to be there for the community," I said and I hated myself for letting the tremor affect my voice.

"That is a naive view, yes. But you must understand we live much differently than you are used to," Eli explained.

"I understand it is a different lifestyle. One that I have welcomed while I have been here," I said and sat a little straighter, trying to sound sure of my statement.

Ezekiel leaned forward and tugged on his long white beard. He peered through his small glasses at me for a long moment.

"Katherine, you would have to leave everything that you know of behind you. If you made this your home, you would not be able to see your family, or your friends," Ezekiel said gently.

I nodded and looked down.

"I am aware of that. There is nothing there for me," I murmured.

I was sure they would not believe me.

"What of your father? Jonah says he is a man of stature. He will come looking for you, will he not? We do not wish trouble. We stay out of the English way. And you seem to bring conflict with you," Eli stated.

"We cannot allow your violence into our community," the Bishop added.

"I don't want to do that either. I don't want anyone to get hurt," I said hurriedly.

It was my greatest fear in being with the Bergers. That Sean would eventually find me.

The idea that he would hurt Emma. Or Abigail.

"You have much to learn, if we were to consider you. Our youth experience Rumspringa to discover how precious our Way is. You ask for it as if you know that you want it, but have not lived long enough among us to understand its meaning," the Bishop scoffed.

211

"Samuel, she has lived her life in what our youth deny. Fannie tells me she remains true and honest in our beliefs. Perhaps she understands better than we think about our Way," Ezekiel said, smiling over at me.

The Bishop looked over at Ezekiel and murmured to him, in the same guttural German he had used in the Sermon, too loud for a whisper in the quiet room. The three of them pulled their heads close to one another.

She tempts our young. You see her with young Fisher.

Yes. He now smiles, Samuel. That is not wrong.

Nathan will leave with her.

It is not our choice if he leaves.

I sat there quietly; trying not to let on I understood most of what they said. I understood more than I could speak and the occasional English word thrown into their hushed conversation helped in the context. As much as I wanted to utter the scant German I knew back at them, I needed this advantage.

"Katherine," Ezekiel said as he pulled away from the cluster. "What have you done here to learn of our Ways?"

He smiled again, a little bit of comfort in the room.

"I have learned to be helpful as it's needed. Others needs are more important than my own. I have stood by Fannie and fed the family, as well as those in need," I started. Ezekiel's smile widened.

"What of your faith, Katherine?" the Bishop interrupted. "What is your belief in God?"

I swallowed hard.

"I believe everything happens for a reason. Because God has a plan," I whispered.

"And God wishes you to remain here? To tempt our youth, to enchant our young men?" the Bishop pushed.

"I... I'm not here to enchant," I stammered.

"Samuel," Eli whispered, a warning to his voice. The Bishop shook his head and continued, his eyes fixed on me in accusation.

"You will tire of this lifestyle. It is difficult enough for our youth. It is not about baking and courting, Katherine. This is not a fairy tale. This is our way of life. And you disrespect it by wishing to join it like a club of your world," he hissed.

I sat there, numb. Terrified to say anymore.

"Katherine," Eli said, his voice more soothing. "We live under God's law. How do you see yourself in the eyes of God?"

I frowned and shook my head.

"I don't understand the question," I replied shakily.

The Bishop interrupted Eli before he could rephrase the question.

"If you were a person from our Book, who would you be?" the Bishop asked, grinning.

I knew where he was going with this.

Jezebel.

But I felt closer to another character. One who had experienced her own trials in faith and trust. I was losing. He was baiting me. Trying to defile the Stranger. As so many did in their Book. Only to find that strangers were to be valued.

Protected.

Why did the Bishop only see me as a threat? When a novice like myself saw that *she* was strong in my head, maybe only from having just read about her.

"I am Ruth."

The Bishop's eyes narrowed and his lips pursed as he leaned closer towards me.

I was sure he had not been expecting that one. And that gave me a little confidence.

"You believe yourself to be Ruth of the Moabites? How so, girl?" the Bishop asked, unconvinced.

I turned to Ezekiel, gaining confidence in his supportive gaze. He nodded gently, asking me to continue with his eyes.

"I have been treated kindly in a strange land, welcomed by a loving family. I am a foreigner, but have been given nothing but kindness. I have worked hard to offer that kindness in return. And I hope to enter this life through trust in God, and those that follow that path," I explained.

I hoped I sounded like I knew what I was talking about.

Did I? I was still learning.

Ezekiel nodded, along with Eli, but the Bishop continued on.

"Do you expect to find your Boaz then, girl? Have you already ensured yourself a place, do you think? Have you claimed someone already, brazen as Ruth was?" he asked, ignoring the men beside him.

"I haven't made any claims, Bishop Yoder. I am grateful for the Bergers and only wish to help them however I can as I find my way," I replied. I could feel the trickle of sweat roll down my back from my nerves.

"And what of the Fisher boy? What hold does young Nathan have on you?" he persisted.

Swallowing again at the intensity of the Bishop's stare, I shook my head again.

"Nathan is part of the family. He has extended his kindness to me," I started, afraid to implicate him in anything.

"He is courting you, an *English*. This is not a path he should take," the Bishop said, a little louder and leaned back as if his words finalized any decisions to be made.

The other elders looked towards one another, and I could see the worry on their face.

I turned my head away feeling the heat on my face.

Nathan was so important to them. More so than simply an Amish man gaining the affections of an outsider. It was obvious that the Bishop had his motives, and sadly it seemed those motives would be more important than me.

"Nathan's choice is his own. I don't know his intentions," I whispered finally.

Ezekiel cleared his throat, drawing my eyes up to him.

"Katherine, it is obvious that he has taken to you. He stood before us and argued quite enthusiastically on your behalf to have you welcomed to our community. He was most insistent. This is troubling to us, only in that he has not taken his Rumspringa. He is a troubled young man who has lost so much. If we were to allow you into our community, and you made a decision to leave, he would suffer. This family would suffer," he said, his eyes suddenly very sad.

"I would never wish to hurt them, Elder Ezekiel," I replied softly.

"If you left child, do you not think he would go after you?" Eli asked.

I shook my head.

"He doesn't belong in my world," I whispered and looked down into my lap, embarrassed of the world I had called my own. Nathan would be lost in it. He didn't deserve that.

"You would destroy him. We have seen it before, you have no idea," the Bishop said harshly.

Ezekiel raised his hand, silencing the Bishop.

"It is his choice, Samuel. It is always their choice. You forget that," Ezekiel said, his voice stern.

The Bishop's eyes seemed to blaze for a moment.

I watched as they spoke again in hushed German murmurs.

You cannot allow her! She is temptation!

You are clouded, Samuel. From your own experiences. Enough.

She will not adjust to our way. She will leave.

She has learned our ways better than many of our own children.

She must not be involved with young Fisher.

That is not our place.

He must make his own choice.

Yes, he must get on with his plans. Maybe then he will see her for what she is.

This girl is kind. I will allow her to try.

You risk losing another boy from our flock!

That is how it has always been, Samuel. She makes it no different.

I do not approve.

I do.

There was a long pause, as Eli looked my way, his eyes thoughtful for a moment before turning back towards Ezekiel.

I will allow her, if she will try to live our way.

I held my breath at Eli's words. Did that mean I was accepted?

"Katherine," Ezekiel said loudly. "You have learned some of our life. You must learn everything. You must embrace God as we do and embrace our lifestyle. We do not wish to turn a daughter in need back into the darkness. But we cannot have the darkness take over."

I nodded, trembling at the idea that perhaps I had finally accomplished something for myself.

"You must prove to us that this way of life is your way of life, Katherine," Eli continued.

"I will," I breathed, fighting back an overwhelming rush of emotions flooding me.

"You must sever all ties with your world when you make this choice, Katherine," the Bishop said. He stared hard at me for a moment and then offered me a tight smile.

"You must let your English father know as soon as possible. And you must have resolute ends with this boy that pursues you," he added.

I felt my breath stutter in my lungs at the idea of confronting Sean any time soon.

I could only nod.

I had no idea how I would resolve anything with Sean, or figure out how to tell my father I was never coming back without him hunting me down. I'd figure it out. I had to.

"Well, I should think you would like to spend some time with your sisters, yes? This is a celebration after all," Ezekiel said brightly, moving to stand. The two men helped him up, their eyes following me as I stood slowly.

"Thank you," I said, stepping up closer to Ezekiel as he neared me on his way out.

"You are a dear child. I know you will not fail us. Jonah and young Fisher would not step up for you if you were not. They were quite insistent," he murmured and patted me lightly on the shoulder as he passed.

Eli and the Bishop nodded my way as they passed me, the Bishop's eyes betraying the frustration I know he felt at losing the chance to be rid of me.

I stood in the room for several minutes after they had left; overwhelmed by the conversation I had just had with the older men. It had gone much better than I had thought, but I was troubled by the Bishop's interaction. I had so many things to be angry for.

At his way of judging me before learning of me.

Of trying to control me, just like my dad had. Or Sean.

Of trying to ruin anything that Nathan wanted.

Why was Nathan coveted so?

"One thing you will learn soon enough, daughter, is forgiveness."

I jumped at Jonah's voice in the doorway, unaware that he had even stepped in. I blushed and unclenched my fists at my sides, letting out a long breath. Jonah stepped in slowly, looking off towards the celebration outside. I could hear laughter and children yelling.

Everyone was having a good time.

"It may appear that you have a mountain to climb, but there are those that will help you to scale it," he murmured.

"I have so much to do. I don't know how to do it all," I admitted.

He smiled and touched me on the shoulder tenderly.

"First, we must find your strength and your purpose. And then we will shed the worry and the doubt," he replied softly.

He looked outside and let out a long sigh.

"Nathan is missing you. Let us put this behind us for now and worry over what we will do tomorrow, Katherine. Come, let us enjoy today," he whispered and pulled me gently towards the door.

I was quiet as we stepped out into the sunlight, the brightness of it blinding me for a moment. I couldn't make out where Nathan was, until

Jonah steered me to the side of the porch. Nathan was there, pacing back and forth. He looked like he had just undergone the interrogation I just had. Hearing our footsteps, his head shot up and his eyes widened when he took me in. I must have looked upset because he rushed over to us and spoke hurriedly.

"Are you all right? You were in there for so long! They agreed to allow you to stay, yes? Kate, tell me you are all right?" he asked in a rush.

I nodded and tried to smile. It seemed to work. The tension in his shoulders lessened and he looked then to Jonah.

"She is allowed to stay?" Nathan asked again.

"So Ezekiel tells me, Nathan," Jonah said with a kind smile.

Nathan let out a relieved breath and offered me the brilliant smile I had only seen in private. Jonah cleared his throat and stepped away slowly.

"You should eat something, Katherine. You look pale. I leave her in your care, Nathan. Just be mindful that she is still under scrutiny," he said and stepped away, his eyes holding onto Nathan's until he turned and walked away.

"What does he mean by under scrutiny? They said you could stay," Nathan asked, his brow puckering with worry once more.

"I don't really want to talk about it right now. My head hurts from it all," I replied.

Nathan touched me softly on my wrist, for just an instant before withdrawing.

"You did not eat. It was not fair of them to steal you away so soon," he whispered, looking down into my eyes.

I blushed at his attention and simply shrugged.

"Come," he whispered. "Emma saved you a plate. We have a blanket laid out in the shade."

I walked beside Nathan quietly, listening to the chatter of the guests as we passed. On more than one occasion, a head would turn our way and watch us as we walked. Perhaps I was paranoid, but after the hesitancy from the Elders, and the mistrust from the Bishop, I felt the judging eyes of people taking in how I walked beside Nathan away from the general celebration.

I saw Emma stand just as I thought to turn and go back to the gathering, her eyes troubled as she stood near John, who was sitting comfortably on the blanket. I tried to smile, not wanting her to worry; although I knew she could read my stress in the way I carried my body.

Nothing got past Emma.

"We were so worried," she whispered when she pulled me into a tight embrace.

"I know. It's ok. They agreed to let me stay," I murmured, feeling her arms tighten before she released me.

"But you are still upset," she stated as she looked me over.

"Emma, let her relax for a moment," Nathan said.

John and Emma settled in on one side of the blanket, Emma patting beside her for me to sit. Nathan sat beside me, letting his legs stretch out off of the blanket. Emma pulled out a plate and offered it to me. I wasn't really hungry, not after the nerves had done me in, but I knew we probably wouldn't eat again that day. It just felt strange to be the only one eating while they watched me. I sat there quietly looking down at my plate for a minute before John finally spoke up.

"I am hungry for some pie. Shall I bring some back for everyone?" he asked, standing and smiling down at me before he turned to head towards the dessert table. Emma followed him with her eyes as he walked away, making me smile in the thought that somehow they had reconnected.

"John seems happy," I mused.

She pretended to scowl at me.

"We are not talking about John. We are talking about you, Katherine," she said.

I fidgeted with my plate, tearing apart the bread.

"They are letting me stay, with provisions," I murmured.

"What provisions?" Emma and Nathan said almost simultaneously.

I shook my head and poked at the chicken on my plate.

"Obviously I need to live like you," I started.

"You do that already," Emma argued.

"I didn't know about the language thing," I grumbled, glancing at her warily.

"What language thing?" Nathan asked, confused.

Emma nodded, understanding.

"The Ausbund," she explained. "And the Sermon. I am sorry, we should have told you. Some still speak our language, but more each day speak as you. It is easier when we sell to the English in town. Honestly most only use it be secretive around the English. Mother and Father do not choose to speak it in the home."

"We will teach you," Nathan offered, an apologetic frown marring his handsome face.

I just nodded, not knowing if I wanted anyone to know just how much I really understood from my interrogation. Would it get back to the Bishop and make him furious that he didn't have that advantage? Would knowing it help me?

"What else?" Nathan whispered, interrupting my thoughts.

"I need to sever ties and make sure Sean doesn't come around. Severing ties I am not that upset about," I explained.

"But they want you to confront your English boyfriend? That would not be wise," Emma said heatedly.

"That's an understatement," I mumbled. I couldn't look them in the eye. I was too embarrassed by the fear I felt over Sean. I was terrified to see him again.

"We will find a way, Kate," Nathan whispered and leaned in to brush his fingers across mine.

"Yes, I am sure Father can figure something out. He has many English friends in town. We will think of something," Emma said soothingly.

I nodded and remained quiet. I knew whatever I needed to do in order for Sean to forget me would take more than a few friends that did not raise a hand in anger. The fact that these people who knew so little of me, would risk so much made me love them that much more. I wouldn't get that support at home. I hadn't at all, which was why I was here in the first place.

That and maybe divine inspiration.

Was I here for a reason?

"Please, Kate. You should eat," Nathan whispered.

I turned to him and smiled up into his worried eyes.

"That is supposed to be what I say to you," I murmured, enjoying his blush.

"Nathan did not eat much either, he was so worried," Emma replied.

"We can share then," I said and pulled a green bean off the plate and offered it to Nathan. His blush deepened and he hesitated before taking it with his mouth.

I felt his lips brush up against the tips of my fingers, the heat of them enough to make me tremble. Enough to make his ears burn and his eyes look away quickly to mask the desire there. I mentally shook myself and turned back to Emma, who was smiling at the two of us.

I distracted myself with a piece of chicken and tried instead to ask Emma about John.

"So you are speaking to John again," I stated, grinning when I noticed her blush and wrinkle her nose at my keen observation.

She sighed and looked back towards where he had disappeared.

"He asked to sit with us just as I brought the last pies out. I had forgotten how persuasive he could be. And how sweet. I do love how he makes me smile," she whispered happily and pouted at Nathan's embarrassed chuckle.

I laughed and took another bite before extending my plate toward Nathan, offering him to pick something. We sat there quietly and ate, until John returned with two plates of pie. He sat down comfortably beside Emma, offering her one plate and Nathan the other.

"They were almost bare. I grabbed what I could and thought we would share," he explained and produced four forks.

We ate our food in silence, the sound of the children carrying on the breeze as we sat there. I watched as Abigail ordered some of the younger girls around, smiling at how precocious she could be and still appear to be that sweet Amish girl. We were not all that different, as I looked around. It was only the darker side of my life that the Amish did not pursue.

Nathan finished up the plate of food, while I picked at the pie. I smirked and handed him the plate when I noticed he still looked hungry. He took the plate with a quiet thank you and grinned when he noticed it was one of my pies. He finished it in no time, letting out a contented sigh as he leaned back on his elbow, stretching out beside me.

"I am afraid I ate too much," he chuckled and slipped further onto the blanket, resting his head carefully over his arm.

John followed Nathan's cue and stretched out beside Emma, sneaking a gentle hand squeeze when she took his plate from him. I set our plates behind us and leaned back, enjoying the sun as it beat down on us through the shade of the tree we sat beneath. Nathan let out a satisfied sigh and watched me as I relaxed for the first time all day. He reached for my free hand and brushed it softly before letting his hand rest on his stomach.

It was difficult to watch him, laid out beside me and not want to just lean in to touch him. He was lean and lanky, and stretched out as he was you could see just how tall he really was. I kept my eyes up high, watching the soft smile play on his lips as he tipped his hat down over his closed eyes. Watching his chest rise and fall, his breathing grew deeper, and soon I knew he was asleep.

I wondered how tired he was, working as he did and probably sleeping poorly when he did sleep. It was nice to see this contented side of him. Glancing over at John and Emma, I caught John watching me. His soft smile widened and he laughed softly.

"I am sorry, Katherine. You seem to be at peace in the moment. It is a nice thing to see," he said quietly so as not to wake Nathan.

I nodded and closed my eyes.

It was weird. I did feel content in the moment. Regardless of all the anxiety I had felt earlier in the day, right then I felt at peace. I was with friends who cared. I smiled into the sunlight and thanked the powers that be for this little bit of heaven we lived in at that moment. I couldn't remember a time when I had felt this at ease.

"You are good for each other," John whispered, my eyes opening up to his words.

Looking down at sleeping Nathan I smiled.

"He is a kind person. I'm glad for his friendship," I replied.

John's eyes didn't waver as he watched me from across the blanket. It was difficult to look away; he seemed to have a persuasive draw about him. And like Emma, he seemed he could read people well. I let out a relieved breath when his eyes moved to Nathan's sleeping form.

"You are bound to him in more ways than friendship, Katherine. You and he need each other. It is like finding the missing piece to the puzzle after ages thinking it lost. It is something to hold onto. Something that was worth the wait," he said, turning to Emma with such love on his face, I knew he felt that same connection with Emma.

Emma touched his arm lightly, a radiant smile like I had never seen before flitting across her face. I watched in wonder, as they seemed to have an entire conversation with their eyes, John's deep and content, Emma's full of joy and excitement.

They had most certainly mended their ways. I wondered if he had asked her to be his wife again. Perhaps it was too soon. John seemed like the kind of man that would wait until the time was right. He seemed patient and giving. And all that seemed directed not just at Emma, but also to those around him. He was the perfect companion for Emma.

He closed his eyes and smiled serenely towards her as he settled into the blanket, much like Nathan. His hand remained in Emma's, a quiet link to one another.

I looked around and could see that most of the women were busy cleaning up, while the men and younger kids relaxed. John had tipped his hat over his eyes as well, a happy smile the only part of his face I could see. Nathan was sleeping well, his chest rising and falling at a steady rhythm. It was nice to be this close to him even in slumber.

It was nice to just sit back and relax, if only for a little while.

There was always something that needed doing. I joined the women in cleaning up, smiling as I worked, and feeling more at ease after having won today's battle.

I would prove that I was made for this life.

CHAPTER 18

"You have certainly made quick work of the house, girls!" Fannie exclaimed when she brought in the last of the linens from the tables outside.

I wiped off the bit of sweat on my forehead and smiled at her happily.

"It is our sister's wedding day," Emma replied merrily. "She deserves a special evening."

Fannie raised her eyebrow and laughed, glancing out into the waning light outside.

"I am sure a certain young man out there was not the incentive, Emma," she chided.

I joined in Fannie's laughter and pulled the linens from her hands to set out on the porch. I walked out on them hugging, Fannie offering soft words into Emma's ear. I didn't know what she might be telling her daughter, but I had a feeling based on her glassy eyes that she was feeling that moment when one child leaves, you are sure the others are not far behind.

Fannie finally let out a heavy sigh as I walked back in.

"Fine!" Fannie said loudly, feigning exasperation. "You may go out and talk a while with that poor boy. But only because he helped Jonah and Nathan with the chairs and tables!"

Emma grabbed me and laughed as she bolted for the back door.

"Thank you, Mother! We will stay close!" she yelled as she dragged me out the door.

The last thing I saw was Fannie's endearing smile as the door closed.

"Where are we going, Emma?" I asked as she pulled me towards the barn.

The idea of any more chores made me cringe. My hands were all pruny and my feet throbbed. More than anything I wanted to just take off my shoes and sit down. But as we rounded the barn, another thing seemed more important.

Spending quiet time with Nathan Fisher.

Nathan leaned against the fence, talking casually with John. His hat was off as he pulled his hand through his hair, causing it to ruffle slightly where his fingers had been. I felt Emma squeeze my fingers at my sigh and shook my head when she laughed at me. John and Nathan looked our way at the sound Emma's laughter, and the world fell away at the smile on Nathan's face.

Emma stepped away from me and joined John, who stood there smiling tenderly down at her. One hand moved up, tracing her cheek softly before he whispered something to her. I was too far away to hear, but it must have been nice, because she smiled up into his eyes and took his hand, leading him away towards the far side of the barn. John glanced back towards Nathan, nodding to him as if in silent conversation.

Nathan shuffled his feet and glanced my way, clearing his throat as I stepped close.

"Did you sleep well?" I asked.

He offered me a shy smile and nodded.

"I have not slept that well in a long time. John had trouble waking me. I was dreaming," he whispered and his smile widened a bit.

"What were you dreaming about?" I asked softly, my heart speeding up at the way he flushed.

"I cannot say," he murmured and looked down at his hands.

I chanced overstepping again and reached for his hand, hearing his soft exhale of breath when I took it into my own and moved closer. His hand closed over mine, the gentle tug pulling me even closer, until I brushed against him. He leaned down, his lips brushing across my hairline.

"It is nearly sunset, would you like to walk a while?" he asked.

My feet cried out in protest.

"Actually, I'd really like to sit somewhere and put my feet up," I said and laughed at his confused expression.

"It's been a long day, Nathan."

He nodded and looked down, a little crestfallen.

"Of course, you need your rest. I can walk you back to the house," he murmured and took a step back.

"No," I said hurriedly. "I don't want to go to sleep. I just want to sit somewhere with you."

His smile returned and he looked off towards the barn, shaking his head.

"John has already claimed where it will be most comfortable," he said and laughed when he noticed me look back towards the barn where Emma and John had disappeared.

His face lit up and he pulled me away from the fence, past the far side of the barn where Jonah kept his farming equipment. He stopped before a large open wagon, still littered with loose hay. One last glance back the way we had come and then his hands moved in to encircle my waist. I didn't have a chance to be alarmed by his touch as he lifted me up onto the edge of the wagon as if I weighed nothing at all. He leapt up beside me with ease, his laughter light as he helped me settle back into the soft hay near the front of the wagon. We were well hidden from the house, the walls of the wagon high to contain all the hay. I felt a moment's apprehension at the idea of being so far removed from the safety of the Berger's home. I was alone, with a boy who obviously desired me.

One moment I was hopeful for something more from Nathan, the next I was nervous of the same thing.

"Kate?"

I flinched when I saw his hand rise up towards me.

Pure instinct. It was ingrained in me, even after a couple of weeks away from Sean's threat.

"I'm sorry," I stammered.

His hand moved slowly towards me, as if towards as spooked animal.

"Kate, I would never hurt you," he whispered. His fingertips grazed my cheek, so soft it tickled the skin until it prickled. He paused when he felt me tremble.

I took a deep calming breath, and closed my eyes to feel his warmth against me, leaning into his palm.

"It's not you, Nathan. I'm just not used to kindness," I said and opened my eyes when I felt his fingers trace along my jaw once more. He was gentle as he stroked my cheek, regarding me tenderly.

"Kindness is what you deserve, Kate. That is all I wish to give you."

This was quickly turning into a serious discussion, when all I was sure he wanted was a quiet moment with me. I could tell by his rigid body; he was strung tightly, surely venturing into uncharted territories for him. And I was flinching at his gentle hand, causing him to refrain from what we both wanted. I wanted him to touch me, even if my innate fear of being hurt lingered in the periphery of my wary mind.

For that I hated Sean, for ruining me in so many ways for Nathan. Nathan had been sweet and kind. He had defended me when I needed it most. He watched me with genuine concern. My hands found their way around his neck, pulling him down so that his lips were inches from mine. He paused, indecision in his eyes.

"I do not wish to frighten or hurt you, Kate," he said nervously.

"I know. I trust you," I replied, looking up into his innocent eyes.

"I want to make you happy, Kate. Like you do me," he whispered against my lips. I pulled him down so that his lips met mine, offering him the chance to explore.

To learn.

His body was so close, the heat and firm presence of it should have made me fearful, but it felt right with Nathan. He kissed me slowly, measured as he leaned in a little more, covering my body carefully. I felt him hesitate, as if to question his own decision. And then his lips softened and he kissed me fully, having learned so much in the last couple of weeks of how to make me breathless. My hands found new places to explore, one rooting deeply into his hair, and the other tracing down the length of his back.

Finally I could touch that which I had obsessed over every time he left me.

Feeling its strength, the muscles tensing as he held himself just far enough away from me to remain separated; I loved the feel of his back under my hand. He moaned into my mouth when his fingers moved to my neck, tracing down the length of it until his hand splayed out across my collarbone. He pulled away and looked down at his hand, breathing heavily.

"Your heart is beating so quickly!" he said in awe. My hand slipped free of his hair, moving down to his chest, so that I could feel his own beating heart.

"So is yours," I replied, matching his smile.

His head dipped slowly once more, this time moving to my jaw, kissing me softly along the jaw before nuzzling into my neck beside my ear. His breath tickled my ear as he breathed deep. His lips ghosted across my skin until they finally touched the beating in my throat. Soft hot lips lingered there on my pounding pulse, a soft hum escaping his lips before he pulled away to look down at me, a smile breaking out across his face.

"I like the way your heart pounds," he said softly.

I laughed and felt along his shoulders to distract me from all the feelings I had swirling in my head.

I liked his pounding heart too. Everywhere I could feel it.

He adjusted beside me, propping himself up on his elbow so that he could watch me more easily. His hand explored, touching along my cheek, down my neck, ending finally at my shoulder. Looking up and away from me, he smiled and nodded to the dark sky above.

"I think we have the better resting spot. The stars are coming out for us," he whispered.

I looked up, at the dark heavens above us and marveled at how many stars had already come out. I hadn't seen a truly remarkable skyline since my days at camp in the national forest, years ago. Here, in the quiet of the night, the stars burned bright even as the last sliver of sunset lighted the western sky.

"There's so many stars," I breathed.

"Wait until it gets darker. The field lights up with all the star light," he said and smiled at my excitement.

Nathan pulled me close, letting my head rest on his arm as we settled in to look up into the sky. It was comforting, lying beside him. He didn't push, didn't claw at me. His hand gently held mine across my stomach, brushing my knuckles in long slow caresses. We didn't speak, it was enough to simply lie there together and feel one another's warmth. As Nathan promised, the sky continued to brighten with hundreds of stars as the night crept in. I lost track of time, happy in my place beside him, the starlight brightening his face as he regarded me.

He wasn't watching the stars. He had seen the stars hundreds of times in his own lifetime. It was nothing new to him. But I was new, and he couldn't seem to keep his eyes off of me. There was a kind of adoration and love in Nathan's watchful gaze. I closed my eyes and sighed, feeling a great comfort wash over me. The heat of Nathan soothed me, lulled me until the night sounds seemed to turn muddy in my ears. All I could hear was his soft breath against my ear, like the distant tide at the beach on top of the cliffs.

Soothing.

I didn't realize I had drifted off until I felt Nathan's fingertips brush across my cheek. I stirred against him, finding myself tucked in close to him for warmth. Pulling away, I blushed at the idea if having all but wrapped my body around him while I slept. Sitting up I looked around and noticed it was much darker.

"How long did I sleep?" I asked worriedly, sure that Jonah and Fannie would worry.

Why hadn't Emma come to find me?

"Only a little while, Kate. I did not wish to wake you, but it is late," he replied and shifted towards the edge of the wagon before jumping off.

I moved to the edge, smiling as he held his hands out to me. I let him pull me off, enjoying the feel of his fingers around my waist again.

He held me for a moment, his head dipping down to kiss me tenderly along the lips before drawing away. His fingers lingered along my waist, and I could feel his thumbs skirt across my hipbones slowly, warming me further.

His hands felt right against me like that.

We walked hand in hand towards the house. As we passed the barn, I had to wonder about Emma. She would be in trouble as well. Nathan seemed to understand.

"Emma is waiting for you up by the porch. They only just left the barn," he whispered, grinning when I let out a surprised gasp.

Well, Emma has some explaining to do!

Sure enough, Emma and John were sitting in the swing by the back door, talking softly until we neared. As soon as we were on the porch John stood and made to leave. He leaned down and squeezed Emma's hand once more before turning to Nathan and me.

"A pleasant day, yes?" he asked, fighting back a grin.

"A pleasant day, to be sure," Nathan replied, holding my hand a little tighter to temper the laughter I felt bubbling up.

Glancing over at Emma, she was fighting hard to keep from giggling.

"There is a gathering this week at the old farm. We could all go together. Katherine has never been to a gathering," John continued, glancing my way.

I felt Nathan's body tense beside me before he shook his head.

"I do not think it would be something to experience. It is not the best time to explore that way. Thank you for the invitation," Nathan said coolly.

I didn't understand the sudden shift. Nathan and John seemed to be close. The idea of another outing seemed exciting. But I remained quiet as the two men exchanged silent words. Glancing at Emma again, I saw the irritation on her face.

"Let me know if you change your minds. I have a friend who can take us," John said and nodded towards Emma before stepping off into the night.

"Come, Katherine. We need to go inside. Nathan, thank you for your help today," Emma said, her voice much harsher than I had ever heard towards Nathan.

He nodded and stepped away from me, retreating down the steps slowly.

I was utterly confused by the polar shift in everyone.

"Pleasant night, Emma. Kate. I will see you in the morning. Thank you for a wonderful day," he murmured and retreated back into the night, refusing to look back.

I wheeled around towards Emma.

"What just happened? Everyone was so happy!"

She rolled her eyes at me and put her fingers to her lips, guiding me into the dark house. I was surprised no one was up to wait for us. We tiptoed into our room and stripped quickly, both of us giggling quietly over the sudden appearance of hay on the floor as we shook out our dresses to hang up. Abigail snorted in bed and turned on her side, still asleep.

Slipping into bed, Emma finally let out a frustrated breath when I asked again about what had happened on the porch.

"Nathan!" she hissed. "He is such a righteous and stubborn man!"

I raised my eyebrow at her and chuckled.

If she had seen him kissing me earlier, maybe she wouldn't think that.

She huffed and continued.

"The gathering John talked about is part of our Rumspringa. Nathan refuses to go because he is afraid. It does not make sense, not with you here now to show him!" she groused.

"I don't understand. It's a party?" I asked, confused.

"In a way, yes. It is a chance for us to experience some of your world. There is music and dancing, we can wear what we want. It is the only time we can do this. I do not understand why Nathan would not want to experience that with you," she continued.

I wasn't sure I wanted to see Nathan experience anything in my world.

Maybe dancing. But the rest was something we both could forget about.

"It's not a good time for me to be going out, Emma," I rationalized. "I need to prove myself to the Elders. I'm sure that's why Nathan doesn't want to go."

"He has never liked going," she continued. "John and Mark managed to get him to go once this spring. And that was the last time he went."

"I'm sure he had his reasons," I murmured, thinking of all he had gone through after his family had died. To say that he hadn't walked away from his lifestyle was a testament to his beliefs. Emma's reaction seemed extreme.

"I will not be allowed to go on my own," Emma pouted.

"You mean with John?"

She nodded.

"Mother and Father can not stop us from going, but they will be upset if I go with just John. It would make them happier if we went as a group," she explained, her eyes pleading.

Now I understood.

"Are you trying to get me to make Nathan go?" I asked, scowling at her.

She had the ability to at least look a little abashed.

"Maybe, yes. Please Kate, I have never been to one. After Hannah," she whispered and closed her mouth, fear of revealing Hannah's secret clear on her face.

"I know about Hannah, Emma. Maybe your parents are right to worry? It doesn't sound like it would be safe," I said softly.

"I know John would watch out for me. It would be easier with you there," she sighed sadly.

"Why me?"

"Because you understand it. You would be able to tell us what is to be avoided," she replied.

I closed my eyes and groaned, feeling torn over this.

"I will see what he says, Emma. I don't know though. Are you sure Jonah and Fannie won't be upset?" I asked.

She hugged me tight and giggled.

"No, they understand the right of passage. I just do not have friends to go with. Thank you, Katherine. He will listen to you," she said happily.

I slipped under the covers and got comfortable, my mind trying to figure out how to ask Nathan to go along with something he was not keen on. Maybe he was just afraid. Maybe he didn't want to know my world. Did he think I would be swayed to go back to it? Did he think I would be that tempted? Or was it something else?

I was distracted from my thoughts at Emma's sudden giggling.

"What?" I whispered.

"Can you not hear them?" she giggled.

I listened for a moment, my ears buzzing at trying to listen to the quiet.

And then I heard it and blushed.

"Oh.... Really?" I whispered and started to giggle alongside Emma.

It was quiet, and you would have to have excellent hearing to make out the sound and rhythm from the other room. We both quieted down when we thought it had stopped, only to wheeze and giggle some more when it started up again a few seconds later.

"I cannot wait until that is me," Emma sighed softly in the dark.

I touched her gently, feeling her hand wrap around mine tightly.

"Me too," I whispered back, feeling an immense sense of love wash over me.

I knew Emma loved John. Seeing them together during the day made me so happy. I couldn't wait for her to experience everything with John.

We listened in the dark, our minds left to drift, as our sister and her husband found one another in the room next door. It didn't feel like eavesdropping so much as finding joy in her joy. Hannah had what she needed. And we could tell he was gentle. It made me tear up, knowing that my sisters and I were lucky in the men we had found.

Emma would find that with her John, I hoped soon.

I smiled at the thought that I might experience that one day with Nathan as well.

I couldn't wait.

CHAPTER 19

I was running through the corn, laughing at the noise Nathan was making following along behind me. Ahead, the corn seemed to never end, but I knew he was getting closer and would catch me before I made it to the house. The rustling broke through behind me and I turned with a smile to reach for Nathan.

Only to see dark eyes and large hands barreling towards me.

I felt the scream in my throat but couldn't release it, to call out for help. Stumbling in the corn I tried to run, to get away from the nightmare that was closing in.

Reaching for me with brutal hands.

"Katherine! We must awake!"

My eyes slammed open, a gasp escaping my lips when I realized where I was.

A dream. Not real.

Sean was not here.

I let out a steadying breath and swallowed to wet my dry mouth. I looked over at Emma as she watched me from the foot of the bed, her eyes narrowed and her hands on her hips.

"Katherine, come. We need to get dressed. There is much to do today. Are you all right? You look flushed and you thrashed around in your sleep," she said, eyeing me a little more carefully.

I shook my head and scrambled out of bed, my legs aching as if I had truly been running as I had in my dreams.

"I'm fine. Just, too much excitement from yesterday," I murmured and tried to offer her a reassuring smile as I dressed for the day.

I was quiet throughout our chores, my mind wandering again and again to the dream. I had not dreamt of Sean in over a week, and then suddenly he was back in my head. I had to wonder if perhaps the idea of going to the gathering had inadvertently made me think of him again. Emma had remarked that English boys would be there. Was my mind trying to tell me something?

Maybe Sean would be there. That fear brought me white-faced into the kitchen, with Fannie turning and coming to me in a rush.

"Katherine? Are you all right? You are pale," she asked worriedly.

"I'm fine, really," I replied quietly and moved to place the milk on the counter.

"Are you sure? Perhaps you are hungry? Emma says you did not eat much yesterday," she continued, her hand moving up to touch my forehead.

"Probably," I replied numbly.

"You can help Abigail set the table then and sit until we are ready," she said and turned to fetch me some juice.

I heard Mark's heavy footsteps and couldn't help but look away, embarrassed when he walked in with Hannah beside him, a bright smile on his face. And Hannah seemed to be glowing. I felt my face heat up more at Hannah's raised eyebrow towards me. At least now I didn't look so pale.

She slipped into the routine of preparing the morning meal, a tender hug from Fannie and Emma before she slipped on the apron and set to work. Mark watched her as she worked for a moment, his eyes turning soft before he turned and sat down beside Jonah. He smiled broadly, catching my blush before he cleared his throat and turned to Jonah, who had watched the interchange between the newlywed couple and I. I couldn't tell if Jonah was amused by it or irritated. His beard always made his lips look like they were smiling with the upper lip bare.

"What are your plans for the day, Mark?" he said, focusing on him.

"I have one of Father's fields to clear. The wheat is ready. My brothers are coming in today to help. Did you need me, Jonah?" he asked, his jovial post wedding night smile slipping into all business.

There seemed to be nothing like honeymoons here.

"I might need your help tomorrow," he started, pausing when Nathan walked in through the back door. "I would like to help Nathan today with his fields and a few other things."

I watched as Nathan paused in putting up his hat, glancing at Jonah questioningly. His eyes were cautious, glancing around the room before he moved to stand beside the chair next to me.

"I am fine Jonah. I do not plan on harvesting for another week or two. I have just the seeding of the autumn crops remaining," he explained in his soft voice.

Jonah nodded and tapped his finger to his bare lip, as if in deep thought.

"I was thinking of perhaps introducing my mare to your stallion, Nathan. It seems she has one more cycle in her this season," Jonah replied casually. I watched Nathan blink for a moment, his face serious as he thought on what Jonah was suggesting.

"What of your stallion, Jonah? You have foaled two from them in years past," he suggested, shifting in his seat.

I listened in silence, not sure how to take in the conversation about horse mating between Nathan and Jonah. It was something so natural for them, and so uncommon for me. And they talked over planning for the day as if it were as easy as clearing a field. Just another duty to complete in the summer. Horse breeding. Easy.

How many of these had Nathan seen?

"This will be my first time helping with something like this," Nathan said aloud, answering my unspoken question.

Jonah nodded and smiled brightly.

"Well, if they are successful we will have something to barter come early next summer," he added and then turned to the meal as it was being laid out. Fannie was shaking her head and pretending to scowl at him as she settled into her seat across the table.

"Let us not talk of this over the meal, please. We have much to do today," she chided.

All conversation stopped and after prayers, we settled into a quiet breakfast. I glanced at Nathan many times, his face a mask of mystery as he chewed silently beside me. It seemed he was still worked up over the mention of the gathering the night before.

Emma openly stared at him for much of the meal, as if she were trying to read his mind while he purposefully ignored her. Hannah and Mark smiled at one another and ate silently as well, except for an occasional chuckle when Mark would wink at her. It was a different world entirely looking at how Hannah and Mark acted, with Fannie and Jonah sitting at the same table.

Was it normal for everyone to know what Hannah and Mark had done last night?

In her parents' house of all places?

From what it looked like, this was perfectly normal. Fannie smiled at them repeatedly, her gaze adoring every time she saw Hannah crack a smile. I supposed it was rewarding to see her daughter finally at peace and happy. Overnight it seemed, Hannah was a new person.

Reborn.

It gave me hope. And Nathan had his own house. Maybe if we ever got married, we wouldn't have to stay with the Bergers our first night. That thought brought the color back in my face for sure. Abigail glanced at me askance when she noticed and I tried to ease her curious mind with a tremulous smile and a wink. She glanced at Nathan and then back to me, a quiet giggle bubbling up from her mouth before she covered it with a large bite of her biscuit, winking back at me playfully.

I somehow knew Abigail understood a lot more than I did at her age.

We cleaned up as the men spoke for several minutes after the meal. Mark bade his farewells, sneaking a quick kiss from his new wife before he walked out the back door, a jovial spring in his step. Hannah smiled after him and winked at me when she caught me looking. I was saved from any comments when Jonah stood and made to leave. He stopped beside Fannie, brushing his fingertips across her cheek before smiling and glancing at me.

"We will be busy today. Will you send Emma and Katherine to us at midday meal? Perhaps they can help Nathan's garden for the afternoon," he asked quietly.

"Of course. Abigail can help me with the afternoon chores here. The laundry can be done in the morning," she said and patted his hand gently before stepping away.

I watched as Jonah left, Nathan lingering for only a second to look back at me before tugging on his hat and following after. His strange expression had me a little unnerved. It was not quite troubled, but more hesitant than worried. Again I had to wonder what he was thinking of to have him behave so strangely.

"Katherine, come. You and Abigail can help me with preserves this morning while Emma and Hannah tend to the wash," Fannie was saying.

I allowed myself one last glance of Nathan as he walked away with Jonah, and resumed the duties I had learned were an important part of Amish life. Today would be preserves and canning. I seemed to learn something new with every new chore. I learned that I had underappreciated the jams I had enjoyed on my toast, and that it took much longer than simply spreading them on bread to make them the delicious nectar in a jar. A few hours of simmering, a lot of sugar and an unfortunate mess all over me was how my morning progressed.

"The stain will disappear from your hands in a day or so, Katherine," Fannie chuckled when she noticed me scrubbing in the sink to no avail.

The berries we had cooked down for jams had left dark stains on my fingertips. I sighed and shook my head at the sight. It reminded me of the time I had gotten into my father's antique inkwells he had collected. The reminder of him only made me scowl harder. I had no idea how I was going to tell him what I needed to. I knew deep down he would be grateful to give up responsibility of me, but I also knew he would find some way to make it exceedingly difficult for me to cut ties. The hardest part would be saying goodbye to my sister.

"You are most quiet this morning Katherine," Fannie said, breaking me out of my train of thought.

I looked up from the dishtowel in my hand and met her sympathetic eyes. Shrugging, I began collecting the jars we had filled to place in the pantry. She stalled me halfway across the kitchen and took some of the jars from my hands.

"You are worried about the future?" she asked softly.

I frowned a little harder and nodded.

"I don't know how to end it with my family, or with Sean. Every time I think about it, I can see the outcomes, and they are all more disturbing the more I think on it," I whispered.

She helped me up the stepladder and handed me the jars while she spoke.

"It is a significant step. One, sadly I think cannot be done by letter or in your case, by telephone. I am afraid to say it, but it is something that will need face to face contact," she said.

I blanched at her words.

"I don't want to think about being face to face with Sean," I mumbled and shuddered.

She pulled me against her gently and kissed me on the temple.

"You will not be alone. We will make sure of that. But I am sad, you will need to travel for this. Jonah and I have already discussed it, just last night," she said and pulled away enough to look into my eyes. I could see the worry in them.

"You want me to go? There?" I choked out.

"It seems the safest. Jonah has already agreed to go with you if you wish it. And I am sure Nathan will want to go as well, although I am sure Jonah will have words with him over that," she remarked, smiling.

"Why would Jonah need to talk with Nathan?" I asked, afraid maybe they thought Nathan would never return.

Fannie let out a soft breath and tried to hide her smirk.

"It is not something we talk about, Katherine. That is a man's business. But perhaps Nathan needs a father to speak with him before he makes a trip with a girl he is courting, especially if he were to consider this his Rumspringa," she replied and laughed when I swallowed hard.

Poor Nathan.

Getting the birds and the bees talk. Suddenly thinking of the conversation this morning, I gasped, only to start laughing.

"Do you mean, right now?" I asked, fighting my laughter.

It was Fannie's turn to blush.

"I do not know!" she exclaimed and joined in with my laughter.

The sisters glanced our way as we returned to the kitchen. I couldn't look at Hannah without bursting into laughter at the thought of what kind of speech Mark must have received before their wedding night. Fannie pulled me close again and let out a happy sigh.

"Well now that you are laughing once more, let us set up a basket for you to take to the men for this afternoon," she said and we were once again busying ourselves with preparing a meal to bring over to Nathan and Jonah.

We ate quickly in the house, and when Emma and I made to leave, Hannah groused about not being able to bring a basket to Mark. Fannie scowled at her and pushed a bundle of damp clothes toward her to hang out to dry.

"You will see him tonight, Hannah. He has family there to feed him. He will not need you every moment of his life. You can tend to him tonight when he returns," she chided.

Emma and I left before we could hear Hannah's remarks.

"Emma? How long will Hannah and Mark stay here, together?" I asked as we started up the hill towards Nathan's house.

Emma laughed.

"Only one more night. Did they keep you up? Is that why you seem so distracted today?" she asked.

"No, no they didn't bother me last night," I murmured; looking away from her towards the field I hoped to see Nathan in. But it was vacant.

"Is it because I asked you about the gathering?" she asked, and when I turned I noticed her worried gaze.

I nodded.

"I'm sorry, Emma. I just don't want to pressure Nathan not knowing why he was so upset last night. I can't help worrying that Sean might be there, too. I had nightmares last night about him," I replied softly.

Emma grabbed my hand and squeezed it hard.

"I am sorry. I should not have asked, Katherine. I let my selfish wants interfere. I did not mean to cause you pain," she said and hugged me quickly.

"It's not your fault, Emma," I replied and let out a breath. "I just don't understand why it's so important to you."

She was quiet for a few minutes and when I turned to see if she had heard me, I noticed a sad far away look on her face.

"You know that world, I do not," she murmured. "I have not experienced much because of my sickness. I know John wants to commit to the Way, but he has also had a chance to see things. I do not wish to regret having not had that chance."

I remained quiet, thinking about her circumstances. I knew she wouldn't pressure me again to go, but it was hard to not try and explain to her that there were more important things in life than an English party. I shivered at the thought of the last party I had been to.

And run from.

I wished I could reassure Emma that she wasn't missing anything, but like any teenager, I knew she'd want to experience it herself, regardless of past histories of her sister or myself.

We walked the rest of the way in silence, nearing the house when we heard a ruckus off to our right by an open pasture. Edging our way towards the noise, I almost ran face first into Nathan as he turned the corner of the house quickly. He was flushed and sweating, and his eyes looked uncomfortable until he took a step back to keep from knocking me over. From over his shoulder, I could see Jonah coming towards us, shaking his head in amusement.

"Are you all right?" I asked, watching his eyes squint uncomfortably before wiping it clear with a tense smile.

"Of course," he replied and side stepped us to head off to the water pump to rinse off.

I glanced back at Jonah who nodded and smiled as he passed. Glancing back towards the pasture, I watched as the great black horse of Nathan's, Magnus, pranced around Jonah's mare, which nipped and kicked at Nathan's horse.

"It appears Patience is not impressed with Nathan's horse," Emma chuckled and pulled me away towards the house.

I couldn't get my head around human courting much less equine relationships, so I let the conversation die as we made our way into Nathan's kitchen to set out their lunch. Looking in the cupboards for plates, I was taken by surprise at how empty his cabinets were. Hardly any food was left in them. Whatever he ate, he was solely dependent on the Bergers. Having seen the state of his garden, I was sure it was simply too much for him. It made my heart hurt for him.

He really needed help.

"Thank you girls! This is a blessing for a hot afternoon!" Jonah exclaimed as he stepped into the kitchen.

Nathan followed behind, smiling at me as I stood by his refrigerator. It had been the first real smile I had seen on him all day, so it made me feel better about his strange behavior. Emma and I excused ourselves while they ate, Emma explaining to me that if we waited too long, it would be much too hot to work in the garden. As it was, when we stepped back out and started hauling water to the side garden, I felt the heat already beating down on us. It didn't take long to start sweating.

We worked for over an hour hauling water to the parched plants. When the soil was moist, we went through aisle by aisle, cutting back anything too far gone and salvaging any of the vegetables still worthy of eating.

It wasn't much.

By mid- afternoon, when the sun was at its worst, Nathan's garden resembled more of a garden than a withered jungle. Emma and I retreated back to the porch and sighed when we sat heavily in the large swing there. She looked out over the yard, shaking her head sadly as she noticed the dead bushes and dried grass.

"This was a beautiful place once," she whispered.

I looked at all the work that still needed to be done. Paint to be finished, new plants to be planted, windows and porch to be washed down. It was too much for one person.

But for two perhaps...

"It will be again," I replied simply, earning a brilliant smile from Emma.

We heard the door open near us, Nathan coming out with glasses of the tea we had brought. He handed them to us and leaned against the railing, looking off towards the garden. He was quiet for a moment, in deep thought as he sucked on his lip. It was difficult not to stare at his lips. The distraction of cold tea helped.

At least until Emma spoke.

"Nathan, I must apologize," she said into the silence. Nathan blinked and turned to watch her, waiting for her to continue. She let out a breath and let the words stream forth.

"I was excited to hear about the gathering last night when John mentioned it. I know you have reservations, after what happened the last time. But I was excited to think that maybe with Katherine there, she could explain to me why the English life is so fascinating to us. I wanted to be able to experience a bit of her world as she has ours."

"That is not her world, Emma," Nathan replied, a little harsh.

She looked down from his heated stare and nodded.

I watched quietly, not wanting to put my opinion in. I didn't want to get involved with her argument. I didn't really care to go, especially if there was a chance of Sean being there. Or having the Elders judge me for going. Finally he looked at me directly.

"Is this something you wish to do, Kate? It is part of who we are, but it is not an obligation to become one of us. You have experienced your ways. It will be nothing new for you by going," he asked softly.

When I didn't answer immediately, Emma turned and darted for the hill, not looking back when I called out to her.

"She cannot go alone. And John is a friend with some, but not so much with others that will be there. It is not wise for them to go alone. I will go with you if you ask it," he whispered.

"Of course I have reservations. But she also wants to go and experience it with her friends. I just don't understand your hesitation," I said quietly and watching him for a reaction.

He glanced behind him towards the house and shook his head, his lips pursed as if still annoyed.

"We can talk this evening when we sit after supper. It is not a simple answer," he murmured and stepped away just as Jonah opened the door.

"I will take my mare back to the barn. Will you escort the girls back to the house?" he asked.

"Emma has already returned," Nathan replied, clearing his throat as he shuffled his feet.

"Ah, well. Then perhaps we can all go together," Jonah replied and went off to fetch his horse.

Nathan let out a nervous laugh and waved me off when I looked at him questioningly.

"Jonah is taking care not to let me stray with you," he chuckled and motioned me inside.

"Are we doing something wrong?" I asked hurriedly, afraid that perhaps our night walks and quiet moments would be taken away.

"Do you enjoy your time with me?" he asked, a bit of heat in his eyes as he looked down at me.

I could only nod; the desire in his eyes was certainly anything but chaste.

"Then it is not wrong. But Jonah has a watchful eye and would see us behave when he can," he murmured and squeezed my hand as he held the door open for me to enter the house.

I made my way into the kitchen, putting all of the food and plates back in the basket to take back. When I turned around, he was watching me from the doorway, arms crossed casually in front of him as he took me in. I was about to say something when he took a step in and smiled.

"I do think about dancing with you," he whispered and extended one hand out, asking.

I laid the basket down and took his hand carefully, watching as his eyes dipped down to between our bodies. One hand in his, the other resting lightly on his shoulder, Nathan started to sway softly, watching his feet as he moved. I had no idea how to dance like this, and neither did he, but our bodies moved together, at a respectable distance. A small smile tugged up on the corner of his mouth and he was moving his free hand to my lower back when we heard Jonah's voice boom out from the front.

"Let us not dally! Fannie will have supper ready when we return!"

Nathan pulled away in an instant.

I grabbed the basket and hurried out, Jonah waiting patiently until Nathan followed along. We escorted Jonah and his mare back to the house in silence, a timid smile on Nathan's lips as he walked beside me. I thought about what he had said about our time together, and had to wonder if maybe going to the party might be a good thing. If we were to go, wouldn't that give us some time alone there? Maybe that was the reason Amish youth went. To be out of their parents watchful gaze to experience those things not permitted. Like being alone together.

I hoped Jonah wasn't worried about Nathan and I too much. Our evenings together were my favorite part of the day. Surely it wasn't wrong what we did. Nathan was the kindest and most gentle man I had ever met. He respected me and never pushed himself on me. That couldn't be bad.

We separated at the house, Nathan and Jonah heading off to the barn, I retreating into the house to help Fannie. When I entered, Emma and Fannie were talking, and I could tell Emma was frustrated by the almost whine in her voice. The more I interacted with this family, the more I saw that they were much like an average English family.

Even petulant Emma.

Amish teenagers and English teenagers were very similar.

Especially when they didn't get their way.

CHAPTER 20

"I know you cannot stop me, Mother, but I wanted you to know. I want to go. I will not stray. I will stay close with John," she was saying.

Fannie shook her head and turned from her.

"It is your choice. But you know your father and I do not approve. It is too soon. I do not like you going alone with John. I am sorry, but I will worry," Fannie argued.

"I do not have anyone else. Not since Rachel died," Emma murmured, and had I not known her, I would have thought she was playing a pity card.

Only I knew Emma had no friends. I knew she was alone in her life.

Except me, and John.

And Nathan.

I sighed and stepped into the kitchen, their eyes looking up to watch me as I moved towards the sink. Emma turned away and busied herself with the plates while Fannie regarded me thoughtfully for a moment.

"Has Emma not asked you to go, Katherine?" she finally asked.

I swallowed and glanced at Emma, who pretended to ignore me.

"Yes, she has," I answered and began washing the dishes from earlier.

"And you do not wish to go?"

"I don't know if I should or not," I mumbled.

Fannie nodded and returned to her work, the matter set aside when Hannah and Mark stepped in, Mark carrying the large basket of clothes for her. She was flushed and grinning and as she looked our way, her smile widened.

"I will set the clothes upstairs if you like, my wife," Mark announced.

"I will go with you and help you sort," she giggled and followed him upstairs.

"Supper will be ready soon!" Fannie called out and shook her head at them.

We didn't mention the gathering again. I finished with cleaning the afternoon dishes and helped lay out the supper on the table just as Jonah and Nathan entered. Sitting at the table, Nathan tried to continue his conversation quietly with Jonah while we finished serving the meal. Hannah and Mark came downstairs, filling the table just as Fannie brought out the last of the meal. Jonah and the men spent most of the meal talking about schedules for clearing the fields, Nathan growing a little uncomfortable when Mark and Jonah both pledged to help him clear his.

Emma remained aloof for most of supper, only perking up when there was a knock at the door at dessert. She leapt up and Jonah called out a welcome to John as he stepped in and took off his hat. The table full, Nathan had to slide in closer to me so that we could fit in John to the table. His hand brushed accidently across my knee.

He pulled it away quickly, murmuring his apologies with mischievious eyes. I somehow thought that perhaps it wasn't so accidental then. Once all the chores were done, we went on our way, John and Emma joining us on the porch. John was stepping off the porch when Nathan touched his shoulder, getting his attention.

"When is this gathering, John?" he asked quietly.

I could tell he was nervous, his lips were tight and he was tense beside me.

John raised his eyebrows in surprise and glanced at Emma.

"It is on Friday," he replied.

Nathan nodded and thought for a moment before letting out a heavy breath.

"If Kate wishes to go, I will go. I know how much this means to Emma. It would be best if we went together, so that she has her friends with her," he mumbled and chanced a glance at Emma.

She bounded up and hugged Nathan tight.

"Thank you!" she cried.

He pulled her away a bit and smiled dotingly.

"I know you would have wanted to go with my sister, and she would have asked me until I gave in. So I cannot deny you your friend on this journey," he replied.

She hugged him again before stepping away with John, taking a long slow walk that I knew well. I smiled at the thought of timing them when they disappeared behind the barn.

"What are you smiling at?" Nathan asked playfully.

I laughed and patted the seat beside me as I sat down in our swing.

"Nothing," I replied, and then more softly, "That was very nice of you to do that for Emma."

He sat down heavily and took my hand in his, rubbing his fingertips into my palm in a quick and nervous rhythm.

"She needs to see it is not our way. I would rather her see it with us than with strangers. I trust John, I just do not want them to go alone," he murmured and looked out after them as they walked.

"Will you tell me why you reacted like you did last night?"

He frowned and glanced my way before pulling me closer, so that he could speak quietly near my ear. His hand remained in mine, his fingers pausing as he spoke.

"If your world is like that, I am glad you have found a life here," he started and leaned in until his nose nuzzled into my hair. He took a slow breath, inhaling me before he continued.

"It was not what I expected. So much unabashed emotion, you lead young people like us into that situation and it is overwhelming. And that one night; too much happened that night to make me turn away from this life. So much hatred, so much pain, so much lust. I do not understand it," he murmured.

"You were there that night, weren't you? The night with Hannah?" I asked, pulling away to see his pained look. He hesitated before nodding.

"I have never seen Mark upset, before that night. He was not himself. A madness entered his body. He was almost too much for us to manage. I do not blame him for his rage. We forgave long ago. That rage is not something I ever want to experience, but I would if it had been you," he whispered and gripped my hand a little tighter.

"I'm sorry, Nathan," I whispered. "Does Emma know about what you saw?"

He straightened up and scowled towards the barn.

"I will not ask. That was her sister I saw. I would not discuss this if not to help you to understand that it is not something I would like to see again," he said and looked away.

I sat there and wondered how parents would allow their children to experience something like what Nathan had described. I was imagining pure unadulterated drinking and sex and partying, like the college parties Sean had tried to get me to go to. If it was similar I had to wonder why Emma would want to see it.

Is that what she thought I had lived through before I came? Did Nathan think less of me because he thought I was like that?

"I think I want to go now to be able to tell you my life was not like what you saw," I said quietly.

He tugged on his chin roughly and eyed me nervously.

"What if you decide to go back? What if you see that you miss your life?" he asked.

I laughed, surprising him. I shook my head and pulled in close to him.

"Nathan, there are only a few things I might miss there. I doubt you will find them at a barn party," I whispered and smiled up at him.

His brow creased and he reached out to take my hand in both of his and rubbed my wrist nervously.

"What will you miss?"

His voice sounded fragile, sobering me up suddenly.

He was afraid I would leave.

"I'm not leaving, Nathan. I have nothing to return to. Really. Electricity is nice, but I don't need it to be happy. This place makes me happy. You make me happy," I whispered.

A small smile crept up on his face and his forehead leaned in to touch my temple lightly.

"You make me happy as well, Kate," he whispered and breathed me in once more.

We sat together quietly for some time, his fingers tracing lightly along my wrist and tentatively along my arm, causing goose bumps where he touched. He seemed to be making progress with feeling comfortable around me. I wondered if Jonah had really spoken with him today about me.

"What did Jonah say today?" I asked softly, feeling Nathan tense slightly beside me before relaxing again and chuckling.

"He thought I needed a lesson in horse breeding," he said, shaking his head.

I looked up into his eyes, seeing the bit of embarrassed discomfort there.

"I would think you would understand that, working on the farm as you do," I said, fighting the smile as he blushed.

"It does not mean I enjoy speaking about it with Jonah," he explained and frowned suddenly.

"What?" I asked.

"Did your father or mother talk to you about such things?" he asked, suddenly shy.

"Um, we don't own horses where I live," I replied and bit at my lips when he blushed again.

"Of course," he said hurriedly, looking out to the garden.

I sighed and leaned into him, drawing his eyes back to me.

"Dad tried to give me the sex talk when I started dating Sean. He bungled it up, though. They teach us that in school in eighth grade. It was more embarrassing for him than for me," I explained.

"Your father assumed you would be intimate with him?" he asked.

I swallowed and closed my eyes for a moment, trying to will away all the emotions associated with the idea of intimacy with Sean.

"I am sure my dad assumed a lot of things," I whispered and looked back out into the night.

Nathan nodded and remained silent. Speaking about Sean made me worry once more about what I had to do and having to face him again.

"Do you think Sean will be at the gathering? I know he hasn't given up yet," I whispered.

I felt Nathan's hand pause on my wrist.

"If he is, we will deal with it," he replied softly.

"I don't want anyone to get hurt," I said worriedly.

"No one will raise a fist to him, but he will be dealt with," Nathan said, his eyes intense.

I didn't want ask him to explain, his feelings were clear in his determined eyes. It was a little alarming, seeing such an intense emotion raging in his eyes. It only lasted an instant and then he was relaxed again and stroking my wrist once more.

"I will not let anyone hurt you, Kate," he murmured and held me closer.

I closed my eyes to the security I felt with Nathan, here in this peaceful community. Fannie was right, I needed to confront my past and start my new life. I liked seeing Nathan happy, and if that meant going back to tell my father and Sean I was leaving for good, then I would. My sister was another story. Stacy would understand I was sure, but she'd be upset to lose me forever and she was the one person I would miss most.

He pulled me out of my contemplative thoughts when his fingertips drifted up my arm slowly. Glancing up at him, his eyes were transfixed where his fingers traced. I held my breath when he gently pulled my arm closer, edging his hand further up my arm into the crook of my elbow. It was easy to touch me there, the short sleeves offering my entire arm for his exploration.

"Your skin is so soft here," he whispered as his finger traced lightly against me.

I watched him, his eyes following along in sweet innocent wonder as he marveled at how the skin goose fleshed at the lightest brush of the rough tip of his finger. A white-hot torrent rushed through me when he skirted just under the sleeve of my dress. I couldn't help the soft shiver that ran down my body, something I was finding I liked feeling when Nathan touched me.

But his touch paused, and when I glanced up into his eyes they were dark, his brow slightly puckered with tortured contemplation.

"I know what it is I do," he murmured. It wasn't an arrogant statement, just an innocent observation.

Dear God, did he really know?

Because if he did, surely he knew this was by all accounts sinful and against the rules. I must have made a noise, for he looked up at me with such innocent eyes I felt lost for a moment.

"Is it wrong?" I asked quietly, stilling his hand as it moved to draw away.

That molten rush ran through me once more at the tiny quirk of his lips.

"Does it feel good?" he offered when his finger slipped once more beneath the fabric.

I could only nod. Every sense was stupefied with that tingling feeling inside of me. His grin widened and his eyes creased up, a hint of mischief in them as he let out a measured sigh.

"Then it must be wrong," he murmured, and let his fingertip linger there under the fabric for a moment before slipping back out to trace down to the inside of my elbow once more.

Hours after he had left, I could still feel the heat of him along the inside of my arm. Just the thought of him touching me offered me that flush I wished for whenever I was with him. If he could do that with just a simple touch, I wondered what it would be like elsewhere.

Most definitely sinful.

CHAPTER 21

I was not sure which was worse. A sulking Emma or an over-excited Emma. Ever since Nathan consented to going to the gathering, every day was full of quiet questions about my world. The world I wanted to forget about. She asked everything from the very basic questions to ones I felt uncomfortable answering, mainly because it made clear just how little I really knew.

I had no idea about current fashion. I had no idea what girls talked about at parties. I had no idea what boyfriends and girlfriends really did either. I felt that maybe I was just as unprepared for this party as the Amish youth were.

Maybe more.

Friday came, and with it came a feeling of trepidation.

The more I spoke with Emma, the more I worried that this party would be a temptation for Nathan and I to go a little further with our relationship. It both thrilled me and terrified me. Perhaps that was some of his reservations also. Each night as we sat together, his hand would trace a little further. He would become a little bolder with his comfort, until last night I felt his touch along my neck, feather light over and around my ear and then down the length of my neck to the edge of my dress.

I would listen to his breathing pick up when he felt my skin heat from his touch, and I would know when he was about to draw away, the temptation too much for him as we sat there on the swing. We let Emma and John spend their time near the barn, never walking far from the house and never having a moment alone.

Nathan continued to respect me in the presence of the Bergers.

Without the threat of Jonah or Fannie there to forbid us any alone time, how far would Nathan take our relationship?

How far would I?

And how would it appear to the Elders that we went together?

Fannie had been quiet about her feelings when she learned we were going. Emma explained it was not up to the parents to allow or deny their children their experiences, only to hope for the best. The idea of Fannie and Jonah not putting up a fight just made me more nervous. So as I sat there watching Emma brush her hair for the tenth time, I fidgeted and thought instead about what might happen at this gathering.

A tap at the window long after Fannie and Jonah had gone to bed had Emma jumping up to check the window.

"It is John!" she exclaimed, covering her mouth at her excitement.

"I want to go too," Abigail pouted from her bed, but her yawn belied her eagerness to go.

"Go to sleep!" Emma chided and grabbed her head covering.

I patted down my hair and pulled my cover back on, my nerves peaking as the moment was at hand. Emma grabbed my hand and pulled me down the stairs, stopping short when we saw Fannie by the door. She was in her shift, her hair down. And a nervous look in her eyes as she took us into her arms and hugged us.

"Be safe tonight," she whispered, and her voice cracked from the strain. We squeezed her tight, offering her a little comfort before stepping away into the night.

As soon as the night air hit us, I paused a moment and looked back at Fannie as she stood in the doorway. She smiled and raised her hand in a singular wave, and then slowly closed the door, sending us on our way. When I turned back, I saw John and Nathan standing by the road. I smiled when I noticed Nathan was still in his Amish clothes, as was John. They understood we would be nervous, and the idea of seeing Nathan in a pair of blue jeans and a T-shirt would weaken me. I took Nathan's hand when we were close enough and smiled when he leaned down to kiss me on the cheek.

"Are you ready for this?" he asked when we started down the road.

I nodded and gripped his hand a little tighter.

"Steve is waiting for us down the road. He will drive us to the gathering," John was saying.

As we crested the hill I saw a car, an old Buick that looked like it had seen the last of its days. And leaning against it was a tall formidable man. He watched us as we neared, his dark eyes following us as he sipped on a soda. When John approached, the man straightened and nodded to Nathan and me.

"I thought it was just you and your girl. It's gonna be tight," he said in a deep southern drawl, and motioned us towards the car. Looking in, I noticed we were not his only ride. In the front seat sat a pretty girl in pigtails and overly done makeup, and in the back seat there was already another couple, lip locked and intertwined in each other.

"Saddle up, kids. Free lap dances tonight it seems!" Steve exclaimed and watched as John and then Emma climbed in, John wrapping his hands around Emma's waist as she settled into his lap.

I could hear Nathan swallow as he contemplated getting in.

"Can't wait all night, Fisher. Now or never," Steve said and slipped into the driver's seat, starting the engine.

"It'll be okay," I whispered and squeezed his hand encouragingly. He shook his head and slipped into the car, his hands outstretched for me to get in. I had told him it would be okay. But I knew this was just the first hurdle we would face tonight. I swallowed down my nerves and crawled into the car, feeling his hands grasp at my hips, keeping me firmly in place on his lap while I tried to adjust to get more comfortable. The car lurched into motion, propelling me back into him, and forcing one of his arms to wrap around me protectively.

Settled in against him, I could feel him let out a heavy breath into my shoulder and felt his hand on my hip try to adjust me forward. At first I thought I might be crushing him, until I adjusted a little against him. And he let out another heavy breath. And he tensed beneath me.

Oh.

I wrapped my hand around his at my waist and squeezed it, hoping I could relay to him silently that everything would be all right. But when he squeezed me in return, pulling me back a little against him and letting out another breath, I knew we were in for an interesting night. He made another adjustment under me, another heavy breath, and a flexing of his hand along my stomach, spreading his fingertips across my quivering belly.

It was my turn to swallow and let out a long breath. Because feeling him under me was something I wanted to feel more of, and I knew that would only upset him more than he already was at the moment. It was as if some higher power truly wanted to tempt us, knowing we would ultimately fail.

I felt Nathan clutch me to him and still his movement beneath me. Even then, the car's journey seemed to keep me moving against him, no matter how tightly he held me against him. We had been riding for some time when we finally hit a dirt road; one that was rough and caused us to move against one another in ways I knew made him uncomfortable. Just when he seemed to have himself in control, the bumps and jogging of the car had me rubbing against him again. I could feel him harden further against me, and I bit my lip to keep from groaning.

Would he be disgusted with me if he knew feeling him beneath me worked me up as much as from a simple kiss?

I knew it was wrong.

His body simply reacted; he couldn't help the instinctual biology. But it was making my body heat up in the most incredible ways. He was so close to me, hard and moving just far enough away to make me want to cry out in frustration. Feeling his hand tighten his hold and his breath warm my neck as he pulled me close on the rough road made me want to do so many things to him. I felt depraved while secretly I enjoyed it.

Gone was the need to prove how I could be respectful and sweet. I wanted more from him and I wanted to give him more of myself. It was not something I was used to. Every time I had been alone with Sean, every time he begged me to touch him, I never felt anything more than revulsion. Nathan sparked something else in me entirely, a deep-seated desire that flared to life at every touch. The need to be with him was slowing consuming me.

Every day I fell a little harder for Nathan Fisher.

Everyday I needed a little more of him.

So as we pulled down the road leading to the barn that was obviously the gathering place with its lights and music playing, I felt my heart leap into my throat. It was truly in the middle of nowhere, the only light for miles it seemed were the barn itself and the cars near it as they pulled in. We were out of sight from any one who might stop us from doing anything against the rules.

We were on our own.

That idea terrified me.

Not because I was afraid of Nathan.

He was not Sean.

I closed my eyes and leaned into Nathan, gripping his hand tightly to feel his strength and his tenderness against me. Nathan was a different creature entirely. He had never forced himself on me. Had never pushed.

I had faith in him.

Perhaps Nathan had healed me in some ways. At the very least I trusted him.

I wasn't so sure about myself.

We pulled into a space and stopped a good distance from the barn; there were so many cars and trucks littering the yard, as well as a number of buggies on the outskirts. It was strange, there was not a house anywhere near the barn. And the barn looked old, falling apart in some areas where the light burst through from inside. It had long been abandoned.

Steve glanced back and shot us a quick grin.

"Be back here at one, or you walk home," he drawled and swung his keys in his fingers as he laughed.

Steve got out of the car, as well as his girl in the front and moved immediately towards the barn. The couple beside us slipped out on their side without a word or a glance back, leaving Emma, John, Nathan and me in the car. Emma slid off John hurriedly and grabbed at his hand, tugging him out from the empty side of the car.

"Come! Katherine! Let us go!" Emma exclaimed and clung to John in a tight embrace as she waited for us to emerge.

I opened the door and shifted my weight on top of Nathan so that I could turn and look at him. His eyes were clamped shut, his lips tight as he breathed through flared nostrils. I leaned in and brushed my lips to his cheek, forcing his eyes to open, the pain and embarrassment clear.

"I am so sorry," he croaked and moved to push me away from him, away from what I knew he was embarrassed over.

I shook my head and leaned in once more towards his lips, one hand drifted up to the side of his head, holding him in place.

"Please don't say you're sorry. It's all right. It's natural, Nathan," I whispered against his lips.

He swallowed and let out a stuttered breath, kissing me quickly.

"I think I need a moment," he whispered and forced an uncomfortable smile when I patted him on the shoulder.

It probably wouldn't do him any good if I had told him I liked it and wanted more, to be closer. I slid out of the car and looked around briefly, surprised by the number of cars parked around the barn. The music carried loudly out from the inside of the barn, something much like hard rock and roll. It was hard to tell, as it was distorted by the building and the screams and laughter mixed in.

I felt Nathan's hand slip around my waist, and I glanced up at him as he held me close, his look a little tense as he took in our surroundings as well. He shook his head and grimaced before looking down at me.

"Promise me you will stay beside me all night? I do not want to think," he stammered, trailing off when I touched his face with my hand to ease him.

"I'm not leaving your sight tonight," I assured him.

"As with you, Emma. You stay with me all night," John was saying, suddenly serious.

She pouted and nodded.

"You are so worried. We will be fine tonight," she chided and pulled John a little towards the barn, motioning for us to follow.

"Are you sure you're okay with this?" I asked as we started to move.

Nathan looked around worriedly but nodded. His nerves set me on edge, enough that I glanced around, looking for whatever trouble he was surveying. I didn't see anything out of the ordinary. We passed a few cars that had occupants in them, the windows cloudy from whatever was going on inside, leaving me to wonder if the occupants were Amish or English. Nathan looked a little longer at the rocking cars until he realized what was going on, and then he turned quickly and held me a little tighter.

I smiled to myself at how innocent Nathan really seemed. I was innocent by my world's standards; I knew what was going on in the cars. But to see Nathan's reaction, I had to wonder if his buggy was big enough for any sort of make out session. No, it would probably spook the horses.

"What are you chuckling over?" he whispered, his lips beside my ear.

I opened my mouth to try and come up with something to say when suddenly I felt Nathan's grip tighten on me and he slowed down. I turned to look in the direction he was staring at. I watched as a tall man made his way towards us. He had nearly black close-cropped hair and his dark eyes were slightly sunken in like he didn't eat enough. His clothes were worn, the old concert t-shirt he wore was nearly threadbare and he had a hole working its way through one knee of his faded jeans. His overall appearance made him look like he was an Outsider, but his words made me question that.

"Fisher, my friend!" he said in a throaty voice, like he smoked too many cigarettes. Nathan slowed to a stop and clutched at me a little harder, staring at the man hard.

"Benjamin," Nathan replied and nodded curtly.

The man slowed to a stop a few feet from us, taking in first Nathan and then his eyes moved over me appreciatively.

"It's Ben now. You know, new life and all. Who is this, Nathan? Are you finally taking your Rumspringa? Come to see the better life?" he said grinning as he watched us.

"How are you Benjamin? Your mother misses you," Nathan said quietly, holding me fast.

The man's smile faltered at mention of his mother and he looked instead to me.

"I have not seen you, has Nathan trekked to another community to find his wife? I know he was never really interested in the girls at home," he quipped.

"What have you been up to, Benjamin?" Nathan sidetracked once more.

"You know, a little of this. A little of that. Working in the mill. Partying it up. Has Father finally roped you into his fold?" he asked, still eyeing me.

I was starting to feel uncomfortable under his gaze. Nathan knew him, but felt nervous around him, if his tight grip on me was any clue. His fingers were beginning to make my hip ache from the pressure, something entirely new, at least from Nathan.

"It is good to see you again, Benjamin. Your family misses you. I can send them your regards if you like?" Nathan continued coolly.

Benjamin frowned and took a step back, shaking his head. He pulled out a joint and rolled it nervously between his fingers, taking another step back.

"They don't miss me. Naomi is here and didn't even say hello. I get it. Remember, I lived the same as you? Whatever, have a good time.

Nice to meet you," he said looking back at me briefly before turning and walking away, lighting up as he went.

Nathan let out a soft breath and pulled me along, away from Benjamin and towards where Emma and John had gone, into the barn.

"Who was that, Nathan?" I asked and glanced back to see Benjamin join a couple of other men in the shadow of the barn. One man was Steve; the other was a tall, thin blond man. All three looked back our way briefly before turning to talk amongst themselves and pass around the joint.

Nathan remained quiet as we walked.

"Nathan? Who was that?" I asked again.

"Benjamin Yoder. The Bishop's son," he replied simply and moved us along.

"So, he left the community?" I asked, wondering how he knew Nathan.

"Some of us find your world more enticing and never return. Benjamin preferred this life rather than following in his father's footsteps," Nathan replied forcefully and drew to a sudden stop.

He shook his head and looked down at the ground.

"I am sorry. I did not mean to infer your world was bad. It is just that Benjamin was my friend. It is difficult to see him as he is now," he whispered and looked up at me with sad eyes.

"What happened?" I asked, afraid to ask. I looked back towards where Benjamin had been, but the space where they had stood was now empty. Nathan took my hand and held it tight, pulling us back towards the barn once more.

"Benjamin went on his Rumspringa early this year, right after my family," he started, pausing at the mention of his family. He cleared his throat and continued.

"He was considered for taking over for his father when he retired. I was also, as soon as we both were to be baptized, it would be the natural plan for us to be voted in as ministers, and from there, one of us would be chosen as Bishop. When my family died, I stepped away, withdrew. I did not want to talk with anyone. Benjamin tried. He was like my brother. I did not want the reminder of family then. He tried everything. Benjamin even tried to get me to come with him on Rumspringa right after I buried my mother, but I could not. How could I?" he asked, his voice a little rough.

"So Benjamin went without you," I guessed.

He nodded.

"I should have gone with him. Mark told me that he had become friends with some Englishers, the ones who supply these parties. He started drinking in excess, and then soon smoking. His friends worked at the mill with he and Mark, so Mark saw how Benjamin began to falter. So did his father," Nathan continued.

"I'm sure the Bishop was not happy with his son living the wild English life," I whispered.

"It was his Rumspringa. That was the excuse at least. But he was overzealous in the lifestyle, openly defying his own life. The final straw for the Bishop was when he found out he had gotten an English girl pregnant. Benjamin was given a choice. Her or the community," Nathan replied.

"He picked the girl," I said, understanding even more why the Bishop hated me. He expected me to pull Nathan away as well.

Nathan let out a harsh laugh and shook his head.

"It was never really about the girl. As far as I know, she ended the pregnancy. Benjamin was in it for the drugs. That one time I came here, that was all he talked about. It was all he wanted me to try. It was tempting, given how I was feeling," he said, his voice trailing off towards the end.

"Is that who Naomi is? His ex-girlfriend?" I asked.

He chuckled and shook his head, looking around.

"No, Naomi is his youngest sister," he said and then frowned. "The Bishop had hoped I would marry her."

"Oh," I murmured and looked down, realizing just how complicated Nathan's life was.

"I was not interested in Naomi," he said and brushed my cheek with a fingertip, tilting my head up so that he could smile down at me.

"No?" I asked, fighting my doubts.

"Like Benjamin said," he whispered and brushed his lips to mine. "I was never interested in the girls of my community."

I smiled into his lips and let him guide me towards the barn ahead of us, his arm wrapped possessively around me. As I looked around, I could now see more of the temptations that were there for the naive Amish as they entered. Beer kegs lined up one side of the barn, couples emerging from the dilapidated stalls, which offered little privacy. A teenage boy near the stalls was handing out condoms to other boys discreetly as they stepped up, their girlfriends sucking down drinks and dancing to the music a few feet away.

It wasn't only Amish couples; there was a healthy mix of English and Amish walking around. A lot of English men had Amish girlfriends. A couple emerged from one of the stalls, the girl a little disheveled, the boy grinning and holding her close as they made their way back into the party. As soon as they had left the stall, another couple stepped in, disappearing behind the door.

It instantly made me remember the nightmare about Sean.

Nathan would never, but there were a lot of boys around looking to find someone willing. All it took was one misstep. I understood better why Nathan wanted me to stay close. All too clearly I could imagine that night with Hannah and I knew she was stronger than me. There was nothing here to protect me.

Except Nathan.

As we stepped inside further, I could smell the pungent smell of cigarettes, as well as the more exotic fragrance of pot mixed in. I turned my head away when I saw the heavier drugs in the darkest corner. It seemed every corner of the barn had some vice that wasn't on the Amish list of rules to live by. This was every temptation they could throw at themselves, with no one to tell them no.

Faith could very well falter amidst so much temptation.

A band was set up to one side, playing so loudly it was difficult to hear inside the barn. I saw Emma and John near the dance floor, Emma's eyes taking in the entire spectacle. She looked a little overwhelmed. She held onto John a little closer and spoke to him near his ear, shaking her head. I tapped Nathan on the arm and motioned towards them, wanting to stay close to Emma given all the diversions around us.

I didn't want Emma to end up like Benjamin, or worse Hannah.

"It is so loud!" she yelled to me when we stepped up to her. I nodded and motioned towards the door leading out the back of the barn. She shook her head and pointed towards the dance floor.

"I want to dance first!" she said. I glanced at Nathan, who was looking around the room as if danger lurked in every corner.

It did, and it seemed Nathan knew that.

Sex, drugs and Rock and Roll.

This was my world to them.

"Please, can we dance?" Emma asked again, tugging on my sleeve.

I nodded, grasping Nathan's hand and moving him to where other couples were dancing. He paused at first, wrinkling his forehead until I smiled and pulled him a little harder and leaned into him.

"Come on, let's dance," I said into his ear.

He offered me a timid smile and moved with us onto the dance floor. The music was too fast for my liking, not that I liked to dance at all. I had two left feet when it came to dancing, but Nathan was just as timid as we stood facing one another. Glancing over at Emma, she was giggling and laughing as John held her close and pulled her around the small space, twirling her around with a smile and gentlemanly grace.

He was used to these parties I supposed, if I understood Nathan right when he had said John had gone to many of them in the past, after Emma had refused him. It made me wonder if John felt a pull towards this life.

I hoped not.

Nathan glanced over at John and mimicked his hands on me, wrapping one arm around my waist, the other taking my hand and holding it to his chest. He pulled me close and swayed softly, ignoring the beat of the music until the band switched songs, slowing it down for the couples to dance closer. Nathan leaned in; his lips close to my ear. I could feel his breath against me as we danced, a gentle exhale as he held me.

"Your world is so different than ours. It is difficult for me to believe you lived like this," he breathed into my ear.

I pulled away to look up into his eyes. They seemed so sad.

"This isn't my world, Nathan. This is the extreme of my world."

He looked around at what he could see.

"You do not have parties like this?" he asked, nodding towards the teens that were drinking from the beer kegs.

"We do, but it isn't our every day lives. It wasn't something I was interested in," I explained carefully, not wanting to dredge up those last few times at parties with Sean.

They were a lot like this, and I had been uncomfortable there. Strangely, I felt much safer at this party with Nathan holding me. Sean had been the danger then.

"Have you tasted alcohol?" he asked softly, pulling me back to the present.

"Yes, once," I said and tried to shove the memories aside.

"Have you?" I asked in return.

He frowned and didn't answer me, turning me towards the corner where the smokers hung out.

"Have you smoked before, Kate?" he asked.

"No, never. You?" I asked, worried that maybe he had done far more than I had that one time he had come.

Maybe Nathan was worldlier than me.

"No," he murmured and pulled me close again. His face was troubled, his entire body tense. "I just wonder what your life was like before. This is what I know of your world."

"I haven't done drugs, haven't stolen, and haven't murdered anyone. I kept to myself mostly, Nathan. I studied hard, and I tried my best to be a good person. This was something that Sean enjoyed, not me," I continued, watching as Nathan's face grew more serious as he listened to me.

I shook my head and dropped the subject, resting my head on his shoulder to avoid looking up into his troubled eyes. He held me close as we swayed. His heated body against mine made me sweat, the inside of the barn too hot to stay for long. Emma tapped us on the shoulder after a few songs and motioned for the far doors outside, where we could see other people gathered. Nathan nodded and pulled me out into the cool night air.

Outside, couples relaxed in small patches, talking softly amongst themselves. A few small groups sat together by a small fire, laughing and smiling. This was much more relaxed than inside, but you could still see the beer bottles and cigarettes being passed around. We settled in to a blanketed spot that had just been vacated by a few teens, the couples moving towards the darkened recesses of the yard and out into the corn field.

"It is too hot in there to stay for long, and so loud," Emma complained as she snuggled into John when they sat down beside us.

"Do you want something to drink?" John asked softly.

She nodded and he stood back up, looking down at us in question.

"Water?" I asked, and Nathan nodded.

"I will see what they have," he said and slipped back inside.

"I doubt they will have anything without alcohol," Nathan murmured and pulled me close. He had leaned up against an old post, allowing me to lean against his chest as he relaxed.

Emma tugged on the grass, her face downturned as she contemplated what she had seen so far. I could tell the party did not impress her. I thought again about Benjamin, and had to wonder how he could choose this style of life over what he had at home. I could only think the drugs must have gotten to him, and maybe his obstinate father. Had his father pushed him away, by his insistence in joining the community? Perhaps the drugs had been a great escape from his father. Associating with an English girl, getting her pregnant must have been the last straw.

The Bishop would surely see me as a threat if that were the case.

I didn't see how I would ever be able to win him over.

"This was not what I expected," Emma said softly, tugging a large clump of grass out of the lawn.

I waited for her to continue, knowing she had much more to say. She glanced my way and shook her head.

"I do not believe this is how you lived before you came to us, Katherine."

"No, not at all. Our parties are much like this, but this isn't a good representation of how I lived, Emma. Is that what you hoped for?" I asked, watching as she frowned and resumed attacking the grass.

"I just thought that maybe it would be more fun, having an expert with us. But you are not having much fun either, are you? I like the dancing, but the music is so loud. It's nothing like the music that Nathan listened to," she muttered.

I craned my neck to look up at Nathan to catch him glaring at Emma.

"You listen to music?" I asked, curious as to why he would listen to music.

It was not allowed. He scoffed and shook his head as if to deny it.

"He has a radio in the barn. He used to sneak and listen to it when he had to muck out the stalls," Emma said, smiling.

"I do not listen to it anymore, Emma. It is not our way," he replied stubbornly.

"I liked that music more. You could move to it better. What did you call it Nathan? Oldies? I liked those better," she murmured and tossed another clump of soil off into the dark.

I continued to look up at Nathan, hoping he would explain, but he shook his head and looked off into the field, his lips tightly pursed. It seemed Nathan still had a lot of mysteries left untold, and with the knowledge that he had listened to a radio made me wonder what other rules he had broken.

Or what rules he was willing to break.

I let out a soft breath and looked away from his strong jaw, wishing for more modest thoughts.

John returned with bottles of water and sat down again by Emma.

"What did I miss?" he said taking in Nathan's sour face and Emma's bare patch of grass before her.

"We were discussing how this isn't like my old life," I said and took a long drink of my water.

"Well of course it is not," John said simply.

"What do you mean, of course it is not?" Emma said, narrowing her eyes at him.

He smiled and wrapped his arm around her.

"Katherine is too soft spoken to be someone from this part of her world. This is what you would expect from a wild party; only she has better sense to stay out of it. Am I correct, Katherine?" he asked, his eyes penetrating mine.

"You are correct," I said softly, smiling at his perceptive eye. He returned my smile and tipped his drink to me in a silent toast.

"So you asked me to come so that I could learn that?" Emma asked in a small voice.

"I wanted you to see this was not the life for you," he whispered softly and leaned in to kiss her.

She laughed and smacked him playfully on the shoulder, surprising him.

"I knew that, John! I thought perhaps maybe we could just have fun here, on our own, without my father watching. I knew I would not find this life better than ours. Why would Katherine leave something better than what we have?" she asked, looking over at me for confirmation.

I smiled and nodded, happy to see that she understood.

"I do like dancing though," she quipped and pulled John up again, giggling.

"Are you coming?" John asked us.

"I think we'll pass," I replied, grasping onto Nathan's hand. "Maybe we'll go for a walk."

John raised his eyebrow and pulled Emma back towards the barn, holding her close.

"Stay close, and do not get lost in the corn," he said as he left, Emma laughing when she looked back to find Nathan blushing.

I stood and offered him my hand.

"Want to take a walk?"

He stood and pulled me close, dipping his head down into my hair.

"I would go anywhere you wish, Kate," he murmured.

My heart stuttered at his words, wondering if in fact he would go anywhere with me. Would he really follow me if his world did not work out for me? I pushed that thought aside. There was nowhere I wanted to be more than with Nathan.

I would go anywhere he would go.

CHAPTER 22

Nathan grabbed the blanket and took my hand, guiding me past couples on blankets trying to ignore the various degrees of undress as we passed. The field drew near, and he walked beside it for a few moments before he spoke. His voice was soft, and trembled a little from his nerves.

"I do not want you to think I am presumptuous, Kate. I came tonight because I knew Emma would be upset if you did not come. But my reaction to you tonight on the drive might have you assume I have other intentions."

"You mean you don't?" I asked, intending on teasing him.

His brow drew together and he slowed our pace until he pulled us to a stop, taking both of my hands in his.

"I do not have expectations for tonight, Kate. Only that you have a pleasant time, as well as we can here," he whispered.

"I understand," I replied and looked down at the ground.

"Did you have expectations?"

I let out a soft laugh; embarrassed that maybe I had been expecting something more. I felt his fingertips brush my cheek, tracing down until he could tilt my chin up to look up into his searching eyes. I could see he was nervous, afraid to proceed. He seemed to be asking what I wanted with his eyes.

I wanted too much.

"I was hoping for a kiss," I whispered.

His eyes crinkled as he smiled and leaned in to kiss me, softly at first. I moved my arms around him, pulling him to me as the kiss deepened. He groaned into me when he felt my body press against him, his body hard everywhere I touched. I felt his hand move until he held my head, not wanting to break off the kiss, our tongues exploring one another slowly. When we did break away, he was panting and holding me tightly against him. This time he hadn't pulled his body away when it reacted.

"I do not wish to go back just yet," he whispered breathlessly, his hand slipping down my back until it pressed against the small of my back.

Maybe he did want more.

I pulled him into motion, closer to the corn and away from the barn. He sucked in a breath and glanced back towards the barn.

"John did not want us to go far," he said, a little nervous.

"We won't go far," I said smiling. "Just somewhere a little quieter, for a little bit, okay?"

He swallowed and nodded, following me closely into the first row. I pushed ahead, the half moon guiding us farther from the noise of the party until Nathan reached for me and pulled me close, his lips moving to my ear, nipping it lightly.

"I do not wish to go too far," he groaned into my neck.

I wasn't sure he meant into the corn or with me. I stroked the back of his head, threading my fingers through the hair there. He hadn't worn his hat, allowing me to feel his hair easily. It had grown since I had first met him, becoming a little unruly. He groaned at my touch and his hands clutched at me, one hand moving down towards my back side, while the other moved up to thread his own fingers through my hair at the base of my neck.

281

He let out a soft moan when he felt me pull away, stealing my hands away long enough to toss the blanket to the ground and pull the cover off my head. He watched with dark eyes as I slowly pulled my hair free, letting it tumble down into his hand. He tugged me to him and kissed me again, all hesitation gone from his mouth as he devoured me, winding his hand into my hair. His long fingers tangled easily, but I couldn't care at the moment.

He lowered me onto the blanket, the heat of Nathan beside me comforting as we continued to kiss. I tugged at him, wanting more. His hand at my hip drew me closer; I wrapped my leg over at his gentle guidance and there we were, closer than we had ever been before. I moaned into his mouth and gripped him harder when I felt him adjust against me, and still he wasn't close enough.

With Nathan, I always wanted more. I had never felt that with anyone before. He just felt right with me. He pressed his body to me tighter, our bodies perfect for one another. Feeling every part of him respond to me made me moan into his mouth. My hands drifted, more sense memory of my past than anything else, slipping down past his waist. My hand found what it was looking for and slid with gentle pressure over the front of his pants, hoping to give him a little relief.

Nathan groaned and for a brief second, pressed himself against my hand before breaking away from the kiss abruptly.

"I cannot. I am not...I want... we should not," he stammered, rolling away and sitting up to scrub his head roughly.

I sat up cautiously and touched him along the back as it heaved from his breathing.

"Nathan, I'm sorry," I whispered. "I just got a little carried away. I thought... Please, will you look at me?"

He shook his head and rocked gently, his arms wrapped around his knees so he seemed curled into himself.

"I should not have let it go so far," he murmured, still curled up.

"I'm sorry, Nathan," I said again, mortified. "I just thought I could ease your tension."

He grunted and shook his head.

"You should not apologize, Kate. I would only disappoint you."

"You couldn't disappoint me," I assured.

He shook his head again and glanced my way.

"I will disappoint you with my inexperience. You understand this more," he mumbled before clenching his eyes shut. I sat there confused at his statement, trying to understand why everyone thought I was more experienced, in anything. A number of times this evening, I felt like they had expectations of me. Truth be told, I was feeling more inexperienced with each encounter I had with Nathan.

"Nathan, I don't know as much as you seem to think," I said and touched him along his cheek, trying to get him to open up.

"You have been with someone, Kate. You make me want more, but I do not know how to do this as easily as you do. I feel like I might burst, and I do not know how to ease it and yet one touch from you and..."

"Nathan, look at me," I said, my voice a lot more forceful than it probably should have been.

But I wanted him to know.

He glanced up at me, his eyes pained. I cupped his cheek to hold his attention.

"Nathan, I feel the same things when I am with you. I want to feel those with you," I said.

He sat up a little, covering my hand in his.

"You are my first, Kate. My first kiss, the first who has made me want, the first to touch. You have a better knowledge of these things. You have experienced this with," he stammered and blushed when I pulled away abruptly.

"Why did you have to bring Sean into this?" I whispered, struggling to fight back tears.

"I am sorry," he said and reached for me as I stood. I took a step back from him, wrapping my arms around myself protectively.

"You all have assumed I am so worldly, but have you considered that maybe I haven't done all you think I've done?" I asked.

He swallowed and held his hand out to me as he sat there, but I had to make him aware of my past- fully.

"Nathan, Sean and I dated for almost two years, and most of that I was terrified to give anything of myself to him. Believe it or not, I believed in giving myself to someone I loved, and most days it wasn't Sean," I said and shuddered at the memory of Sean's hands on me, of him wanting more of me.

"Kate."

I shook my head and continued.

"Eight months into our relationship, Sean made it clear that he was done waiting. Do you know what he gave me for my eighteenth birthday?" I asked, watching him shake his head slowly. "A bruised jaw, Nathan. You know why? Because I wouldn't give him what he wanted. Every time I said no, I received a little something for my trouble. And every time he demanded, I felt myself giving up a little bit at a time. That night, the night I ran? The only reason I pleaded not to give in was because his friends were there, and I had no idea if Sean would stop his friends from…."

He shifted and reached for me again, and I retreated a step. Instinct always had me retreating.

"Kate, I would never do that to you," he said and I shook my head to silence him again.

"I know you wouldn't, Nathan," I whispered. "That's why I know with you, I can trust my feelings. Don't you understand that? I feel these things with you that I didn't with him, and more than anything I want to share them with you."

I took his outstretched hand and knelt down in front of him, placing his hand to my heart.

"Do you feel my heart beating?" I asked, and continued when he nodded. "That's you, Nathan. I feel this because of you. What we feel is not wrong. What you want, what I want, is not shameful. I'll go as fast or as slow as you want, because I want this with you. You are my first too, in so many ways, do you understand that?"

He nodded and looked down at where our hands interlaced over my heart.

"I promise to never hurt you, Kate," he whispered and looked up into my eyes, his pledge clear. "I will not let anything happen to you."

He let out a long sigh and shook his head, his eyes closing tight.

"I want more with you. So much more. You are my temptation, Kate," he said into the night, his voice rough.

"I'm sorry," I whispered.

His eyes opened halfway, a lazy grin spreading over his face.

"Please do not be sorry, Kate," he murmured and stretched to kiss me. "I only mean that I want this to be more than what we have here alone tonight."

"I don't understand," I said, looking down at his clearly worked up body.

He did want me, right?

"You are more than a thoughtless romp in the cornfield, Kate," he whispered and tipped his head up to kiss me. "I know temptation. And I know what I want. But I will do this right. I am happy with what we have at the moment. I will not disrespect you because of my desires, Kate."

He kissed me again, slow and sure, relaxing back into the blanket until I could feel the blanketed ground at my back. He let his fingers work their way into my hair, the gentle pressure of his fingertips against my scalp made me hum softly.

"I like your hair down," he murmured and continued to stroke it slowly as he watched it slip through his fingers.

"It's not proper," I teased.

His grin widened and he shook his head.

"No it is not, but I can enjoy this."

"One step at a time," I whispered and kissed him slowly, happy to feel him relax some against me.

We lay like that for a long time, just taking one another in under the moonlight. My hands explored over his back, his own finding their way along my back and down, pressing me against him over and over, offering a little relief to each of us. Never completely. He was so very tempting, as I was sure I was to him. I was amazed he never pushed further for his own relief.

With every heated kiss he offered before drawing away to take a breath, with every push of his middle against my thigh and deep-throated groan as our bodies pressed, those would be our temptations not to take it further. But with each touch, we grew more comfortable with one another, until he could lie there beside me, smiling as I had rarely seen him before.

We returned to the others some time later, finding Emma and John searching for us amongst the groups of people outside the barn. When she saw us emerging from the corn, she took notice of my hair and shook her head.

"Come on. We have all the corn in the world back at home. I want a little more dancing time with my sister before we have to leave," she said, grinning.

I scowled at her as she pulled me along, glancing back at Nathan as he ran his hands through his hair, trying to straighten it.

"I'll remember this when you and John disappear behind the barn next time," I retorted, earning me a wide-eyed look from her. John stepped in to take Emma from me, a wide grin on his face when he looked at Nathan's relaxed posture and my uncovered hair. I shook my head and motioned for the barn.

"Fine, let's go back to dancing," I said and felt Nathan's arm come around my waist, drawing me close.

"I like your body against mine. I will miss that after tonight," he murmured and kissed me before following Emma and John up to the barn.

We slow danced to the music, regardless of the beat. Nathan held me close, groaning into my ear now and again when I would brush into him, feeling him stir against me. I tried not to be cruel, but his hands had become more adventurous as we danced, one drifting lower and lower until he guided me to him with it, just a slight pressure on the top of my rear to draw me in. He kept his head tucked close, laying soft kisses by my ear often. He was much more at ease as we danced together.

I would have been happy to dance with him all night. Unfortunately, John was signaling us that we had to head back to the car. I sighed and wondered how the night had sped by. It seemed like only an hour or two, but as the thought of going home settled in, the fatigue hit. I fought back the yawns as we slowly made our way towards the car. I was jarred awake when Nathan caught me by the arm and pulled me close, just as I heard his name called out from across the cars.

"Fisher! What the hell are you doing here?"

I turned to see whom Nathan was staring at, zeroing in on the thin blond man Benjamin had been smoking with before. Nathan tensed up beside me, wrapping his arm around me a little more protectively. The blond made his way over to us, leering at Emma and me before narrowing his eyes again at Nathan.

"I didn't think I'd see you again, Fisher. After the last time you were here. Did you keep the ox at home? He and his slut?" the man said.

"We have nothing to say to you Jeff," Nathan hissed, his eyes shooting daggers at this man. I was instantly on edge by Nathan's uncommon anger.

"What? I thought you all were the forgiving kind. That buddy of yours, Mark, is lucky I never pressed charges. You haven't been around, so I thought you guys were done."

The blond then turned his attention towards me, his grin lascivious. I instinctively shrank back into Nathan. I knew that look. It was the same predatory look that haunted my dreams.

"But I see you just needed to bring fresh meat here. Who's this? Is this the new girl some of the girls have been talking about?" he asked, edging slowly towards me.

I felt Nathan draw me closer to him, shielding me from this man.

"Forget it, Jeff. We are done with you," John said, his eyes trained hard on the Englisher.

Jeff put his hands up, pretending to surrender.

"No big deal. I just thought I would make conversation. Meet the new girl that has stolen Nathan's heart here. Keep an eye on her. Lot's of unsavory people around here. Wouldn't want your little Amish girl to go astray," he said, laughing as he stepped back.

"I am well aware of the unsavory people here," Nathan grated.

Jeff chuckled and turned away, heading back up to an English girl with red hair. He glanced back one more time, straight at me and leaned in to talk with his girl beside him. Nathan started moving again just as the girl turned to look for us. And her eyes narrowed. I remembered her. Joanna, the girl that had sneered at me at the Wittmers, nearly a month ago.

She must have been here on her Rumspringa, wearing all English clothes to fit in. She frowned at me and turned away, speaking with Jeff. I had an unsettling feeling in the pit of my stomach at her seeing me.

"Let us go, Nathan," John said beside us. "Steve will be waiting."

Nathan took one final look towards Jeff, his eyes narrowing before he guided me with him behind John and Emma back towards the car. I chanced a look back, a cold shiver running down my back when I noticed Jeff and Joanna both looking my way. Benjamin had joined them, but his eyes seemed less predatory.

Maybe a little wistful.

I turned and tried to put his eyes out of my mind. Because I had to wonder if maybe Benjamin did regret his decision after all. Maybe he wanted to come home, but couldn't. That idea made me incredibly sad, and it made me like the Bishop even less.

"Are you all right?" Nathan whispered as we neared the car.

"I feel badly for Benjamin," I whispered, looking back at Benjamin.

Nathan frowned and glanced back towards the trio in the distance.

"He chose that life. He chose those friends. We cannot change that," he murmured softly and nuzzled his nose against my temple, as if to calm himself as much as to ease my mind.

I was quiet as we climbed back into the car, Nathan's hand more sure against me as I settled in. His lips traveled along the base of my neck and he held me close, letting me relax against him as we started off. The other couple had chosen to remain, so there was more room in the backseat, but Nathan had pulled me into his lap, a boyish smile on his face. I couldn't deny him, if it made him happy.

I watched as Emma slowly fell asleep in John's arms, his eyes watching her lovingly as she slept. He looked up once, catching me watching them and he smiled. I liked John, he was more settled than Emma, and seemed to ground her in a way that suited them both. He wanted the best for her, even if the gathering had been a strange idea at proving to her that the Amish way was the right way. I knew he wanted her to be able to make that choice he had already made. I could see it now; in the way he held her and respected her and that he wanted a life with Emma.

I tucked into Nathan's shoulder, kissing his neck softly before snuggling in. His arms wrapped around me, a contented sigh from his mouth as he buried his nose into my hair. He was relaxed, and holding me with ease. I smiled into his shirt at that. Small as it was, we had opened up to one another simply by being close, without any pressure to go too far. I had no idea what would come next, what with returning to the prescribed rules of the Way.

But we would figure it out.

Together.

Chapter 23

I felt like I had just put my head to the pillow when I was getting back up again. Emma lay asleep next to me, but hearing footsteps outside our door, I knew it was close to time to get up. I had to wonder if being allowed to go to the party allowed for us to sleep in.

I doubted it. There never seemed to be a time when you could sleep in. I stretched and smiled as I thought on the events from the night before. Well, not all of the events. Because that party had been crazy. But my time with Nathan had been spectacular. Last night had been the most carefree I had ever seen Nathan.

Dancing with him.

Kissing him.

Offering him some time alone, for us to explore. Knowing that Nathan wanted to take things slowly, and to respect me. Sean had never done that. Nathan wanted to please me. Maybe that was why I felt more with Nathan. He was willing to explore more with me, rather than being selfish like Sean had been. Nathan was true to his word in that he would never disrespect me.

I sighed when Abigail stirred and slipped out of bed, going into the bathroom to wash my face and get ready for the day. My shift from the night before hung on the door, still a little damp where I had scrubbed away the dirt from lying in the cornfield. I wondered if Fannie would ask about it.

I wondered if Nathan would act differently; feel more emboldened now that we had spent some more time exploring one another. I let out a contented sigh and got changed, sure that the day was going to be amazing. Even with little sleep. I was excited to get started, so that I couls have the evening alone with Nathan.

"My daughters are up!" Jonah exclaimed when Emma, Abigail and I stepped into the kitchen a half hour later.

Emma glowered and moved to get the milk buckets. She had been the difficult one to wake up for a change. Abigail and I had to get her up by jumping on the bed. Fannie came and hugged us tight, relief clear in her face when she pulled away.

"I am pleased to see you up. We will make a simple breakfast this morning," she whispered.

"We'll get the cows settled and come in and help, Fannie," I replied, my smile never faltering. I felt like I had so much energy today. Fannie regarded me when she touched my cheek.

"You have some color in your face today, Katherine," she commented, and I swore there was a twinkle in her eye.

I blushed, thinking back to Hannah' glow the morning after her night with Mark. Fannie only grinned and patted the two of us before letting us go for our chores, sending Abigail for the eggs. Emma slowly woke up and became more animated as we milked the cows. She had many questions about the night before.

"You never did anything like that before?" she asked, and it took me a moment to realize she was talking about the party and not Nathan.

"No. We have parties like that, but I think we are more reserved because it is more readily available. I was really surprised by all the drugs," I said quietly.

"I was surprised by all the sex," she retorted.

I almost dropped my bucket.

"Yeah, there was certainly a lot of that going on," I murmured and blushed behind the cow, wondering what Emma would think of sex in general.

"John is driving me mad. He kisses me and then I melt. I just wish he would let me touch him soon," she said.

I leaned out behind the cow's hip and looked at her in surprise.

"What do you mean?" I asked, not sure I wanted to hear about Emma's exploits with John.

"Katherine, you know what I mean. You were not looking for worms in the corn last night with Nathan," she admonished, raising her eyebrow at me. "Or maybe you were."

I coughed and quickened my work. Did she honestly think that Nathan and I had been doing more than what we had been? Well, I had wanted to at the start of the evening, so perhaps there were expectations. She glanced back towards the barn door; to be sure we were alone before she scooted her stool to my side, leaning in to talk.

"It is just that John confounds me. He is so attentive. He was before I became ill as well. But we seem to have taken a step back, even when he makes me feel good when we are alone," she whispered and raised her eyebrows as if to emphasize something.

I blinked at her, clueless.

She rolled her eyes and continued.

"John is a gentleman. His kisses make me lightheaded. His hands worship when he touches me. But lately I have wanted to offer him some pleasure, like he does for me," she explained.

"What does he do for you?" I asked, curious.

Surely, Emma hadn't gotten more from John than I had from Nathan.

293

"I should not say. It is not exactly proper."

I looked at her pointedly from the side of the cow, amused.

"Neither is kissing, but I know you do that. Your lips are always redder when you come back from your walks," I said, laughing.

"So are yours, Katherine! They were quite red last night! And your hair was down. What did you really do last night in the corn?" she teased.

"Kissed, and talked," I said, avoiding her eyes.

"Of course," she said and winked.

I blushed furiously and concentrated on the cow again. She glanced towards the door again and leaned in.

"John touched my breast last night," she confided, almost giggling.

My eyes widened and I cleared my throat.

"No, really?" I asked, suddenly thinking that John was perhaps a little more forward than I assumed, and I was wishing that Nathan would be just a little more forward now that I knew what Emma and John had done.

"Does that surprise you, Katherine? We are not so different. Of course I am sure Nathan has not ventured past a kiss, but I am sure he would offer more if he knew you wished it," she said and giggled when I spluttered.

"I didn't figure John as a groping sort of guy, that's all," I replied, not looking up at her.

"He is very affectionate. Tender and supportive. I just want to give him something back. He has been so wonderful and patient and kind. I want to make him happy," she said, her voice a little wistful.

I smiled and thought of them when they were together. John was definitely happy.

"You make him happy by just being with him, Emma. I don't think you need to do more for him. He is happy to bring you joy," I replied, enjoying her blushing giddy smile.

"He makes me happy," she sighed, and her face definitely had a glow to it I had never seen before.

We finished the work, making our way back to the house with two full containers for our work. I glanced up at Nathan's hill and my heart skipped a beat when I noticed his silhouette making its way down towards us. Emma chuckled and leaned into me.

"I am not the only one that is happier these days. I suppose we will have to discuss who gets to sit on the swing and who gets to walk evenings," she said, smirking.

"Yes we will, Emma. We need to make it more equitable for everyone," I joked.

"First one done with chores then?" she challenged, sticking her hand out.

I glanced back at Nathan and took her hand, gripping it tightly. We laughed and stepped inside with the milk, bottling it up for Fannie before helping her pull out the breakfast casserole she had made for the morning. I was distracted from slicing the casserole when I heard the door open and Nathan walked in, a pleasant smile on his face.

I was certain everyone noticed it.

Fannie smiled brightly as he put his hat up, Jonah smirked and concentrated on his coffee. I looked away before my blush thoroughly gave me away to what we had done the night before and concentrated on cutting up servings of casserole. I could feel Nathan's eyes on me as he settled in next to Jonah, and I could feel the flutter in my stomach when I heard his soft voice. I chanced a glance at him when I set the plates, and fought my smile when our eyes met. The joyful glimmer in his eyes made me want to jump for joy.

I was completely taken with Nathan Fisher.

Breakfast was business as usual. Nathan and Jonah talked about when crops would be cleared, and Fannie detailed the plans for the day. I was surprised when Jonah volunteered me to go with him to Nathan's for the day. I looked up from my breakfast, trying to stay out of the conversation for fear of blushing and saying something telling. But my name and then hearing work at Nathan's woke me up.

"What?" I asked meekly.

Jonah smiled and eyed Fannie with a knowing look.

"If you can spare her today. She can tend to Nathan's house while we clear the near field. We will have mid day meal there," he suggested.

"Whatever you would like, husband. The girls can help me here today," Fannie replied, unfazed.

"I do not want to burden Kate with my chores, Jonah," Nathan started and then closed his mouth suddenly. Perhaps he realized I would be there all day for him? It was what I had been thinking. A stolen kiss, having him near me. We just needed to distract Jonah somehow.

"It is settled then! And I will bring Patience as well. Give your stallion another chance," Jonah exclaimed and made to stand. Nathan cleared his throat and looked a little uncomfortable, but stood as well and stepped past me, his fingers tracing across my shoulder as he brushed past me.

Immediately I felt the rush course through me at that simple touch. Nathan would be able to figure out so much about me. I rushed about to gather lunch for the men while they waited outside, Fannie pushing me out the door before the breakfast dishes were even cleared. Nathan waited on the porch for me, Jonah gone to the stables. Nathan's smile in the early light made me feel lightheaded.

"Jonah said he would meet us there. Walk with me?" he asked, his voice soft and sweet.

I smiled and fell in step with him. He took the basket from my hands holding it in one hand so that the other could take my own as soon as we had crested his hill. His fingers interlaced with mine warmed me to the core. We were quiet for most of the walk, his face relaxed and content as he looked ahead towards his home. When we crossed the yard, he finally spoke up.

"Did you sleep well?" he inquired quietly.

I shook my head.

"No, I had trouble sleeping," I replied, fighting a grin.

"I am sorry, what made you sleepless?" he asked, concern in his eyes.

"Thinking about you," I murmured and winked at him. He grinned and pulled the door open to his home, letting me in first.

"I had the most amazing dreams last night. I think that was the first night I have slept and remembered my dreams," he said.

"What did you dream about?" I asked as he set down the basket in the kitchen.

He turned and offered me a devastatingly brilliant smile.

"You."

I moved a step towards him, wanting to kiss him. His hands reached for me, pulling me close. His lips were close, leaning in.

"Nathan! Let us get the horses rigged up so we can be done early!" Jonah called in from the front door.

Nathan pulled back with a sigh, looking off towards the front of the house.

"Have a pleasant morning," I said, chuckling.

He laughed and stepped away, running a hand through his hair nervously.

"It would have been had we just a few more moments," he said and took another step towards the front door.

"I'll see you at lunch," I said and offered him a sympathetic smile.

He looked back once more before disappearing, leaving me alone in his house. Looking out the window, I watched as Jonah and Nathan worked to strap their horses into the machinery for harvesting the corn. Nathan brought out his two Haflingers, strapping them into the wagon while Jonah worked on the larger piece of machinery that looked like a giant reaping machine. I watched until I remembered I had things to do. There was no time to daydream.

I was supposed to be tending his house. I had never been more excited to do chores in my life. Perhaps because I knew Nathan would appreciate a clean house. I put the food I had brought into the refrigerator and grabbed a large sun tea pitcher from Nathan's cupboard, filling it with water and setting it up on the edge of the porch to steep in the sun. Looking at the disarray of the exterior of his house I let out a heavy sigh and dove into the task at hand, figuring I would clean outside first while it was still cool out.

Stepping out onto the porch, I realized this would be a great idea. I could watch them work while I cleaned. I just had to remember to actually do something, rather than watch Nathan standing tall in the wagon, distributing corn as it was pushed through the contraption that Jonah handled from the ground in front. Nathan was very distracting as he turned and pushed and shoved, already sweaty and flushed from the hard work.

Too many times while I swept, or while I tossed out the mop water into the dying grass, I would find my eyes searching for him. Time and again he would be there, doing something to make me smile and think about how good he was in his element. One instance that had me grinning was when he went to water his giant black horse, Magnus late in the morning.

The great beast nodded its head, bumping against Nathan as if to insist on something that Nathan had in the satchel he carried. I watched while he patted the horse softly and pulled out a small apple, which he offered Magnus. It disappeared instantly, his hand reaching for a second one to offer his hungry horse. He paused, eyeing the red apple thoughtfully for a moment. Nathan brought it to his nose, his eyes closing for a brief second before opening again, a brilliant smile flashing across his face before he took a bite of it.

I smiled to myself when the horse batted his head at Nathan once more, swallowing up the offered apple with no thought whatsoever. But Nathan's smile remained. As if he had felt my eyes on him, he looked over his shoulder towards me, his lips upturned and his eyes happy. He took another apple out of his bag and took a large bite out of it, winking at me before Jonah called for him.

I turned from watching Nathan and busied myself with making the front of his house look clean, wiping down the dusty windows that had many months of sediment on them. The first floor windows completed, I set to scrubbing the porch deck. It was well worn, but dirty beyond measure. It took several buckets of water from the water pump and a rough scrub brush to knock down the dirt until I could begin to see the painted floorboards. I hadn't realized how late it was until I heard the heavy footfalls of Jonah and Nathan coming up the porch steps.

I looked up, sweaty and wet from scrubbing on my hands and knees, to see Nathan and Jonah regarding me. Nathan looked pained, while Jonah looked pleased at my work. I stood up quickly and brushed myself off, pushing the hair that had come loose behind my ear as I moved towards them.

"I'm sorry. The time got away from me. Let me go get cleaned up and I'll get your meal ready," I said hurriedly, rushing inside without letting them answer.

I scrubbed up in the kitchen, splashing cold water against my face to cool off. I heard them walk in behind me, Nathan stepping in beside me with the container of tea. He handed me a towel to dry off and stepped in to wash his hands, quiet while Jonah spoke.

"The porch looks almost new, Katherine! And I believe it is lighter in the house now that the windows are clear. You have done more than I expected! Nathan will have a sparkling home in no time. Thank you, daughter," he said proudly.

I busied myself with pulling out the preparations for sandwiches to hide my embarrassment.

"I'm happy to do it, Jonah," I said softly and blushed when I heard Nathan sigh behind me.

I glanced back towards him and watched as he poured glasses of fresh brewed tea into glasses. He settled in beside Jonah at the table, a thoughtful look on his face as he watched me finish the sandwiches. We ate in silence, Jonah concentrating on his plate while Nathan and I repeated exchanged glances. Jonah would need to be blind and unfeeling not to see the tension between the two of us.

I wanted to reach out and touch Nathan, to assure him I was truly happy to be here helping him. He didn't need to do it alone. When Jonah pulled away from the table, Nathan followed him, stretching from the meal.

"It will be too hot to do much more. We should get the corn stored from today and work perhaps on your stalls while the horses are out to pasture. Katherine, perhaps you can work inside the remainder of the afternoon?" he suggested and I simply nodded.

Nathan offered me a soft apologetic smile and followed after Jonah, leaving me in Nathan's house on my own once again. I set to work quietly, cleaning the kitchen first, which was in good shape from the last time I had cleaned it. It wasn't used much really. I made quick work of the first floor, dusting and wiping down anything that wasn't covered. Looking towards the stairs, I swallowed hard and took the steps slowly. I had never ventured upstairs.

I knew immediately which room was Nathan's.

Of the five bedrooms upstairs, his was the only with the door open. I hesitated in opening the others, out of respect for his family. What would I find? Rooms left just as they had been when the occupants died? Pristine shrines of people he loved?

It made me sad to think once again of Nathan in this large house all by himself.

The house was entirely too quiet.

I slipped into his room and took it in. A small bookshelf with a dozen worn books, a few trinkets that looked like might be old wooden toys, and scraps of papers stacked neatly. My heart beat a little harder at the sight of the papers; similar to the ones I had seen that day when I first cleaned. Perhaps he had brought them up here, in the privacy of his room, so that I would not happen across them.

His simple wood slatted bed seemed too short for his tall frame. But he kept it tidy and was neatly made. The dresser under the window held no defining mementos on it that reminded me of Nathan. The room was very plain, except for the books and scraps of paper. He lived quietly. This was his sanctuary.

This was his room, his private place.

I suddenly felt like I was invading.

There was nothing for me to do here. Nathan's house was quiet, lonely and really very melancholy as I looked at it more closely. He kept himself to only a couple of rooms, his bedroom and the tiny table in the living room. I fought the urge to uncover the furniture in that room, to make it more lived in. It was quite possibly that he kept things covered because they hurt too much to look upon. With each observation, my feelings for the man who lived here grew. His smiles and his contented countenance were more important than anything now.

He deserved to be happy.

I made my way back outside and decided I would spend the remaining part of the afternoon in the garden, regardless of the heat.

Inside by myself, I could almost feel the eyes of ghosts watching me in their home.

Today was not the day to confront his ghosts.

I'd save that for another day. Today, I gave Nathan a home.

"Katherine?"

I lifted my head out of the wild jungle of the bushes by the house, avoiding the thorns as I stood and stretched. Jonah came to me and surveyed my progress. I had managed to get one side of the house tamed, watering and trimming down the long abandoned bushes. They still looked a little forlorn, but they were more green than brown now. He smiled and patted me lightly on the shoulder.

"You have done much today. Come; gather up your basket while I collect Patience. You will walk with me back to the house. Nathan will be along in a while," he said and turned to walk back to the pasture to fetch his horse that was grazing on the far end with Nathan's black.

I dusted myself off and went inside to get my basket. I was walking back down the hallway when Nathan came down the stairs, dressed in only his pants, the suspenders dangling at his sides. He stopped at the first step at seeing me, his eyes large and his hand in his mussed hair. He was dirty from the field, his face marked and his arms darkened with the corn dust. It was an extreme contrast to his pale bare chest. That chest I had seen from afar, but now couldn't pull my eyes from as I stood there a few feet from his beauty. Broad from farm labor, a thin smattering of hair on his chest that thickened on a dizzying trail south across a taut stomach and disappeared into the waist of his pants, I flushed at the thought of what that trail led to.

"I am sorry, I thought you were Jonah," he said quickly, pushing his hands deeper into his hair.

"Jonah wants me to go back with him. I just came in to get the basket," I replied and tried to pull my eyes away from him.

But it was impossible. Even dirty, he was beautiful. I found myself moving closer, my body drawn to his. He looked around the house, suddenly very shy.

"I did not wish you to tend to me, Kate. Thank you, you did too much," he whispered.

"I wanted to," I replied, stepping up to the step he fidgeted on. It was then that I noticed he was barefoot. Long elegant toes peeked out from the bottoms of his pants.

"I was going to wash," he murmured, tensing when I leaned in slightly. "I am filthy from the field."

I nodded and closed my eyes, taking in his scent as he stood there. As dirty as he was, he was still alluring. He smelled like sweat and dirt and the crispness of freshly cut corn. When I opened my eyes again, he was regarding me strangely. His eyes crinkled and he let out a nervous laugh.

"I must offend, Kate," he whispered.

"No," I murmured, my voice husky and tipped my head up to look up into his heavy lidded eyes.

I felt his hand wrap around my waist, drawing me close while his lips searched me out, capturing mine hungrily. I felt a thrill shoot through me at his needy claim, happy that he was becoming more adventurous with me. He moaned softly, his mouth opening up for me to explore. I could taste the salt of him on my lips from the day's hard work; the taste of him had me sinking into him.

Just as I thought I would pass out from the overwhelming need for him, Nathan drew away slowly, his eyes taking me in as he held me loosely to him. He let out a long contented breath and reached up slowly to stroke my cheek. Glancing towards the door, he shook his head and regarded me with apologetic eyes.

"You should go. Jonah will be waiting and I must clean up," he said with a small smile.

I nodded and took the last step down a little shaky, preparing to leave.

"I'll see you in a little bit? Are you too tired to sit with me tonight?" I asked, not wanting to ask him to stay if he was exhausted from the long day.

"I would never miss a chance to sit with you, Kate," he replied.

I grinned and made my way outside, trying to fight the giddy need to giggle like a girl. Jonah came around the corner just as I stepped out and we made our way back towards his house. He continually glanced my way, fighting a smile.

"Katherine, may I speak with you openly?" he asked as we climbed the hill.

I tensed and looked at him worriedly, but nodded.

Was he preparing to give me the same speech he had given Nathan?

"Are you happy here?" he asked, surprising me.

"Of course I am. I have never been as happy," I replied, a little confused.

He smiled at me and continued.

"You have been with us for almost a month, Katherine. And you seem happy in this life. I wished to ask you before we discuss your family," he said, his face suddenly serious.

I sobered up quickly, knowing we had to talk about that eventually.

"Your father will need to know soon. If this is truly where you want to be, if you see your future here, we will go and speak with your father after Nathan and I have cleared our fields," he said.

"This is where I want to be," I replied quietly, looking out over the fields that lay between the Berger's and Nathan's home.

This was my home. I could feel it in my heart when I looked on the two houses that felt more real to me than my home back in California. I hadn't lived before coming here.

"And if your future were to include Nathan? You would be happy?" he asked a little more softly.

I smiled bashfully towards Jonah, unsure how to respond.

He chuckled and grinned at me with a twinkle in his eye.

"He is rather fond of you, Katherine. And as your father figure, I would have to agree to this match. If that is what you wish," he explained.

"What about the Bishop?" I asked nervously. "Doesn't he have to come and ask me too?"

I didn't like that idea at all.

Jonah sighed and nodded.

"He is only a messenger, Katherine. He cannot say you can or cannot marry. It is up to you and Nathan. And me," he replied, his tender smile returning.

"I am just afraid of being denied eventually," I murmured.

Jonah slowed down as we crested the hill, looking back at the Fisher house.

"You have found us for a reason, Katherine. This I know. You were lost, as was Nathan. Now you are found. Regardless of what may be said of our laws, we know faith and understand that we must follow His intentions. The elders know this. And they will see what I have seen."

I swallowed at his words.

"What have you seen?"

He raised his hand slowly, so as not to scare me.

"I have seen an angel come and bring light to our world. You have brought hope and renewed faith into this family. If it is your path to stay and make this your home, it will be so," he replied and looked back towards the Fisher farm again. "Your good deeds will not go unnoticed. You will make a good home. You have already begun. You and Nathan are a good fit."

I nodded and thought about what Jonah was suggesting. He was already hinting at marriage. I wondered if Nathan had spoken to him about that today while they worked, or if Jonah was preparing himself. Things were moving awfully fast.

Did that scare me?

Maybe just a little. But perhaps that was how they did it here. And the idea of marrying Nathan did make my heart speed up.

"Just remember my daughter. There are some things that must be held true until the wedding day," he said, his pointed look not lost on my scarlet face.

I nodded and inwardly cried out in relief when we made it to the house. The last thing I wanted was the sex talk from Jonah. I didn't want to bear witness to that. And I think perhaps Jonah understood that Nathan and I would respect one another.

At least I hoped so, judging by his mischievious smirk towards Nathan all through dinner.

That or there would be a lot more time spent with Patience and Nathan's horse to drive the point home.

CHAPTER 24

"If we hurry, we can beat Emma and get a walk in," I whispered to Nathan as he helped me wipe down the table.

I glanced back at Emma, who was drying the last dish and looking out the window for John, who had yet to arrive. She turned and pretended to scowl at me, knowing what I was up to. I grinned and rushed to rinse out my washrag, drying my hands on my apron as I pulled it off hurriedly. Fannie snickered beside the stove and nodded to Nathan while he played nervously with his hat by the door.

"Go, Katherine. We will finish up until John arrives," she chuckled.

I was outside in no time, Nathan trailing behind a little more slowly, blushing. He glanced back towards the kitchen before following me down the steps and into the yard. His smile flashed in the sunset, making me smile even more. I slowed down as we neared the barn, trying to pace ourselves.

I was failing miserably.

So was Nathan.

As soon as the house fell from view, he was pulling me close and kissing me. His arms wrapped around me, his breath heaving hard in his chest when we collided with the wall of the barn. He leaned into me, his lips moving to my cheek, taking huge gulps of air as I clutched at him and let my lips edge to his jaw. The stubble there from the day burned my lips, but I didn't care. I could still taste him on his jaw.

"A few minutes is not enough," he groaned, burying his nose into my hair by my ear.

I sighed when I felt his hands wrap around my hips, pulling me closer. I kissed him again, searching him out. He opened his mouth to me willingly, moaning softly when he moved against me. When he finally pulled his lips from mine, we were both breathless. I could feel his heart beating through my chest, something that seemed to beat in perfect rhythm with my own. Looking up into his eyes, I saw nothing but joy in them.

I did that.

I let out a soft breath and traced the hairs along the nape of his neck, enjoying the moment. His soft breath, and then his quiet voice melted me further.

"This is not wrong," he murmured.

"What?" I asked, my brain cloudy.

"What I feel for you. What we do. It is not wrong. God would not make what I feel with you sinful. It is renewed life I feel when you are with me," he whispered and kissed me softly.

His hand moved up slowly, cupping my cheek lightly before slipping down my neck. His fingertips grazed my pulse point, pausing as his eyes travelled there to watch my throat pound. And then his eyes travelled lower, searching out the source of my pounding pulse. His fingers dipped lower, tracing along the neck of my dress as if in contemplation to move further. I swallowed and waited, breathing raggedly when his hand slipped lower, pressing firmly along my chest above my heart. I hummed softly; drawing his eyes up to gauge my reaction.

"Is this all right?" he asked.

"Yes," I whispered, watching as his eyes pulled down once more, his bottom lip slipping into his mouth as his hand slipped with staggering slowness across the fabric of my dress.

The pressure of his hand lessened, until just his fingertips traced tentatively, my breath catching at the incredible thrill running through me when I felt the back of his fingertips brush along the underside of my breast. He adjusted against me, and my eyes fluttered closed at the sensory overload of Nathan against me.

I should have felt trapped. I should have felt threatened with the way he had me pinned up against the barn door. But instead I felt a fire working its way through me. Across my neck as I felt his breath on me, in my stomach as his arousal hardened further at the gentlest nudge against it, at the tingling madness that was engulfing me at the feeling of his fingertips getting closer to where I ached in my breast.

And he gently cupped my breast, capturing it in his large hand, squeezing with gentle pressure. This was like nothing I had ever felt before. This was not pawing, like Sean. This was worshiping. Exploring, loving. His thumb shifted delicately, purposefully avoiding my hardening nipple.

"Is this all right?" he asked, his voice deep and gravelly in my ear.

I could only nod.

"So soft. You are so soft, except right here," he whispered and let the pad of his thumb brush with gentle pressure over my aching nipple.

I cried out at the pleasure it elicited. He pulled away suddenly, his hands shifting to my shoulders to hold me up. I covered my mouth and looked around; sure I had alerted the Bergers to what we had been doing. I licked at my dry lips and fought to swallow a sudden urge to laugh from the nerves. We stood there looking back at the house for a moment before he turned back to me, chuckling. His eyes shone with awe as I caught my breath, not realizing I had lost it in the first place.

His eyes crinkled up tight as he leaned in to brush his lips along my cheek.

"I do not think they heard. Are you all right?" he asked, his eyes hopeful and smiling.

I laughed softly and nodded, loving his joyful air.

"You took me by surprise," I replied. "We're getting our chores done first every night."

I couldn't wait for him to do that to me again, and maybe a little more. He leaned back in to me and hugged me tight, holding onto me for a long moment before groaning and pulling away.

"We should return. They will be missing us," he said, taking my hands in his and pulling my shaky body from the wall.

"Are you happy, Nathan?" I asked, worried maybe that again, we had stepped into something too quickly. And unlike Sean, Nathan wasn't demanding satisfaction. Was he satisfied with only a brief touch? Had it been Sean I would have been made to feel guilty.

He touched my cheek where it still felt flushed.

"I am more happy now than I have ever been. I have been blessed with an angel to bring me back to life," he whispered and kissed me one more time before pulling us back around the front of the barn.

Our hands separated when the house came into view, but I could still feel him on me, even from a few feet away. We were linked to one another, of that I was sure now. We shared something that could not be broken by distance. Emma and John sat on the swing, talking quietly when we slowly made our way up the steps. It was getting late, and I knew our night was coming to a close. Emma leaned in and pecked John on the cheek, his smile widening at her touch. I felt Nathan's fingers capture mine, turning me around to face him.

"I will let you get some sleep, Kate. We can have tomorrow together," he murmured and squeezed my hand gently in his.

"I enjoyed our walk tonight, Nathan. Sweet dreams," I replied, smiling.

"Pleasant dreams, Kate," he said as he pulled away, back towards the night.

I watched him go, Emma standing beside me as John walked off in the opposite direction. The moon gave us enough light to watch them until they disappeared behind the hills, the two of us letting out a sigh when they had gone. We turned to one another and burst into laughter, hugging each other tight as we turned and made our way upstairs to bed.

Settled in for the night, Emma snuggled up under the blanket when she finally spoke.

"John asked me again tonight," she whispered, her eyes glassy and her smile wide as she watched me process. I wanted to shake her. I looked at her expectantly, at her beaming smile.

"You said yes, right?" I exclaimed, practically bouncing off the bed.

She shushed me and giggled as she pulled me back under the covers, hoping not to wake Abigail.

"Of course I did, Katherine! There is nothing I want more than to be with him. Now we just have to get Father's blessing," she said, beaming.

"He'll say yes," I said confidently and hugged her tight. "I am so happy for you, Emma."

I closed my eyes and felt my heart twist a little. I was so happy for her; she would be getting married, going off like Hannah and Mark to start their new life together. And I would be here. I had no expectations that Nathan would ask me to marry him after knowing him for less than a month, even if I couldn't see myself anywhere else. I would be here when Emma and Hannah were off starting a new family. At least there was still Abigail who would be sure to stick to me like any little sister might.

Emma pulled away and touched me lightly on the cheek, her eyes taking me in.

"Nathan cares for you. He will ask in time," she whispered.

I snorted and pulled away, closing my eyes to her knowing gaze.

"It's a little early for that," I replied and laid my head on the pillow, feigning exhaustion.

"It will happen," she said. "I know it will."

I felt her settle in beside me, holding my hand tight in the dark. I let my mind drift, thinking about that quiet house, and how much better it would be with more than just Nathan in it. The happiness I had seen in his eyes made me believe that perhaps he was thinking about a future. And that maybe, if everything went well, he wouldn't be alone for much longer.

CHAPTER 25

Time spent with Nathan sped past, always much faster than when he was not with me. Sunday was a whirl. We finished our morning chores early, and I spent most of the late morning helping Fannie prepare a roast for supper, as well as what she was calling my signature pies. Nathan remained with us throughout the day, sitting with Jonah to discuss the future of the farm when he wasn't sitting with me as I read from his mother's Bible. He liked to watch me read, and his expert knowledge was helpful when I had questions.

Afternoon came and went, Emma and John spending much of their time in the yard. I was fine with that; Nathan and I found pleasure in just being next to one another, and Emma and John had so much time to catch up on. I watched them briefly, grinning when I noticed John touch her hand as if in askance. She smiled and took his hand, in the open for all to see. It made my heart flutter.

"They are good for one another," Nathan whispered near my ear.

I blushed and looked away from the couple, up into Nathan's contented gaze.

"Yes they are. I like how sweet John is with her. He loves her," I said looking back out towards them.

"How do they court in your world?" he asked, drawing my eyes back to his.

I shrugged.

"I don't really know, Nathan. We go out for dates, we talk, we fall in love. He asks her, she says yes, happily ever after."

He smiled and pulled my hand in his, leaning in closer than he usually did while we sat in view.

"So it is not much different from what we do. That is good to know," he whispered and snuck in a quick kiss before pulling away and going back to reading out loud.

But he smiled more, and he read inspiring passages on love until late into the evening.

Time flew too quickly. But I cherished every second I could make Nathan smile and look at me like I was his whole world.

He was every bit mine.

Every day with the Bergers was another day away from the horror of my old life. Every day with Nathan was another day of me learning that love could be tender and reciprocal. Nathan cared as much about me as I did about him. Every evening Nathan showed me a little more beauty that was his world. By his soft words, his gentle touch, and an openness to let me please him that I had never experienced before falling into this life. Never did he push, never did he insist.

Never did he hurt me.

He was gentle. He was willing to try, and he was willing to bend the rules just a bit, never too far. We explored one another slowly. With the little time we had, it was more important to talk than to feel, as much as both of us wanted a little more physically, we never ventured further than what we had already experienced. The barn was our refuge when Emma had not staked a claim, but we found ourselves simply enjoying one another in a kiss or light touch in quiet splendor for a few brief minutes before someone missed us.

He wanted a slow pace. I wanted to see his smile.

He wanted to learn everything about me.

I wanted to learn everything about this new life.

I grew more confident in myself with each new lesson learned. I stepped up to the challenge of trying to be what I needed to be in order to win the hearts of the Amish Elders.

I smiled more at the how the simplicity of this life made me feel whole. And I stressed over having to end my old life. With every foot of Nathan's field harvested, I knew the time would come soon for us to leave and say goodbye to my family. And confront Sean.

I was fine with saying goodbye. I was just scared of the reaction.

I was scared of him fighting back. Jonah had volunteered to go, to serve as a witness and to help cushion the blow for my family. He wanted to represent the community. Nathan wanted to go because he worried for me. I think he worried I would not return. It killed me to see the insecurity in his eyes whenever we discussed my need to leave to deal with things. It unnerved me to think I needed to go in the first place. But I loved these people, and the threat of Sean coming in to ruin things wore on me.

Nathan reassured me every night that I would be safe.

God would protect me.

My epiphany came as I was gardening with Abigail and Emma late on Thursday. Looking around at what the Bergers had, I realized how much I wanted that as well. I wanted a house, with a garden just like theirs. I wanted a man, who cared for me just as much as Jonah cared for Fannie.

Or John to Emma.

Hannah to Mark.

Nathan to me.

It was right here.

Everything we did was a gift. In my old life we took it all for granted. In this world it was accomplished with thanks to God and honest hard work. I smiled over at Emma as she stretched and grabbed the last of the string beans on the vine.

"I can't wait to cook these," I said, grinning at the idea of cooking what I had gathered today.

Abigail and Emma both laughed at me.

"You are excited about cooking beans, Katherine? I think the heat has gotten to you finally!" Emma replied and hoisted the basket onto her hip, full of vegetables.

I shrugged and remained quiet. Of course maybe she didn't understand. It had always been that way for her. But for me it was a new start.

A new life.

I felt like I fit in, finally.

I felt accomplished. And that was more than I had felt ever in my life. I closed my eyes for a moment, turning my face up to the afternoon sun. The warmth was welcome, regardless of the heat of the day. I felt touched.

By God? I didn't know. But I felt blessed.

I would pray to whoever that made me feel like this.

"Katherine?"

I opened my eyes and turned to Emma, who smiled softly.

"Just offering a bit of thanks," I replied and picked up my basket to walk beside her towards the house as Abigail rushed inside. Fannie stepped out and gathered up my basket, nodding towards the barn.

"I will take this, Katherine. Will you gather up the eggs for me? There were so few this morning when Abigail checked. So many things to do now that Hannah is gone to stay with the Bowmans," she said, her voice catching a bit as it did regularly now since Hannah had left with her husband.

I touched her arm to soothe her and nodded.

"Of course, Fannie. I'm happy to," I said enjoying her brilliant smile.

"Thank you, daughter," she whispered and turned back into the house, leaving me to make my way towards the barn.

I smiled into the sun again as I walked, smelling the air and sighing at the quiet. I could hear everything. I could smell everything. I could hear the birdsong in the trees that rustled in the afternoon breeze. I could smell the horses, could smell the hay and grain as I passed the open barn door. I heard the crunch of hooves as the horses stamped and nickered as I passed.

Every sense was tuned in to the world around me.

I was alive here.

The sun blazed in my eyes and I welcomed it as I stepped up the ramp to the chicken coop, their chattering getting louder as I stepped close.

"Don't give me any trouble you noisy birds. I'm taking your eggs whether you like it or not," I admonished the squawky chickens.

They seemed more skittish than usual, perhaps because we had waited so long before taking their eggs from them. I grabbed the eggs quickly; their beaks leaping at me and then retreating like the chickens that they were. They startled me when I went to reach in again and they all burst into a flurry of feathers and angry voices.

I didn't have time to react.

Because I was shoved roughly into the wire with my hand still in the cage, the other releasing the basket of collected eggs on the instinct to defend myself. Eggs tumbled out over the basket, breaking and spilling at my feet.

I made to cry out, but a large hand covered my mouth with an iron grip.

I knew instantly. I could feel, could smell, and could sense everything in that second.

Aftershave, hot meaty hands, the harsh breath that wafted over my neck.

"Found you."

I struggled in his tight grip, feeling the wire from the chicken coop pinching my cheek. My eyes were wide, trying to process.

Trying to find an escape.

Sean had found me.

"Going domestic, Kate? Funny, this wasn't what I imagined it would be like," he said and shoved me harder into the cage, the small building shuddering under his weight against me.

My free hand flailed beside me, at the wrong angle to grab at anything as he pinned me hard. His mouth drew close to my ear, laughing low.

"Do you have any idea how obstinate these people are, Kate? It took me going from house to house asking about you and still they didn't say anything. Well, except a pretty little red head. She seemed more than happy to tell me things, she and her boyfriend," he hissed, slipping his hand down my back until it palmed me roughly along my hip.

I shook my head and whimpered through his hand, trying to see him as he pushed against me.

"They seemed perfectly happy to help me find you. They don't like you so much here, Kate. You're an outsider. You don't belong here. You belong with me," he growled and dragged me back, his wandering hand suddenly wrapped around my waist, tugging me back as he retreated from the chicken coop.

I struggled in his grasp, feeling my feet leave the ground as he pulled me close against him, jerking me towards the near field. I knew as soon as we were in it, I would be lost. I kicked, grabbing at his thick arm that was clamped over my chest, desperate to get his hand from my mouth.

To bite, to scream, to do anything but get lost in the corn.

I scratched him along the arms, feeling the skin give, but he held firm, even when I broke the skin of his forearms with my nails.

"Knock it off, Kate, or I swear!" he grated, and hoisted me a little higher off the ground.

Airborne, I was high enough to kick him hard on the inside of the knee to cause him to stumble. His grip weakened around me as he faltered, his hand slipped from my mouth just enough and I screamed with every ounce of energy that I had. I could hear it echo off the house and the barn before his hands returned, my teeth digging in between his thumb and finger before silencing me.

Just one scream.

And the angry rustling corn was so close.

I tried to dig my heels into the dirt, but he pulled me up again, carrying me. I tried to trip him, tangling my legs in his to cause him to fall. But he remained clear of my meddling. I needed to do something; mere feet to the corn and I would be gone forever. I fought as best I could against him, kicking, scratching, anything.

We were steps from the corn.

"Katherine!"

Sean whirled around, flinging me with him like a ragdoll in his arms, to see who had called out. I saw Fannie on the porch, her hands to her mouth and her eyes wide. Abigail was leaping from the steps, running with amazing speed towards us.

"Abigail! No!" Fannie shouted and vaulted after her, much slower. Emma passed by her as well, catching up to Abigail and grabbing at her to slow her down.

Sean moved his hand to my neck, clamping hard as Emma and Abigail approached, Emma's skirt pooling around her legs as she stopped hard, realizing quickly what Sean intended. She clutched at Abigail who fought in her arms. Sean's grip squeezed harder, the air gone as he cut it off from my lungs. I was left flailing in his grip, choking and scratching desperately as I watched through watery eyes Abigail and Emma's helpless expressions.

"Please! Let her go! You are hurting her!" Abigail entreated, her hands clasped before her in a desperate plea and still struggling with Emma.

"I'll snap her neck! Don't come closer," he grated, twisting my neck to the side a bit as if to prove his intent.

I was gagging, the pressure was too much. My eyes were losing focus. Had to get free.

Away from him.

Had to. Run.

"Please, just let her go! It does not have to be this way!" I heard. I was losing focus but I knew it was Fannie.

"I'll kill her if you follow us. I mean it. I'll kill her!"

"No please! Do not take her! Please! NO!"

The voices were growing faint, and there was a new noise, the angry rustling of the corn all around me. Suddenly the air rushed back in and I was thrown hard over his shoulder.

"Bring back my daughter! Please!"

I tried to struggle again, to get back to the voice, but the grip around me was solid. I could make out green and brown of the corn as it whipped past me, as I tried to right myself. Light and darkness flitted across my vision, but the darkness seemed more oppressive now in his grip.

A sudden drop and I felt the bite of the pavement on my palms. I lay there gasping for a second before I heard a car door open and his hand grabbed me by the hair, ripping the prayer cover off in the process. I struggled again, seeing my terrified reflection in the window as he tried to shove me in the car. I threw my hands out, bracing against the frame of the car door.

"No!" I gasped, my throat searing at the pain of being practically crushed moments before.

"Damn it, Kate! Get in the fucking car!" he screamed and grabbed at me a little harder, I could feel his knee in my back shoving me roughly.

I slipped free and whirled around, tripping over myself as I tried to keep my head from spinning. Hearing fabric rip I was pulled back against hot steel that burned my shoulder where my dress must have torn.

"No!"

I had to get away.

Back to Nathan.

I tried to push away.

"Damn it Kate! Stop being so difficult!"

"No!"

Claws out I scratched against his jaw. I watched in horror as the switch went off in his head. His eyes blazed. Jekyll to Hyde. Man to beast in an instant.

And then the all-familiar crack.

My head spun, the pain shot through my jaw and into my skull. I fought to keep my eyes from losing focus.

No. Fight. Get away. Run. Must run.

"No," I gasped and reached out with fists to hit whatever I could.

"Stupid whore, get in the car!"

Another crack, this time my temple roared.

"No!" I cried out hoarsely, waving at the blurry vision in front of me, pushing away.

Corn. Back into the corn. Back to…

"Get in the car!"

Crack.

I felt my knees jar against the road.

Dizzy.

My lips tasted like iron.

"No," I croaked and grabbed at fabric, trying to pull it down with me.

But I was losing focus. Spinning. Trying to crawl.

Crack.

I couldn't tell you where it hurt.

Because blackness finally took me away.

Away from everything.

Life. Love. Happiness.

The last thing I remember was the acrid scent of motor oil and car vinyl. Smells that were foreign to me and yet so familiar.

And absolutely terrifying.

CHAPTER 26

I was drifting, my body leaden and unable to move. I couldn't open my eyes; the throbbing in my head was too unbearable.

But I could feel.

I could feel something soft under me. My cheek rested on fabric, and the room was cold. My temple felt numb, as did my cheek and a chill dampness leaked down my neck causing me to shudder. I felt the cold move slightly, confused how the cold would migrate lower towards my jaw. I tried to open my eyes to figure it out. But no matter what, my brain didn't want my eyes to open. So I lay there and listened as my body woke up from a blackness I wished I could return to.

Smell came next.

Bleach and bad fabric softener, maybe cheap soap invaded my nostrils, making them burn. I tried to place where I was, the smells unfamiliar to where I had been the last few weeks. It didn't smell like my old house.

Not the Bergers.

Sean.

Fannie. Emma.

Little Abigail wailing.

Gone.

Everything came back to me in a rush.

How long had I been gone?

Was anyone looking for me?

Where was Nathan?

Nathan. Oh God, Nathan.

"Why would you say that, Kate? After everything I've done for you? Why would you say his name?"

I shivered at the sound of Sean's voice, just behind my ear as he moved the cold from my jaw line. I tried to move but his hands came around and held me close, the heat of him oppressive in the cold room.

"Why can't you see I love you? You are all I want, Kate. I'll do anything for you, and yet you run from me to him. Did you think you'd just go off and be a little farmwife for your farm boy? When you know you are mine?" he whispered into my ear.

"Sean," I croaked, my throat ruined from his squeezing. I coughed and winced at the pain it caused.

"You made me do it, Kate. You make me so angry sometimes. You think I like punishing you? Do you think I like having to hunt you down? Why do you have to be so stubborn? Why can't you be the good girl with me? I want you to be a good girl," he groaned and moved in closer, his body lining up against my back.

I jerked, trying to get away, but his hands held me tighter, moving to my hip to hold me to him. I tried to open my eyes. I could manage to only crack open one, but everything was blurry. The light pierced my eye and I clenched it shut again at the pain. I heard a noise in the room, and realized it was my damaged voice.

Broken whimpers as he touched me along my waist, moving up.

"Shhh, baby. Just relax. I want to show you I can be good for you. I helped you, Kate. I took care of you. The swelling has gone down. I can take care of you. I can be everything you need. Please Kate, I can show you I am better than he is," he whispered hoarsely into my ear, his mouth capturing it roughly.

I shuddered and tried to pull away again.

"No," I gasped.

"I want to show you," he murmured, his hand moving up over my dress trying to undo the closures at my breast. I felt his lips along my throat, sucking hard on the skin there.

I struggled to open my eyes again, to move, to flee but my body was useless. It hurt to move, it hurt to defend. I managed to strike out, my fists landing on hot fabric against steel. His hands grabbed at mine, shoving them over my head.

"I'm better for you. I'm better than he is," he growled and moved in closer, twisting my body so that I was forced onto my stomach.

I felt his hands at my ankles, tugging on them. My body reacted on instinct, pain be damned. I was in survival mode. I flinched, my legs pulling in close and my back tensing in understanding to what he planned.

"Hold still," he hissed and pushed the skirt up my legs past my thighs.

"No, please, Sean," I whimpered and struggled to roll away.

"Hold still!" he said again, forceful as his hands gripped my hips hard, holding me in place.

"No. No, no, please no," I whimpered, shaking and struggling again.

I felt his hand in my hair, tugging me back to him. The other was moving behind me, and I jerked away as best I could when I felt him move behind me. My hair burned on my scalp as he gripped me, as I struggled under him, while his hand squeezed the fleshy part of my hip and grabbed a fistful of fabric there.

"No!"

I was desperate now, my arm swinging back to hit him. At the angle he had me trapped, I could only hit the air. He pressed my face into the pillows, the pressure making me cry out in pain.

"I love you so much, Kate. Let me do this. I'm better than he is. I know I'm better," he growled and clawed at my dress, the cotton straining to yield in his grip.

"Please, Sean. Stop! Please, I'm sorry! I didn't mean to run! I'm sorry! I'll be good! I promise! Please just don't!" I babbled, anything that would stop him.

"I'm tired of you running away, Kate. This ends here. You're mine, not that farm boy's. I'll make sure you're mine for good," he hissed and I heard the fabric ripping.

I felt it cutting into me as the dress tried in vain to remain together. Hannah's stitches were strong, but Sean was proving to be stronger. Always stronger. I let out one last whimper and went limp, lifeless under his hands. There was no fighting it. This would happen. I had no power. I never had. Sean proved that time and time again.

"Please, no. No, no. Not like this. God, help me. Please," I sobbed brokenly.

The best I could hope for was darkness and I wouldn't feel it. But my senses were overly alert. I could not see, but I could feel. I could hear. I could smell.

The air was cold. My skin trembled from it. The tears on my face felt icy on my hot face. His hands were scorching as they paused over my limp body, his body slumping away somewhere behind me. His breath was ragged. Mine rattled in my lungs as I sobbed through my damaged throat. The cheap fabric softener was over sweet in my nose where it was buried deep in the bedspread.

And then his choked words.

"Why...Why can't you love me?"

And then I was alone. He was off the bed with a whimper. I heard the door open, felt the warm night breeze in the artificial air before it was shut out to me. And then it was quiet. He had left me there, half dressed in the darkness of a strange place. I gripped the bedding under me, trying to move, to get up. But my body was useless. I had hardly any strength to move.

To flee. To escape. I was broken.

All I could do was manage to slip off the bed, my body shivering on the cold hard carpeting of the room I lay trapped in.

I let the quiet envelope me, the darkness following.

He'd come back, I knew. Would he try again? Would he succeed then? I just wanted the darkness. I didn't want to be awake for that.

Dear God, please. Just let me stay in the dark.

Please. End this.

I'm sorry, Nathan. I don't have the strength to fight.

Please God. End this.

CHAPTER 27

I could feel the heat of the sun on me, and the air was hot as it blew past me. And there was music. How long had it been since I heard music? I tried to swallow and open my eyes, but the sunlight hurt when I tried to open them. I moved to shade them, feeling the tremendous ache in my joints as I moved.

"Good morning!"

I jerked at the sound of his voice, my eyes squinting to open a crack regardless of the pain around them. It took me a moment to focus.

Sean was smiling at me as he drove.

I looked around to see the jagged mountains and rough scrub brush along the highway, the passing highway signs telling me where we were headed.

Redding.

We were back in California.

How long had I been out?

"You slept great, hardly a sound out of you," Sean continued contentedly, looking back at the road ahead of us.

I swallowed and shifted in my seat, when I noticed I was in over sized sweats. He had changed me. He seemed to notice my distress, and cleared his throat nervously.

"I couldn't bring you home to your dad in those clothes. I didn't look... much," he said, his lips quivering into a chilling leer that left my stomach turning.

"How long?" I whispered, my throat still feeling a little tender.

"You've been out most of the trip. I got a little worried when you didn't wake up at first in the motel. But you mumbled in your sleep, so I knew you were okay," he replied, turning away from me to look straight ahead, his demeanor suddenly serious.

"You look better now though," he continued. "Once we tell your dad about how he hit you, everything will be all right."

"He who? You hit me, Sean," I said, backing up into the side of the door at the flash of his eyes, threatening to throw the switch to the monster inside.

"We're not going to tell him that though, are we? He hit you, Kate. And I took you away. You're coming back home. Things will be good again. Your dad will be so happy to see you back with me. You're safe now," he said, nodding to himself as he spoke.

"I'm not going to say that, Sean," I said heatedly.

He laughed low in his throat. The look he gave me sent a cold chill through me.

"You're going to say what I tell you to say," he hissed. "See, I know all about your little farm boy. I saw you with him. I watched you, with him. I watched you at his house. Did you like playing happy little homemaker for him, Kate? You let him touch you. You think I'll let that go?"

I sat there, frozen as I listened to him. His eyes burned as he looked out over the road.

"You're mine, Kate. Not his. You're coming back to stay, and your dad will believe me when I tell him you were seduced into some cult by him. You're going to tell him I saved you from him. Because if you don't, I'll make sure that farm boy has a little accident. I've got friends there, Kate. He's not well liked by my friends. It would be easy for them.

Buggy accident, or maybe he falls off barn roof. Easy. Look at how I got to you, and you weren't alone," he spouted, grinning at the last.

I couldn't speak for fear of crying.

Sean was threatening Nathan.

He had seen us together. He had made friends, undoubtedly with Jeff and Joanna. Would they really hurt Nathan? What about Benjamin? Surely he wouldn't hurt his friend? I couldn't know. I really didn't know them.

"You understand, Kate?" he asked darkly. "You get it? You play happy-to-be-home-Kate and everything will be fine. You don't, and I hurt him."

I stared at him, terrified.

"GOT IT?" he screamed, his eyes commanding.

I nodded and remained quiet.

He laughed and relaxed his grip on the wheel once more.

"We'll forget about all of this, Kate. You'll be better now that you're away from them. He won't come looking for you. Wouldn't even hit me he was such a coward. Can't believe you fell for someone weak like that. I can protect you, Kate. And that's what your dad will believe," he continued like he had to convince himself.

I had no doubt Sean would protect me. Possess me. And hurt me. I had to think of how to get away again, to tell my father so he would believe me. But he would need undeniable proof. He would need evidence. Sean's father would insist on it so he could deny any wrongdoing. Or they'd cover it up so as to avoid scandal. Otherwise it would be my word against Sean's.

I glanced his way, my eyes zeroing in on his arms as they strained against the steering wheel. Scratches ran up and down his arms, scabbed and jagged. I remember clawing at him.

Were those from me?

I looked away and glanced down at my hands, still dirty from yesterday. Fingernails blackened from digging into something. Could I still have evidence on me? Or was it just the dirt from the garden? How long did evidence like that survive? Could I finally have irrefutable proof, more than my word?

"Things will be better, Kate. You'll see. Because I love you so much it hurts," he said, startling me to look back up at him.

He was grinning, happy as a clam. His Jekyll and Hyde switched again. Unfazed by me, beaten and disheveled beside him.

"We'll tell Mr. Hill I took you away from all that, Kate. Took you away from him. I took care of you," he repeated, as if trying to drill it into me.

"Say it, Kate."

I swallowed down the bile.

"Say it."

"You took care of me," I whispered.

He pulled me to him and kissed me on the top of the head, wrapping his arm around me protectively as he drove through the redwoods.

"I took care of you," he repeated happily into my hair.

I sat there, uncomfortably folded up into his side while his heavy hand brushed my head absently. I needed to get my father to believe me. I had no idea how I was going to do that.

The familiar surroundings of the coast came into view ahead of us. I sat there in a suffocating haze, trapped under Sean's arm. He chattered on about going to see his friends at the university, taking me out for dinner and the movies, and asking my dad to make it official. He spoke like nothing had ever happened. Like the circumstances of the last month didn't exist.

I stayed silent and watched the world pass by; a world that I recognized but wanted no part of. I watched cars and cargo trucks beside us, had felt a pang of loss when we passed some of the dairy farms inland, and then the fog of the coast engulfed us and the sun was gone.

I shivered at the dark oppressive feel of this place, no longer home. I refused to acknowledge him when Sean offered me his sweatshirt. I would rather embrace the cold than smell of him. I concentrated instead on figuring out how to get away again. To somehow find my way back to the town somewhere in rural Iowa.

I didn't even know where in Iowa he was.

Nathan.

I swallowed and closed my eyes to the rolling grey and the town as we passed through. It was not mine any longer. Mine was far away. I missed the heat and the green fields.

I missed home.

Nathan.

What was he thinking?

Was he okay?

I pondered that while the last few miles sped past, taking me one step closer to the life I had run from, and a father that would take Sean's word over mine. I was once again in my prison. We pulled up to my old house, the grey siding even more foreboding in the lackluster afternoon sunlight. My old Suburban looked like it was still in the same place I had left it, and my father's freshly washed sedan parked neatly in the driveway. Everything was foreign to me.

I stepped out of the car before Sean could come around for me. He pursed his lips and pulled me roughly to him, his mouth close to my ear. The bite of his fingertips along my hip made me wince.

"Remember, I saved you from him, Kate. Remember what I told you. Think about what I can do if you don't," he whispered close.

He pulled me up short and hugged me tight, his grip almost unbearable.

"You're mine, Kate. Remember that. Your dad wants that. My dad wants that. Think about how upset they'll be. How it will mess up everything they worked for," he said once more.

The door opened, and as Sean pulled away, my father came rushing out of the house. I was surprised to see my sister Stacy close behind him, coming straight for me.

"Kate!" she cried out and grabbed me, pulling me into her arms and out of Sean's.

I felt her arms wrap around me and hold me tightly. I stood there numbly, shocked that she was here. I only had a moment before my father was reaching for me, his unfamiliar hug jarring me out of my shock. He pulled away and looked down at me worriedly. His eyes took in the bruises on my face, at the cuts that had not yet faded. Normally all show and smiles to the public eye, his grey eyes seemed stormy when he looked me over. He looked like he had aged years, his brown hair peppered with a lot more grey.

Everything was grey here.

Even my sister's usually bright demeanor was deadened as I glanced at her while our father held me tight. Her normally warm brown eyes were dull and the circles under them told me she hadn't slept in probably days. I instantly felt the weight of guilt at having pulled her back into this life.

Had she come back just because of me?

"What happened, Katie? Who did this to you?" my father asked, his voice disbelieving as he looked from me to Sean.

I took a breath. Torn to tell him or not. Everything in my body told me this was the moment of truth. I paused, mouth open. I watched as Sean's eyes, so full of confidence one second, faltered.

"Kate," Sean whispered warningly.

"Kate?" my sister asked, suspicion clear on her face. My heart hammered in my chest, fear for Nathan weighing out any fear I had for myself.

Would he really be able to hurt Nathan?

Please God, keep him safe.

"I don't feel well. Can you just take me inside, Dad," I said, stalling for time. I needed him alone if this was going to work at all.

Sean had other plans.

"Yeah, we should take you inside, Kate. You've had a difficult time. What with that guy hurting you and everything," he said, staring me down to force me to say his lies.

Always his lies.

"What guy?" my sister asked, her voice steely before she looked to me. "Kate, tell us what happened? What guy?"

Sean stepped close and held my father's shoulder, like a buddy breaking bad news.

"This guy she was with. He hit her, Mr. Hill. I got there before he could do anything else, but he's bad news!" Sean explained.

"Is this true, Katie?" my dad asked, turning to me. Sean so easily swayed him.

I closed my eyes, feeling my jaw tighten at the notion of lying. I would not say that it was Nathan.

Never.

"Thou shalt not bear false witness," I whispered, feeling my heart tighten at the thought that I could very well hurt Nathan by standing up now. I opened my eyes to see Sean's own harden.

"What was that? Kate, you look sick. Maybe I should take you to the hospital," my sister suggested, pulling me gently from my father's arm, and away from Sean as he tensed near me.

I held Sean's intimidating stare, willing myself to be brave enough to stand up to him. I needed my father to believe. But just the thought of Sean going after anyone else made my whole body shudder in fear.

"Kate, come on. I'll take you to the hospital," Sean said suddenly.

Sean stepped forward, causing me to flinch in towards the only comfort I had at the moment, into my sister's side. Stacy's hands pulled me a little closer, tightening around me. My father blocked me from Sean looking confused, glancing from me to Sean trying to read us.

"Sean. I think you better go home, son. I'm grateful for you bringing her home, but we should get Katie checked out. We can take care of this," he said in that voice he used when he addressed his opponents.

Sean watched me for a second, his mouth open to argue.

"Go home, Sean. You father is worried about you. Katie's home, that's all that's important," my father said, his voice level.

There was no room for Sean to argue. With my sister and father there staring him down, all he could do was leave. Sean took one last look at me, the stern meaning clear in his eyes, before backing away and jumping in his car. I let out a soft breath as his car disappeared down the street.

My knees weakened at the thought of what I had just done.

"Katie? Honey, are you all right?" my father asked tentatively. I looked up to see the concern in his eyes, something I had rarely seen in the last few years, but something seemed to have struck him since I had left.

Or it was because finally, I stood before him bearing proof of something he had long ignored.

"No. No, I'm not," I whispered and struggled to remain standing.

All the fear of retaliation, the fear that Sean was on the phone right that minute calling in his attack on Nathan, I was dizzy and sick. I felt their hands hold me up, my sister helping me into the car, and I closed my eyes when I heard the car start. I kept my eyes closed as I felt us move out.

"Where are we going?" I asked wearily.

"To the hospital. I want to get you checked out. We need to deal with this," my father said, his voice gravelly as he tried to remain calm.

"Deal with this? How are you going to deal with this?" I croaked, the anxiety of Sean's actions slowly winning over.

I needed to get away; back to Nathan before anything happened to him because of me. My dad let out a strangled sort of noise, shaking his head slowly.

"I can't really make sense of anything right now, Katie. You're home. But look at you? Sean brought you home like this? And you were with some guy? Did this guy do this to you?" he asked, glancing at me with that uncomfortable expression he wore when we had family talks.

"Nathan didn't do this," I whispered.

He let out an angry breath and smacked the top of the steering wheel hard, making me jump.

"Why would Sean say that, then? Who the hell is this Nathan? Where the hell have you been this last month? No calls, nothing! Sean called me every single day to give me an update. But you? You didn't even consider how your little trip might affect things here? You just thought you could vanish? For what? A boy? When Sean is heartbroken? You don't think about others, Katie! Stacy was worried. I was worried. You just disappeared. I just... I just don't know what to think," he mumbled and continued to look ahead at the road.

"Believe your daughter, that's what you should think," I murmured and turned into the door of the car, away from him.

"I want to believe you, Katie. I just need you to open up your damned mouth and talk. Who did this? Sean loves you," he insisted, looking intently at me.

Would he listen? He never had before. I looked at him, trying to judge the level of irritation. He was plenty irritated which meant he would think I was lying. He wouldn't want to hear he was wrong all this time.

"Dad," Stacy interjected from the back seat, "Let her tell the nurses that. And you should call Deputy Stevens."

"Why Deputy Stevens? Sean's father is a Deputy Sheriff!" he exclaimed, the harshness of his voice forcing me to shrink into the side of the car.

"Deputy Stevens deals in domestic abuse, Dad," Stacy continued, placing her hand along my shoulder as if to give me strength. "I told you it wouldn't be a good idea to include Deputy Miller."

"Well he wanted to know what the hell his son was doing for over a month," he grated and pulled up to the front doors of the hospital. He turned and looked at me, his eyes wincing when he took in the bruising around my eyes.

"Are you going to tell me, or are you going to protect this guy who hit you? You can trust me," he asked, his voice showing his frustration.

Now or never.

Swallow.

"I've been trying to tell you for months, Dad," I whispered, shaking with fear.

"Tell me what, Katie?" he asked, growing more frustrated. I could tell by his narrowed eyes, he would not believe me. I let out a breath and reached for the door.

"I'll tell you when you call in Deputy Stevens," I replied and got out of the car, heading straight through the ER doors, Stacy guiding me in with a careful hand on my arm.

"Wait a second," my dad growled and grabbed my other arm roughly.

I winced and he let go instantly, realizing his mistake. He looked around the lobby and found no one watching.

"Dad. I will tell you everything, but I want a female officer here. Assault victims get that don't they? Do you really want to hear how your daughter was assaulted, Dad?" I asked, a little loudly.

That got his attention. He swallowed and looked at me again with new eyes. He looked down at my bruises, at my neck, down my arms. When he looked back up into my eyes, I finally saw it.

Fear.

He was afraid finally.

I had to wonder what he was afraid of.

That he would have to deal with it?

That it would somehow tarnish his political career?

That he hadn't been able to stop it?

Did he know, deep down that it was Sean all along?

"I'll call her as soon as we check you in," he whispered and turned to speak to the nurse on duty.

"Everything's going to be all right," Stacy whispered near my ear. "I'm just glad you're safe."

"Why are you here?" I asked and winced at my tone. "Sorry. Thank you for being here, I was just surprised."

She smiled and for a second I could see the old Stacy, the beautiful blonde prom queen in just that smile. But it was only an instant and then she was worried once more.

"I couldn't get ahold of you," she whispered and pulled me over to a group of chairs to sit. "Sean called me and then Dad, threatening to take away my tuition. I'm sorry Katie. I didn't know what to do. Then Dad called yesterday saying that Sean was bringing you home. I knew you'd need someone here for you."

I nodded and tried to swallow, thinking of all the ways I had fouled up my family's life.

"I'm sorry I pulled you out of classes with this mess," I started and leaned into her for support.

"We don't start back for a couple weeks yet," she said and pushed some of my hair aside, her brown eyes narrowing as she took in the damage. "He really did a number on you this time, sis."

I pushed my hair back in place over my temple, hiding as well as I could.

"Who was the boy he was accusing?" she asked and leaned in to look at my downturned eyes.

I shook my head and stood when I heard my name.

"Doesn't matter now," I mumbled and choked back the tears as I walked with the nurse towards the back of the exam rooms. I settled in to wait, changing into their hospital gown. As I stripped, I took in the damage.

I swallowed painfully and eyed myself in the mirror. The image there before me was frightening. The bruises and inflammation around my right eye was the worst on my face, where my eye could only now start to open. The eye itself was blood red. I touched at my jaw tenderly, wincing at the yellow lump there. I had a clear bruise around my neck, a wide band that seemed to wind entirely around. Splotches of purple and yellow dotted my body, where hands had pushed and grabbed.

I closed the gown and turned from the mirror, sickened by what I saw.

How would my father react to this? Would he believe me when he saw the damage?

Had he seen the scratches on Sean?

Could he make the connection?

I balled my hands into fists and rocked on the exam table nervously waiting for the doctors and the police to come in. It seemed to take forever. Every second felt like another way for Sean to alert his friends to hurt Nathan. There was no way to get a hold of Nathan to warn him, and with each moment away from him I felt the peace I had known slipping from me.

A knock at the door made me jump and a tall woman stepped in, carrying a case with her. Stacy and my father followed in after her, my father's eyes bunching up when he saw more of my marks. Another woman stepped in, carrying a camera. Behind her, Deputy Stevens came in.

She was new to the police department, a strong woman with an excellent criminal justice background. The city council had jumped on board to wholeheartedly welcome her to the force, which still irked Sean's father. He had said he was only worried about having a woman on the force for her protection, but I knew Sean's dad hated the thought of her because he felt she was simply weaker. I didn't think she was. I had seen her stare down angry drunk men. She was short and looked small next to many of the men in the department, but it was deceiving.

She was tough.

Which is why I knew she was the one I needed to tell. I had liked her immediately, because she was determined to make this town a better place to live. Her presence had helped a lot of women out. She didn't take domestic violence lightly. So many times I had wanted to go to her, but the fear of the police covering up for Sean always stopped me. And Sean's threats kept me quiet.

I had a reason now. Sean would hurt others.

I took a deep breath, preparing myself for what I knew would come.

"Kate?" Deputy Stevens asked, surprise showing in her widening ice blue eyes.

Had my father not told her it was his daughter she was taking a statement from?

"Hey," I murmured, trying to smile. But even that hurt.

She turned back towards my father, her face hardened as she stared up at him.

"I need to talk with her alone, Councilman Hill," she said quickly.

My dad shook his head and made to argue, but she held up her hand, which silenced him. I had no idea he was that intimidated by her.

"I'll fill you in, but she needs to be able to talk freely without her family here to judge. This needs to be an objective investigation without politics or preferential treatment," she said.

"What does politics have to do with my daughter's assailant?" he shot back at her, his face reddening.

"If you push this, Councilman, you could have an investigation on you. I need this to be done by the book, and since you have affiliation with the department, I need you to step out," she said, her body tensing when he made to move toward her.

My father looked at me for another moment, then nodded and stepped towards the door.

"I'll be right outside, Katie. It'll be okay," he murmured, retreating quickly.

Stacy reached out and held my hand for a second before nodding to the deputy and stepping out as well.

Deputy Stevens sighed and turned back to me, her eyes taking me in.

"I was wondering when you would finally say something, Kate. I wish it had been before we came to this, but I'm proud of you. It takes a lot of courage to speak out," she said softly.

I looked at her in shock.

"You knew?" I whispered, feeling the tears burning my eyes.

She nodded and sat down next to me, her gun belt creaking slightly as she sat. I understood her words to my dad now. She knew that he would protect his best friend's son any way he could.

"I suspected. I asked your dad once or twice when I saw the signs, but he denied it. Said you were just clumsy. I am sorry. I should have pursued further."

I closed my eyes and let out another cleansing breath.

"He wouldn't listen. He'd rather believe the lies than me," I whispered and opened my eyes back up to a much more determined Deputy Stevens.

"This is going to be difficult. I just want you to know that, Kate. But I am here to help you. You don't need to be afraid anymore. It's my job to make sure you are protected, not your father," she said quietly.

I shook my head.

"No, I need to do this. I know that now."

She pulled out her notepad and looked up at me with sympathetic eyes.

"Let's get to it then. We'll need to collect whatever evidence we can, and we'll have to take pictures. I am going to have to ask you some painful questions, okay?"

I nodded and held out my hands.

"I scratched him. I don't know if that will help, it was a couple of days ago. He has welts and cuts on his arms," I said, biting on my lip to keep from crying.

"Good girl," she whispered with an encouraging smile and moved aside as the nurse began the task of scraping under my nails.

I could only hope it helped.

"Can you tell me what happened?" Deputy Stevens asked gently.

I nodded, and for the first time, told my story, feeling such relief knowing finally, someone would hear. And maybe someone would finally make it right.

Chapter 28

"Do you want to grab something at a restaurant?" my dad asked on our way home.

I shook my head and remained quiet, looking at the last of the weak sunlight as it disappeared in the trees as we drove up the coast towards home. Stacy held me a little closer as I had retreated to the backseat with her after the exam.

"Or maybe we can order in?" he suggested, glancing back at me worriedly every chance he could.

"Whatever you want. I'm not that hungry," I replied numbly.

"You have to eat, Katie. We can order Chinese. Maybe watch a movie?" he said and tried to smile. I finally looked up at him and watched his forced smile slip in the rearview mirror. He was looking at me with that uncomfortable grimace again.

"You don't believe it, do you?" I whispered, looking him in the eye.

He frowned and he returned his gaze to the highway. He hadn't spoken about what Deputy Stevens had told him since I had come out of the exam room two hours later. I had heard the heated discussion between them about arrest warrants and bad press going public. I heard her suggest he wasn't trying very hard to bring his little girl's assailant in fast enough. He had threatened her with a lame accusation of insubordination. She shot back something about a judge and going with news coverage. It was election season and my dad caved quickly, allowing Deputy Stevens to call in a warrant to pick up Sean for questioning.

I knew my father would be defensive, and as he looked at me uncomfortably from the mirror repeatedly, he only confirmed it. How could he go against his best friend's son? He was protecting Sean, over me. He doubted me.

He shook his head and kept his eyes on the road.

"I think it's best to let the police deal with the evidence," Stacy interjected, earning another put out look from our father.

"It's not that I don't believe you, Katie. It's just hard for me to think that Sean would do that to you. He adores you," he argued.

My confession to Deputy Stevens had given me courage. She had offered me hope. She had promised to look into speaking with the West Grove police in an effort to protect Nathan and the Bergers. She was what my dad should have been, months ago. But he hadn't. He had practically encouraged Sean. Having known the Millers for years, he had wanted nothing less than the families to be that much closer.

"I was a possession to him, Dad. I ran away for a reason. He didn't have the right to take me like he did," I replied, my throat tightening at the idea that I had lost what I had found.

I thought again about the Bergers and Nathan, and how they had to be worried sick.

"I just thought he would be able to get you back. I couldn't go, I had campaigning here and if I left I would forfeit my chair in council. When he asked for help finding you, I thought I was helping. He wanted to find you. Bring you home," he stammered.

"How did you help him?" I asked, aghast. Stacy held me a little tighter and whispered my name as if to warn me.

He shrugged and let out a long exasperated sigh.

"I sent him money, Katie. He needed money to stay out there looking for you. And I had his father call the Sheriff there in Iowa, trying to get information between two law agencies. You were completely off the grid, not even the sheriff could tell us where you might be. Who knew you would shack up with a bunch of Amish? The sheriff said you could be anywhere. But the Amish? You're joining crazy religious orders now? Seriously Katie, you do the most ridiculous things!" he said, looking at me like I was crazy.

"You paid for him to hunt me down?" I whispered, dumbfounded.

I didn't believe Deputy Miller had even bothered to contact the Sheriff in West Grove, but the fact that my father had paid Sean cut deeply of his betrayal of keeping me safe.

"A hefty portion of savings that should have gone to tuition for you and Stacy," he grunted as he pulled into the drive. "No chance of you going to that cooking school now."

"Then you are to blame for what happened to me as much as he is," I spat out and jumped out of the car before he even had it in park in the yard.

"Katie! Wait! Katie! Come on! We'll eat and we'll talk," he called after me as I ran up the stairs to my room.

I closed and locked the door and turned on the light, squinting at how bright it seemed. Digging into my foot chest, I found my candles I had for when the power went out. I lit them and turned out my light, slipping into bed and watched the shadows as they played across my bedroom walls.

Even my room seemed foreign. Nothing here seemed to suit me anymore. The small television, the computer on the desk, the pile of CDs. I tucked deeper into my covers wanting to hide from it all. Nothing of my life here felt like home anymore. I was suddenly homesick for the creaky little bed and the warmth of my adopted sisters.

Stacy knocked on my door half an hour later, after some muffled arguing downstairs. When I let her in, she took in the candles and quietly slid into the bed behind me, hugging me close to comfort me. She let me lay there quietly for sometime, working out all the thoughts jumbled in my head.

About the Bergers. Fannie and the girls.

What were they doing right now? Had they run to find Jonah and Nathan? Could they even begin to look for me? Would they? Or would they decide it was in God's hands, as I had come to learn was their way?

Nathan.

I let the tears fall quietly as I thought of him and what he must be feeling with me gone. Someone else, taken from him. He was alone again. I closed my eyes and lay there in the dark, seeing in my head the face I missed most. He had to be hurting. I could feel the deep ache in my heart, and knew it was not just mine.

I had to get back somehow.

Stacy stroked my hair and let out a soft sigh behind me.

"I can't stay here, Stacy," I whispered in the growing darkness.

She sat up and regarded me thoughtfully.

"You can come back with me," she suggested. "I have a couch to sleep on. With some time, we can get you into classes."

I shook my head and shifted in the bed, holding back a groan from the aches and pains.

"I had a place, Stacy," I start and closed my eyes, trying to figure out where to start.

"With this Nathan," she said, prompting me easily.

"He is great, Stacy," I started and couldn't help the slow smile on my face. She chuckled and leaned up against the headboard, drawing my head into her lap.

"So tell me all about him," she said and listened as I launched into my journey.

Broken down busses.

A scared but intriguing young man with a magnetic pull to my heart.

A simpler life.

Happiness and love. Purpose and family.

All the things I had wanted to find at the beginning of that trip.

"And you can see yourself there?" she asked gently. "Even with the crazy religious beliefs and patriarchal structure?"

My sister was always one to defy gender roles.

"It's not like that," I argued, looking up into her eyes. "They have religion, yes. Their life lives by it. But it's more. I can't explain it. And Jonah and the men I have met are respectful of their wives. And Nathan is sweet and not overbearing. He's more. It's just...there's more love there."

She laughed and shifted under me, slipping out of bed and shaking her head.

"You haven't had that many good role models, Kate. You were there for a few weeks; I don't think you could experience everything about them in that time. I wouldn't jump into the first bed you find that seems sweet and innocent. You'll find yourself with twelve kids and no painkillers," she said, her voice a little wistful.

"I can't stay here," I said again softly.

"I know," she replied and leaned down to kiss me on the head. "Let's give Deputy Stevens a couple of days to find and arrest Sean. Let you get healed up too. I leave the day after tomorrow. You can always come with me."

I nodded and blew out the candles after she left. My room darkened as the sun disappeared, and all I could think of was what I might have been doing at the Bergers. Dinner done, dishes washed, maybe out on the swing already.

What was Nathan doing with me gone?

I fell asleep with him in my head, the image of his back as he walked up his lonely hill following me in my dreams all night long. Tossing and turning, never finding myself comfortable in my old bed, I found myself awake before the dawn. I couldn't fight my internal clock. I had grown used to waking up early, and even with the time change and my battered body, I had to get up.

Turning on the overly bright fluorescent light to the bathroom I washed up, feeling the strange vibration of my old toothbrush drill away at my head. I glanced in the mirror, grimacing at the bruises. The swelling around my eye had gone down considerably, but the evidence was still there, even if my dad refused to believe it.

I looked at myself again, willing myself to be strong. I'd be here long enough to see Sean arrested. I hoped they didn't want me there for the trial. I frowned in the mirror at the thought of being here for months while we waited. Months of dealing with my dad's uncomfortable looks, months without Nathan.

I couldn't do it.

I needed resolution. I needed my dad to understand, and then let me go. Perhaps this was the means I needed to do as the Elders had asked. To finalize my goodbyes to the English world.

Making my way down to the kitchen I sighed at the disarray I found there and set to work cleaning it up. I would have never worried as much before, but Fannie kept a clean kitchen, and my father's embarrassed me. I had the room cleaned from floor to ceiling; trash taken out to the can outside, and breakfast nearly done by the time my father came down at his usual six thirty. He stopped in the doorway, his mouth open wide when he saw what I had done.

"Katie, this is cleaner than it's ever been. How long have you been up?" he asked, looking around to find I had even wiped down the cobwebs on the ceiling fan.

"Before dawn," I mumbled and slipped his plate of food onto the table before he had even sat down.

I poured myself some juice and brought his coffee to him before sliding in to sit across from him at the table. He eyed the meal in wonder and shook his head in amazement.

"You made all this? What are these?" he asked and pointed to the corn cakes.

I averted my eyes and concentrated on buttering my toast with the margarine.

"They're corn cakes. I didn't have everything I needed, but maybe they're all right," I whispered, feeling my throat burn.

"Mmm, they're not half bad. Could use some honey or jam, though. Kind of bland," he replied and dug in to the eggs.

I watched quietly as he ate, barely touching my food as I thought about how Nathan had smiled and thanked me every time I had made him food. Never a complaint. Just grateful to be eating.

I missed his smile.

I missed the simple things.

I had been gone for three days now.

"So what do you want to do today? I thought I would take the day off," he said, just as Stacy shuffled into the kitchen.

"Don't you have to go pressure Deputy Miller about finding his son?" I asked, a little harshly.

He laid down his fork and watched me for a minute, as if what I had said was inappropriate. Stacy hung back by the coffee pot, ready to intervene. I was glad for her presence, and for her silence. When he saw I wouldn't back down, my father pulled away from the table and leaned back.

"He has people looking for him. Bill promised to bring him in for questioning when he came home. That's all I can do, Katie," he replied stiffly.

I remained quiet and distracted myself by looking around the kitchen, at the freshness there and thought of the rest of the house.

"I want to clean today. This house is a mess," I replied and stood to clear away the dishes.

He glanced around the room and let out a sigh.

"You don't have to try so hard, Katie. We can take it easy today. Watch a movie or something. I'd say we could all go out but," he said and grimaced, watching me carefully.

Of course I wouldn't be acceptable for public appearances, looking the way I did.

I looked out the kitchen window at the fog and rain lightly falling. It had been that way since I had come home. No sun, no heat. Just the cold wet California coastal dreariness.

"It's raining. I'd rather not go out when it's raining," I replied coolly and turned to start the water for dishes.

"We'll stay in," Stacy suggested. "You can help me with some things on the computer."

I nodded and concentrated on the dishes, the room growing silent except for the running of water. I had thought our father had left until I heard his voice a few minutes later.

"I'm sorry, Katie."

I paused in scraping the dishes to turn and look his way. He sat there, slightly hunched in his chair and looking down at his hands in his lap. He was a tall man, much like Nathan, but now he seemed small in comparison. He seemed so insignificant as he slouched there, so unlike Jonah or any of the Amish men who would have sat tall and protected their family.

Frank Hill was nothing but a coward, all show for his public audiences, but in his home, he was lost.

I waited for him to continue.

"I can't begin to think of what you have gone through," he started.

I laid the plate down and leaned against the counter, waiting for more. Waiting for him to acknowledge what I had been trying to tell him for so long. How his neglect had made me feel insignificant. How his attitude towards Sean had made me think he cared for him more than me.

His words surprised me.

"I'll make this right, Katie. You don't need to run anymore. I'll get this figured out. I'll take care of Sean," he said, his eyes narrowing as if in determination.

"Then you should have had him locked up when we first got home, Dad. He's gone, probably hiding with friends on campus or down in San Francisco. Probably using the money you gave him," I replied, my voice a little rough in my ears.

He looked up and shook his head vehemently.

"No. Sean wouldn't run. Bill told me last night. He'll bring him in. And if this DNA comes back positive," he began.

"When the DNA comes back positive, Dad!" I exclaimed, Stacy stepping in to hold me back as I advanced on our father. "When it comes back! Still you don't believe me! What will it take? Him beating me in front of you? Me dead? Why can't you believe me?"

"I believe you, Katie," he murmured, looking down again, uncomfortable.

"You believe me because I went around you. The evidence is there now. Neither you nor Mr. Miller can hide it now," I said.

"Bill would never hide anything, Katie," he spat out, his eyes hardening again. "You were the one that hid. Ran away instead of facing your problems."

"Not anymore," I whispered and turned back to the dishes.

"I'll fix it, Katie. I'll keep you safe."

"I was safe where I was, Dad. Until Sean came. I won't be safe until he is locked up," I replied and plunged the dishes into the hot water, fighting back the tears.

"I'll make sure no one hurts you again, Katie. Now that you're back, I'll be here more. We'll do more things. I'll quit the council," he started only to pause when I shook my head and laughed again.

"I'm not staying, Dad. As soon as Sean's in jail, I'm leaving," I said. "You can keep your council seat. It was always more important than us. Mom knew. I know now."

"That's unfair," he said and stood. "My work has kept a roof over your head and kept you happy."

"Not happy, Dad," I replied, never looking back. "Kept, yes. But never happy. I was happy in Iowa."

I could feel him moving behind me, and I closed my eyes, bracing for him to hit me. Or push me. Anything.

"I don't think it's a good idea for you to go traipsing back to wherever Sean found you. You belong here. This is your home. You belong here," he argued, his voice only a little closer. He knew to stay away it seemed.

"I have nothing here. As soon as I can, Dad. I'm gone," I whispered and returned to cleaning.

He was quiet as I worked, and when I looked back several minutes later, I saw both he and Stacy had gone, leaving me to the quiet to think. I didn't want the quiet to think though. Thinking only made me remember those I had left and what they would be doing. I needed to keep busy or I'd go insane.

I finished up the dishes and made a list of chores to accomplish. The list was long as I looked through the house. Laundry to be done, dusting, vacuuming. If it were not raining, the carpets would have gone out to be beaten clean. I sighed and went to work, happy for the work to occupy my time.

The things I had done before I had found the Bergers didn't interest me anymore. My father stayed clear of me, watching television or talking on the phone with Deputy Miller about Sean. I caught a few words: surveillance, warrants, tests needed to be processed faster than they were. I wondered if maybe he thought I was right with Sean disappearing, or that Sean had already run. I wondered if Deputy Miller had called him with news of Sean conveniently gone. A cold shiver ran through me at the thought that he could show up at any time.

Or he was on his way back to deal with Nathan.

How far would Sean go to get back at me?

I cleaned a little harder, trying to forget about the fear and loneliness that gripped me. After only a month with them, the Berger's had become such a part of my life. Nathan had become everything. I missed them desperately. And I was afraid for them.

Stacy ventured to help me with lunch, trying unsuccessfully to cheer me up. In the end she and my dad ate their lunch in silence in the kitchen, and I retreated up to my room to sit and wait for the laundry to finish. I felt restless as I lay there on my big plush bed. I wasn't used to having so much free time. I moved around in my room, straightening up, sorting through my clothes to find something I felt comfortable in. I tried to read but I couldn't, a headache coming on from the grey light in the room. I sighed and made my way back downstairs, desperate to do something, anything that would get my mind off the tortuous thoughts of what the Bergers and Nathan would be doing, and if they had tried to find me at all.

I made dinner, something simple and lackluster that my dad merely grunted and shoveled in.

Business as usual.

Stacy tried again to pull me from my solitude by offering to play a board game, but I refused her. I could see the hurt in her eyes at my refusal, but every moment I spent with my family made me wish I were back in Iowa.

I went to bed early by my father's standards, late by my new ones. But the fear of Sean coming for me made me restless. I had trouble closing my eyes until exhaustion took over, only to be confronted with paranoid visions as I slept. I dreamt of running through the corn, up a familiar hill, to find myself lost, pushing and shoving through endless rows dry, rustling stalks that grabbed at me. I woke up several times in the night, sweating and tangled in my sheets as if I had truly run in my sleep.

My dad retreated back to work the next day, promising to come home early. Still no news of Sean, and still no test results. I grew more restless, needing something to do. But the house was clean. And the rain poured outside, trapping me indoors. I was scared of being ambushed should I walk outside the house. Sean had friends here too.

The house became a prison of sorts, leaving my mind to drift over scenarios that included Sean coming after me or of Nathan being harmed because of Sean's jealous rage. I grew more worried that Sean had left to go back to Iowa when I overheard Stacy arguing with my dad as soon as he came home late in the afternoon. My dad went so far as to slam the front door when the conversation turned to my sister accusing my father of helping to hide Sean from the law. Stacy soon stomped to her room, her own door slamming to end the argument.

I pulled away from the window in my room, tired of all the rain, wishing for the warm sunset over Nathan's hill. I hoped I would be able to see it again soon. I could feel the distance between us. I could feel my heart growing heavier at the length of time away. Four days now, and no way to comfort him. No way to tell him I was even alive.

He would think the worst.

Hunger finally drove me back to the kitchen, my only refuge from my restlessness. I was contemplating spaghetti when I heard a knock at the front door. I heard my father walk towards the hall to answer it. Fear gripped me and I paused in the kitchen doorway when I saw him frown at whatever he saw through the door.

I held my breath and pushed myself back into the doorway of the kitchen, scared that perhaps it was Sean. Or the police to tell us that Sean was indeed gone. My dad glanced at me and put his hand up as if to warn me to stay away. I grabbed a hold of the doorframe to brace for the worst as he opened the door.

The smell of the rain assaulted my senses as the cool wind blew in.

And a voice.

"Pleasant day, Mr. Hill? I am Nathan Fisher. I am here to bring Kate home."

I felt my heart jump in my throat at the words.

Nathan was here.

Nathan had come to bring me home.

CHAPTER 29

I was shaking.

His voice.

Nathan was here?

I couldn't get my head around it.

I took a halting step forward, terrified that my mind had suddenly snapped and that I was imagining things.

My father stood in the doorway, blocking my view. But I knew that voice.

"Please, Mr. Hill. I have come a long way. Is Kate here?"

Maybe it was the pain in his soft voice. Maybe it was the magnetic pull I felt whenever he was close.

Maybe it was the desperate need to be comforted again.

I found myself slipping around my father to find Nathan standing before me. His eyes widened a second before I had my arms around him, wanting to feel him against me.

Please be real.

"Kate."

His voice was choked as his arms wrapped around me, cold and wet. He was standing there, on my porch, drenched from the rain.

Away from his home.

In English clothes.

It didn't even faze me.

I couldn't appreciate the beauty of him, because he was trembling from the cold California coastal chill that must have caught him unawares. I pulled away to look at him. To be sure it was really he, because my head had hoped and imagined such things before too many times.

He looked different in these clothes. Taller and thinner, and his face looked different.

Pale and drawn.

Blue lips.

Trembling.

"You're soaked," I breathed, feeling the rain that soaked through his clothes bleeding into mine as he held me.

"It is raining," he murmured, his dark eyes taking me in, seeing everything. "I did not think about the rain."

His teeth chattered and I felt his body shudder again.

"You need to come in out of the weather," I replied, my mind swiftly thinking about caring for him in his need.

Had to get him dry. Had to get him warm.

Had to know he was real.

I reached for his cold hand and pulled him towards the door.

"Kate," my father said roughly behind me. "Who the hell is this?"

I tugged Nathan inside, towards the stairs, never looking away.

"This is Nathan."

Wasn't it obvious?

I pulled him up the stairs, his eyes never leaving mine as he stumbled behind me. I heard my father below, calling my name in agitation, but I didn't care. Everything in me was saying Nathan was here, and I needed to get him out of his wet clothes.

I switched on the bathroom light to which his eyes squinted at the harshness of it.

"I know, you'll get used to it in a minute," I whispered and moved to turn on the shower, to get the steam going.

"Kate," he whispered, his voice quivering. He was looking at me again, at everything about me with pained eyes.

I shook my head and looked at his chest, at the buttons I was unfastening quickly to get rid of the wet shirt that clung to the t-shirt underneath.

"We have to get you warm. I know it's not that cold out, but you're not used to it. Your lips are blue. You'll get sick. I couldn't stand it if you got sick," I said, seeing only the task at hand.

Get him warm.

Take care of him.

Pulling off the soaked t-shirt to reveal shivering skin.

"Kate," he said, a little louder.

I felt his cold hands on mine, stalling me at his half unbuttoned jeans. The gentle pressure of his hands broke me from my trance so that I could look upon him and see that he was really there, standing before me shivering and bare-chested.

He gently pried my hands away, frowning as he looked down at me.

"I can do this, Kate. You do not have to tend to me," he whispered gently, his cold fingertips tracing along my cheek, just under the bruise that lay there.

I looked down again, embarrassed at what he saw and nodded.

"Sorry. I don't know what I was doing. I just. You're here," I choked out and put my head in my hands, feeling my breath catch at the immensity of having him there with me. I felt his arms around me once more, cementing it for me.

Nathan was here.

"Kate!"

I jumped at the sound of my name outside the bathroom door. I wiped my eyes and stepped away hurriedly, looking down at my feet as I took a step towards the door.

"I'll get you a change of clothes. And then I'll make you something to eat," I said hurriedly, avoiding his eyes, before cracking the door open and slipping out to face Dad who seemed to loom just outside the door. Stacy was coming out of her room, her eyes wide when she noticed someone else in the bathroom behind me just as I closed the door.

But our father wasn't in the mood to wait for answers.

"Care to tell me who exactly this Nathan is? And why you think it's a good idea to have him taking a shower in my house?" he hissed, pointing towards the bathroom.

"A shower?" Stacy interjected, her eyebrows rising as she looked at me expectantly.

I pushed away from the door and moved past them, down the stairs to where the laundry lay folded up. I found a t-shirt of my father's, and a pair of sweat pants. I paused over the boxer shorts, thinking in bittersweet reflection of the last time I had dealt with Nathan's underclothes.

Turning around, my father was hovering again.

"Who is he, Katie?"

I couldn't step away from his intimidating stare, but it was difficult to explain who Nathan was to me in this world.

"He's her boyfriend," Stacy answered for me, glancing back up the stairs with a curious look on her face.

The news that I had a boyfriend other than Sean confounded my father; I could tell by his open mouth, his disbelieving eyes.

"You ran away from Sean and got yourself a boyfriend while you were gone? While you were figuring out life, you find this kid?" he asked, incredulous.

I lifted my chin a bit in defiance.

"I figured out a lot of things while I was gone, Dad. But you haven't once really asked me about what happened while I was gone, have you?" I asked, my eyes challenging him to argue with me.

He blinked and stood there looming over me as if to say something else, before he took a step back, surrendering. He swallowed and glanced up at the ceiling, as if he could see Nathan above us in the shower as the water shut off.

"Well don't expect him to stay here tonight," he grumbled and turned to walk out.

"Then I'll leave too. I go where he goes," I said, my heart hammering in my throat at the conviction I had in my voice.

My father turned back to me, gauging the authority in my voice. I stood there, trying not to shake. I had no doubts that I would leave with Nathan if my father refused him. It was just the simple fact of leaving the house, with Sean still on the loose that scared me. I needed closure with all of this before I finally did leave.

And I knew without a doubt now that I would leave this all behind.

"Katie," Stacy intervened once more. "This is the perfect opportunity to let us get to know him. I'm sure Dad sees that. We don't want you to leave before we know where it is you're going, right, Dad?"

She looked at him as if to persuade him to let Nathan stay.

"He can sleep on the couch," he grumbled and started towards the hallway. "I'm not happy he's here. I don't like the idea that you turned your back on Sean for some kid I don't even know. If he stays, I expect answers."

"Nathan wasn't the one I was running from, Dad," I said, feeling the anger bubble up inside of me once more.

"Then your boyfriend won't mind answering some questions to clear things up," he said and turned back down the hall, disappearing into his office.

"Don't worry, Kate," Stacy whispered. "If he is anything like you say he is, I'm sure this guy can handle our father. And besides, I'm curious."

I couldn't help the small smile when I looked up to see Stacy's eyes shining with mischief. She shrugged and wiggled her eyebrows before disappearing down the hall after our father. I took a calming breath and made my way back up stairs, knocking on the bathroom door quietly, and intent on taking care of the man that was most important to me.

"Nathan?" I said softly through the door.

The door cracked open, his face peeking out. I could tell his chest was still bare, the reflection in the mirror behind him showed off a lot more than he realized. I looked back into his eyes and quickly thrust the clothes towards him.

"I have a change of clothes for you. We can dry the other ones," I murmured.

He took the clothes from me and looked down at them in his hands, bashful.

"Thank you, Kate. I will be out in a moment. Do not leave?" he asked, his voice sounding rough.

"I'll be right here."

A small smile appeared on his lips and he nodded as he closed the door. I could hear him in the bathroom, fumbling around until less than a minute later; he was opening the door and stepping out, clean and dry, except for his hair that was damp and finger combed haphazardly. I took the bundle of damp clothes from his hands and motioned him to follow me back downstairs. He stayed close, his hand brushing along the small of my back until we reached the kitchen, where I tossed his damp clothes into the dryer. I was turning around to face him when I felt his fingertips along my arm, tracing along the bruises I knew were there.

"Please forgive me," he whispered.

I looked up into his tortured eyes as they took me in again, studying and wincing at the damage he saw there. I looked back down, away from the sweet eyes I had dreamed of. They had worried over me in my dreams as they did now. The pain in them was too much to bear in person.

"Please don't. It's not your fault. Please, just don't look at me like that. I'll heal," I said quietly and laid a hand over the worst part of my bruised face, ashamed at having him see me as I was.

"I promised to keep you safe," he choked out and took my hand away gently. "What he did to you. I cannot forgive myself for what has happened. I should have been there with you."

His fingertips stroked across my bruised jaw, up to where the swelling was almost gone by my temple. I felt his gaze on me, seeing all that had happened.

"So much hurt and I could not stop it," he continued whisper soft.

Whispering soft words into my ear to comfort me, I couldn't handle much more.

Too much.

"You're here," I finally managed and leaned into him so he couldn't see me cry.

"I am here. You do not have to be afraid anymore, Kate," he whispered gently and wrapped his arms around me, drawing me in closer to his warmth.

"I thought I'd never see you again," I cried into his shoulder and gripped him harder.

He stroked my hair and held me up as I cried softly, my breath evening out as I felt his energy soothe me. He offered me the support I needed, holding me up when he must have been utterly exhausted. I could hear the fatigue in his voice when he spoke.

"I was so afraid I would not find you. The journey here was a trial in patience. And not knowing if he had taken you here. I was afraid I would be on the wrong trail," he murmured and touched his nose to my hair, inhaling softly.

"How did you know where to find me?" I asked, looking up into his worried gaze.

"Emma gave me your bag. Your identification was in it. The sheriff station printed out a route for me to take to get here. And I had help," he confided, smiling.

"Who helped you?" I asked, curious.

Nathan arriving was a surprise enough, but having travelled in the English world, and having on English clothes told me he had to have had help.

"Benjamin helped me," he replied. And in his eyes I could see a fondness in his old friend. I remembered Benjamin from the Gathering. The Bishop's son.

"Benjamin?"

He nodded and looked down at our hands intertwined.

"I accused him of telling your Englisher where you were. He had not known what had happened. He told me about how Jeff and Joanna had talked at length about my new girl and me. Benjamin knew that meant you. The English had been with Jeff one night when Benjamin was there. He was riddled with guilt, so he offered to drive me to the bus station and help me get to you. He was the one who told me that your English intended to take you home. I owe Benjamin much," he said quietly.

I closed my eyes and inwardly prayed that Benjamin would be all right. That Jeff would not retaliate.

"Even still. Fannie and Emma described how he took you," he choked out, closing his eyes once more.

"Are they all right? Why didn't Jonah come?" I asked.

Nathan shook his head and looked up at me with sorrowful eyes.

"Emma wanted to come with me, she was frantic. Fannie and Abigail were inconsolable. Fannie could not speak when we first arrived. She was like I had never seen her. And Abigail would not stop crying. I think Jonah knew he would need to stay for them. He wanted to come, he is upset for not coming," he replied.

I started to cry again, the pain I had caused my new family overwhelming me.

"It will be all right, Kate. We will call them in the morning and let them know you are safe," he reassured me. I looked up in confusion.

"How will we call them? You don't have phones."

He shook his head and chuckled.

"We do have phones, Kate. They are just out in the field where many can use. Jonah has had Emma wait by the one near our home since I left," he explained.

"I'm sorry I caused so much trouble," I said quietly, the magnitude of how much I had changed their lives finally crashing down on me.

"I prayed every moment that he would not hurt you. That he would not harm you in such a way as you would lose yourself," he stammered, clenching his eyes shut at the thought I know filtered in his head.

I squeezed his hand.

367

"He...He...tried," I stammered and stopped, afraid to go into it.

I felt him tense, his hand tightening around mine until he pulled it away, perhaps afraid he'd hurt me. I could see the question in his tortured expression.

"He stopped...He tried... right after...he wanted to prove I was his. I fought but," I stammered, ashamed.

I couldn't say much more, at that moment we heard a tremendous crash at the entryway. I jumped at the sound, clutching at Nathan's hand when I saw Dad's glare at the doorway.

"You didn't tell me that part," he grated, taking a step into kitchen. In his hand were the remains of a glass he had been drinking from. "Deputy Stevens told me the rape kit was clean. Sean assured me... He tried to rape you?"

I stood there dumbstruck.

Sean had assured him? I couldn't form the words, because discovering that my father might know where Sean was would be the worst betrayal of all.

"Did he touch you like that?" he yelled, causing me to shrink towards Nathan. I could only nod; trembling at the rage I could see in his face. He threw the broken glass into the sink and stormed off down the hall. When he came back, he had on his jacket and ball cap, keys in his hand.

"You are not to leave, you understand me? I will deal with this," he grated and slammed the door behind him as he left.

We heard the car pull out, screeching tires as it sped down the road. I sat there breathing hard, confused by my father's sudden shift in moods. For two days, he had made me think it was my fault. Now he was out the door and I assumed off to hunt down Sean.

Had he known where he was all along?

"What the hell is going on?" I heard Stacy exclaim from the hall.

Stacy appeared in the doorway, looking back where our father had disappeared. When she noticed Nathan standing protectively beside me, she turned red and immediately stepped in to introduce herself.

"Sorry," she started, clearing her throat as she extended her hand to him. "I'm Katie's sister, Stacy."

Nathan took her hand politely and offered her a timid smile.

"I am pleased to meet you, Stacy," he replied and held me a little closer. "I have heard many nice things about you."

Stacy quirked her eyebrow at me and grinned, the old flirt emerging.

"Oh really?" she teased. "Well all of it was true, I'm sure."

I pulled away from Nathan to grab the dustpan, intent on cleaning up the broken glass in the hall before one of us stepped on it. Nathan ghosted behind me, bending over to pick up the bigger pieces while I swept up the small shards.

"Your father is a very troubled man."

I looked at Nathan, his face serious as he looked towards where my father had left, and I burst out laughing. His eyes widened in alarm and I couldn't help it, I laughed harder. It certainly wasn't funny, and the tears weren't happy tears. Maybe it was because someone finally saw it. Everyone thought my father was a star citizen and pillar of the community. Nathan's simple words drove it home. Finally someone understood. Or I was just finally losing it.

Nathan pulled me to him and held me tight as I fought to bring the laughter under control. I clutched at him hard, gripping my dad's old shirt in my hands and tugging him closer, needing his warmth around me. His heat calmed me, and soon I was hiccupping in his shoulder, quiet at least for the moment. His hand smoothed my hair, his lips brushed across my temple as he whispered softly.

"You will be all right, Kate. I will take care of you. We will go home. We will leave this behind. This is not your world."

"I'm so glad you're here, that you came for me," I whispered, weeping.

"I will come for you always, Kate," he murmured and pulled me away so that he could look down into my eyes. "You are my everything. I will not lose you again. We will go home."

His fingers traced over my cheek, his eyes more determined than I had ever seen.

"I will protect you. I will not allow anyone to separate us again."

I leaned in and touched my lips to his, barely there as I tried to temper the need to simply kiss him hard and hold him forever. Stacy was in the kitchen watching after all. She cleared her throat to remind us.

"You must be hungry," I whispered, happy for the timid smile on his lips. As long as I had known Nathan, I had wanted to feed him.

"You do not need to tend to me," he murmured, the amusement glittering in his eyes.

Finally, a moment when I saw the man I had discovered beyond the heartache.

"Yes, I do," I replied and brought him over to the table, settling him in a chair while I turned to rummage through the cupboards for something fast to make. He watched as I moved around, but remained quiet as I prepared a quick bowl of soup and simple sandwich. Stacy sat at the table across from him, quiet as she regarded us together. She finally spoke when I turned from the stove.

"So, Nathan," she started, glancing at me cautiously before continuing. "Kate tells me she wants to go back. But it means that she would need to sever ties with us."

I grit my teeth at her directness and took a step towards them, halting when I noticed Nathan's contemplative face.

"The issue is not you, Stacy," he said quietly. "In order for Kate to live amongst the Amish, she must give up her English ways. Our Elders are concerned with the violence and neglect from her father and the Englisher, Sean. I do not think it applies necessarily to you."

"Our father won't agree to it," she said, looking at me to confirm her statement.

"It's not his decision, Stacy," I said, feeling defensive.

"He won't just let you leave to live in some community that doesn't allow us to be a part of your life," she said, and turned to Nathan again. "Surely you understand if someone told you that you couldn't see your family ever again?"

He looked down at his clasped hands and let out a sigh. I stepped forward to him and put my hand on his shoulder in the hopes to comfort him.

"His family died last year, Stacy," I said softly.

"I'm sorry, I didn't know," she stammered and blushed. "She's all I have. I don't want to lose her."

He nodded and offered her a sad smile.

"I would speak to the Elders on your behalf. I would agree you should not lose your only sister."

"Is that how it works? Your Elders tell you what to do?" Stacy asked.

"They make our laws," he said simply, straightening a little at her inquiries.

"The Elders will decide whether I can join their community, Stacy. It's their way," I replied.

"So there's a chance you won't be allowed to stay with him," she said and I frowned at the thought. I had thought of that many times, but had chosen to work at proving myself.

"I have faith she will succeed," Nathan replied, the determination clear on his face.

"And if she isn't?" Stacy pressed.

"Then we will see," he said and squeezed my hand. "I have faith."

She nodded and made to stand.

"Well, I appreciate you understanding that I want to keep in touch with my sister," she said and looked at me meaningfully before excusing herself so we could be alone.

I let out an irritated grunt and moved back to the stove to pour his soup into a bowl.

"She's not one to conform to old fashioned views," I explained.

"Not many understand our ways," he replied. "She is concerned for your well being. I understand her fears."

"I'm old enough to make my own choices," I grated.

"It is always your choice. I would never force you to do something you did not wish," he replied, looking up at me with those deep eyes I had missed.

"I know. It's why I feel safe with you."

He murmured his thanks when I set his meal before him, cocking his head to the side when he saw I hadn't made anything for myself. I sat down beside him and pushed the plate towards him.

"I'm not hungry," I said, easing the concerned pout on his lips. He hesitated before nodding and reciting meal prayers quietly before digging in to the meal eagerly, his eyes closing for a moment at the first bite.

I watched him as he ate, the events of the last few days taking a back seat at the sight of the man before me. This felt right, being with him, smiling at the contented expression on his face while he ate what I offered him. He complimented me again and again with each bite. Gone was the proud man I had first met who refused help. Now we got on so easily. I could see myself with him by his side so much more clearly with each moment he was there with me. He had taken a risk to come for me, against all odds. He had made my well being his priority, something I had encountered little of with anyone else.

The choice was clear to me.

I would go where he went.

Nathan let out a relieved sigh and wiped at his lips when he had eaten everything I had given him, his tired eyes drooping from the effect of a full belly, and perhaps a long journey with no sleep.

"We should get you to bed," I whispered, laughing when I saw his eyes widen and his ears burn.

I laughed a little harder and pulled him up out of the chair.

"I meant that you've had a long trip and you looked tired. What were you thinking?" I teased, enjoying the gentle tug of his lip as he shook his head.

I held his hand and walked him out towards the living room, eyeing the couch.

"Dad says you have to sleep on the couch," I stated, thinking.

"Of course. I would certainly do as your father wishes," he replied quickly.

He followed me to the linen closet in the hall where we kept the spare blankets and pillows. We set up his bed in silence, my thoughts wandering to what it would be like to have him with me every night. I shook my head at the thought.

One thing at a time. We needed to get out of here first, and then deal with the rest.

I leaned over and kissed him softly as he settled in, his eyes already growing heavy as he lay down in the comfort of his makeshift bed. I hated to leave him. Having him here with me once more, I never wanted to be away again, but there were rules, in his world and in mine. I made to stand, ready to leave when his hand came out and held mine, pulling me back towards him. His eyes caught mine, deep and thoughtful as he looked on me.

"Will you stay here for a little while? I would like to feel you close. To know this is real. To know you are here. That this is not a dream and I am still on that bus," he murmured.

As if he knew what I needed, I lay down and tucked in next to him, almost on top of him to keep from falling off the edge. He adjusted some to give me room, but his hand slid down to pull my leg over him, holding me there firmly as he let out a soft breath and closed his eyes.

"In my world, parents would allow young couples to sleep together sometimes. It is not common and frowned upon in some communities. It is expected that the courting couple behave, knowing that the girl's parents are in the next room. But maybe," he whispered and yawned, holding me a little closer.

I smiled at this little bit of new Amish culture I was learning.

"I don't think Emma or Abigail would like it much," I giggled, and hugged him closer.

He laughed softly and brushed his lips against the top of my head, breathing in deeply.

"I missed your touch. I missed your scent. I missed all of you. I will not let you go again," he sighed and let out a long breath.

"Me too," I murmured and listened as his breathing slowed.

He was out almost immediately, exhaustion finally settling in. I lay there watching him sleep, his mouth curved in a contented smile, his eyes moving as he dreamt. I wondered what he dreamt about, if his dreams had been as dark as mine these last few days. His body twitched beneath me and I thought to slip away, but I didn't.

I was selfish.

Lying there with Nathan, with his warm body against me provided me the comfort I had needed these last few days. I knew things had changed between us. I could feel it. Things were more intense, like he and I both had come to realize that this last week had been the worst of our lives being apart. I saw it in how he looked at me, even with the pain. He needed me as much as I needed him.

I needed him close.

I could not spend another moment away. I lay there and watched him sleep, unable to bring myself to sleep as I waited for Dad to return. I fought my heavy eyelids, until fatigue won over. I dreamed of fertile fields, and a large house that was bright and sunny. And the man in my arms as he smiled and kissed me, showering me with all his love.

One day soon.

CHAPTER 30

I shook myself awake at first light and slipped carefully from Nathan's embrace, his body turning away as he settled in without me in his slumber. I peeked outside to see if my father had returned and noticed his car was there. A moment of dread crept through me at the thought of my father finding me with Nathan in the living room, but he had not disturbed us. I wondered if he had simply gone straight to bed.

Hearing a noise in the kitchen, I found him, seated at the dining table, his jacket still on and staring at the beer in his hand.

He looked defeated.

I felt Nathan behind me, silent but comforting as he waited behind me, his arm wrapped loosely around my waist. Dad looked up and saw us in the dawn's light in the doorway. He averted his eyes and stood, making his way to his office. We followed him where he slumped into his chair and closed his eyes.

"Dad?" I asked needing to know what happened.

"It's done," he replied, so quiet it was almost lost.

I took a halting breath. What did that mean?

"What's done? What happened? Is he...dead?" I asked, having mixed feelings about the idea of him being dead.

Dad opened his eyes in shock, shaking his head at me.

"Of course not, Kate! But I am sure he wishes he were. He lied to me and betrayed my trust," he replied roughly and took a deep drink.

"What do you mean?" I asked, feeling my own sense of betrayal that he had known where Sean was all along creep through me. "You knew where he was, didn't you?"

My father turned and looked me in the eye hard.

"I got him for you. I took care of it. And now he's in custody in the emergency room. It's over, Kate. You're safe. He won't hurt you again," he said, rubbing his bloodshot eyes.

"How did you find him?" I asked. "How did you take care of him, Dad?"

He turned and looked up at his pictures on his wall; at all of the sailing trips and political campaigns he had done with Sean and his father. It had been my father's wall of fame, and sadly there were fewer pictures of his family there.

"Can't you just be happy that he is no longer a threat? It doesn't matter how I found him or what I did to him. He's in custody, Kate. And if those tests come back positive, then he'll be put away for a long time and you can do whatever you want," he said and waved towards Nathan who stood just behind me.

I felt Nathan straighten up beside me.

"I need a moment alone with him," my father said.

"Dad," I started, afraid in his present mood it would lead to Nathan getting hurt.

"You want to go away with him?" he asked. I nodded. "Then grant me a few minutes alone to talk to him. Go make some breakfast or coffee or something."

I felt Nathan's hand press against my shoulder.

"It will be all right, Kate," he whispered. "We have not had a chance to meet and talk. It is necessary."

I let Nathan move past me and watched as my father stood half way to extend his hand to Nathan. I tensed on reflex, unsure what my father's intentions really were. Nathan remained straight-backed and polite as ever.

"Frank Hill. We really didn't get a proper introduction," my father started, seemingly civil.

Nathan stood a little taller and took his hand firmly, shaking it man to man.

"I apologize, Mr. Hill. I had travelled for a few days with little sleep. I do not know what you must think of me, given my intrusion. I am Nathan Fisher," he said formally.

I could see Dad sizing him up as he sat back down, eyeing him carefully.

"There's a lot I don't understand," he said and leaned back in his chair. "But I'm sure you'll answer some questions I have."

"Of course, sir."

My dad motioned me out the door then and I reluctantly made my way to the kitchen to make something for breakfast. I kept an ear out for yelling, or some kind of crashing. When I had breakfast mostly done, I snuck down the hall again to see how things were going. But more, I watched as Nathan took in the small room and answered Dad's questions without pause. I watched Nathan because I still could not believe he was here before me.

I had been in a state of shock until this moment, seeing him respond to my dad's questions. Sitting straight, slightly uncomfortable in my father's office with all of its distractions. His profile showed off his angular jaw, darkened with several days growth from not shaving. His eyes seemed a little sunken in, as if he had slept little. I could understand, having not slept much myself since my forced departure. But his strong back was just as I remembered it from all those days of watching it retreat from me.

"How do you do everything without modern machinery? And electricity?" Dad was asking.

"We manage. As was done before electricity tied you to the world around you, we live simply. We live by our own means and are happy with what we yield. We do not try to show off our accomplishments. We are there to do as God bids," Nathan replied simply, looking my father in the eye with the confidence of a man beyond his twenty years.

"So you are religious then. How Kate fell in with you I can't figure out. We're not a religious sort," Dad rebuffed, shaking his head.

"Perhaps she only needed the chance to see for herself," Nathan replied, and I could tell he was a little more guarded when he spoke. He was trying to be respectful, but still hold onto his convictions. So far he was standing up well to my father.

I smiled for what felt the first time in days, seeing him there in Dad's old t-shirt, one that was maybe a little tight across the chest and biceps, showing off what honest hard labor did for him.

"So you farm. Is there money in it? Or do you have to take handouts from the government?" my father asked.

"We make our way without outside interference," Nathan replied smoothly.

I was proud of him for speaking so well in front of my dad.

"And your family? What do they think about you rushing off to find some girl?"

"My family is gone, sir. I have no one but myself to tend to," Nathan replied.

And then I was so sad for him, knowing what a brave and frightening thing it was to come find me. He held himself surely, and it weighed on me that he had taken this journey alone, without Jonah or an elder. I frowned and thought of the Bergers. They had to be worried out of their minds.

"You manage a farm on your own?"

"Yes, sir."

"How? You're just a kid," my father said, looking a little shocked. My dad had always complained about how kids today didn't know the worth of good honest work. I had been offended by his complaints, until I met Nathan and realized it was true. Nathan was rare indeed.

"I manage, sir. It would be easier with more hands."

I smiled again at that. Because I wanted to be one more set of hands for him.

"And it's your farm? You own it?"

"It was my family's farm. I inherited it when they died, yes."

Not once had my dad offered his condolences to Nathan. Grilling him on his property. Material things. Never about what good came out of Nathan's hard work. It made me so mad; he was acting like a father from the stone ages.

"So what are your intentions with Kate then?" I heard from the room, my eyes widening at Dad's brazen question.

Nathan didn't even flinch.

"I am here to bring her home."

"This is her home," Dad replied, his eyes narrowing at Nathan's calm demeanor.

Nathan nodded and looked off towards the wall of pictures for a moment before speaking.

"I am here for whatever Kate needs. She was happy there. She was safe. I only want that for her again," he replied softly, avoiding my father's glare.

"She's safe here. Regardless of what you might think; whatever you think might have happened. She doesn't have to worry about anything while she is at home," Dad grated.

Nathan turned his eyes back to Dad, and I felt my body tense when I saw the steely determination in his eyes.

"Kate deserves to feel safe no matter where she goes. She has the right to choose where she goes, be it here or there. But it is apparent that she is not safe in her current situation," he said, his voice much more steady than I thought it would be.

"And you think you will keep her safe?" Dad pressured.

"If she will have me, yes," he replied, whisper soft, and my heart sped up.

He wanted me.

Dad chuckled and shook his head.

"Well we'll have to see about that, son."

"Yes, sir."

"I won't just let my daughter go away with anyone. I have my principals."

I watched Nathan's jaw clench, his eyes flash. And I knew he was thinking about how my father had practically thrown me at Sean. Nathan opened his mouth to speak; I knew to say something that was not in his character. I jumped when I heard Stacy's voice right behind me.

"Breakfast is ready!" she called, touching my shoulder and nodding before turning to the kitchen.

My dad stood and made his way past me while I waited for Nathan who rose stiffly from his chair. I could see the anger in his eyes, but as soon as I held out my hand, the anger faded. We walked in silence back to the kitchen, where my father was already eating what Stacy had served him. He watched Nathan from across the table as I placed our breakfast on the table, ignoring me when I sat down beside Nathan.

Nathan broke his eye contact with him as he bent his head and recited meal prayers, my own head dipping as he did so. We both murmured our thanks and amen, and when I looked back up, I found my father and sister both eyeing us awkwardly.

"Amen," my dad said, clearly uncomfortable with the word.

We ate in silence for a few minutes, while my family continued to watch us. When my father finally spoke, he turned his attention to me.

"He lives on a farm."

I looked up and wondered where my father was going with this.

"I know. I've been to it many times," I replied.

"That's why you've been getting up early, and cleaning?" he asked.

I nodded.

"You know how much work a farm is?"

"Yes."

"And you know you'll be cooking and cleaning and washing this man's clothes. No cooking school for you with him," he said, and there was a bit of a sneer on his face when he noticed Nathan's back straighten.

"We will work together to provide for one another, Mr. Hill. That is our way," Nathan said.

"But she won't go to college," my father pushed.

"I wasn't going to go to college with Sean either. I was going to be forced to stay at home while he worked," I shot back.

My dad's smile broadened.

"So why is this situation better then?"

"She has a choice, and will have love and respect with me," Nathan replied, his voice carrying that dangerous tone in it once more.

My father looked from him to me, shaking his head.

"You'll see, Kate. You're just going from one man to the other. It'll be the same with this boy as it was with Sean."

"I would never raise a hand," Nathan started, but my hand on his arm stilled him.

I turned to my dad and stood up.

"Nathan cares for me, Dad. More than I have ever felt. He's a gentle person, from kind people. My place is there," I said.

My father leaned back in his chair and seemed to think about what I had said. In that brief moment, I thought that perhaps he understood. I thought that finally he might wish me well and want the best from me.

"Well don't expect to come crawling back here when he isn't as kind and gentle as you say he is," he rebuffed and stood from the table. "No one's forcing you to stay. So go whenever you want."

He tossed his napkin on his plate and walked out, leaving me disappointed and embarrassed in his wake. We heard him head back to his office, the door slamming with a sense of finality. Stacy slowly rose from her seat with Nathan immediately following. She hugged me tight, and I could tell she was watching Nathan as she spoke.

"I don't understand everything about your kind, but I know you love my sister," she said and then pulled away to eye me. "I have to leave this morning to go back to school. I don't want to leave, but I want more time with my sister. If this is the last time I get to see her…"

Nathan stepped close and rested his hand lightly on her shoulder. She looked up at him, surprised.

"I will see to it that you may visit your sister. Please know that I would want nothing less than your support and love for your sister," he murmured and was surprised himself when she reached for him to hug him as well.

When she pulled away, she excused us so that she and I could speak alone. She hovered by the door, glancing at her bags and shaking her head.

"Do you want this? To live with him and live that life?" she asked.

"I was never like you, Stacy," I said and chuckled when she pursed her lips at me. "I like the quiet life. And I care for Nathan more than I have anyone, except maybe you and Mom."

Mentioning our mother made her nod slowly and look back to see Nathan cleaning up our ruined breakfast. She laughed quietly and reached for me, hugging me again.

"If he's what you want, I can't argue. Just promise me you'll write or call," she whispered into my ear. "I don't want to leave until I know you'll be all right."

"I'll be all right," I assured her and pulled away when I heard Nathan drawing near. "I found my home."

He blushed at my last comment and slid in beside me, smiling that tender smile I loved so much.

"Then, I've got a plane to catch," Stacy said and moved to grab her bags. Nathan moved in quicker and took her bags for her, the three of us moving towards the door. I hadn't noticed the rental car parked on the street when Sean had delivered me, and now I was sad to know that I was saying good-bye to my sister.

Nathan put her bags in the trunk while I hugged her one last time, trying hard not to cry. When he approached, she pulled him close and hugged him again.

"I'm holding you to your promise," she said. "I want to see you both again."

"You will," he replied simply.

Stacy let out a breath and slid into the front seat, starting up the car and rolling down the window to offer one last bit of encouragement.

"Get out of here as soon as you can, Kate. This isn't where you're meant to be. I love you," she said and put the car in gear, waving as she pulled out.

I felt Nathan's arms around me again, his lips brushing along my hair to comfort me as I watched my sister's car disappear at the curve in the road.

"Your sister is right, Kate. This is not your world. It is time to go home."

I nodded, feeling his words soak into me.

I was ready to go home.

CHAPTER 31

With my father's blessing to leave, as Nathan put it, I realized there was a lot to do before I could actually pick up and leave forever. Nathan sat with me at the table while I wrote down all the things to do, smiling in encouragement whenever I would get frustrated at just how much I needed to deal with.

I needed to pull out the rest of my savings from the bank.

I had to pack and decide what to leave behind, although that seemed to be the easiest task as I had little I could bring back with us.

I needed to be sure Sean would stay in jail, speak with Deputy Stevens about what came next.

I needed to do so many things when all I really wanted to do was simply leave.

"Things will be better, I promise. We will leave this place and our lives will be ours again," he whispered and kissed me on the forehead before allowing me to retreat upstairs to shower.

I let my thoughts ramble as I washed my hair, feeling my fear and confusion slowly disappear down the drain. With each moment closer to leaving, I found more courage to do just that.

I would leave, and start anew.

I felt a surge of energy course through me at the thought. I smiled into the mirror, seeing the bruises had faded more, a sign that I was indeed moving on. I stepped out of the bathroom full of hope. I retreated into my room and changed quickly, wanting to find Nathan and get out of the house, finally. I found him in the living room, standing in the middle of the room, his eyes transfixed on the television. I smirked and stepped in the room, Nathan coming out of his daze and shaking his head apologetically.

"I turned it on by accident, then it would not shut off. It is troubling what they show on your television," he said and let me take the remote from his hands. I patted the back of it, jarring the batteries before shutting it off.

"I won't miss TV. It rots your brain," I retorted and laughed when he could only nod.

He was dressed already, having found the clothes in the dryer. I took a moment to appreciate him in his English clothes, now that I was less distracted by the events of yesterday. He stood there and smiled sheepishly, looking over his own outfit and glancing at mine.

The T-shirt he wore was cut nicely for his broad chest, the v of it allowing some of his chest hair to peek through. I hadn't registered last night how beautiful he was when we had been in the bathroom. But the English clothes revealed his strong arms, his long neck that needed a shave, and his strong legs whose jeans form fitted to him just so.

He really was quite...

"Beautiful."

I looked up in surprise at his voice.

"You are so very beautiful, Kate," he whispered and shuffled in place, bashful once more.

I didn't know how to react.

I never thought of myself as beautiful, but from the first moment Nathan had looked on me, he had been transfixed. Even if at first it had been fear of what he did not understand. We had grown so much in the last month, and had this detour in our lives not occurred, I wondered where we would be. I tried to look at the positive to having been taken from him, to acknowledge that it had made us stronger in our relationship. I would be able to show him some of my world, for good or bad before we committed to his.

"We should call Emma before we go out," he murmured against me.

From his pocket he pulled out a small scrap of paper, and smiled shyly.

"I have never had to call the phone before," he explained. I handed him the house phone and watched as he dialed the number, holding the phone to his ear.

I could hear it ringing as I stood close to him, anxious to hear Emma.

Two rings and then Emma's excited voice boomed out of the phone.

"Nathan! Have you found her?"

"Emma," he said and I could hear in his voice the strain of finally speaking to her.

He cleared his throat and looked towards me, tugging me closer to him as he spoke.

"I found her. She is safe. I am sorry I am just calling. I arrived last night."

"Can I speak to her? Oh please, I do not mean to be rude, but I need to hear her voice!"

He paused a moment and grinned as he handed me the phone. I took it gratefully and felt the lump in my throat when I said her name.

"Emma."

It took her a moment through her crying before she could say anything. Hearing her so upset made me hurt that I was so far away and could not comfort her.

"Are you all right, Katherine? With what happened when you were here, we were so worried," she asked quietly.

"I'm okay, Emma. Really. Are you okay? How is Abigail? Is Fannie all right?" I asked and choked up again when I heard her clear her throat.

"We will be well when you are home again. When are you coming home?" she asked, almost desperately.

"As soon as we can," I murmured and closed my eyes tight. I felt Nathan take the phone from me gently and talk softly with Emma.

I hadn't realized how torn up I was until I felt his hand rub along my back, trying to console me. First my real sister leaving and then to hear my adopted sister upset, it was too much. I looked up into his eyes as he watched me while speaking with Emma.

"I will call again tomorrow, Emma. We are still waiting here to finish up. We will know soon," he was saying.

But once again, I just wanted to get into the car and head back.

I wanted to get there and put the Bergers at ease.

He quietly ended the call and pulled me into an embrace while I pulled myself together. We had things to do, and crying over it wouldn't get us there any faster. He took my hand, smiling as we neared the door. Nathan opened the door and stood beside me, looking out at the sunshine.

"It is a beautiful day to start anew," he whispered.

I looked out, seeing the sun as it shone bright. It was not the same warm brilliance of Iowa; it held something a little cool being so close to the ocean. But it was bright. And it offered a newness I hadn't felt in the last few days here.

"A beautiful day," I repeated and held his hand a little tighter and stepped out into it.

I breathed a sigh of relief at the feeling of freedom and laughed when he paused beside my car. Sliding in to the driver's seat, I motioned for him to get in. He looked dubious for a moment before getting in, touching the front dash lightly before smiling.

"I am not sure I want to know this part of your world, Kate," he said and laughed when I scowled at him.

"Is it because I'm driving? It's not true what they say about female drivers," I retorted.

"I trust you. Just do not tell my horse I did this," he replied with an amused look on his face and leaned back with his arm at on the window ledge.

I rolled my eyes and put it in gear before pulling out onto the road at a careful pace. I had to admit the one thing I had missed was driving my car. I had worked hard on weekend shifts at the diner to buy the car in the hopes of being able to work in the city. It seemed strange to think that after I left, I would have no need for it. I'd have to sell it, but perhaps that was a good thing. It could help to pay for anything we needed in our new life.

I pulled into the police station and killed the engine, turning to Nathan to catch him eyeing me in amusement. He chuckled and looked away briefly.

"It is interesting to see you like this. I like it," he said and slid out of the car to come around to open my door.

"I'm still me," I whispered as he held my hand and closed the door behind me.

"I know. But you are more confident when you have your mind set on things. I cannot wait to see you like this when we get home," he replied.

I wondered if I would be like this when we got back. Had I really changed? I didn't feel so different. But Nathan seemed sure of himself in regards to my confidence, and his faith gave me the courage to see things a little better.

Deputy Stevens was walking out from the back rooms when we walked into the police station, her smile quivering when she took in Nathan beside me.

"Kate! So glad to see you! I was just going to call, but figured your dad might have filled you in on some of what has happened," she said and came up to us, looking again to Nathan.

"He told me some," I replied and then motioned to Nathan. "This is Nathan, Deputy Stevens."

Nathan extended his hand to her and shook it cordially.

"Very nice to meet you, Nathan," she said, smiling again.

"Thank you for assisting Kate with this," he replied before stepping back to hold me loosely.

"It's my job. I am just glad she has someone to be there for her," she said and motioned us toward her desk, off to the side of the station.

I sat down carefully, noticing the folder sitting on her desk labeled with my name on it. All the sunshine from the drive over seemed to disappear at the thought of why that folder looked thicker than it should. She noticed me looking at it with trepidation and slid it to the side, drawing my attention back up to her.

"You know that Sean is in custody?" she asked carefully.

I nodded. She let out a sigh and rubbed her eyes, trying to hide the fatigue I could see there. She looked like she had been burning the midnight oil.

"Did your dad tell you what happened?" she asked, not moving her hand from her face.

"Just that he took care of it and that Sean was in custody in the Emergency room," I replied, not sure if I should say anymore, because Deputy Stevens simply grunted.

"What happened?" Nathan asked, taking the lead. She opened her eyes and looked off towards a darkened office to the side. From where I was sitting, I could see Deputy Miller's name on it. A moment of trepidation filtered through me, having not realized I could have walked in to find him here. I didn't think I could handle seeing him. Deputy Stevens pulled me back into the conversation with a clearing of her throat.

"You dad came in last night, upset about something you had said at home. He confronted Sean's father about it. Something about Sean going too far. Which, if you ask me was obvious when you were at the hospital. But your dad seemed more upset at Sean last night. He went into Miller's office and they argued for a bit before your dad came storming out, Deputy Miller close behind him," she said and shook her head again.

"A call came in about three hours later, asking for an ambulance. When I got there, they were loading Sean into the back. He was unconscious and pretty beaten up. Broken nose, looks like they'll have to wire his jaw. Some stitches. And your dad simply said he took a fall. Sean's dad looked like he may have taken a little of the same fall as well. And there's more, Kate," she explained, tapping on the file folder lightly.

I nodded for her to continue. For her to get it over with so I could be done with it.

"The Feds are involved now. Because this originated in Iowa, I've contacted the FBI. Between them and the district attorneys, they'll be figuring out where to try Sean. Most likely, it will be in Iowa, because of the conflict of interest here with his father being a law enforcement officer. Your dad unfortunately may be implicated," she said, and paused to gauge my reaction.

"What do you mean implicated?" Nathan asked for me again.

He seemed to know I was having trouble speaking.

It was too much.

She looked from me to him, perhaps trying to evaluate how much she should say with him there. But then she nodded and opened the folder, revealing so many things I had no desire to see. I felt Nathan tense next to me when he saw a flash of the pictures of me when I had arrived, before she closed the folder again, a piece of paper in her hand.

"There are receipts from your father's company that pay for Sean's travel while he was searching for you. They can add him as an accessory to your kidnapping because of it. There's also proof that your father willingly assisted Deputy Miller in hiding his son while the warrant was out for him."

I struggled to come to terms with the fact that my father had been involved all along. He'd say he was doing it because he was worried, but I knew he was just looking for a way to keep it quiet. If anything good had come of this, it was that I could finally step away from all of the nonsense, and never look back.

This was not my life anymore; I had a family in Iowa that cared for me.

"It doesn't matter. As soon as you say I can, I'll be returning back to Iowa," I said, trying to appear strong.

She glanced at Nathan again, this time a little more carefully. She seemed to come to a decision when she smiled and looked back at me.

"I think that's a good idea, Kate. You seem happier with that decision," she murmured.

"So I guess I just need to wait for the test results? Will Sean stay in jail until they figure out where to have the trial?" I asked, wanting to wrap this up and get moving on my new life.

"You don't need to stay for the results if you don't want to. We can send you those results back, but you and I both know what the results will be. As far as him getting out? There is always the chance of bail, but I doubt his father can afford it, especially now that he's on suspension for hiding his son. No, Sean will be in custody until they extradite him to Iowa," she replied.

The idea that he could possibly make bail didn't sit well.

"He won't make bail, Kate. I think it will be set pretty high, and maybe not at all given the fact that he hid while we looked for him. You're safe now," she reiterated.

I felt Nathan squeeze my hand in encouragement.

"Now," Deputy Stevens said and pulled out another piece of paper. "If you are going back to Iowa, we'll need some way to contact you. The FBI will want to interview you, as will the local district attorney. I believe the sheriff there already took statements from your family there."

"You can take down my address," Nathan said, blushing slightly when I looked his way. He returned the smile and bent over the paper to fill out the address for me.

"I should be getting the test results soon. With the FBI involved and Sean in custody, that has helped to speed things up. I can send you any information you want at this address," she said.

We stood and shook hands with her, one step of my journey complete.

"Thank you, for believing me. And for doing so much. I'll never forget this," I said softly while she held my hand.

"It is my job, Kate. You take care. We'll see an end to all of this. I hope you have a good life where you are going. I have a feeling you will," she said and grinned at Nathan once more, who took her hand and shook it lightly.

"I will take care of her, Deputy Stevens. I promise," he murmured and pulled me out of the station.

Hopefully for the last time.

CHAPTER 32

I stepped out of the bank, irritated with the news I had been told.

"What is wrong?" Nathan asked as I slid back into the driver's seat.

"Dad took most of my money out of my savings," I grated, pulling out into traffic once more towards home. I had some things to say to him.

Nathan kept quiet, knowing that I was angry by the way I gripped the wheel. I shook my head again and let out a bitter laugh.

"Nice to know he could finance Sean's little trip but wouldn't allow me the chance to go to school with the money I had earned," I spat.

Nathan soothed me with his hand on my arm, willing me to calm down.

"It is in the past, Kate. We do not need the money. We will get by," he said simply.

"I had almost four thousand dollars in the bank, Nathan," I said and watched his eyes widen. "How much grain and hay is that?"

"It is done, Kate. It cannot be undone," he replied softly. "We will manage fine."

I sighed and concentrated on the road, trying to do as Nathan said. But every second closer to the house, the more frustrated I became. My hard earned money had dragged me back here, and now we had barely enough to make it back to Iowa. I wasn't sure Nathan understood how much it would cost to drive back.

Perhaps I would need to sell the car now and we would take the bus back.

All my hopes of being able to show a little of my world to Nathan had evaporated with my empty bank account. I gritted my teeth when we pulled up to the house, seeing my father's car still there. I knew I would need to confront him, to say my goodbyes. But now there was the fact that he had stolen from me to deal with.

"It will be fine," Nathan assured me at the door. "What is done is done. You can only forgive him and move on."

Forgiveness was not on my list, even though I knew it was Nathan's way. And would soon be my way as well. If I hoped for any closure from this life, I knew I would have to forgive and forget. We walked into the kitchen to set down the groceries we had bought while we were out, yet another expense I was suddenly worried over. It was another minute when we heard Dad moving around upstairs. Nathan slipped away and watched me as I finally put away the groceries, a frown on his face. When I put the last of the items in the refrigerator, he spoke up.

"How long would you like to stay before we leave?" he asked quietly.

I laughed quietly and shook my head.

"If I could we'd be there already," I retorted.

"I know that, but how long would you like to say your goodbyes to you father?" he asked, and his eyes held mine intently.

I thought about it, about the finality of saying goodbye, and knew, it wouldn't take much.

As much as I needed to forgive my father, it wouldn't be drawn out.

"Not long, Nathan," I whispered and turned toward the hallway when we heard my father coming down the stairs.

He came in, glancing at us for a moment before reaching into the refrigerator to grab a drink. He didn't say anything for a moment, taking a long sip.

"Stacy left, so when are you leaving?" he asked.

I blinked at his abruptness, although I shouldn't have been surprised. I could tell in his eyes he knew I was leaving for good.

"As soon as I'm packed," I replied, watching as he nodded and waved me with him towards his office.

"I have a few things to say, alone," he emphasized, glaring back at Nathan as he retreated.

I looked at Nathan, who simply offered me an encouraging nod.

"I will be right here if you need me," he whispered and sat at the table, while I went off to speak with my father.

He was sitting in his chair, looking at the blank computer screen while he waited for me to sit. When I was situated, he took another long drink and pulled his eyes from the screen to look at me. His eyes were hard but vacant.

"So you intend to really go away? And let the charges against Sean stand? This boy is that special?" he asked, and I could hear the bitterness in his voice.

"He is. I'm happy with him. And Sean brought on the charges himself," I replied, trying to sound calm.

My father snorted and shook his head.

"You leave and that will be it. I won't be around to help you out," he replied curtly.

I wanted to say so many things in rebuttal.

"I'll be fine where I am going," I said instead. It was better that way.

"Well, I just want you to be sure. If things don't work out there, you're on your own. I have enough to deal with here when you leave," he murmured and I could tell he meant he knew he was in trouble.

I looked away and shook my head.

"What you did, Dad. With Sean. That was your doing, not mine. Whatever problems that come up because of that are your issues and not mine," I said, my voice struggling to sound sure.

He was quiet for a while, and at first I thought perhaps that was all he had to say to me, until he spoke again, this time much more quietly.

"I should have been the one to bring you home. Then maybe he wouldn't have gone too far. Maybe then you and he would still be together," he whispered.

I stared at him hard, trying to understand how he rationalized anything.

"I ran away because I was afraid of him, Dad. That night before I left, he tried to rape me. His friends helped hold me down. Did he tell you that? And then he brings me home a mess, and that was okay? I don't get it. You never once questioned my injuries. Instead, you couldn't see he was the dangerous one, that he hurt me over and over. And then you send him to find me? Everything about that is wrong," I spat and moved to get up.

He leaned out and took my arm carefully, indecision on his face when he noticed me flinch.

"He should have known better. I made it clear he was just there to get you to come home," he stated. "I didn't know about the rest."

I yanked my arm away and stared down at him in disbelief.

"And that makes it all right? You paid for his trip, with my savings, and you expect me to be all right with all of this?" I asked heatedly, feeling the tears rising up in my eyes.

He slumped back in the chair and shook his head, not saying a word.

And with that, I knew. Dad would never be the father I needed.

We were done.

I let out a defeated sigh and sat back down, watching him as he stared ahead blankly. He would end up a lonely man, without anyone to care for him. And it would be his fault. I sat a little straighter and knuckled down my courage. I was ready to get this over with.

To close this door, for good.

"Dad, I forgive you."

He looked at me in surprise but I raised my hand before he could speak.

"I need to finish. I forgive you for being blind to how much your daughter needed a father when her boyfriend decided to possess her. I forgive you for not being here when I needed someone to protect me all those times he got angry with me. I forgive you for thinking he was more important than your own flesh and blood when it mattered. And I forgive you for not believing in me when it mattered most. I forgive you for taking what little I have of myself to give to those that would hurt me. I forgive you for abandoning your daughters after their mother died, and I forgive you for never thinking that family was more important than your career. I understand now, because I have that chance with Nathan. I forgive you," I said, my words seeming to come out in force as I thought them.

He looked at me wide eyed for a moment before I stood and made to walk out.

"And I hope you understand, that I am going someplace that I will be happy. I will be loved. I will have a family that cares about me. And for that I have to thank you. Because had you stepped up and been the father I needed, I would have never left, and I would have never found love. Some would call it fate, I think I'd like to think someone guided me there," I murmured and walked out, leaving him to sit alone to dwell on his own failures.

Nathan was by the hall door to the kitchen, his hands in his pockets and a worried look on his face as I walked swiftly past him to grab my car keys.

"Are you all right?" he asked, following me as I pushed past the front door to outside.

"I think we should see a little of town. Get out one last night before we leave," I suggested and started the engine as soon as he closed his door.

"Are you sure?" he asked.

I nodded and pulled out onto the road, towards Arcata.

"I said what I needed to. I can move on. It's too late to leave today so we'll enjoy what we can before we head back to Iowa," I replied and let out a long breath when McKinleyville faded away behind us.

Nathan let me have my silence for a while, and took in the coast as it passed on the side of the road. His soft chuckle brought me out of my numb haze.

"I did not think you would forgive him in quite that way," he said, looking over at me finally.

"What do you mean?" I asked nervously.

The last thing I wanted was to have to do it again, in some acceptable fashion.

"I mean that you were direct and strong. There is nothing you cannot do, Kate."

I shook my head and looked back out on the road.

"There's a lot of things I can't do, Nathan," I whispered.

"I do not think so, Kate. It is what I admire about you. You are stronger than you think you are," he replied and held my hand a little tighter.

I couldn't deny that I felt a little stronger since meeting he and the Bergers.

Perhaps he saw more than I did.

Perhaps he made me so.

"Do you not feel healed from your proclamations to your father?" he asked.

I thought about it and nodded. I did feel better in a strange way.

"Faith has a way of healing many things," he said and looked off towards the ocean once more. "I was healed by your presence when you came to live with the Bergers. You healed my faith in finding a purpose. I have faith you will find yourself healed of much when we leave here."

"So do I," I replied and looked ahead of what was to come.

It really was a good day to start anew.

CHAPTER 33

It was early afternoon arriving into Arcata and we were starved.

Nathan stood beside his door and took in the bay, awe written across his face.

"It is so immense," he breathed.

"Have you never been to the ocean, Nathan?" I asked, surprised.

He shook his head and continued to stare out over the water.

Suddenly there were so many more things to do with him before we went home.

"Let's get something to eat, and we'll take it to go. I have someplace you should see," I said and tugged him up the main street. When we neared an electronics store, I felt Nathan slow as he looked at all the gadgets flashing in the window, I couldn't help but to laugh.

"You want to go in and look around?" I suggested.

"Are you trying to show me everything before we leave, Kate?" he mused, his eyes twinkling.

"Yes I am," I quipped, squeezing his hand a little harder. "To show you it's not all booze and loud music. And to see some of what I enjoyed but am willing to walk away from."

He chuckled and took my hand in his, glancing back at the store as we continued.

"There are so many distractions in your world. I find it difficult to concentrate on what matters most," he said with a smile and leaned in to kiss me.

When we pulled apart, he started moving again, allowing me to lead the way down the street. He looked again and again at the window displays as we passed, but never seemed to need to linger long. He had seen most of what we had whenever he went to town for supplies, but now that he could spend time investigating it without fear of judgment, he simply chose to walk away.

We walked into the local deli, ordering up sandwiches and drinks before climbing back into the car and heading along the coast.

Nathan kept his eyes on the water, enchanted by the rolling waves as they crashed along the rocks. The coast on the north side of town didn't offer as much beach, but I knew of a part of south bay that would allow us a lovely view of the sunset on a sliver of private beach few knew about. It would be perfect and judging by Nathan's bright face, I knew he would enjoy it. How often would he get to see the ocean in Iowa?

Pulling off the road, I parked the car and had Nathan gather up the food and drinks. I grabbed the blanket behind the seat and took his hand, walking us down a narrow path leading to the beach.

"What are we doing here?" he asked as we wound our way down to the roaring sound of the ocean.

I nodded towards the sun as it started its descent.

"Have you ever watched the sun set over the water before, Nathan?" I asked just as we made it to the soft sand. Barely a hundred feet beyond us, the waves crashed along the beach.

He looked out over the bay again and his mouth opened in amazement. I felt his arm wrap around me, pulling me close so that his lips brushed against mine. My hand moved up to cup his cheek, the whiskers tickling my palm enough to make me giggle.

"What?" he murmured against my lips.

"Your whiskers tickle," I giggled and squirmed when he rubbed his cheek against mine.

"I have not been able to shave. Does it bother you?" he murmured and kissed my jaw, sending a shiver through me at the dichotomy of his soft lips and rough beard.

"No," I whispered and tugged him closer, nearly toppling us over into the sand.

My hand drifted, reaching up to graze the nape of his neck and feeling the softness of his hair there. My own lips moved against him, feeling the burn of his cheek as I made my way towards his ear. He let out a soft breath and hugged me tighter to him, and I could feel his hands slip across my back to feel me better. I tossed the blanket to the ground, sinking into it with Nathan close behind, sunsets and food forgotten. We rolled until I straddled him, my hands sliding over his tight t-shirt while his lips grew more adventurous over my mouth. I felt him tug against my hips, drawing me closer over him where I felt him hardening beneath me. He groaned and pulled his lips from mine, licking them as if he wanted to devour me.

Looking down into his eyes, his need was clear. His tight grip on my hips as he held me tight against him proved it as he adjusted.

He swallowed and tried to calm his breathing.

"You are so much. I want so much with you, Kate," he groaned and let his eyes close when my hands traced down his neck and to his chest. I let my lips drift along his throat, enjoying the feel of his heartbeat against my lips at his throat.

The sunset was fast approaching, and I didn't care. We were alone, something that rarely happened, in his world or mine. It was a moment that we could explore, and not be judged or called out.

His breath came a little faster when he felt my hands slip down his shirt, drawing it up a bit to expose his bare stomach where I could run my fingers through the thin trail of hair there. He moved beneath me again, sending shivers through me. He watched me with heavy eyes as I leaned back a bit, feeling him adjust again.

"Kate," he murmured and sat up to kiss along my throat his hands moving up along my ribs. I pushed myself into his hands, feeling the warmth of his palms cup my breasts tentatively. I whimpered when I felt his fingertips graze across the hardness of my nipple and then capture my breast again in a gentle squeeze.

The scraping of his lips against my throat, the hardness of him against the heat of me, his strong hands as they moved across my body made it sing with need. I felt the warmth seeping into my limbs, and trembled against him when I rolled my hips, wanting to find the right spot to feel him. When I found it, we both sighed and moved against one another with a little more urgency. I could feel a tightening in my stomach, and gasped when he rolled us over, trapping me beneath him. He groaned and kissed me deeply, the heat of him a delight in the waning light. When he pulled away, he was panting.

"If we go much further, I will lose myself, Kate," he said with his eyes clenched tightly.

I relaxed my hands around his neck and let him roll to the side, separating us. I knew it was wrong. I knew he was trying to be respectful, but touching one another felt too good to deny. I wanted it as much as he did. How he could pull away and resist, he had superhuman restraint. He wrapped one arm around me and kissed me softly by the ear before sighing.

"I am sorry, Kate. I just want this to be right. I do not want you to regret us," he murmured in my ear.

I groaned and tugged on his shirt in frustration.

"I don't regret you, Nathan. Believe me, I don't," I sighed and tried to cool down my body as he held me and touched me along my waist once more.

"Well, let us be on our way home and away from this place before we do anything more," he mumbled and looked out at the darkening sky.

"Don't tell me my dad scares you," I said, incredulous.

He shook his head and laughed low.

"No. I am not afraid of your father. I just want us to go home. I am tempted here with these surroundings. I want to do right and respect you. Even if I am tempted to stray every time you are near me," he mused, the twinkle back in his eyes.

I rolled my eyes and slid from his hold, standing and offering him my hand.

"Come on," I said. "I think we both need something to cool us down and you can't leave here without getting your feet wet."

He followed me curiously as I walked us closer to the approaching waves. He mimicked me when I pulled off my shoes and socks, and rolled up his jeans just as I did. Taking my hand again, he followed me to the water, pausing for a moment as the water moved dangerously close to his bare feet.

"The sand is freezing!" he exclaimed.

"So is the water," I said and let go of his hand to skip into the oncoming wave.

I let out a startled cry at how cold it was, but waved him on. He looked at the water for an instant before stepping into the next wave, his eyes going wide when he felt the water slosh over his ankles.

And then he laughed.

A beautiful and carefree sound that bounced back and forth against the rocks, again and again as he jumped and ran through the cold water, kicking it up at times that I knew he'd be wet above the ankles. I rushed for him, feeling him catch me as I sped by, laughing with him as he spun me around and splashed again and again. He pulled me close and kissed me deeply, all the joy and excitement clear as his body held me as the waves moved in.

The cold water finally made us retreat back to the blanket, drying off enough to relax and enjoy what we came for. I tucked back into him, offering him his sandwich finally. We sat there in the quiet watching the sunset as we ate, alone in our thoughts. I was surprised when he finally spoke up in the silence.

"Thank you for sharing this bit of your world with me, Kate. This moment is something I will remember all my life," he murmured near my ear.

"This is my favorite part of this life," I replied quietly, watching the sky turn pink above us. "But I'd give it all up so I could see you every day. I'm glad I could share this with you."

"Coming to find you was the best thing I have done in my life. And the hardest, Kate. Because there is not a moment that goes by that I do not want everything from you. I will refuse to let them keep us apart when we are home," he said, his voice determined.

"What about the Elders?" I asked worriedly. "And Jonah and Fannie?"

He slid his hand up my arm to my face and traced the side of my cheek lightly.

"Jonah and Fannie understand. The Elders? We will show them you are meant for our world. You came for a purpose, and they will see. I promise," he said and pulled me closer to his side, looking out over the deepening sunset.

We were quiet for a long time, watching the sky turn from a light blue, to turquoise, to a deepening lavender and red, until the blue began to darken and the last bit of fire lay at the top of the ocean. As the breeze turned cold, we slowly made our way back up the trail to the car. I let the heater warm up the car some before we had to leave. Nathan held me close and let out a long sigh, looking out at the purple and red sky ahead of us.

"Is there anything else you will miss here, Kate?" he whispered into my hair.

I thought about it for a moment, trying to imagine what could possibly be more tempting that being in Nathan's arms. I couldn't think of anything.

"Nothing?" he asked when I shook my head. "Not even this car?"

I laughed and nodded.

"Okay. I'll miss the car maybe. But not much else," I sighed and leaned up to kiss him.

"Coming to see your world has made me realize how little we know of it, Kate. There is such beauty here that I would not have dreamed possible. But having you here beside me, watching this bit of God's work, I know this is right. I'll be everything you need," he said.

I felt his hands tip my head up so that I could look into his eyes.

Everything I felt for him I saw there.

He kissed me slowly, allowing the last of the sun to fall away. When it grew too dark to see one another, I regretfully pulled away from him and started us back towards the house.

The drive home was distracting.

Nathan continued to trace his fingers along my arm that he held. He had grown so comfortable with me in the short time since arriving; I didn't want that to diminish when we returned. More so I didn't want to miss it while we traveled back home. And I kept thinking about all the things we could do if we drove back to Iowa instead of taking the bus.

"Nathan?"

He hummed and slowed his gentle stroking, looking over at me sleepily.

"What would you say to driving back to Iowa? Spending a few days extra instead of taking the bus," I suggested.

He frowned and sat a little straighter, thinking it over.

"How long do you think it will take to drive? It would be nice to get home as soon as we can. I left Jonah on his own," he replied.

"It's three days by bus, with all the stops. But with the car, and spending the night somewhere, maybe four days," I thought, not really sure.

I knew he'd want to get home. I was being selfish. I wanted just a little more time alone with him before strict courtship rules were enforced again. He was thoughtful for some time, until his fingers resumed their path along my arm and he smiled.

"By bus we would not be alone. And it was not very comfortable. Someone would need to pick us up at the bus station. Perhaps driving would be better. I'd like to see more with you, Kate," he said and grinned again.

I was pretty sure he meant more than the countryside. I turned back to the road, excited for the trip back, because I wanted much more as well.

When we pulled up to the house, I immediately noticed my father's car was gone. Nathan glanced at the bare spot and eyed it as we stepped up to the porch and unlocked the door. It was dark inside, and quiet. Perhaps he had gone to work, him not being here until late at night wasn't uncommon.

But when we walked into the kitchen, I knew. He wasn't planning on being around when I left. An envelope sat on the table, and beside it a note. I took a breath and hesitated in taking the note in my hands, afraid to read it. I felt Nathan behind me and gained some courage from his warm hands on my shoulder as I opened up the note to read.

Kate,

I won't be here when you leave tomorrow. I'll save you the need to pretend to be kind, when I don't deserve it. I left you what I took from your account in the envelope. Use it for your new life.
I hope that you truly meant what you said about forgiving me. I do love you. I know you needed someone and I never came through for you. I know now that you have someone who will truly look out for you.

I am sorry. For everything.

Dad

I reached slowly for the envelope, pulling out the large wad of cash that was in there. I couldn't bring myself to count it, I knew he'd be honorable and pay his debt. And it left me feeling sad for him, to know that this would be viewed as a business transaction more than an honest wish for a better future.

"Are you all right?" Nathan whispered.

I nodded and closed up the note.

"He is trying in his own way to make amends. He is not without honor," he whispered.

411

I nodded and put the money back in the envelope, feeling that this sense of closure was not as happy as I would have wanted.

"Perhaps he will come home in the morning. We can wait to say goodbye to him."

"We'll still leave tomorrow. I want to go home," I whispered and walked upstairs to my bedroom, hearing him follow after me.

He remained silent when I lay down and held out my hand to him. He slid off his shoes and lay down beside me in the big plush bed and held me close, his hands remaining on my shoulder as I wept quietly. As much as my father wasn't a part of my life, I knew I would still miss him. I hugged myself against Nathan a little more firmly, knowing that his warmth was my new solace.

Tomorrow we'd leave, and I would start my new life with him.

Tomorrow was the start of everything.

CHAPTER 34

I awoke well before dawn, yet again set to my new ways.

I knew Nathan was awake behind me, his body was warm against me and his fingers had slipped into my hair, stroking it lightly with his fingertips. I stretched beside him, feeling him back away from me slightly as my body rubbed against him. I turned onto my back so that I could see him in the dim light, laying on his side with a tender smile as he propped his head on his elbow to look down at me.

"Pleasant morning," he murmured, his smile widening.

"Pleasant morning," I whispered back and touched his fuzzy cheek with my fingertips.

He dipped down and kissed me lightly along the cheek, letting his growing whiskers scrape lightly before pulling away. He let out a sigh and adjusted beside me again, one leg brushing over my knee. I let my hand ghost down his chest, his breath catching when I neared his stomach. I could see the indecision in his eyes, the desire mixed with the fear, making me pause. He rolled towards me and slipped one leg in between mine as he settled against me with a soft moan. The weight of him was enticing, and to feel him hard along my thigh made my heart speed up. His hands moved to my head, thumbs stroking across my cheeks as he gazed down into my smiling face.

"There is nothing in this world that is as beautiful as you are. The warmth of your body, your fragrance as it fills me with desire. You are my weakness, Kate," he murmured low and kissed me along my jaw, moving to my ear where he could hum softly.

I felt my smile widen in joy at his words. Even without a pen and paper, Nathan could say the most beautiful things. My desire for him had no limits. It seemed every moment we were together, I loved him more.

There was no doubt in my mind that Nathan was the man I would spend my days with. I wanted to tell him, to express it openly, but one small part of me was afraid to say it.

What if the Amish didn't say it?

Maybe that was why Nathan had not said it.

Surely he loved me?

Everything he did suggested it. He had come all this way to find me; I was sure it was love and that he wanted to be with me, committed and together forever.

"What are you thinking?" he whispered against my ear, his nose tracing along my temple.

I swallowed and looked up into his eyes as he pulled away slightly to regard me. I let my fingers trace nervous circles along his shoulders while I gathered up the courage to speak the words. It was more difficult than I thought. I had never said them to anyone before.

"Did I do something wrong?" he asked, his worried brow making my nerves spike.

"No, no you didn't do anything wrong," I said quickly.

His brow loosened and his lip turned up in an amused smirk. He slid to the side of me and leaned casually there, propped on his elbow once more while he waited for me to continue. I turned along my side and let my hand toy with the collar of his shirt, avoiding his eyes so that I could say what I knew I needed to.

It wouldn't sound nearly as poetic as his words, but it was from my heart.

"You mean so much to me. I'm not sure if I ever thanked you for letting me into your life," I said softly.

"I must thank you, Kate," he started, only to stop when I placed my hand on his warm lips. He raised his eyebrows at me but let me continue.

"I mean, you didn't have to. But you took a chance with me. You pursued me and showed me that a man can be gentle and caring. I've never had that. I've never felt what I feel for you," I continued, and felt his lips curve up against my fingers.

His hand wrapped around mine, his lips kissing my fingers before pulling them away slowly.

"What we have is a gift from God, Kate. We were both in need of love. And we found it in one another," he replied.

"Love," I whispered, feeling my throat close up a little at the word.

He nodded simply.

"Of course. The love I feel for you is more than I have ever felt. And it grows by the day. From the first day I met you, I knew," he whispered.

"Knew what?" I sighed, feeling an overwhelming surge of warmth pass through me at his declaration.

"That you were for me. That we belonged together. That I loved you," he replied, his eyes joyful as he looked down at me.

"You love me?" I asked hoarsely and let out a small laugh when his eyes crinkled as his smile broke out.

"Of course I love you," he said easily, his laughter bubbling up from deep in his throat.

He made it so simple in his declaration.

Every worry I had fell away at his conviction.

"I am so in love with you," I breathed and reached up and kissed him hard. I needed to show him just how much he mattered to me. He held me close and kissed me back, moaning into my mouth when he felt me move under him, wanting him closer. He didn't flinch or jerk away when my legs wrapped around him; instead he seemed to take it as a sign to venture further. The heaviness of his body as he moved over me only made me wish that we weren't in my father's house, and that there was less between us. His breath came faster, his mouth urgent like his hips while they moved in time to me beneath him. Wanting more, always more.

When he finally pulled away from my lips, we were breathless and clutching one another tightly. He hugged me close and rolled over once more, pulling me against him as we rested in the early glimmering of morning. We held one another like that for a long time, Nathan's fingers playing through my hair while I traced lazy patterns across his chest. When the room finally started to lighten, he let out a long sigh and hugged me a little tighter.

"We should rise if we plan on leaving," he murmured. I nodded and slipped out of bed, intent on getting the day started.

Nathan excused himself to the bathroom while I looked through my father's room to find clothes for him to wear. I found an older pair of jeans in the closet, well worn, clean and soft, as well as a few shirts that I hadn't seen him in for some time. Dad had more than enough that would fit Nathan, so before making my way down to the kitchen, I laid out the fresh clothes for him to choose from.

I smiled at my choices.

I was growing rather fond of Nathan in those tight t-shirts.

Four more days and then back to his traditional clothes.

I grinned at that, knowing I loved him more as an Amish man than in his Englisher clothes.

Breakfast was nearly ready and I had ventured to make a quick pie dough while he was in the shower. By the time he entered the kitchen, I had started cutting up some of the apples we had bought.

"What are you making?" he asked, smiling as he looked over my shoulder while I cut.

"I thought I'd make apple turnovers. They're easier to travel with than pie," I replied, grinning.

He hummed and pecked me lightly on the cheek before pulling away to pour some juice.

Finishing up the apples I covered them and threw them in the refrigerator, and pulled out the egg dish from the oven. It was an improvisation of Fannie's, but as Nathan took a bite and grinned, I knew I had managed to make something good. We ate quietly, enjoying the peace for once.

I set to making the turnovers while Nathan cleaned up. It was a little strange to have him in the kitchen with me. Not that I was trying to separate our gender roles in any way, but I had never truly seen him work in the kitchen. Nathan seemed happy to help, and when he had washed everything I dirtied, he turned and watched me as I made my small triangular pastries.

"How do you do that with such ease?"

"What do you mean?" I asked, confused.

"You are so quick with it. It is natural for you. I watched my sisters do something like this, and they would be much slower," he replied and for a moment I saw that hint of sadness in his eyes in speaking about his family

I swallowed hard and tried to smile to comfort him.

"I enjoy this. It's like writing for you I guess. It comes naturally," I replied softly and moved to stick the pan full of turnovers into the waiting oven.

When I turned to look back at Nathan, he seemed thoughtful as he looked around the kitchen.

"My mother would have loved you, just as Fannie does. She was not much different than Fannie," he whispered, and frowned. "Perhaps that is why it is so hard to say no to Fannie most days."

"She loves you very much," I said, knowing just how much Fannie seemed to care for Nathan. She had so much love to give.

He nodded and offered me that bashful look once more.

"She was always that way. She was made to be a mother," he said and frowned again, straightening up and looking around once more. "We should pack whatever you wish to take. We do not want it to get too late before we set out."

I wanted to know more about why Fannie only had her three daughters. I knew enough about Amish traditions that said that the larger the family the easier the work. I had my theories, but assumed it was rude to ask. I wouldn't push where it was not my place.

I made my way upstairs into my bedroom, looking around to see what I could bring. I threw my duffel bag onto the bed and dug around for a few shirts and shorts for the trip, Nathan sitting awkwardly by my computer table, fingering the keyboard and trying not to watch as I pulled out bras and underwear. I looked again at the computer and thought about our trip.

I'd need a map.

One last hoorah with technology and maybe I could show Nathan one last thing about this world I had enjoyed but would not really miss. I leaned over him briefly, his eyes widening before turning curious as the computer whirred to life. He eyed the screen as the background sprung up, a picture of the mountains at sunset. I leaned over him as I clicked on the Internet, tapping my fingers as the page loaded.

Nathan looked up at me and raised an eyebrow, smirking.

"I wanted to search out our route, get it set and printed so we wouldn't get lost," I explained and moved to sit in his lap.

He straightened a bit and wrapped one arm around my waist as I settled in to type out directions to home.

"Do they not make maps anymore?" he asked, fighting a grin.

"I thought I would show you how they do it in the 21st century," I shot back, laughing.

He watched as I pulled up the maps page and laid in a course for us. His eyes went from comical to amazement as the map laid out our path.

"That is impressive! What else can you do?" he asked, looking more closely at the page as I sent the map to print.

"You can find out all sorts of things on the internet. Think of it as an unlimited resource, like a library," I said and clicked on my homepage.

"What would you like to know?" I asked, looking down at his contemplative face as he thought for a moment.

"What should I plant when we get home?" he asked and squeezed me gently.

"All right."

I typed a search on crops for fall planting.

Nathan's eyes widened at the sudden listing of sites to visit. He leaned forward, his eyes transfixed as he watched me click on a few and read over briefly anything that might be of use. I touched his hand that was wrapped around my waist and slipped from his lap, placing his hand on the mouse and instructed him through the simple workings of the Internet.

"I can look for anything?" he asked, biting at his lip as he looked up in awe.

"Just about. But I'll warn you, some things might send you to something perverted. If that happens, don't worry. Just click the little " x" at the top there and start over. There's really too much out there on the Internet. You could get lost pretty easily," I said and laughed when I noticed him blush.

I patted him on the shoulder and excused myself to check on the turnovers. I glanced back at him as he turned back to the computer and clicked on the next link. Smiling at the wonder on his face I busied myself with putting another batch of turnovers into the oven and packing the few things I wanted from my kitchen to take with me.

Cook books, my recipe cards from my grandmother of her cakes and casseroles, and the few decent dishes I had bought when I thought I'd have a career in baking. I laughed to myself at the realization that in many ways, my future would include a lot of baking. I found a large plastic container in the front entry closet and emptied it, returning to wrap my dishes up in some towels.

All my worldly belongings managed to take up most of the trunk, but that was all. We dug out the sleeping bags from the storage shed in the back yard, wedging them into the back as well. I packed us a cooler with drinks and a few sandwiches for the road, and put the turnovers into a secure container. We loaded up the inside of the car, my phone and my mp3 player going on the dash, our pillows and blankets piling up.

I walked through the house once more, taking in the odds and ends.

Dad's worn chair. The dust on the television. The ridiculous plaques on the wall for service to the community while on city council. Hardly any family pictures to speak of. Nathan remained by the front door, allowing me to say goodbye in my own way.

I glanced at the note I had left for my father on the kitchen counter, noticing another piece of paper attached to it. Curious, I picked it up.

Mr. Hill,

I feel I should somehow apologize for how we met. It was never my intention to do so under such circumstances. But God works in mysterious ways. Had it not been for events that Kate will put behind her, I would not have met her. And I would have never known love and kindness from such a gentle creature as your daughter. Kate will find beauty and happiness where she is going, I promise you that.
I give you my word that I will take care of her.
I will love her, for the rest of my days, as God wishes.
I am a simple man. But I know what I want. I know what is right. Kate is right in her choice to find love and peace.
As her father I hope you take solace in that.
I wish you peace from your demons, and pledge to you that I will respect and honor Kate.
Forever.

Respectfully,
Nathan Solomon Fisher

On the back of the note, Nathan had left his address.

Regardless of what Nathan may have thought of him, he had left my father a way to make amends, to remain a part of my life if my father chose to. I took a deep breath and replaced Nathan's note beside mine.

His was so much more eloquent.

But then again, it was Nathan.

The Amish were right about him.

He was a faithful and good man.

And as I locked up the house, he remained at my side, taking my hand tenderly as I stepped away from this life and into his. I sat in the car; looking at the house I had lived in all my life and saw it with different eyes.

It was no longer home.

It was the past.

I gripped the wheel tightly, took a deep breath and pulled out, never looking back.

We were quiet as we made our way through town, Nathan tracing his fingers over my arm as it rested on top of the pillows that rested between us. It was a welcome feeling as I silently said goodbye to everything I had known here. It didn't take long before we were driving south towards San Francisco, Nathan's hand in mine and the sun above us that peeked out of the trees as we veered east and south towards the Humboldt National Park. I smiled at his wide eyes of wonderment at the trees, as they grew progressively larger, until the Redwoods took over. We pulled off onto Grand Giants Avenue that ran parallel to the 101 freeway, knowing he would enjoy the sights of the large majestic Redwoods there. I opened up the sunroof, and his smile only grew.

Nathan spent most of his time with his eyes to the skies, blotted out by the tall trunks that were easily as wide as the car, if not more. I had seen the forest many times as I had grown up, but seeing him experience it for the first time brought back all the good memories of my childhood in the trees.

"They are so big," he breathed as we passed close to one particularly large redwood.

"They are hundreds of years old," I said and recited the history of them to him, having heard the tale so many times on fieldtrips.

He listened and continued to take in the experience, a bright smile on his face as we drove. At times his hand would squeeze my thigh, and he'd look back at me and grin. This was the part of my world I wanted to share with him. The beauty and majesty of it, and funny enough, he would say that it was all the things God offered that were the things I enjoyed most in showing him. The more I thought on that, the more I began to believe that faith had existed all along inside of me, it only took finding Nathan and the Amish to recognize it.

We stopped at a small tourist store near the end of the forest, Nathan insisting he buy a few postcards for Emma and Abigail.

"They will not believe it otherwise," he said and wrote a quick note on each before putting them in the mail. He tucked the rest in my backpack and relaxed into the seat once more and we were off.

We enjoyed the quiet for a time as I concentrated on the twists and turns of the road. The coolness of the fog still lingered along the coast, but Nathan still enjoyed the air as it passed across his hand from the window as we continued south. Back and forth along the coast we drove, the sun sneaking in through the fog and the tree line, until the distant city appeared ahead of us.

And before that the red arches of the Golden Gate Bridge.

He sat up a little in his seat, marveling at the large structure ahead of us. The lingering fog that was burning off in the sunlight obscured part of the bridge, but the city and the far tower beyond were crystal clear. It was the perfect portrait of how I would always envision San Francisco.

"Are we going there?" he asked, and I could hear some of the trepidation in his voice.

I nodded and took his hand that had been resting on my leg.

"Welcome to San Francisco," I replied and filed into the line of cars making their way slowly onto the bridge.

We had arrived in the late morning, and traffic was not as bad as it would have been near rush hour, but it was still slow going across the bridge and into the city. Nathan seemed a little nervous on the bridge, as we felt it sway and rock in the breeze. I held his hand and talked about the things we could do while in the city to serve as a distraction.

"Chinatown is impressive, as is the wharf. And if you're hungry there is all sorts of places we can go to," I explained.

He swallowed and shook his head.

I wasn't sure talking about food while we travelled on a swaying bridge was the best idea, so I changed subjects.

"There's a number of museums and places to see here too. We don't need to drive right through without seeing at least something," I said.

"This is where you wanted to study cooking," he said as we made it to the other side of the bridge. There was a soft smile on his face as he took in the brightly colored row homes, and the hustle and bustle of the cable cars and milling traffic.

"I love this town. There is always something to do here," I replied and took it all in one more time.

"You will not miss this?" he asked and waved to the city.

I shrugged and thought about it.

"Probably, but I had given up on it a while ago when Sean wouldn't let me come down here. I think I can miss it but still appreciate the wonderful things I will have in return," I said and winked at him.

Nathan over San Francisco and all its diversions?

I could give it all up.

We decided on the Wharf and I parked at the closest parking garage, sensing Nathan's tension at the underground structure. But as soon as we stepped out onto the street, he was transfixed by all the buildings, and the busy pedestrian traffic all around us. Holding his hand, I guided him down the street, closer to the Aquarium and the few restaurants I wanted to go to. It might be my last chance to get crab or clam chowder, and I wasn't driving out of San Francisco without some sourdough bread.

Every new thing caught Nathan's eye, and I relaxed beside him as he seemed to enjoy himself. I had feared it might be too much for him, but he took it in stride, even though he admitted to not liking the clam chowder much. He stopped to watch the sea lions on the docks, and was particularly interested in the arts and crafts market along the street.

There were so many things I wanted to show him.

But so little time.

Was it wrong to wish for just a few more days with Nathan in my English world?

CHAPTER 35

As the afternoon drew closer to evening, I knew we'd have to be on our way. Getting out of the city would be hard enough with the traffic, let alone wanting to stay and show him everything. He was quiet as we made our way out on the road again, stopping and going in the afternoon traffic towards the Bay Bridge into Oakland. The traffic made my body stiff, and I cringed at the idea that we still had about four hours to go before we made it to Reno.

I inwardly berated myself for wanting to show him the city, cutting into our precious travel time. The tension of the drive worked through me and I didn't even realize I was hunched a little until I felt his hand slip up and rub gently on my back, his brow furrowed as he watched his hand move.

"I should share the load of this trip with you. I feel badly that I am not driving," he murmured.

I laughed and shook my head.

"Maybe when we get to Utah. It's all open roads there. But here, it's all bridges and busy highways. I'm all right," I said, hoping to ease his worry.

I let him continue to rub my back lightly. It helped by leaps and bounds. As soon as we passed through Sacramento, the highway opened up and the trees and mountains took over, allowing a bit of peace to wash over us once again on the drive. Nathan talked to keep me occupied as we made the long stretch through the eastern part of the state. He asked about my childhood and more about my mom.

"Before the depression, she was very attentive. But as my father worked more for the city, she became really detached. She started taking antidepressants and drinking a lot to forget. She forgot a lot of things, sometimes even being a mother," I explained when he looked at me in horror when he learned of one memory where she had left me at the grocery store.

It had been several hours before she finally made it back get me.

"But to leave your child and then not worry about coming to get you for hours?" he asked in disbelief.

"She gave up a lot to be with my father. She quit her job teaching when she had Stacy. She had to always seem put together and the pearl of the community when she went out with my dad. I don't really blame her for anything. She just couldn't handle being in his shadow and not appreciated for what she did at home," I said and thought about how insignificant my father had viewed her role in their marriage.

"She didn't want to be just thought of as the housewife. I don't think she understood just how important her role was for us. We didn't understand either, until she died," I said quietly.

"You said she died in a car accident," he stated, offering me sympathetic eyes.

"That was the second time she tried to leave us," I said and shook my head at how much her life and mine mirrored one another. I had run too.

"Why would she leave you and your sister?" he asked, shocked.

I shrugged, which did nothing to ease him.

"She wasn't well, Nathan. She was sad and lonely and drank when she shouldn't. I know she loved us, it just wasn't the life she wanted," I replied.

I had forgiven my mother years ago when I had felt the first urge to run away to San Francisco.

He finally shook his head and let out a strangled noise.

"I thought my losses were unbearable. I can tell you love your family, but I can also see why you would leave it behind. You deserved more love than you received," he said quietly, continuing to gaze out the window as Lake Tahoe passed by.

"I didn't know what I was missing, Nathan. Maybe that's why I don't know if I'll miss anything I am leaving behind. You knew the love your family had, and that is hard to part with," I said and looked over at him, to see if he understood.

He turned and I could see the sadness in his eyes over his lost family.

Something I wanted to ease but had no idea how.

I didn't know his family at all. We never really spoke of them until this morning.

"Family is very important in our lives. I can imagine a life without them, Kate. It is what I know. It is not a good life," he whispered and held my hand a little tighter.

He remained quiet for a while, the daylight falling behind us and the landscape growing more barren as we neared Reno. I wanted to ask him about his family. But I didn't want to do it while we drove. I wanted to give him my full attention.

He had other plans.

"When I was a boy," he started, whisper soft, "I thought the world was so simple. We had our school, where we learned a little of your world. But my life was as you see it. My father, my older brothers and I tended the fields, my sisters helped around the house, and it was all very structured. My mother was happy, because she was close to her sister, Fannie. And my father was happy because he had a loving wife and many children. We were prosperous, if not in money, we had an abundance of love."

"How many brothers and sisters did you have?" I asked, afraid to interrupt, but very curious about the size of his family.

"There were eight of us in all. My father and mother. David was the oldest, then the twins, Mary and Ruth. Then me, Rachel, and lastly my little brother, Jason," he rattled off and sighed and scrubbed at his hair.

"I'm sorry. We don't need to talk about this now," I said hurriedly, feeling the tension rolling off of him at his memories.

He shut his eyes and tried to smile, but it was forced and his voice was tight when he spoke again.

"It is selfish of me to not tell you about my life. You have told me yours. And I want you to know my family. It is the first time I have spoken of them since they passed," he explained and opened his eyes again with more resolve.

I nodded hesitantly and he continued.

"David was much older. My mother had troubles having children after he was born. Something about her childhood had made it difficult. Fannie will not discuss it," he said and frowned as if he had said too much.

"Is that why Fannie only has three daughters? They're adopted, aren't they," I ventured.

I had my theories, seeing that the three sisters looked distinctly different from one another, and little like Jonah or Fannie.

His eyes were distant but he simply nodded.

I felt even more for Fannie; to have issues with bearing children, with as much love as she had to give. I could understand her open arms to let me stay now so much more. And to have adopted children when they could not have their own, it made me understand her affection even more.

"My mother lost another son and daughter before Mary and Ruth were born. But with my sisters, she was thankful. Twins run in her family. When I was born, the mid wives thought they would lose her. But she pulled through and a year later gave birth to Rachel," he continued, and smiled fondly at the memories playing in his head.

"Rachel and I were inseparable. Until Emma came along," he said and smirked at me.

I could only imagine what trouble Emma got Nathan's sister into when she was little.

"The winter that Jason was born, David died," he said, his voice heavy with pain.

"How?" I whispered.

"Buggy accident," he said simply. "It is more common than not. He was working late and was hit by a drunk driver coming home. Mother was devastated."

There was so much tragedy and horror in Nathan's life. He wondered about my strength; I had no idea how he had managed to be so kind and gentle. Many would have become bitter and angry.

"When I was fifteen, I was chosen, along with my friend Benjamin, to be groomed as future deacons of the community, with the hopes that one of us would become the next Bishop if chosen. It was a way to draw us into remaining a part of the Amish way, to offer us an esteemed position upon baptism. My mother was proud. She knew how much I enjoyed following the Word. My sisters would be starting their

Rumspringa that summer, so the death of my brother slowly healed as we continued to grow and prosper," he said.

I waited quietly as he gripped my hand, preparing himself for what I knew was the worst of it. His thumb moved over my knuckles repeatedly. And then a soft breath and the words I knew were the hardest for him.

"Some say it was the new strain of the flu, others food poisoning. Whatever it was, it was swift and fierce. My father went down first. He grew sick, my sisters following soon after. I had just left on a missionary trip with Benjamin and the Bishop to Minnesota when my father fell ill. But he insisted I go. The harvest was in. Things were taken care of," Nathan said, his voice monotone as if reciting a story in his mind.

Detached from it somehow.

But his thumb continued to skirt across my knuckles roughly.

"Did they go to the doctor?" I whispered, afraid to break him from his trance.

He shook his head.

"When I left, it was snowing. We had an early winter. I learned from Jonah that by that first night, it had become difficult to get from house to house, much less into town to the clinic," he whispered.

"I'm sorry, Nathan," I said and tightened my hold on his hand.

"Fannie and Jonah did not know my father had died until my mother came to their door, delirious with a fever and Jason dying in her arms."

He closed his eyes and swallowed again repeatedly.

"I was called home as soon as Fannie and Jonah learned of their illness. It took me two days by bus to get home. I returned in time to say goodbye to my mother and to bury them," he whispered and pulled his hand away from mine, leaning into the window of the door, letting the wind blow across his face to calm himself.

I knew of his tragedy. But to hear it now from his lips was too much.

I pulled off the road, just outside of Reno and stopped the car, tossing the pillows that had been between us to the side and hugging him close. I whispered softly in his ear as he held me, his voice silent but his breath labored as he struggled with the emotions he had held inside for almost a year. When he finally relaxed, he pulled away and closed his eyes as he let his head rest on the back of the seat.

"I have not talked about that to anyone. I am sorry to let it weigh on you," he whispered.

"It's what I am here for, Nathan," I said and smiled gently when he opened his eyes to regard me.

I leaned in and kissed him softly against his cheek.

"We're here for each other. You came for me. You supported me. Now it's my turn," I said and kissed him again.

He sighed and hugged me close again.

"We do not have to hurt anymore, Kate," he sighed into my hair.

"Never again," I confirmed and let him enjoy the moment of the two of us there on the side of the road as the trucks and other cars passed us by on their way to their destinations.

When I finally slipped back into the drivers seat, Nathan's hand was firmly gripping mine once more and a gentle smile played on his lips again.

"Let us make the rest of this trip about happy memories. For both you and I," he said as I pulled back onto the road.

"I like that idea," I laughed and felt my smile broaden at the idea of happy memories with Nathan.

I had never been to Reno, but from the lights on the horizon as we drove towards it, it seemed bigger than I had imagined. The bright lights of the city looked similar to the pictures I had seen of Las Vegas, and I wondered how Nathan would feel about staying in such a place. Every sign we passed mentioned gambling, or dancing girls, or shows that made him blink at the suggestive pictures.

I was too tired to hope for someplace less glitzy though. After driving for eight hours, I was feeling my body's rebelling muscles as I struggled to stay focused on the road leading up to the bright lights. We found a small motel on the outskirts of the city, Nathan chuckling nervously when a woman in bright red lipstick and short shorts tried to proposition him. When she noticed me come out of the rental office, she immediately disappeared wherever she had come.

I began to wonder if maybe it would have been better to continue on.

Nathan simply held me a little closer and helped with the key to the room.

We turned on the lights and looked at our room, clean and quiet despite the glowing lights coming in from the curtains. I collapsed onto the bed, laughing when Nathan flopped down beside me. We lay there for a few minutes, side by side, not touching until I heard his stomach rumble. As much as I wanted to simply get in my pajamas and go to sleep, I knew we needed to eat. I let out a long sigh and groaned as I sat up, looking down at him as he lay flat on his back beside me, grinning at me as I took him in.

His t-shirt had ridden up, offering me a view of his stomach and hair that disappeared into the jeans that were a little low on his hips.

I really wanted to stay right where we were.

I could starve.

"Hungry?" I asked, meaning every use of the word.

"Very much so," he replied and chuckled when I blushed.

He rolled off the bed and took my hand; grabbing the keys and dragging me back outside.

"We will eat and come back. You need to rest," he replied softly and wrapped his arm around my waist to guide me down the street.

I was going to miss having his arm around me when we got back.

I was still thinking about it when we settled in to our table at the restaurant, a small diner tucked next to a brightly lit casino a block from our motel. The waitress took our order and left us alone, Nathan eyeing everything around us curiously as I sipped at my cola.

"Are you all right here?" I asked.

He turned from the busy traffic on the street and smiled timidly.

"This is more like what I see your world as," he said and laughed softly. "It is very busy here. And the people are distracted by the colors I think."

I looked around and took it in as he would. People rushed past in tight clothes, wearing flashy jewelry or talking on their phones, oblivious to the world around them. Even in the restaurant, we could hear the casino noise, with its beeping and clanging of the slot machines. It was a foreign place to me when I looked at it from his viewpoint. Too much noise and not enough peace and nature. I shook my head and returned to stare at his innocent face.

"I could definitely give this up," I said and laughed with him all through dinner as we watched people come and go. We didn't dally while we ate, both of us exhausted from the travel.

"I'm so tired," I sighed yawning as if to prove my point when we closed the door to our room.

"We should go to sleep, then. Tomorrow is a long day by your map. Are you sure you want to go that far tomorrow?" he asked as he sat in one of the guest chairs and untied his shoes.

I dug through the duffel bag and found my sleep shorts and tank top.

"We have to. Besides, there's not a lot to the rest of Nevada and into Utah. I'd like to get through it as fast as we can," I admitted, scowling at him when he laughed. We both were anxious to get back home.

I excused myself to the bathroom and changed, brushing my teeth and washing my face quickly so that he could have his time. When I stepped out, he was already changed. Sleep pants and a new t-shirt, and a bashful look on his face as he avoided staring at me. I looked down and remembered his reaction to me that one day coming home from town, in my shorts.

"Sorry, I didn't think," I rushed out. "I'll find my pants and put them on."

His hand stilled me from digging through the bag, and when I looked up into his eyes, I could see the decision there.

"It is fine," he murmured and leaned down to kiss me slowly, his hands moving around me to hold me close.

I felt the heat of him as I leaned in, moaning at the dizzying feeling that coursed through me. He let out a low moan and traced his hand down my hip, fingers splaying across the flesh of my thigh before pulling away to look down at his hand as it fingered the bottom hem of my shorts, just below my rear.

"I should prepare for sleep," he mumbled but made no move to leave, only stared at his fingertips as they teased across my skin producing goose bumps.

When his eyes finally turned back to mine, they were dark with need. He leaned in for another searching kiss before stepping away slowly, one hand in his hair. He disappeared into the bathroom, and I all but leapt into the bed, tossing off the blankets and slipping the sheet over my legs.

He came out a few minutes later, scrubbing at his hair still as he made his way towards the bed. He shut off the light, a soft glow of light peeking in from the curtains, but enough to see him. He slid in beside me, his hand resting gently over my stomach as I moved in to spoon against him. He let out a measured breath and couldn't help adjusting behind me.

"We should sleep," he said near my ear although he seemed unconvinced when his fingers flexed along my stomach and his hips pushed gently against my backside. I was tired, but his heat felt wonderful. I took his hand and moved it closer to my heart, feeling his fingers flex under mine when they drew close to my breast.

"I'm not tired," I murmured.

"Yes you are," he chuckled and squeezed himself closer against my back, his arousal evident. He let out another soft groan and nuzzled his nose into my neck.

"We have time, Kate. Sleep, and tomorrow will be a pleasant day," he murmured.

"Today was nice, with you," I mumbled, sighing at his hot breath near my ear.

My eyes felt heavy, his heat was lulling.

"Pleasant sleep, Kate," he whispered and held me gently as my eyelids finally won over and sleep took me.

CHAPTER 36

Nevada was a long state to get through, and I knew it would be a rough leg of the trip on my own, so when Nathan begged to let him drive alone the long path through the middle of Utah, I couldn't say no. I had spent most of the morning instructing Nathan on how my car worked. He wanted to drive, and judging by the excitement on his face once he was behind the wheel, I was in for a ride.

"Brake! Brake, brake, brake!" I hollered as a semi-truck passed by while we slowly drove along the shoulder.

"I am fine, really! I did not see him in the mirror!" Nathan exclaimed, laughing brightly as he finally merged onto the road.

I let out a breath and tried to hide my grin, but his joy was contagious and pretty soon we were driving down the road at a good pace, Nathan laughing and grinning as he concentrated on the road. It wasn't as fast as the rest of the world wanted us to go, but it was safe for both Nathan and the car. I relaxed in the passenger seat and watched him as he drove perfectly, hands at ten and two, looking at his mirrors and keeping within the lines at all times.

It was adorable really.

He was like a guy who had just gotten his first car.

And as the minutes ticked by, his smile remained. It was a joy for him to do this.

He chanced a glance over at me, but only for a brief instant and then he was back to eyeing the road. I leaned in close to him, the pillows and blankets tucked in the passenger side so that I could lean into him while he drove. We talked all day, about what we saw, about how Jonah and Fannie would react when we returned home.

About what would happen when we got home.

Nathan was avoiding the topic, but I knew he had to be thinking about what came next in our relationship. He had not even asked me and I was already feeling nervous over it. He was so sure about us. Perhaps like his saying he loved me, it was something that the Amish just knew. Emma had said something about the Bishop asking the intended, and I knew that would be a trial in itself. But so much of what Nathan and I had been through, I just needed to know how we would get through the next hurdle of our trip.

Because I was finding it so much more difficult to stay away from him and remain respectful to his pure intentions. I was not so naïve that I didn't know he was battling his own demons. Since he had come to find me, his touch was more willing, and his body more tense when we lay down at night. I knew he was tempted.

We both were.

When we stopped in the evening at a hotel just outside of Evanston, Wyoming, I decided to confront him about it. I struggled with how to ask him his intentions, well after dinner and into the late evening as we settled down to go to sleep. Nathan held me close, lying on his back as he lightly fingered the strap to my tank top absently. It had been another long day, and we were both tired. But my mind was spinning at the idea that in two days, things would change.

"Kate?"

I looked up at him as he chewed on his lip as if uncertain to speak. This was the first time all day he had seemed less than joyful.

"What is it?" I asked, suddenly worried.

"I have been thinking about when we arrive home."

I took a breath and nodded.

"Me too," I said, relieved and yet also a little nervous of his thoughts.

He smiled and laughed.

"I know that you have. You have been quiet most of the evening. Every time we settle in to sleep, you think about it, do you not?" he asked.

"It's kind of necessary when we are lying next to each other and I want to kiss you and touch you and know I won't be able to in a couple of days," I conceded, embarrassed.

He sat up and looked at me thoughtfully.

"Kate, I will not be able to go back to what we were before. I want more," he urged softly, his eyes closing as he seemed to check himself

I held my breath and waited for him to continue.

"I want so much more with you. This trip has made me see just how blessed and cursed I am for wanting you so badly," he whispered.

His thumbs skirted across my cheeks, his eyes opening to stare intently into mine.

"Is that something you have felt?" he asked.

"Yes," was all I could manage.

He swallowed and watched his fingertips as they traced down the side of my neck, his voice throaty as he continued.

"I imagine many things I should not, Kate, when I am with you. Things I should not think on without disrespecting you in some way. But I cannot help it. Especially at night when my body wishes I could forget the rules, and then I feel remorse for thinking such things as I know they are not mine to take."

I touched his lips to silence him, his eyes landing on mine once more, dark and turbulent.

And hungry.

"I want you too," I said and put my finger over his mouth again when he made to object. "And if it's disrespectful then I have done the same, Nathan."

He groaned against my fingers and I let him press his hard frame close to mine.

Moving slowly, to keep him from retreating, I placed his palm over my breast. He let out a low groan and took the chance to be bold, enveloping my breast with his large palm. My hand moved down further, until it landed on his hip, drawing him against me tight so that I could wrap my leg over his.

"If this feeling is wrong, if what we are doing is wrong, why would you be allowed to explore on Rumspringa? And is this not something like a Rumspringa for both of us?" I whispered.

"Kate," he whispered against my lips.

I moaned into his lips at the slow grind of his hips into me, his hand squeezing me with more need. He rolled us over onto my back, his lips searching me out until I gasped when his hips rolled just right. He leaned back a bit and looked down at me cautiously.

"Is this too much?" he said huskily.

I shook my head and placed my hand over his, to encourage him further. I laid a little pressure on his hand as if to urge him along before releasing it and slipping it across his chest and down until I traced the hard outline under his pants. He closed his eyes briefly at the pleasure he felt as I touched him, his hips rolling so that my hand was trapped between him and me.

"I want more with you, always more," he whispered softly and his hand moved again, ever so slowly edging under my shirt so that his hot fingers came in contact with my breast. I whimpered and fell back into the bedding, his body following to line up with mine in the most delightful way.

"I do not wish to disrespect you," he murmured. "I just want to feel you."

Lips brushed along my collarbone and he groaned when he grazed his thumb across my hard nipple.

"This is not wrong."

His hand cupped my cheek, his mouth moving everywhere he could. On my mouth, along my jaw, to my ear where he groaned when his hand slipped down along my ribs on its path south.

"I want to be everything for you," he whispered and let his lips move along my throat.

I let out a moan, wanting him to go further. My hand in his hair spoke for me as he dipped back down, hot lips leaving an electrifying trail down my throat and to my shoulder before his hand grasped along my hip. He paused over my breast, the heat of his breath causing me to shiver. He glanced up at me and then back, before laying his soft lips against me, just over my heart. I sighed and melted in his touch.

Another kiss closer, along the edge of my tank top.

And then another.

And then another pause, just long enough to make me whimper when I felt the light tug of fabric before it turned into a moan as his lips brushed against my nipple. I held his head a little harder, trapping him there.

I wanted him to kiss me there again and again.

His mouth opened and he kissed me more openly. I moved against him, needing more. I was aching and I needed to feel him. My hand found his, and I guided it down once more, fingers slipping under the waistline of my shorts and beyond.

He pulled his head away to watch as our interlaced hands slipped deeper and I moaned at the welcome pressure of his fingers with mine as they grazed down. His breathing picked up as we dipped down, into wet warmth. I laid my fingers over his and offered enough pressure for him to see how I liked to be touched, watching his face as he concentrated on our hands under the fabric. He followed my fingers carefully, the gentle pressure making my legs shake, the brushing of his thumb across my clit making me jolt against him. He paused and swallowed as he took in my reaction.

His thumb brushed across me once more, with a little more pressure and I groaned at the warm flush rushing through me. I pressed against his fingers, groaning as he circled me slowly. The build up was maddening, and so unlike anything I had ever felt. The heat running through me was picking up. Gaining speed.

I opened my eyes to catch Nathan watching my hand as it moved along the front of his pants; searching him out to offer him the same pleasure he was giving me. His mouth was open, panting as he worked a little faster, responding to my hand as it slipped under the fabric of his pants and found him. He let out a deep-throated moan as I stroked him, and then he moved against me, the two of us a writhing mess in the sheets as we pleasured one another. When he leaned in to offer me a panting kiss, his eyes were dark but his smile was proud as I groaned and trembled against him at the mounting tension in me. He added more pressure with his thumb as it rubbed against me until I felt all the tension explode in my body. I stiffened against him, the air in my lungs leaving me in a strangled cry.

Washing over me in a hot rush.

Shaking, falling away, gasping. Swirling.

And then I was limp in his arms, gasping for breath while his fingers moved to cup me almost possessively. When I could focus, his lips were on mine, searing and desperate as my hand continued to work him towards his own release. He broke off the kiss in a long groan and together we watched as I brought him pleasure, his hips moving to my movements this time until he let out a gasp and a low-throated moan. We collapsed into one another, lips touching, breath ragged, legs intertwined, and completely content.

"That was better than anything I imagined," he said when he could speak again. He had a dazed look on his face. I giggled and traced my hand along the long length of his torso, enjoying the sight of him in the dim light. His chest beat at a faster rate, and there was a slight sheen of sweat on it as he struggled to calm himself. When he could breathe without panting, he rolled onto his side and smiled bashfully at me, his eyes continuing to take in my nakedness until I started to shiver in the cool air. When he pulled the blanket over us, he let his hands wander over my body, tracing over every curve, every dip. It wasn't until I heard his soft chuckle that I dragged myself out of my euphoric daze.

I looked up into his eyes and saw something I had not seen in a long while.

Mischief.

"What?" I asked, laughing nervously.

His eyes darted off into the darkness and his laughter grew.

"It is just that I have imagined that for so long. To bring you pleasure. But I was unsure how to do so," he said and ducked his head into my neck, laying sweet kisses along it to try and distract me.

"You did just fine," I replied, squirming a bit as his whiskers brushed against the sensitive skin of my neck. When he pulled away, he was grinning widely.

"Your computer has more information than it should," he confided, and I burst into laughter.

"You didn't!" I sputtered and clutched at him as he nodded and laughed softly with me.

"Pleasing you is much more important than crop forecasts," he said and his smile softened. He settled in against me, one arm tucked beneath his head, the other moving across my bare skin in a gentle caress.

"You are so beautiful, Kate. Beauty made by God. Every part of you should be exalted," he whispered in my ear as he lay against me.

"I am so happy because I'm with you," I sighed, wanting him to know, he was everything I needed.

"Forever, Kate. Be mine forever," he murmured against my lips.

I nodded and tried to kiss him again, but he pulled away to look down at me, his eyes intense. He held my head in his hand, purpose driven to say what he intended.

"Forever, Kate. Be my love, my partner. My wife. Everything," he said breathlessly.

I felt my smile fighting to take over my face.

This was Nathan's way of asking. And to me it was better than any sappy English proposal.

Because I could see it in his eyes, and feel it in his trembling frame against me.

"Yes, Nathan. Everything," I promised and let him kiss me until we couldn't keep our eyes from crossing.

He smiled and settled in beside me, squeezing me gently and whispering into my ear playfully.

"Be my wife."

"Yes."

He laughed softly and hugged me a little harder.

"Be my wife."

I giggled and fought the urge to swat him for his silliness.

But he was happy. And that was everything.

"Yes."

"I will love you always, Kate," he murmured; sleep making his words a little garbled. "I will be there for you, forever."

"I love you, Nathan. Forever," I whispered back and heard his soft hum as he drifted off to sleep.

He held me as I slipped into slumber, content and at ease as my mind drifted at thoughts of what I had planned for his house when we returned.

We still had hurdles to jump, but I knew his heart.

And it was the same as mine.

CHAPTER 37

Wyoming was a blur.

Little things stood out.

Nathan's smile.

Nathan's repeated request for me to be his wife as we stood filling the gas tank at the truck stop or grabbing snacks in the store.

Nathan's hand in mine as we walked at every stop along the way.

Nathan's happy laughter as we ate ice cream at the soda fountain shop when we stopped for lunch in Cheyenne.

Nathan's wide-eyed wonder at the Western Museum. We strolled hand in hand, enjoying the break from sitting for so long in the car. Families passed us as we toured, and Nathan's hand pulled me close and he whispered in my ear playfully.

"Be my wife."

"Yes."

And we'd smile and continue to walk amongst the English. Our presence going unnoticed.

Nathan's contented sigh as we breathed in the clean air as we continued east.

The heat of the day allowed us to roll the windows all the way down, and I relaxed in the hot wind as it whipped across my face and through my hair as we continued east. We stopped at a campsite in Nebraska, setting up our gear by the Maloney Lake. We seemed to be the only ones there, as the season had ended and many travelers would continue on to Omaha. But we were exhausted, and the sun had set. We couldn't think of another couple hours drive. So we made camp, eating the last of our turnovers and finishing off sandwiches we had bought somewhere along the way. This was our last night together, before we went back and pledged our life to the Amish way.

Before I pledged myself to Nathan, forever.

I climbed into the sleeping bag, the air finally cool enough against my skin to want to snuggle against where Nathan laid, his head resting on his arms as he watched me move. He was smiling as I slid in under the warm cover, against the heat of him in his boxers.

I didn't feel strangely in just my tank top and underwear. We were beyond the awkward embarrassment of nakedness with one another, and we were alone on the lake. But we had achieved so much the last couple of days. My hand found its home over his heart; my head nestled against his shoulder as we lay there taking in the beauty of the sky above us.

It was like a million pinpricks in the night sky, the Milky Way big and clear above our heads. The half moon offered just enough light to see, but the stars seemed to light up everything around us.

And it was quiet, save the soft rustling of wild grass and the occasional creak of the trees nearby. It was just the two of us. Alone under the magic of the Nebraska sky.

Nathan moved against me, his lips tracing across my forehead until I looked up, and his lips found mine, searching. He rolled us over, groaning at the feel of my bare legs against his. The kiss deepened as he traced one hand down my side, reaching under my knee to pull it up, opening me to his warmth as he moved in closer.

Slow.

Searching.

Discovering the heat between my legs.

His own firm heat adjusting against.

Moving.

Sighing against lips as fingertips slipped up my thigh, finding the hem of my shirt and trailing beneath.

Tracing.

One rib.

Second rib.

Another adjustment against me.

My own hands searching.

Through hair that felt so soft between my fingers.

Down the soft cotton of his back, feeling the muscles slide under my hands as he groaned and moved over me.

Stars so bright.

Heat so seductive.

Fingers searching.

Lips moving down my throat.

Fingers finding.

My lips whispering his name in adoration.

Our last night together, we worshipped each other in the moonlight. Soft words, searching kisses, and hands that explored in order to memorize every part to tide us over until the next time we would have to ourselves.

Who knew when that would be?

So we savored one another until late into the night, fighting fatigue and simply sharing the love we both felt.

Being together.

As we lay there, content and relaxed, Nathan held me close and stroked my arm lazily. It had become a habit for him as he drifted off to sleep against me. To feel me there, and his fingertips lulled me as much as they comforted him. He sighed and buried his nose into my neck, snuggling into my warmth.

"Kate?"

I opened my eyes and hummed in response.

"Tomorrow will come too soon."

I hugged his arm that lay around me.

"I know."

"But we will be home. We will show them. This is right. I will ask Jonah when we get home. I want to marry you, Kate. Soon. I want us to start this life together. I do not want to wait longer than we must," he sighed and held me closer.

I closed my eyes and hoped that the Elders would see.

This was right.

We wouldn't know until we got home. Tomorrow would come, and I both looked forward to it and dreaded it.

They had to see that this was right.

The sun was setting as we drove through town. I smiled as we passed the general store.

It had all begun there.

I was seeing the town with new eyes, and new hope.

Nathan drove past, his arm leaning casually out the window as he took in his surroundings. He had grown quite used to driving, and I had a suspicion that inside, he had grown to love my car.

It would be sad to get rid of it, but we had no use for it, and hopefully it would fetch a decent price.

We had things to buy.

A farm to get running.

It was my gift to our life.

I grew anxious as the fields came into view, many cleared away in the week we had been gone.

It had felt like a year.

My breathing picked up and I straightened my skirt again in preparation to seeing the Bergers again. I had dressed more appropriately today, my one and only skirt from my former life and a loose shirt to cover myself discreetly. Nathan still called me beautiful and smiled every time he looked my way as we traveled.

I had the feeling that he preferred me in dresses, which I supposed was good, since I would be wearing one for the rest of my life. I'd miss shorts and jeans.

But I loved Nathan more.

"Are you ready?" he asked as he paused at the road leading to the Bergers. I took a deep breath and nodded, the wait almost unbearable. I couldn't wait to see my family again.

Nathan leaned over and pulled me close, his lips finding mine easily after the few days alone. I kissed him tenderly, his lips moving against mine as if to memorize their taste and texture before pulling away smiling.

"I needed one last kiss before we must hide behind the barn again," he mused and held my hand lightly as he turned onto the road.

My heart raced as I saw the house come into view, the lantern light in the kitchen bleeding out onto the porch swing. It would be suppertime or shortly after, and suddenly I was starving. Nathan had called Emma the day before to let her know roughly when we would be home.

We were a little late, having slept in this morning.

As the sound of my car drew near, the back door opened, Jonah's profile in the light as he stood there watching our car move closer. Abigail and Emma were next in the doorway as we drew to a stop, but Abigail lingered only a second before she was bolting for us, Emma following right behind her.

Fannie and Jonah stepped through after with Hannah and Mark, Fannie rushing out with a cry as she saw me open the door to the car. I was barely out of the door before Emma's arms were around me and I was hugging her to me. I couldn't breathe, between her strong grip and the emotions that washed over me.

Arms wrapped around me, Fannie's soft sobs and Jonah's strong arms enfolding us into one. Mark seemed to surround us and Hannah's grip was tight around my waist. Nathan stood to the side for a moment before Fannie tugged him close, her tears streaming down her face as she looked us over and hugged us tightly once more.

Jonah broke the quiet sobbing with his soft voice, the voice of a father I had missed so much.

"Welcome home, my children. Thank you, Lord, for bringing them home. We are all together again. Thank you, Lord."

I held onto my family and cried with them, so overjoyed to finally be where I belonged.

Every worry and sad thought washed away at the feeling I felt in my family's arms.

I was where I belonged.

I was finally home.

~~~~

Follow Nathan and Kate on their continued journey in the second book of the In Your World series, coming late 2013.

EXCERPT OF BOOK TWO OF THE *IN YOUR WORLD SERIES*

Nathan leaned in and held my head in his hands, the gentle touch soothing after the events of the day.

"You do not need to be afraid anymore. I will be here for you through everything," he said.

"Together, right?" I asked, my heart full by his pledge.

He grinned and stood.

"Always. No matter how long it takes," he said and stretched. He was leaning in to offer me a kiss when we heard voices inside. He pulled away hurriedly.

We watched in surprise as the Bishop came through the back door, followed swiftly by Jonah and Fannie. Jonah glanced our way, his eyes travelling over us as if to be sure we weren't doing anything the Bishop would find inappropriate. Had he been here a few moments earlier, perhaps he would have had an argument.

"It is late, Samuel. This can wait until tomorrow," Jonah said.

"I must say what I came to say tonight," he demanded and turned to me. "Katherine, I will speak with you in private," he said.

I blinked at him, all fatigue gone as I tried to figure out if he was upset or just being direct.

"She does not need to be alone while you speak with her," Jonah started but the Bishop waved him off.

"What I have to say to Katherine is for her alone. And God."

Nathan stepped a little closer to me, his hand moving to encircle my shoulder.

"Please," the Bishop requested, his voice much softer.

I looked up at Jonah, to ask him silently if this was safe. He hesitated before nodding and holding the door open for Nathan.

"Nathan, come inside and have some tea with us," Jonah said and waited for Nathan to move. He seemed reluctant; his eyes on the Bishop before he let go of me.

"I will be just inside," he whispered.

I waited until they were safely inside before I directed my gaze back at the Bishop. I couldn't read his face. It was a cross between agitation maybe even resignation. He gestured to the swing and followed me to it, sitting after I had sat. He kept his distance and pulled off his hat, looking off into the evening. When he spoke, his voice was rough, surly almost.

"I must ask your forgiveness for my actions today."

I blinked at his words and nodded.

"You have it. I understand why you did it," I replied quietly.

"But you are not upset with my reason?" he asked, keeping his eyes on the field.

"I can't understand why you treat me badly when you don't know me," I confessed.

He was quiet for several minutes. I waited for him to continue.

"You seem to have won over everyone around you."

I straightened and held my head a little higher.

"I haven't won anyone over. I am just trying to make a life here, Bishop Yoder," I replied.

"Are you? Or are you here simply for Nathan?" he asked, refusing to look my way.

I took a breath, struggling to remain calm.

"I am here to find peace and a life I can understand. Nathan is part of that, yes. But it goes beyond that," I started, but he put up his hand to stop me.

"And your trust in God? You come from a world that is Godless. How can I trust that you are not here to hide, and have not found God?" he asked.

"I may be new to this community, Bishop Yoder, but the outside world has God as well. If you are asking if I have found Him while I have been here, the answer is yes. I may see it a little differently than you, but I have found it here," I replied.

"To live with us is to live with God," he said haughtily.

I pursed my lips and eyed him carefully, not sure if I should say what I felt. But he had judged me, without knowing me.

"To live with God is to follow his words. Words like love and forgiveness and acceptance, " I argued. "To know God is to open your heart and your home to others, to help those less fortunate, to offer friendship and peace to a stranger. To forgive those who have wronged you, to know that God will send justice to those, not man. God rewards those that follow his path."

My heart was beating fast as I waited for his response. So much of what Nathan spoke about at night were these things exactly, things I had witnessed every day. But the Bishop had shown me none of that. He was farther from what he preached than I was.

"You speak well, but do you mean what you say?" he whispered, skeptical.

"I have always been honest and true. That has never changed. Not all English are bad, Bishop Yoder. I wish you would see that. Whatever your prejudice, it's not fair to judge me based on whatever you are basing your hate on," I whispered and stood.

He sat there looking out at the field while I stood waiting for him to speak. When he did, it was barely a whisper.

"Your world corrupts the innocence in ours. I have not seen any good come of your world."

"That's like the outside world saying that the Amish are all occultists and narrow-minded zealots," I replied, watching his face contort in anger at my words.

"It's not what I think," I added softly. "But you see the prejudice? It's not fair to compare me to that world when I so desperately wish to live apart from that view."

He shook his head stubbornly.

"You are too worldly for this life. You will tire of it here. And you will drag Nathan with you out into that evil, just as I have lost my son, we will lose Nathan," he hissed.

"Nathan is old enough to make his own choice. I won't tire of this life. You don't know what my life was like before. This is what I choose. Even with you making it difficult at every turn, you will not dissuade me, Bishop Yoder. I will do my best to make you believe I am worthy," I said and moved to leave.

His next words made me pause.

"I do not approve of you, Katherine Hill, because you are a woman with strong opinions. Your world has made you willful, and that is not our way."

"If anything, Bishop Yoder, it has made me more determined to seek out what will make me happy. That world made me run, and I found this place. It made me see where I needed to be. There is nothing I desire from that world. Not when I can find peace and joy here," I replied and stepped inside.

I heard him following after me; saw the looks of surprise on the Bergers' faces as I stepped inside. I put myself at a safe distance from him, close to Nathan as the Bishop lingered in the doorway. He looked at each of us, holding his hat tight in his hand.

"I was told to meet with both of you weekly, so that we may complete your baptism classes before first frost. I will do so, but it is under duress," he said, refusing to look at me.

"Samuel, you know this is right," Fannie said as she stood beside Jonah.

He shook his head and turned to leave.

"The community has spoken. Therefore I will abide by their wishes," he said and paused in the doorway, looking back at us.

"I will expect you at my home this Tuesday evening. We will meet for an hour, and then discuss a time to meet from there. It is inconvenient, but it must be done," he said.

"Thank you, Bishop Yoder. We will try not to burden you," Nathan said, stepping forward to offer his hand to shake in pledge.

The Bishop glanced over his shoulder, eyeing Nathan hard.

"We will see. But you must remember your baptism brings responsibilities, Nathan," he said and disappeared into the night.

I looked up at Nathan, whose eyes were now downturned and thoughtful.

"What did he mean, Nathan?" I asked quietly.

His smile seemed a little sad as he looked out after the Bishop.

"It means," he murmured, "that you may soon be a Bishop's wife."

~~~~

ACKNOWLEDGEMENTS

This story would not be possible without the love and support of my friends and family, and my incredible readers that have stood by me through every word.

To my loving and patient husband, for believing in me and being patient while I diligently researched. Thank you for eating all those corn cakes and pie. Thank you to my dear son who patiently waited for many a burnt meal while I tried to finish that last paragraph.

To Leah who nudged me to take the first step.

To Jess for reminding me of what was important and providing sanctuary.

To my girls on Twitter and Facebook and the forums- thank you for providing so many hours of love and support, laughter and inappropriate inspiration to keep me going.

To Claudia, Teddi, Traci, Terri, Staci, Sarah, Kris and Mandy for the moment of conception on this sweet boy: suspenders and big black hat, shy smile and all.

To Barbara, Amy, Mary, Ava, Jules and Jayme for holding my hand through the editing process and lending me your most trusted opinions.

I love you all, and I am so blessed to have you all on this journey.

ABOUT THE AUTHOR

Jennyfer Browne has always been a sucker for a good love story- a complex recipe with a dash of dashing, a pinch of heroism, and a hefty dose of outside forces that test young lovers. Seasoned with tears and laughter, followed by a sprinkle of happy sighs fill out the perfect recipe.

Jennyfer also enjoys pie.

Ms. Browne lives in California with her wonderful husband and adoring son, where she enjoys the beach and sailing off on further adventures. A member of the Romance Writers of America and blessed with an overactive imagination, she writes sweet and savory romances with a twist of tart that always come to a happy ending.

You can visit Jennyfer Browne on her Facebook page at https://www.facebook.com/jennyferbrowneauthor

Made in the USA
San Bernardino, CA
02 November 2013